MORE PRAISE
ALAMO HOU

"A great story of comic female friendship and solidarity set against a backdrop of collegiate lowlife. Her characters? I know them well—the student lounge lizards, moral misfits, lost souls in the halls of academe (they all live in my dorm). Sarah Bird had me rooting for them. A woman's hilarious answer to Animal House."
—MIMI POND
Author of *Splitting Hairs*

"Beyond her humor is Bird's understanding of modern relationships."
—*Houston Post*

"Considerable humor and a quick narrative line."
—*Austin-American Statesman*

"Bird is a remarkable Texas writer to watch."
—*Daily Texan*

"Sophisticated wit . . . Endearingly eccentric characters."
—*Kirkus Reviews*

ALAMO HOUSE

Women Without Men, Men Without Brains

i

ALAMO HOUSE

WOMEN WITHOUT MEN, MEN WITHOUT BRAINS

SARAH BIRD

Ballantine Books • New York

A Ballantine Book
Published by The Random House Publishing Group

www.ballantinebooks.com/BRC/

Library of Congress Catalog Card Number: 2003093932

ISBN 0-345-46007-3

This edition published by arrangement with W. W. Norton & Company, Inc.

Cover art: Image of neon sign © Harold Sund / GettyImages; image of house © Photodisc Collection / GettyImages

Manufactured in the United States of America

First Ballantine Books Edition: September 2003

10 9 8 7 6 5 4 3 2 1

ACKNOWLEDGMENTS

For those without whom . . . Kay Dee,
H. Hinzmann, Annie Rooney, E. Sharpe,
Suzanne, Nurse Bird and the Doctor, Clare,
Lee, Nancy, Marian, and, always, George.

ALAMO HOUSE

WOMEN WITHOUT MEN,
MEN WITHOUT BRAINS

1

MAYBE I EXPECTED too much from Roger Halpern and our live-together trial. I knew when I moved in with him that he was as ignorant about housework as Louis XIV. What I hadn't bargained on was ending up as the entire janitorial staff at Versailles. At twenty-seven I had close to a quarter of a century of field experience on him. I probably should have started him off with a basic understanding of dirt, what it is and why we do not like it in our houses.

I'd run the gamut of approaches for coercing Roger into shouldering, if not half, at least a fraction of the care and maintenance of the shelter we shared. I'd started off very New Age with a contract dividing duties: Roger take out trash. Mary Jo mop kitchen floor. Roger mow lawn. Mary Jo vacuum and dust house. Roger pick up his socks. Mary Jo clean bathroom. The terms were generous. Roger agreed to them. As soon as I'd moved in, however, he paid as much attention to his contractual obligations as a Trobriand Islander.

In the few months I'd cohabited with Roger in our single-family dwelling in bucolic Travis Heights, I'd systematically trimmed away all the flourishes. I was down to the essentials of sanitation. They represented less housework than I'd have done if I'd lived alone. The problem was I *wasn't* living alone and I *was* doing all the work. The real problem was, I felt like a chump doing it.

Maybe the housework issue was only the messy symptom of a much greater ill.

Such were the thoughts that wheeled through my mind as I pedaled past Alamo House, pumping my fat-tired bike further into the overheated miasma that settles upon equatorial Austin for three-fourths of the year. A sign swinging from the porch roof read "Vacancies for Graduate Women." Half a block later I remembered that *I* was a graduate woman, not Roger Halpern's live-in domestic. I started classes in photojournalism next week. Alamo House applied to me. Though I'd ridden by it on my way to work at the Lyndon Baines Johnson Library every day for a month, I had never really looked at the house until that moment.

She was a dowdy dowager out of place on a street full of Greek-columned fraternity and sorority houses with BMW 320i's out front interspersed with condominiums bought by Dallas daddies looking to get a tax write-off and an education for Bubba at the same time. Alamo might have been marginally regal a hundred years ago with a horse and carriage out front and an acre or so on either side. Now, with her grounds sliced practically up to the porch and one motley pecan tree, naked and scarred from the ground up except for its leafy top, on what remained of a brown and abused lawn, she looked distinctly frumpy.

I didn't know anything about architectural periods and styles, cupolas and portcullises. Alamo House was just a huge old house painted the drabbest of olives. Still the moldering edifice held a certain charm for me. I was certain she would be cheap. Cheap enough to make Roger start believing in the possibility that I might actually leave. I leaned my bike against the one surviving tree of those that had given the street its name, Pecan. A member of the nut family. *How often in life do we ignore the obvious?*

I entered planning only to gather basic facts about things like rent. All I wanted were a few details to add a bit of ballast to my increasingly empty threats about throwing in the towel (and the sponge mop, and the toilet brush), and moving out. Since I was merely gathering props for my *Potëmkin emancipation*, I was spared the jolt that other graduate women earnestly in search of reasonably priced shelter must receive upon entering Alamo. The living room looked like the lobby of a welfare hotel. It was steeped in the shabby gentility of graduate students whose sole luxuries are their recherché dissertation topics. The room was dominated by a poster of a cow's head staring with mournful Elsie eyes. The caption: "Love Me, Don't Eat Me." A flurry of notices about Campus Co-op League meetings and U.S. Out of El Salvador, Nicaragua, Honduras, and South Africa protest marches were tacked to the wall next to a pay phone. It was like walking into a sixties time capsule. Only the names of the Third World countries had been changed.

A small, wiry woman uncurled herself from her perch on one of the greasy armchairs and approached me. From a distance her eyes seemed darkly outlined in kohl. Closer inspection revealed that the coloring was natural; a kind of permanent bruising of the lids made her gaze sensitive and haunted and piercing. Your basic borderline schizophrenic.

"Hi. Looking for someone?"

Those eyes. Pits of perception. She seemed to know all, judge nothing. I came close to telling her about my life as an indentured servant, about my search for the man within the man I loved, who would happily massage Pledge into our furniture.

"No," I stammered, pointing behind me to give her a clue as to my mission. "The sign. I saw your sign."

Her laser stare did not waver. I spewed out more clues.

"You have a vacancy listed."

She nodded sagely.

"Well, I was wondering, just wondering," I added tentatively, "how much is rent?"

Her eyes held mine. "Two-twenty a month."

In the university area that was approximately what a converted barbecue pit went for. Her eyes bore more deeply.

"That includes meals."

My jaw slackened, but I did not allow it to swing open. She moved in for the kill.

"We all share duties. Cooking. Cleaning. Everything. It's all written into the contract."

After a summer of Dumpster Love the vision was irresistible: beaming graduate women, shoulder to shoulder, comrades in cleanliness, scrubbing out the tub together, inching the fridge forward to delve behind it for some deep cleaning, cracking fresh sheets over a bed.

"My name's Judith Feldman. What's yours?"

I hadn't planned to divulge that, but Judith's eyes drew it out of me. "Mary Jo Steadman."

"Listen up, folks." Judith raised her voice to capture the attention of the half-dozen residents draped over books at various spots around the living room. They had the pasty phosphorescence of those whose daylight hours are spent in library carrels and stacks. "This is Mary Steadman."

Mary Steadman? Isn't Mary Jo dreary enough? I didn't bother to correct Judith. I wouldn't be around long enough for any of these escapees from *Night of the Living Dead* to call me anything, much less Mary Steadman.

"That's Hillary." Judith indicated an emaciated woman with long, straight, carroty hair parted down the middle and lankly framing one of the gauntest faces I'd ever seen outside of a Dorothea Lange Dustbowl photograph. Hillary had the sickly, drawn-out look of fanatical vegetarians. I assumed Carrot Girl was responsible for "Love Me, Don't Eat Me."

"And Toni and Barb." Judith's hand swept over to a couple clumped together on the middle cushion of a lumpy three-cushion sofa. Both wore denim overalls and both had the kind of scalped-to-the-bone gamine haircut that Mia Farrow had once made popular. One in blond, Barb, one in brunette, Toni. Mia with her delicate bone structure had looked like a big-eyed waif in her pixie cut.

Barb and Toni, big, meaty gals, looked like hillbilly gas station attendants.

"Toni is House Maintenance Person and Work Manager. She's the one you see about work duties." I smiled. Work duties. Yeah, right. They nodded in my direction and went back to thumbing through a book of David Hamilton's gauzy portraits of young girls.

"And Josie Guzman." A curly-haired Chicana in a string T-shirt glanced up from her *Analog* magazine and waved a cigarette in jaunty circles at me by way of a greeting. She took a long tug on the Lone Star long-neck at her side before diving back into the science fiction story she was reading.

"Josie's in law school," Judith whispered approvingly. "And Byung Duk Soo." From across the room a chunky Oriental woman in her early twenties bounded forward, her hand extended. She gripped mine and give it three tick-tock-the-game-is-locked shakes. Her smile creased her eyes into two happy parabolas floating over her cheeks. "I am very hoppy to make your acquaintance," she announced, releasing my hand and stepping back expectantly. A whooshing sound accompanied the announcement as though she were trying to suck her words back in even as she spoke them.

"Yes, me too." I was overcome to find such vitality here amidst the undead. "Where are you from?"

"Seoul, Korea."

"I'm from Albuquerque. New Mexico."

Byung Duk Soo beamed as if my point of origin was a source of vast merriment. Unspeakably pleased with our exchange, she nodded and returned to her chair.

"And I'm the house disgrace," a woman in her mid-forties volunteered.

"Heh-heh." Judith sawed off an imitation of laughter. "This is Esme," she said. "Esme is working on her dissertation in philosophy."

Esme, well into her forties, was curled up with a copy of Hannah Arendt's *Origins of Totalitarianism*. She was decked out in a hot pink and turquoise mini-skirt that exposed ghastly yards of varicosed leg. A torn sweatshirt bearing the message that "The Fab Butthole Surfers Ride the Rim!!!" slid off her wrinkled shoulder. Her hair, hennaed to a violent purplish orange, had been terraced into an upside-down stairstep cut like an inverted ziggurat. Meeting this menopausal woman in her abrasively trendy gear was like seeing a progeric, one of those prematurely aged kids, bald and wrinkled as a lizard, beneath a Cub Scout uniform.

I twinkled my fingers in hello, but Esme was too engrossed in Hannah Arendt to notice.

Judith faced me, took a deep breath, then launched into a soliloquy that had the canned flavor of many past renditions. "We're a community of women here. What we're about here is growth—personal and academic. Alamo House is a sharing, giving kind of a thing."

I tried to look like I cared.

"If it's a concept in living that you think you could be comfortable with, that you feel you could invest some of your energy and your self in, come for dinner this evening. We eat at six. Everyone in the house has to meet and approve new residents."

Fat fucking chance, I thought as I left. Alamo House sheltered the largest collection of academic eccentrics, sixties throwbacks, and social retards I'd ever seen at one time. I was more than ready to leave them behind when I was stopped dead on the porch by an overpowering clove-scented cloud. It was coming from the stairwell off the porch that led up to the second floor. I peeked up.

For the first time in my life I understood what it meant for a person to be stunningly good-looking. A Scarlett O'Hara-era Vivien Leigh, with her hair turbanned in a towel, was crouched on the top stair talking on the phone. She was far too engrossed in her conversation and in chain-smoking clove cigarettes to notice me. I took the opportunity to inventory Towelhead: a face straight out of the forties which made her look all that much better in the eighties. Luminous skin, I mean a glow you could read by. Perfect eyebrows, dense arches over dark eyes. Bambi eyelashes. A couple of acres of cheekbone and nose and lips off a cameo. What on earth was such a creature doing here at *Moldering Arms*?

All I could think was, good thing Roger isn't with me. Towelhead made me feel that perhaps my rightful place *was* down in the trenches doing hand to hand with the cockroaches. I didn't need to have Roger suaving all over himself to confirm my worst fears.

As I chugged up the long hill leading to the Lyndon Baines Johnson Presidential Library and Pyramid, I decided I couldn't wait to toss Alamo House at Roger. Since I made my own hours, I simply wheeled around and headed for our shared abode, the Love Hovel.

A word about Roger. He was a professor of the lowest rank in a discipline that the University of Texas held in no great esteem— anthropology. One of the bearded buck privates in the armies of academe, he actually confronted things like freshmen and papers needing to be graded. Overall he was fairly aware, cared more than most people, and, for a time, I did love him.

Unfortunately so did his mother. Roger had never experienced the horrors of making his own bed or swabbing out a commode. Until he left home at eighteen, he was convinced that elves and fairies whisked his clothes away at night to the Elfland Laundry then brought them back pressed and sweet-smelling the next morning. A not uncommon male belief. All of which left me in the role of charwoman that I was trying to shuck with empty threats about moving out.

Like most everything else I tried in those last weeks, Alamo House was introduced strictly for effect. What I had in mind involved Roger blanching visibly at the tragedy of losing me, then looking off into a dimming horizon as he choked out, "God, no, Mary Jo . . . there's no life for me without you."

As it turned out, Roger and I were working from radically different scripts.

"So, Alamo House?" Roger repeated after me in that way he used to draw out his less-than-brilliant students. "Why would they name a woman's co-op boardinghouse after the place where all those Texas heroes were massacred? There's something disturbing about that."

"Roger, it's not Santa Anna House," I reminded him. "They name everything down here after the Alamo." One of Roger's more annoying traits was that he saw radical feminism everywhere.

"Are you seriously considering it?"

Roger's tone alarmed me. We were discussing my moving out, not whether to order in pizza. The emotional pitch was far too low. Roger's litter of socks and boxer shorts gave me courage.

"Roger, I can't handle the situation around here. Because I know it makes you break out in hives, I won't mention the exact nature of our problem but it does have to do with a one-woman struggle to turn back the ever-cresting tide of filth we live in."

Roger squinted painfully. "That is an entirely cultural perception, Mary Jo. I mean the whole construct is cultural. Filth is far from an absolute."

"Roger, save your insightful anthropological analyses for the coeds. The cockroaches are, at this very moment, massing for an attack on our kitchen."

Roger shrugged and gave me a beneficent, enlightened smile. "Cockroaches don't bother me. There is no conclusive evidence that they are carriers of human disease. For God's sake, Mary Jo, when I was doing my field study on that baboon troop in Kenya colubrid snakes would crawl into my sleeping bag with me. They were not poisonous. They did not bother me. If cockroaches bother you, do something about them."

"I have, ever since I moved in and you welched on our deal, and I am about ready to resign." That was when I uttered those fateful words: "Maybe we shouldn't live together for a while." I tensed, ready to spring into action in case the thought of life without my constant companionship should throw Roger into a state requiring cardiopulmonary resuscitation.

Instead he tilted his head to one side and looked at me like some genius cocker spaniel trying to puzzle out my motives. He has big, sorrowful Albert Einstein eyes that he knows make me goofy as a game show contestant. He *should* know, I've told him often enough. Anyway he had them turned on me now as if I were one of the baboons he'd slept with snakes to be around. I was afraid he'd start making field notes.

"How much is rent?" he probed. "Is it close to the university?"

Why was he asking logistical questions? He should tear his broken heart from his chest and hand it to me if only I would stay.

"Two-twenty. Two blocks away." I threw those bald facts into the pot like they were the deed to the farm. Roger called my bluff.

"You say you feel isolated here. It would be a way for you to meet people."

I nodded numbly. I was bleeding to death on the emergency room floor and the doctor was telling me to try another hospital where I could meet nice young people my own age. I was frozen. One thing I'd learned is that you can't demand that someone love you. They either do or they don't.

I gave up on "working" on relationships after David. David and I worked on our relationship like it was the Great Wall of China. Hours of gut- and soul-wrenching confrontations in which we rooted around for the noxious growths within ourselves that were choking the life from our puny passion.

After three weeks of this I found myself with an itch that wouldn't stop. It was pubic. It left tiny pinpricks of blood on my underwear. It was, as probably the average third-grader could have told me, crab lice. I, however, had to pry one of the wee beasties off a follicle and take it to David for identification. He told me what to buy to kill the little creepers. The Kwel box produced the name of the parasite I was hosting. *Our Bodies, Our Selves* revealed that they were a surer sign of carnal betrayal than lipstick on the collar and hidden VISA receipts.

In heartbroken desperation I turned to my best friend, Alice. As I burst into tears, so did Alice. She had something to tell me, we were too close to keep this hidden. She was the crab lice donor. I didn't know if I was supposed to grant absolution or share my Kwel. It was the last time I put in heavy labor on a relationship.

So I didn't wail and rend my garments with Roger. Instead I went for the grand gesture, played my trump card, pulled out the tranquilizer gun and aimed it at the spot right above the horn on the charging rhino. If this didn't bring Roger to his knees, nothing would—I began sorting the albums into two piles.

In the silence that fell I heard Roger rustling behind me. Surely now his strong hands would grip my shoulders in a Rhett Butler embrace which would sing of love and need and devotion. He would beg me to reconsider. I held my breath.

"The Bruce Springsteen and the Talking Heads are both mine. Why are you putting them in separate piles?"

The tumbrels had started rolling and I was on board. We had our belongings disentangled in a few hours. When Roger had gotten a contract to teach at UT, we'd come down from New Mexico with only as much as we could pack into his secondhand Audi. I'd stored most of my things, so there were only my few boxes of clothing, the series of early 1900s *Ladies Home Journal* covers I'd framed, the bleached-out turtle shell I'd found at camp when I was eleven and had used for a soap dish ever since, and the sheets I stripped right off the bed. I pulled my other set off the bathroom shelf. If Roger was going to be mingy about Bruce Springsteen, I was taking my sheets. Both sets.

We weren't speaking by the time we pulled up in front of the co-op. In the evening shadows it looked as homey and inviting as the House of Usher. On the porch, I noticed a hand-painted sign I'd missed earlier: "Graduate Students, Don't Litter. Pick up the Shards of Your Frustration." I sleepwalked inside. Only then did I remember about coming to dinner and being approved by the other residents. Dinner was clearly long over. A few denizens were in the living room studying or lingering over coffee at the dining-room table. I spotted Carrot Girl, the terminal vegetarian, and waved feebly to Byung Duk Soo, who burst into her megawatt smile complete with a couple of vigorous head nods. Judith of the snake-charmer eyes, I remembered. She uncoiled and came forward.

"We missed you at dinner."

"Uh, sorry. I couldn't make it." This could be my break. They'd reject me now on a technicality and I could return to Roger with the news I wanted to believe he was hoping for, that I was coming home. "I guess this means I can't move in," I prayed.

Judith pressed forward and drew me further into the house like a Juarez shopkeeper with a warehouse full of onyx burros and black velvet paintings to unload. "Not necessarily. We might be able to negotiate something here. You *are* a graduate student, right?"

"Well, I haven't actually gone to any classes," I equivocated. "I've only registered."

"What college?"

"Communications."

"Hey, that's terrific!" Judith bobbed her head enthusiastically. I think she was "reinforcing" me. Even knowing what Judith was doing, though, didn't stop me. I was starved for a few bobs of approval. "I'll be in the graduate program in photojournalism."

Again she rained nods on me.

"How about you?" I asked, pretty sure I already knew the answer.

"I'm finishing up my dissertation in clinical psychology."

"What's your topic?"

The dark eyes lit with a strange fire. "I'm doing a study based on my internship work at Student Counseling on the inherent fallacies of conjugal and quasi-conjugal dyads."

"You mean, like, why relationships don't work?"

She narrowed those suffering eyes. "Something along those lines," she allowed.

It was my turn then to bob approbation and we both stood there bobbing and grinning like a pair of hula dolls in a car window. Outside the Audi containing one-half of the quasiest of conjugal units tooted in its peremptory, Germanic way.

Judith lowered her voice and raised her eyebrows expectantly.

"Someone waiting for you?" Her eyes were twin black furnaces demanding constant loads of dark grief to keep them fueled. I fed them.

"Yeah, the man I was living with." Promoting Roger to "man" felt like fraud. He'd always been a "guy" before but talking to a head-bobber makes you say that kind of thing. Judith's eyes melted into pools of professional commiseration.

"I sensed you'd been through some emotional devastation. Would it be invasive of me to ask what happened?"

"He wouldn't share . . ." I paused. Judith froze mid-bob. How could I say "housework"? I was supposed to be emotionally devastated. ". . . himself," I finished. That response won the Head-bobber's Palsy Award. Judith boinged herself silly.

"Why is it so difficult for men to allow themselves the privilege of opening up? Of being authentically intimate?"

Of even flushing every time, I wondered? Outside, the Audi tooted again. "About moving in?" I made my question neutral, undemanding, easy to refuse.

"No problem. I'm thinking we can draw up a contract on a probationary basis and get you settled in tonight." She turned to the study group and asked, "That okay with all you folks?" No one so much as twitched in response. "Great!" She dug out a piece of paper from a nearby desk entitled Alamo House Residency Contract. It looked about as probationary as the Magna Charta.

"Can't we look at the room first," I stalled.

"Oh sure." Judith gave a silly-me laugh and led me out of the living room through a kitchen equipped with restaurant-sized accessories—a stove with eight burners, five-gallon vats of mayonnaise, a skillet large enough to fry slices of giant redwoods—into an alcove that opened in back of the kitchen. It led to a bedroom with all the charm and lightness of a boiler room. It also smelled like all the fried, boiled, and burned meals that had been cooked in the kitchen for the past century. My depression deepened. Judith put the full range of her years of postgraduate training into an analysis of my mood. She perceived that I was not pleased.

"There's another double upstairs and several singles," she volunteered.

"Singles?" It hadn't dawned on me that the quoted rate came with a roommate. "How much is a single?"

"Three-twenty."

Some quick calculations revealed that, on top of tuition and books, a single would necessitate more hours at the Presidential Mausoleum than I cared to cram into a month. I frowned. A non-intimate roommate at age twenty-seven was out of the question.

"In all likelihood," Judith dived in, "we won't be getting any more new folks this semester. If you take a double, you'll probably end up with a single. At least that's what I've been seeing for the past two years that I've been House Coordinator."

"Let's see the other double."

We had to go outside onto the porch to reach the stairs. I flagged a limp wave down to Roger. He didn't return it. What a switch this was from the way we'd started. He was a teaching assistant in the anthro department the summer I spent photographing a dig at a sixteenth-century Spanish mission outside of Albuquerque. I was tan and lithe that summer and Roger was just one of a half-dozen guys I'd dated. I started out with a strong lead in our relationship, but somewhere along the line the balance had shifted and I ended up on boxer-shorts patrol.

My balance-of-power reveries were wiped away as I glanced up and saw that Towelhead was again installed beside the upstairs phone, only this time she wasn't wearing a towel. She had on one of those wig caps that skin your hair back and a drastic amount of makeup. The combination would make most mortals of any sex look like a female impersonator between shows. Towelhead managed to look even more dramatically beautiful.

As we slid past her, young Vivien Towelhead turned away to muffle an intense exchange. "You heard me, I'm not coming back. Not yet. I can't, you know that."

Of course, someone was begging for the return of *her* radiant presence.

The room was as much of a surprise as young Vivien. It was open, light, and airy. Windows ran the entire length of the street side. Alamo's one leafy treetop edged the view. It was a tree house.

In the car below, Roger was sunk behind the wheel in a sulk I could spot two stories up. He pissed me off. He really did. He needed a chance to miss me. To wallow up to his eyeballs in his cultural constructs.

"I'll take it." If I'd considered for two seconds more I never would have uttered those words. "Did you bring the contract up?"

Judith whipped it out and I signed.

"Great!"

A trail of ink dribbled down the bottom of the page as Judith whisked the contract out from under my pen. Just as abruptly, her tone changed from reinforcing cheeriness to a dreary monotone. "Okay, we'll get your duties assigned tomorrow. Toni does work scheduling, you can talk to her. Everyone gets their own breakfast and lunch. Dinner is at six. If you have a class or are going to be out, leave the cook a note and she'll make a Save Plate for you. That's probably all you need to know for tonight. Toni can explain the rest of it to you tomorrow. Okay, here's your keys. This one's for your room, and this one's for the side door. Anything else? I've got to get back to my dissertation."

The bobbing and beaming cut off abruptly. Suddenly I felt like I'd rudely intruded on Judith and hauled her away from higher pursuits to pander to my selfish demands. I shook my head no.

"Good," Judith exhaled.

It didn't take Roger and me long to wrestle my boxes up the stairs. The job would have been even shorter if Roger hadn't tripped over his tongue every time he passed Towelhead.

When I saw his spaniel eyes mist over for Towelhead the way they used to for me, I couldn't take any more. I shut down and tried to excise my feelings right at their core. We were like two Mayflower movers on a job. After the last silent trip, Roger sank onto one of the twin beds. That was usually my signal to get horizontal, the faithful hound that collapses at the foot of the Barcalounger every time her master takes his ease. Tonight, I took the wooden chair in front of the rickety desk. Such were the furnishings.

"What's wrong, babe?"

I tilted my face and gave him a look of disgust that it wouldn't have taken a baboon expert to decipher.

"Look, we're not splitting up or anything," he whined.

A slow burn of annoyance was melting the novocaine block in my chest.

"I thought this was what you wanted," he added.

"Right," I snipped. "It's a dream come true for me. I always wanted to do 'Little Women Go to Grad School.' "

"Come on, Jo-Jo, you haven't been happy with me for a long time. Not since we moved to Austin at least. Maybe before. I haven't known what to do, how to make you happy."

Try picking up your underwear, slob, I almost snapped, but Roger had already whammed me with one of his meltdown gazes. Even with his standard-issue anthro prof mustache and the tiny corrugations crinkling around his eyes, you could still tell that he had been a heartbreaker of a little boy. I flashed on him in elastic-waist shorts and scabby knees and, right when the situation was most critical, my gullible body started beeping out the All Clear.

I went for the spot Roger patted on the bed beside him. Maybe this would work out after all. For the first time in months, I looked at Roger and saw a person instead of the first link in the Filth Chain. He looked at me in the same muzzy way and lightly brushed my lips with his. It was that look, those feather kisses, which had kept me saying for the last couple of months, okay, this is what it's about, ignore the small stuff. Then it hit me: I really could ignore the small stuff, the microscopically bacterial, the many-legged: I didn't have to live with them any more. I could have the best of Roger and our relationship up here in my treehouse without having to feel like a chump. What a great deal I'd blundered into. He started chewing on my neck and my nipples went into Red Alert. So had his crotch.

He scooped me against his cumin-scented chest. I stiffened.

"What's wrong?"

You smell like a Number Three Enchilada Dinner, I thought. Your pheromones have Vivien Towelhead's name on them. You didn't cling to my ankles when I left. Before I could choose my answer, the door to the room burst open and in wiggled—Marilyn Monroe?—that is, the reasonable facsimile created by Towelhead in a cotton candy blond wig, black beauty mark, strappy sundress, and spike heels. She made her entrance, ascertained that she had captured our attention, bunny-wiggled her pert nose, did some complex undulations with her mouth, and husked out a whispery "Hi."

Roger jumped up. "Well, hi back at you."

I wanted to send Marilyn away for a nap with a large bottle of barbiturates.

She looked around the room then faced me, all the Marilyn kittenisms gone. "So Judith stuck you with Hell Week Heaven."

"This room? Hell Week Heaven?" I asked, but she'd flitted away and was positioned now in front of the prints I'd push-pinned into the wall. There were about half a dozen. I'd taken them at the Princess Beauty Shoppe, one of my favorite places in the world. My Great-Aunt Inez at seventy-five had been one of the younger patrons. Blue rinses and bouffants were the stock-in-trade at the Princess. The way I'd printed the photogs, just a touch dark, on fiber-based paper, then sepia-toned, gave the sweet, old women I'd grown up with a timeless quality I loved. I could just look at those pictures and smell the ammonia tang of permanent solution and the menthol Kools that Pearl, the shop's owner, chain-smoked.

"Uh, don't touch the emulsion," I requested as Towelhead ran the chewed-off stump of a fingernail along my name at the bottom of the print.

"That you?" she asked, reading out the name. "Mary Jo Steadman?"

I admitted it was.

She didn't say anything, just turned to the adjacent wall where

I'd tacked up the shots of the mission Roger and his crew had un-earthed the summer we'd first met.

"Where's this, Mary Jo?" she asked.

Roger had been hovering at the point of near-drool for just such an opening. He folded his arms and reared back proprietarily. "That's the dig I supervised at Towatchi down there south of Inchuna."

Towelhead beamed at him. Roger spread his legs apart into a sturdy, manly pose and pointed a finger toward the photo of the nave that he'd excavated. Before he could launch into the recitation of his finest moment in the field, Towelhead interrupted.

"That's incredible," she gushed.

I hated her.

Her effusiveness threw Roger off his pace a bit. The gush of praise was supposed to come later, after he described how he'd single-handedly unearthed the key to Spanish Colonial civilization in the New World. "That I could preserve the entire nave intact?" he fished.

"No," Towelhead answered, her face still rapt with beaming admiration. "That you're named Mary Jo too. I mean, I did ask *Mary Jo* where this place was. It's not often you meet couples with the same name."

For one moment, just for the way Roger's Colossus of Rhodes posture shriveled away, I loved Towelhead. Of course, the next second she was back to Marilyn, making bass mouth maneuvers with her lips and saying, "Mary Jo . . ." (pant-pant) ". . . it was really great meeting you . . ." (pant-pant, nose wiggles, bass mouth maneuvers) "bye."

How did I instinctively know that she was a drama major? Maybe it was the way Roger and I felt after she made her exit, like two minor character actors after the star has taken the audience out with her, stage left. It suddenly seemed very quiet and stultifying in my new room. I began bustling, ripping things out of boxes and putting them anywhere. It was either that or cry, something I was determined to do no more of in front of R. Halpern. He caught me as I was stuffing underwear into the typewriter well of the desk.

"Bun-Bun." He hadn't used my nickname in months. He grabbed my hand.

I shook off his hand. "Don't call me that. Bun-Bun has died."

"Mar, don't be this way." He pulled me to him. "I told you, nothing's changed between us." He dipped his face down to look at mine tucked stubbornly into my clavicles. "Has it? Really? I'll still be coming by to see you."

"To see Wiggles in the blond wig, you mean."

"That schizoid? Never." His words were muffled as he'd begun speaking them into my neck. "I'll come to see my steady. My Numero Uno."

"Why do I get the feeling there will soon be doses, tresses, quatros . . ." My ability to count in Spanish was seriously impaired by the nuzzling Roger had begun to apply himself to with his usual admirable energy. He hauled me in closer to his crotch so that I could take the full measure of the boner bleating in his pants. I felt myself succumbing and pulled away.

"No, Roger. I can't. I need time to think. I'm confused. I'm hurt. My diaphragm's packed."

Roger heaved a sigh and gave a resigned shrug as if to say he'd done all a man could be expected to do. He was turning away from me when an amplified male voice boomed through the room.

"Oh, man, don't wuss out. You know she wants it, man. Make another run on her, hombre."

I lunged for the window. Directly across the street I found the home of the Sigma Upsilon Kappas. Where all the other frat houses in the area looked like Tara, the Sig Up's resembled a decaying Motel Six. A dozen brothers were sprawled out on the second-story balcony, tanning, swilling beer, and peeping on Roger and me through binoculars. I reached up to pull the curtains shut, then remembered I didn't have any. A beefy brother put the bullhorn he held back to his mouth.

"Don't fight the feeling, baby." He was speaking to me! I

turned to hide but stared at a solid bank of windows. "You got the bug. You know you wanna mug. This is The Bub telling you to, go ahead and GRUB!!!"

He kept the trigger on the bullhorn depressed long enough for me to hear a hearty burst of male laughter with tinkling undertones of giggles from the bikinied retinue of "Little Sisters" in attendance. A banner furling in the wind above them read SIGMA UPSILON KAPPA: HELL WEEK. The last two words were written in a fiery orange script with the letters composed of flames.

Roger peered, agog, at the beer-swilling crew. "No doubt, half of my survey class is over there."

He didn't notice me slump down onto the floor beneath the windows, the only spot in the room shielded from their binoculars. Nor did he hear me repeat Towelhead's words, in a dazed mumble. "Hell Week Heaven." I now knew whence my room drew its enchanting nickname. I wondered what other surprises the olive-drab dowager had in store for me.

2

ON MOST DAYS I drag into work like a woman on a chain gang, but, after a night at Alamo House, LBJ's library seemed pretty good by comparison. I skipped breakfast and pedaled off, dodging the empty beer bottles tossed into the street by the Sigma Upsilon Kappas the night before as they'd roared off to some inter-fraternity sporting event. Probably a doubleheader tractor pull and cock fight. Between Alamo House and the library lay Longhornland, the Forty Acres, the University of Texas. It swarmed with students registering for school. Something about seeing that many rich white kids in overpriced T-shirts with reptiles or polo players on them driving around in BMWs reversed the action of my peristaltic waves.

The non-Greek guys who weren't prepped out all looked like they'd just gotten in from safari in their baggy khaki shorts and oversized camp shirts. The coeds mostly had Louise Brooks haircuts and wore sunglasses that turned them into movie stars, heedless, cruel, and dying to sleep with other people's boyfriends. Mine in particular.

Forget him, I thought, huffing up the hill that fronted the library. Roger can sleep with anyone he wants. Let them sample Dumpster Love. I was out of it. I pumped up that hill with piston legs. So Towelhead was beautiful; I had exceptional cardiovascular endurance.

I locked my bike to one of the aggregate rock columns that ring the LBJ Library and noticed, not for the first time, that the edifice resembled nothing so much as a mammoth marble computer chip. On my way in, I passed by two shallow, square pools with fountains that looked like trout-hatching pools. I tried to fan some of the sweat off my face as I walked toward the library. It was hopeless. Fungus infections do well in Austin in late summer (a period that lasts roughly until Christmas); daintiness is a lost cause.

A polar blast hit me as I pulled open the library door. It was so cold inside the Presidential Mausoleum that I expected someday to discover the Big Bopper himself laid out in a remote corner waiting for cryogenics to advance to the point where Lady Bird could thaw him out and start pumping life into those Buddha earlobes and back under that gallbladder scar. I pulled on a sweater before my extremities could ice over as I passed a glass showcase containing a mannequin of one of the two interchangeable daughters in her wedding gown. The case beside it contained the red satin bathrobe of George Foreman, the 1973 world heavyweight champion. The wedding gown I could understand, but the bathrobe? Every day, as I rode the public elevator up to the third floor, I formed new hypotheses about why the bathrobe of a heavyweight champion might be enshrined in a presidential library. Someday I would read the official explanation.

On the third floor, a swarm of federal bureaucrat-librarians buzzed over the dried turds dropped during the Johnson administration and strained to create from the waste something that would withstand the vagaries of time, something that, in a world of impermanence, would endure—a job for themselves. Compared to them, the Galapagos tortoises of the tenured civil service, I, a minimum-wage temporary appointee, was a mayfly. It's hard to imagine that the few months of odd hours I'd already put in had registered very heavily with any of them outside of my immediate supervisor, Mr. Smythe (rhymes with writhe), and his fellow old maid, Dorothy Fenecke.

Mr. Smythe was the one lone male on the third floor supervising a harem of professional anal retentives, all of them garbed in three-piece suits in a rainbow of hues running from clam to cement. There was something wistfully ironic about seeing them all dressed for success and laboring in the two fields to which the term has no relevance—library science and civil service.

The one spot of color in the group was provided by Dorothy Fenecke's wig, a creation of glistening chestnut Dynel. It looked like it had been discarded by one of the Supremes and created the same problem for Dorothy that Ronald Reagan's vividly colored tresses create for him. In contrast, the lump of aging flesh beneath had all the ruddiness of a bowl of oatmeal. Unfortunately Dorothy didn't have access to the services of a makeup man as skilled as Reagan's to balance the effect. A twitch of a smile lifted the corners of her mouth a fraction of an inch off her dentures as I passed through headed for the private, employees-only freight elevator that delivered me to my duty station on the fifth floor.

I exited into the permanent dusk of the fifth floor that I shared with a fellow temp, Tommy Chastain. From the marble floor on the ground level the patriotic tourist can gaze upward at floor upon floor of classic Johnson memorabilia and coprolites. From that angle the fifth looks quite grand. Shelves of mandarin red buckram boxes the size of unabridged dictionaries line the entire glass front of the floor and contain what the tourist brochure describes as "31,000,000 historical documents used primarily by scholars and the Museum." The bare concrete floor and the single bulb over the work area were slightly less grand from my vantage point.

Our job was to sort through the Johnson Social Files. The nature of these files can best be ascertained by reflecting on two facts: First, they had lain dormant for close to two decades with no discernible effect on the chronicling of the Johnson years. Second, two minimum-wage workers with absolutely no training, and even less interest, in library science had been hired to catalogue them. These files appeared to have been created with liberal contributions from the White House janitorial staff. On the days when everyone was simply too pooped to hike all the way out to the dumpster, old hands must have advised, "Just stick it in the Social Files."

Tommy and I were paid to unpack the heavy-duty brown boxes and catalogue the material therein. Next we reshuffled it into the smaller mandarin red display boxes. Two categories immediately suggested themselves as we dug through that first box—Flotsam and Jetsam. They, however, were far too descriptive.

As we emptied the big brown boxes, we broke them down and piled the flattened carcasses around our work area. A shoulder-high fort of eviscerated boxes paid tribute to our industry. Truth to tell, Tommy's industry had flagged markedly once our stack had grown large enough to enclose an area six feet, three inches long, or slightly longer than the length of his supine body.

As I approached our work area, a snore issued from the other side of the brown-box barricade: my colleague's signature greeting. Tommy had obviously had yet another long night. In the life he considered real, he was Kenny, lead singer of Kenny and the Distractions. The current gig was Club Foot, always a grueling experience from Tommy's reports, what with the controlled substances and uncontrolled women forced upon him.

The lack of zeal Tommy displayed for entombing the Social Files didn't bother me. Unlike Roger's laziness, Tommy's slack-off didn't add to my own work load or make me feel like a chump. I catalogued at my own unremarkable rate and Tommy slept. Mr. Smythe never commented on the fact that our output had dropped by precisely one-half after the first two weeks.

This wasn't my first government job so I was already acclimated to the pace. As government workers ascend from city to county to state positions, altitude sickness sets in: exhaustion upon the slightest exertion, glazed eyes, mental fogginess. This condition becomes so critical at the highest, the federal, level that top-level administrators suffer a Guillain-Barré-like condition that renders them incapable of making decisions or sustaining any activity during those few hours of the week—ten to three on Wednesdays and Thursdays—when there is any chance at all that they might be found in their offices.

I pulled my trolley up to a back row midway down the line of shelves and hauled down a brown box from the top shelf. Ability to lift heavy objects from tall places had been the major prerequisite for a position as an archivist technician, which is, technically, what I was.

I'd originally heard about the job at the Texas Employment Commission. Right away I knew that lies were the only route. In the weeks preceding my first encounter with Smythe, I'd already learned that my bachelor of arts impressed employers slightly less than citizenship papers. I'd just finished a month-long engagement at K-Mart. They hired me for my singular ability to both read *and* speak English, then put me to work proofing the ads for Kotex Stayfree Deodorant Pads and 100 percent polyester fashion blouses. The LBJ Mausoleum represented a major step up. I walked into the interview, résumé hastily rewritten, determined to get the job.

"So you're a government major." Smythe peered at that very résumé. From across his huge desk wafted the insipid scent of his after-shave, Lilac Vegetal.

"American government," I interjected peppily.

Smythe plucked a stiletto-sharp pencil out of a bin containing a dozen others, any one of which would have been adequate for performing eye surgery. They all had perfect, unblemished erasers. Either Mr. Smythe never made mistakes or he threw out his pencil if he did. He made a tiny, neat notation, "Am.," beside my "major," government.

"Yes," I elaborated in my perky, I'm-a-high-energy-gal, job-seeking voice, "with an emphasis on Great Society programs and the civil rights initiative of the sixties." Now that I'd started there was no reason to hold back.

Mr. Smythe further amended my application. I was on the verge of adding that I'd taken special courses on Texas presidents and barbecue technology, when Smythe asked, "Do you have any back problems?"

"Back problems?" I echoed.

"Injuries, strains, slipped discs, crushed vertebrae. Back problems," Smythe elaborated peevishly.

"None." I shook my head trying to get a fix on my interrogator. He squared up the papers in front of him, whisked away nonexistent specks of dust, and wrote in my negative reply. His fidgety preciseness suggested not a man who cared for his own sex, but one with no interest in sex of any kind. Sex being simply too impossibly unfastidious. In short, Smythe was the perfect library scientist.

"Can you lift heavy objects?"

This line of questioning was totally unexpected. I checked further Johnsonian raptures and stared blankly. Smythe peeved-out again.

"Boxes. Full of papers. Can you lift them?"

"Yes, of course," I enthused, catching his drift at last. At that moment the store of energy I'd laid in to expend on my fictitious past as a Johnson scholar diverted itself into proving to Mr. Smythe that I was, in fact, a power lifter.

"See," I burbled as I grasped the edges of his typewriter and, using only my fingertips, lifted it easily off his desk. Though I didn't recognize it at the time, my display had sent Smythe into the near-catatonic state that seizes him when more than one pair of eyes strafe him simultaneously. All across the third floor, my untoward exuberance was attracting attention. Meticulously coiffed heads turned in our direction. Smythe submerged deeper and deeper within himself. I thought he was unimpressed with my performance. His silence sent K-Mart Bluelight Specials flashing in my brain. I stood and took a firm hold on the typewriter. I lifted it higher and higher; I curled it up and down. I finished with a demonstration of power pulls from the tallest shelf.

Smythe turned a trembling ashen gray under the scrutiny I'd attracted. "Fine," he hissed. "That's fine. Start Monday."

I lowered the typewriter back to his desk, still not sure what he'd whispered.

"Monday," he squeaked through clenched teeth, flashing me a look of desperation. It was the last time we enjoyed direct eye contact.

Tommy's snore brought me back to the present and I pulled a box off the shelf above me. It rattled on the trolley as I wheeled it over to the work table to unpack. The contents therein exuded the musty smell of the many bureaucrats who had fingered them. I groaned as I pulled out the first bit of incompletely discarded trash—an eight-by-ten glossy of the Big Bopper wearing his Mr. Potato Head cowboy hat and yanking his pet beagle, Her, up by the ears. For the past week I'd been cataloguing and red-boxing the fallout from this twenty-year-old incident. I'd unloaded letters from outraged dog lovers, letters from animal humane associations, letters from veterinarians, letters from Snoopy fan clubs, letters from stricken schoolchildren. Entire classes had taken up Crayolas to scrawl touching missives.

Dear Mr. President,
　　How wood you like it if a big giant came down and holded you up by yur ears? Even if you do have big ears like a dog it still wood not feel to nice. So quit it NOW!

Matthew Jacobs
Third Grade
Miss Walmer's Class

I could see Miss Walmer exhorting her little savages to the first bleedings of their young hearts for poor defenseless Her. I shoved thirty-three letters, one from every outraged pupil in Miss Walmer's class, into a red box, noted the box's number, and wrote beside the notation, "Beagle Controversy, cont." This was subsumed under the larger heading, "Letters to the President, From Third-Graders." When I'd filled half a dozen red bombers from the brown mother ship, I piled them onto the trolley and wheeled them back to the berth left by the emptied box. As I attacked the next brown box on the shelf, I prayed that Miss Walmer's had been the last class in America to cry out against presidential puppy abuse.

To clear a spot on the worktable for the new box, I broke down the newly emptied one, squashed it out, and added it to the pile enclosing my slumbering associate. Tommy was tucked away as usual in a cozily comatose state gargling air. He hadn't washed the mousse out of his hair after last night's performance and it stood out in aggressive spikes. Tommy really shocked the third-floor lifers when he stopped coming to work in job-hunter drag. After the first week he'd abandoned his work-procurement costume of pressed jeans and oxford cloth shirts in favor of lemon-stiffened hair, camou pants, skinny ties, and Ray Charles wraparound sunglasses. Sort of what the average commando junkie would wear on "American Bandstand." Of course, for Tommy, this wasn't mere fashion. No, dress and do were fundamental expressions of his true self, spontaneous flowerings from the deepest wellsprings of his being. Of course.

As I added another half an inch to Tommy's cardboard isolation tank, the door creaked open behind me. It was sneaky Smythe. I could already smell the Lilac Vegetal. The elevator made too many warning noises so, to catch us unaware, he occasionally crept up the stairs to conduct an inspection. Just as he poked his twitchy ferret nose into our domain, Tommy honked off a snore that would have made a Kodiak bear proud. Almost simultaneously I clapped my hands on the top of the wall of collapsed boxes and hacked out a cough loud enough to cover the sound of artillery fire. Tommy and I finished our duet and Mr. Smythe spoke.

"Aren't the filters working?" He hastened to check the elaborate apparatus that gave continual readings on the temperature, humidity, and dust levels in the mausoleum. They were all maintained according to scientific standards designed to assure the longest life technology could guarantee for the collected letters of Miss Walmer's third grade.

"They're working fine," I answered in a mucoid voice. "Id's just that I'b gedding a code." I sounded like I was coming live from La Brea Phlegm Pits.

Smythe backed away precipitously. Bacteria and viruses weren't what bothered him, it was the human who hosted them he found so appalling. From a safer distance he asked, "Where's Chastain?"

"Bathroom," I answered.

"Spends a lot of time . . ." He paused, pursed his lips, then spat out, "there," as if he personally had never made such an expedition.

My sinuses cleared miraculously as I moved on to an even more repellent topic. "Yes, well, as I've mentioned to you before, he has a chronic bladder infection which necessitates these frequent trips. It causes a continuous urge to void," I explained with the frankness of a public health nurse.

Smythe began bobbing his head to signal that I needn't go on.

"You see, the bladder itself is not actually full," I continued, intent upon my educational mission, "but as the bacteria irritate the lining of the urethra . . ." I grated my right hand over the balled fist of my left to illustrate.

Smythe waved the white flag of his pale hand.

". . . they produce that same feeling of fullness we're all familiar with . . ."

Smythe backed away toward the door, reaching out behind himself for the knob.

". . . which would mean under normal circumstances that we have to . . ."

The door banged shut.

". . . piss," I completed my lecture. The inspection tour was apparently over. Tommy's spiky tufts and sleep-reddened eyes periscoped up over the corrugated enclosure.

"Good morning, Sunshine—" I began but was cut off as Tommy bolted all the way up and slammed his hand across my mouth to silence me. He gestured toward the door and whispered, "The sneaky prick's probably still out there."

I crimped my mouth into an "O" of recognition, nodded conspiratorially, and gave the metal trolley a gentle push. In the silence known only to dead presidents and those who work in their libraries, the trolley clanged against the metal door like a venetian blind factory in an earthquake. The furtive brush of shoe leather on concrete steps ended with the rattle of the third-floor door opening and closing.

"The stepladder," Tommy hissed urgently.

I handed over the implement intended for our use in reaching boxes on the uppermost shelves. It was used exclusively by Tommy for crawling in and out of his boudoir. We both scurried to the elevator shaft.

Smythe was reporting to Dorothy. Like Smythe, she too was utterly loyal to library science and the memory of the Big Bopper. "He wasn't there. As usual." Smythe's words came through in all their peevish perfection via the acoustical accuracy of the elevator shaft.

"She said he was . . ." I could see Smythe puckering up, ". . . in the men's."

"Well, she always does. Doesn't she?" Dorothy mirrored Smythe's petulance.

"What eludes me," Smythe intoned, "is how one human being could possibly spend that much time in . . ."

"The men's." Dorothy spared him the completion of the sentence.

Tommy's shoulders began shaking dangerously. I yanked him away before he could erupt into his patented hyena laughter.

"Careful of your bladder," I cautioned.

Tommy pinched his nose and turned red, suppressing his mighty guffaw. Hunched over in a flaming coral shirt, his black jeans tight on his daddy-longlegs limbs, he looked like a demented flamingo.

"Really, Tommy, calm down. You know how hard it is for you to get back to sleep once you've become overexcited."

He let out a long hiss of air and regained control. "Hey, no. I'm awake today. We're cutting some tracks next week and I've got to come up with a dozen new songs."

"Is that all?"

"Yeah."

I nodded and retrieved my trolley pondering as I did how to shuck chumphood and whether turning in my toilet bowl brush would ring down the curtain on Roger and me. Tommy sensed the nature of my preoccupation.

"You still on latrine duty for the Sun King?"

As one of the few people I'd met in Austin, Tommy had been the sole recipient of my confidences for the past few weeks. He was five years younger than I, twenty-two, and made me feel a slightly dowdy aunt with my complaints about Uncle Roger. Still, I qualified as the second most interesting person on the entire floor, so in between naps he listened. He didn't reciprocate though. Tommy was saving his material for his memoirs, or the movie they'd make of his life after he died, tragically young, in the crash of a light plane.

"I moved out yesterday." I noticed my breath was bunching up in a strange way in my chest, almost as if I cared what Tommy thought.

"The Chastain charisma finally got to you, eh? You're ditching Roger for me, right?"

"We both know you're way too much man for me, Tommy."

"You're right, after The Raj I'd blow out all your circuits in one majestic night of love."

"I'd be ruined for mortal man." Tommy and I had riffed around like this from the first day I'd come up to the fifth. It was infantile, but it helped pass the hours at the mausoleum.

"Well it's about time, darlin'. Where'd you move to?"

I told him.

"Women only? What is it? A bunch of dykes?"

"What a scurrilous thing to say."

"Hey, don't blame me. It happens. Ain't my idea. Wait a minute." A slightly dazed and frantic look came over Tommy's features. "Alamo House? That's not, like, right across the street from the SUKs, is it?"

"Come again."

"The SUKs, the Sigma Upsilon Kappa house."

"Indeed it is," I trilled out with mock enthusiasm.

"The SUKs!" Tommy exploded with the most emotion I'd ever managed to provoke. "Fuck, they're the biggest gang of droogs on campus."

"I got that impression."

"At least you're slightly safe from them though; you're the wrong gender."

"Gender? I'm the wrong *species* for those troglodytes."

"No, really. Didn't anyone tell you about the latest in a long line of SUK scandals? The house just got off suspension this year."

"No, no one told me anything," I answered, thinking darkly of Judith and her caring, sharing community. "Not one word."

"Jeez, it even made the papers. An unsuspecting freshman blundered into their rush frolics, and the SUKs hit him where he used to live with a cattle prod."

"You're joking," I prayed.

"Newp."

"And all that happened was the house got put on suspension for a year?"

"That and some frat daddies ended up forking over big bills to settle out of court."

"That is disgusting."

"Welcome to Texas."

"Anyway, the important thing is, I'm out. Roger can forage for his own undies."

"Fucking A. It's like the song says."

"What song's that?"

"The latest from Kenny and the Distractions, that's 'what song.' It'll be our next release. Watch for it." Tommy turned away singing under his breath, "Lie down, doormat, and I'll STEP on you." He nodded his head a few times in tune to the melody running through his head, and, gripped by his Muse, began writing.

Great, every girl wants to inspire an artist. But as a doormat? I thought again of the olive-drab dowager. Of Judith with the snake charmer eyes. Of the couple in overalls ogling the David Hamilton book. Maybe it *was* a notorious lesbian haven. I tried not to think about the SUKs and the rural freshman and dug into the box I'd just unloaded. A stack of letters on Big Chief paper greeted me.

Dear President Johnson,

How could you be so mean? Your doggie was not bad and even if Her was bad dogs do not no it when they are bad. You are the most mean president I no.

Your friend,
Beth Ann Pearson
Second Grade
Mrs. O'Day's Class

3

I COULDN'T DEAL with another traumatized tyke that day. I went to say good-bye to Tommy, but he was already back on snooze control. I checked the digital travel alarm he kept beside his cardboard dorm. How forgetful, he hadn't set it. I punched in five o'clock—wouldn't want Tommy working late—and left. I took the elevator down to the basement so I could sneak out without running into Smythe.

I pedaled back to the Alamo. As I locked my trusty newsboy bike to the scabby pecan the SUKs across the street called out greetings: "Hey, lesbo-dyke-bitch-whore!" I returned a cheery wave and bolted upstairs just in time to witness a new tragedy being played out in my room. There, in Hell Week Heaven, along with Judith, were four of the fattest humans I had ever seen. Two appeared to be the progenitors of the junior hulks beside them, one male, one female in her early twenties and not quite as obese as the other three. The father and son duo looked like Tweedle-dee and Tweedle-dum in their matching overalls. The female hulklet was whining, "But, Maw-Maw, I don't want a double room."

To which Maw-Maw, casually attired in a muumuu that fit like a sausage casing and a pair of tennis shoes with the sides cut out to accommodate her corns, replied, "We ain't paying for no single room and we ain't paying for that nigger hole behind the kitchen neither. This here's a nice room. You kin see the sky."

I saw then the enormity of the catastrophe unfolding before me. Judith was about to parcel out half my living space to the whining blob! I fought to avert impending doom.

"You would not believe how noisy this room is," I said in as close to a conversational tone as I could manage while simultaneously fighting down panic. Judith shot me a reproving look of vexation. It didn't stop me. "There is a fraternity house right across the street and they yell things at you through bullhorns and cattle-prod rural freshmen. You can't sleep up here. Can't study. It's terrible."

Papa Hulk gave me a country shrewd look from behind his glasses, fixed at the temple with a blob of black electrician's tape. "How come you're living here then if it's so all-fired turble?"

I didn't think they would want to hear about Roger's boxer shorts.

His wife joined the counteroffensive. "Baby Girl's used to noise ennyhow. We're rat on the innerstite in Why-ko."

Was that, "Right on the interstate in Waco?" I wondered.

"Listen, here, Baby Girl," said the father, "You kin either live here or we kin turn right around and you kin live at home and sign on at Baylor where you shoulda oughtta be goin' to school in the first place."

Baby Girl ripped the contract out of Judith's hand and signed her name, Fayrene Pirtle, in a faint, spidery script across the bottom.

I sat in stunned silence as the lardy crew sweated up and down the stairs bringing up Fayrene's wardrobe of maternity tops and polyester, elasticized waist, pull-on pants; her Bible with the gold lettering on its white leather cover; her picture of Jesus—Mel Gibson in a blond wig, shepherding the lambs; and what Maw-Maw called the Treat Box. This last contained emergency rations of faded red peanut patties, Chicken Bones sprinkled with toasted coconut, moonpies, Mary Janes, Little Debbie cakes, Bruce's fried pies, and a couple of cans of Pringle's potato chips.

"Whew," Mr. Pirtle heaved a gusty breath as he dropped the last box. "Used to be a person'd move they's only but two things they had to do: Call the dogs and piss on the fire."

Fayrene's eyelids fluttered shut and she blushed pink as cheap lipstick.

"Paw-Paw, you know I don't 'preciate that kind a talk," Mrs. Pirtle reprimanded her husband.

"Well, we'd better git," Mr. Pirtle said, wiping the back of his hand across his sweat-drenched forehead as he peered out the window. "Looks like them fraternity sumsabitches are after Baby Boy."

"His looks are a curse that way," Maw-Maw observed, joining him at the window. "He's just too pretty," she sighed.

I peeked out. The SUKs were shaking up beers and spraying them on Baby Boy waiting on the street beside his family's Vega station wagon.

"Well, come on, we got a long drive ahead of us."

Mrs. Pirtle turned to her daughter with a stricken look and began blubbering. She threw her arms around Fayrene and both of them shook with her sobs. "Oh, baby, don't you go to the bad down here," she pleaded. "Turn away when the heathen rage. Shun fornicators, blasphemers, and idol-worshippers. Put idolators, adulterers, onanists, and anti-Christs behind you."

Mr. Pirtle dragged his wife away, but her danger list echoed up to us as it faded down the stairs. ". . . secular humanists, evolutionists, money-changers, cabalists . . ." On the street Mrs. Pirtle's warnings were drowned out by the mocking hoots and catcalls of the SUKs. Baby Boy, who seemed a tiny bit feebleminded, was mesmerized by the SUKs, who had graduated to pouring beer directly over his large, round head. Mr. Pirtle swatted the brothers away and pulled his son into the Vega. With the telltale scything sound of a clutch about to go, they drove off.

Fayrene was still perched on the bed. She had chosen not to witness the departure and seemed to be concentrating very hard until she heard the scything sound and the sputter of the overburdened station wagon pulling away, then she relaxed a tiny bit. The tiniest filament of a common bond linked us—neither of us wanted to be in the other's company. I dredged up a little graciousness.

"What are you studying?" I asked.

Fayrene answered in a soft voice sweetened by her Baptist Jesus and Maw-Maw's Treat Box—"Library science."

I smiled and nodded, trying to disguise the fact that she'd just laid the final straw on my back. I could not live in the same room with a library scientist, with one of Smythe's and Dorothy's brethren. Maybe, in the farthest stretches of my imaginings, I could learn to endure Judith, Towelhead, and the SUKs, but a library scientist? In my own room?

"Oh, gadzooks!" I looked at my watch. "Gotta run. Big appointment with a professor. Faculty adviser," I muttered, backing precipitously out of a room I prayed I would never have to enter again. "Got to plan out my course of studies. Real important. Vital," I continued babbling until I was on the stairs.

Outside, I was momentarily diverted by the sight of a pack of SUKs clumped on their front porch. What unsettled me was that they didn't immediately begin to hurl their signature brand of Cro-Magnon abuse. I kept them under intense surveillance as I edged toward my bike. I was still watching them as I felt for the back wheel I had laced the chain through. It wasn't there. I looked down. The wheel *was* in fact there, but, along with the rest of the bike, it had been wrapped around the tree. Tears jumped into my eyes at the sight of my mangled bike. Across the street a chorus of brawny har-hars rang out.

I put my head down and started walking. I didn't know where; I just couldn't deal with Nut Street anymore. It was late evening when I found myself back in Travis Heights, my old neighborhood. After one day of co-op living, our rent house did indeed look like the Palace at Versailles. I was halfway ready to return to domestic duty if only I didn't have to endure any more Alamo depravities.

Funny, I thought, the door was locked. That was very unlike Roger "Property Is Theft" Halpern. I peeked in the front window expecting to see Big Mac wrappers and dirty socks littering the floor. The living room was immaculate. Actually tidier than it had been when I'd left. What was going on? I marched to the bedroom window. Nose pressed against the mesh of the screen, I saw a moiré-screened Roger tucked into our bed. Nestled against his neck was either a large hamster of the long, fluffy-haired Teddy Bear variety, or a head of blond hair.

"Roger, you donkey dick!" I screamed through the screen. The full benefit of growing up with three brothers makes itself felt at times of acute distress.

Roger jerked up holding the sheet daintily under his chin with one hand while he frantically tucked in the bundle beside him with the other. What was he trying to do? Make me believe that he'd merely dozed off with a rolled-up rug beside him?

"This is what I get for giving a worm an even break," I sputtered. "You, you, you . . . Enchilada Armpit." It was lame but the best I could do before shock laid me out. "Don't bother calling me, Halpern."

I marched furiously for several blocks before the full implications of Roger's betrayal hit me: I really couldn't go home again; I was condemned now to Alamo House.

4

I STOOD OUTSIDE the door to Hell Week Heaven for several minutes unable to turn the knob. Finally I detoured into the bathroom. I turned on the water and flushed the toilet repeatedly to cover the sound of my weeping. A half-dozen tenderhearted cockroaches crept out of their hiding places. They gathered at my feet like the kind mice who were the movie Cinderella's only friends. The little guys waved their wee antennae at me in a touching display of interspecies commiseration.

I hope they knew how much it cheered me to dispatch four of their number to Valhalla with my sandal. The two survivors scurried away to spread the tale of human perfidy (a tale that would cause my toothbrush to be peppered every night thereafter with tiny black roach turds). I was left alone again to contemplate the prospect of returning to a room with two hundred pounds of library scientist beached within and fraternity Visigoths encamped without.

Oh, the inexpressible tackiness of the scene. The four smeared roach corpses. The toilet seat worn down to bare wood by the bums of countless graduate women. The shower curtain patterned in an intricate plaid of cracked plastic and mildew.

I thought of the bathroom back in Travis Heights. Of the swans that glided serenely across the glass shower door. I wondered if the Teddy Bear blond would scour their etched bodies. I missed those swans. Tears burbled over my cheeks. I'd never again bathe under the haughty regard of those lost swans. I reeled off a big wad of toilet paper and honked into it. The sinus-resonated sound was almost enough to make me miss what came next.

At first I thought that the bathroom had incredible acoustics, echoing back the sound of my liquid grief with perfect fidelity. I was momentarily impressed. I had no idea of the passionate breadth of emotion I could generate. The sound of it struck me in the heart like a Brassai photograph of a Parisian demimondaine who lets the camera glimpse the disappointment and hurt behind her sharp Cupid's-bow lips. Then I realized that the sound had not originated in the bathroom. It was coming from the bedroom wedged between the bathroom and my boudoir where the lardi-tudinous Fayrene waited.

In her old age, Alamo's grand salons and majestic sleeping chambers had been divvied up into a warren of interconnecting rooms by the slimmest margins of Sheetrock and plywood. The bathroom addendum I sat in had all the solidity of a Porta-Potty. It was no wonder I could hear The Weeper in the next room. Probably if I'd listened hard enough I could have made out her pulse rate too. I wondered which Alamo inmate was on the other side of the plywood. I was certain I hadn't met her. You can tell so much from the sound of a person crying. The Weeper could not possibly be any one of the zero-based personality deficiencies I'd already run into.

My own salty wet ones were staunched by admiration. The Weeper was shedding tears that made mine seem as pretentious as Perrier water. She was weeping the tears of all women who have ever sorrowed. In the face of such epochal suffering, I saw my own travails as wispy and fleeting things, a mist that would clear in the morning sun. Why, a tropical rain forest of unhappiness lay on the other side of the plywood. I almost felt as if I could leave off being depressed now because there was someone doing the job so much better. Someone with a depth of emotion I couldn't even approach.

With curiosity supplanting bereavement, I trundled back to bed. First thing tomorrow I would find out who The Weeper was.

Fayrene had already turned out the light. I found my way to my bed in the darkness aware that my new roommate was not asleep and gratefully joined in the charade that she was. What the hey? After last night's dusk-to-dawn serenade by the Sigma Ups, I was ready for an early night. Just as I lay down, though, the SUKs cranked up the party machine. My head touched the pillow at the same moment that heavy metal screamer, David Lee Roth, began shrieking his version of the old Beach Boys' song:

> *I wish they all could be California girls*
> *Dah-dah-dah, dah-dah-dah, dah-ah-dah-ah-dah-ah*
> *Ee-yow!*
> *I wish they all could be California girls*
> *Well I been all around this great big world*
> *And I seen all kind a girls*
> *But I couldn't wait to get back in the states*
> *Back to the cutest girls in the world*
> *Ee-yow-w-w-w!*
> *I wish they all could be California girls!!!*

When the floor stopped trembling between songs, I could make out the faint sounds of The Weeper. My bed butted up against what seemed to be a nonfunctioning wooden door. A quick moonlight inspection revealed that it had, in a more elegant incarnation, been a French door, but that the panes were now painted over with Alamo's sodden green. Hell Week Heaven had probably been a porch or breezeway a hundred years ago. I tapped a pane. Sure enough, beneath the paint was glass. And on the other side of it was The Weeper. It sounded as if she were tapering off into some light snuffling, sort of like a master running the scales. I was oddly comforted, as if she grieved, like a great, mothering Pieta, for all women everywhere who'd ever gotten the shaft.

As my breathing slowed and deepened, Fayrene must have

thought I was actually asleep. As soon as she deemed it safe, she too began sniffling in the dark. Soon graduate-woman grief was coming at me in stereo. I was about ready to make this duet into a trio when the voices of frat rats high on beer and hormones penetrated the gloom.

"Look out, the Brew Blaster is fixing to unwind again!" a beefy voice bellowed.

"Dive, dive! Brew Blaster Attack!" The shout was taken up by half a dozen braying voices. It grew louder as the voices approached.

"Brew Blast on the dykes!" they chorused from a position directly beneath our window. I could hear the odious clods trampling the shrubbery beside the porch downstairs. Fayrene stopped sniffling and peered into the night. I crept over to the window and joined her. There, illuminated by the front porch light, were a cluster of SUKs supporting one of their pack by his flaccid arms. As we watched, the slumping member hunched over. A great, resonating retch reverberated up to us followed by the unmistakable cascading sound of used beer waterfalling over foliage.

"Way to go, Kytes," the brothers enthused. "Good spray. You got at least a five-by-five coverage offa that one."

Kudos delivered and recorded, they shouldered their spent comrade and dragged him away.

"All right, Kytes," they chorused. "That blast deserves a brewski." They charged back to Motel Six for beer and noise.

Well, the midwest farmer's daughter
Really makes me feel all right
And the northern girls
They keep their boyfriends warm at night
I wish they all could be California girls

California girls. (A reason to like skin cancer.) The music pounded us. For a minute it filled the silence in Hell Week Heaven with a dense bombardment of noise molecules. Then it was over. In the moonlight, I saw Fayrene's pink lips pucker and push deep folds into her chubby cheeks. Then they unpuckered and expelled two words:

"What assholes."

I couldn't believe what I'd just heard whispered by the Baptist library scientist.

"Pardon me," I prompted.

"What . . ." Fayrene paused, and in that fraction of a second I felt the weight of her half ton of family, her blond Jesus, and the Dewey decimal system tugging at her. Surely she'd sink beneath their combined tonnage. She didn't. "Assholes," she repeated in as affirmative a whisper as I'd ever heard, knowing that no other judgment would be truthful.

"My sentiments exactly."

After a lengthy silence, again the soft whisper. "This room really is terrible."

"I tried to warn you. They call it Hell Week Heaven."

"This whole place is pretty terrible."

"A bad attitude," I said. "I'm glad to see it."

"What other kind could you have around here with the cockroaches and all the weird people who live here and fraternity guys vomiting in the front yard?"

"Not a particularly charming picture, is it?"

"It's gross."

"But the price is right."

"Why else would anyone live here?" Fayrene asked.

I fell asleep before I could think of one other earthly reason.

5

BREAKFAST IS a brutal time to meet new people. As an introvert who's learned to compensate, it's something I do best around midnight with an assortment of chemical crutches. It took a few days before I could face *le petit dejeuner chez Alamo*. I studied the dozen or so women seated at isolated spots around the mead hall-length dining room table and was relieved to discover that none of them looked like they wanted to meet anyone either. Their faces, all locked into newspapers, school books, or comas that wouldn't lift before noon, alternately assaulted me—each face too distinct and intruding for seven in the morning—then blurred together in a muddy sludge. My housemates, or most of them anyway. It was like walking into the Greyhound coffee shop and signing on as a regular.

Forget surviving two years of graduate school while dwelling in the hairy bosom of Panhellenism, I was living to save enough to make Alamo a memory. I shoveled in another spoonful of granola, the only remotely breakfast-type edible I'd been able to locate in the kitchen amidst the forty-pound sacks of whole grains stored in steel garbage cans and hunks of frozen meat that looked like they'd been torn off a mastodon. I hadn't eaten granola for ten years since I discovered it was calorie antimatter. Saddlebags in a bowl.

Tiny, charred sesame seeds, black against the bluish white of the reconstituted powdered milk I'd found in the restaurant-sized, double-door refrigerator, floated to the top of the bowl of homemade granola. They looked like sugar ants after a forest fire. I shoved the bowl away.

A prissy type flounced past in a "housecoat." She carried a plastic bucket containing a sterling silver egg cup, a tiny hourglass, her own personal Creuset saucepan, and a monogrammed linen napkin. She performed a stylized ritual, the end product of which was *the* perfect three-minute egg. From the moment she decapitated her creation, her day would have to go downhill. So few things in life can be controlled as neatly as an egg.

"Constance. She does that every single day." I turned toward a face right out of Beauty Makeovers. She was an After with a vengeance, one who was never going back to Before, not even for breakfast at Alamo House.

"You're the one Judith got to sign up for Hell Week Heaven, aren't you?" After asked brightly. Without waiting for a response, she went on, "I'm Alexis Hartwell."

Alexis presented a Technicolor contrast to the grad-school grunginess of the rest of the breakfast crowd. Her eyebrows were tweezed into two slender arches over a rainbow of eyeshadows running from Plumfrost to Dried Blood. Her lips glistened as if she'd just eaten a pound of Vaseline. Two streaks of brown slanted across her cheeks attempted to create the illusion of shadows from the cheekbones she didn't have. Mostly they made her look like Geronimo on a peckish day.

"Mary Jo Steadman," I answered. She sliced up a banana, then speared each section on a fork and passed it through the petroleum by-product barricade shimmering around her mouth.

Words formed on the oil slick. "I'm in RTF. Radio-Television-Film," Alexis elaborated in response to my blank look. "I've already had quite a bit of radio experience. Started out doing IDs during baseball games. I'm interning now at the *Daily Texan*. Print experience gets you big credibility dividends. Of course, they don't pay shit, which is why I have to live here."

I nodded.

"I've made a tape to take around to show the station managers in town. I'll get a job in news for a while, for the exposure, to get my name known. My five-year goal is to have my own talk show."

Alexis undoubtedly would make it. She was a Black Hole, an egomaniac whose attention is focused so intensely inward that not a glimmer is allowed to escape outward. I excused myself before she launched into the complete exposition of her five-year-plan.

Across the street a black man in a rumpled white jacket was gathering beer cans off of the SUK's yard. The wad of granola in my stomach turned to concrete when I saw my bicycle, my sole means of transportation, pretzeled around the pecan. Band of droogs, they'd get theirs. I stomped off to the library under a cloud of dark thoughts. I rounded up a rotating cast of characters and took turns staking them each out on the anthill in my mind. It alarmed me that there were so many candidates—the SUKs, Roger, the Teddy Bear blond, Judith, Smythe, Dorothy Fenecke, I even gave Towelhead a turn just to see how beautiful and heedless she'd look sweating on an anthill.

As I got off the elevator at the fifth floor, I could have sworn I heard maracas. I followed the sound back to the work area. Tommy was there in the drizzle of light, his hair dyed black, brushed sleekly back and held in place by a bandana headband around his forehead. The beginning of a hairline mustache was sprouting on the thin edge of his upper lip. He had on blackout Ray-Bans, an oversized Pendelton plaid shirt buttoned up to his chin, and a pair of work khakis and was shaking maracas. He stopped when I appeared.

"Orale, huisa," he greeted me in breezy barrio slang.

"Tommy?"

"Chuy to you, mamacita."

"Chuy? Tommy, why are you dressed like a lowrider?"

"Hey, it's the way I dress, esse." He started shaking the maracas again, accompanying himself as he pounded an imaginary

Farfiza organ and sang the title of his latest anthem, "Ninety-six tears. Ninety-six tears."

"You're in a new band," I guessed.

"Chuy y Los Nuevo Wavos. El maximo, no?"

"Oh, si," I agreed. "The maximal most. What happened to Kenny and the Distractions?"

"DOA, baby. Too early eighties."

"When did you decide that?"

"I've known it for a long time, I just got confirmation is all. From Allan."

"Allan. The guy who's sleeping with the scout for that MTV show?"

"Yeah. It's supposed to be some big secret, but she came to the Foot last night and told Allan what I knew already."

"Too early eighties."

"Yeah. They're trying to capture the 'real flavor of Austin music' or some such horsepucky. Anyway, what could be more flavorful than Chuy y Los Nuevo Wavos?"

"But the Distractions had a big following. At least Kenny did. With the women anyway."

"Girls you mean," Tommy snorted. It was the first hint of discontent he'd ever displayed in my presence with his role as a reigning sex god of Austin. "Women, someone with a brain, would consider me a joke."

"A joke. I don't know about that."

"So tell me how seriously *you* take me."

I looked warily at Tommy; he was venturing into territory far outside of our bantering limits. What would happen if I told him that I wasn't immune to dark eyes and long lashes? Or that joking around with him amidst the detritus of the Johnson administration was the one bright point in my increasingly dreary life? My morale could not withstand seeing him transformed into a crazed, laughing flamingo by the hilarity of having suckered an honest answer out of me.

"Oh, hey," I answered, "guys in headbands and pencil-thin mustaches just put me in hormonal overdrive."

There was a half-second when I almost thought Tommy might have been serious, but he shook the maracas and yipped like a vaquero joining the coyotes on a lonely night under a Chihuahuan moon. "Ay-yi-yi-yi-yi! Ay-chee, madre! Chuy's gonna be on MTV."

I left him doing "Before the Next Teardrop Falls" and went back to the shelves, hoping for something a bit meatier than more beagle letters. I needed material that would occupy my mind. I had a lot I didn't want to think about for a while. I approached the rows of brown boxes feeling like a stevedore on the docks ready to break down a cargoload of bananas. I'd put off the top row of boxes for the past week, but today I was ready for them. I yanked the first one off the top shelf with a mighty tug and ended up hurtling myself into the next row of shelves. Instead of the hernia-producing load I'd prepared for the box felt empty. I brought it back to the lighted work area.

I hauled the box off the trolley, dumped it onto the worktable, and flipped back the top. Inside the big brown box were dozens of small heart-shaped, white satin boxes monogrammed with curlicued red initials.

"What the fuck?" Tommy expressed my sentiments exactly. He put down the maracas and watched as I opened one of the heart-shaped boxes. Inside the box was yet another tiny parcel resting on a white doily and done up in red foil. I cautiously unwrapped the wee bundle. It contained a slice of something the color and consistency of beef jerky.

"Eat the sucker," Tommy urged.

Like one of Roger's baboons I sniffed the presidential mystery compound, then bit into it. After two decades wrapped in foil, the cake was thoroughly metallicized. It set up a charge between the fillings in my back molars worse than if I'd just eaten the foil.

"LJN," Tommy said, tracing the initials on the heart-shaped box. "It's Luci Presley's wedding cake." Tommy insisted that LBJ's youngest daughter was really the product of a liaison between Lady Bird and Elvis Presley. He'd come to that conclusion during his first week when he was still sorting through boxes alongside me and had unearthed a picture of Luci that highlighted her jet black hair and a certain sultry sullenness which, Tommy maintained, could only have been transmitted by the King himself. He'd also conducted a genealogy study on Lynda and had traced her true paternity to Big Bird.

There were three more large boxes filled with tiny boxes—all containing tiny slivers of Luci's twenty-year-old wedding cake. I put the last of several dozen mandarin red boxes buzzing with electrified fruitcake on display. Stood back and was mighty proud. Proud that I wasn't yet paying any tax dollars to support wedding cake preservation.

I grabbed for the next box on the shelf eager to find out what precious artifacts waited within and trolleyed it over to the work area. Tommy was seated at the far end absorbed in creation. He mouthed some words to himself, shook the maracas, mouthed the words again in time to the shaking, then wrote them down. I hauled the box onto the table, broke it open, and, for the first time in nearly twenty years, the collected recipes of Lady Bird Johnson saw the light of day. I pulled out a stack of photostats, yellow and crumbling, marked with the notation: BIRD'S RECIPES. MAIL UPON REQUEST TO PRIVATE CITIZENS. SEE ME FOR NATIONAL PUBLICATION. The recipes themselves were of the same down-home, western character that had flavored the Johnson regime.

I nabbed copies of Bird's recipes for Bunkhouse Chili, Ranch-Style Enchiladas, Campfire Beans, Roundup Biscuits, Saddle Blanket Stew, and Lucy's (this was from the days before she'd become a Luci with an i) Double Chocolatey Brownies. There were easily a hundred copies of each recipe. I figured that a couple wouldn't be missed. Probably Luci herself never even whipped up batches of Double Chocolateys anymore. I made quick work of the culinary contributions of the Johnson women and trolleyed them over to their resting place on the back row.

I stowed the last box and glanced down. On the ground floor, a Winnebago-set tourist in powder-blue polyester stared reverently up at the impressive tiers of red boxes extending five floors above him. I could see him imagining the vast historical significance of all he beheld. What great things, he must have wondered, were his tax dollars enshrining? The blueprints of the Great Society? Secret correspondence with Ho Chi Minh?

Would he stare with such reverence if he knew the boxes were stuffed with metallic wedding cake, a complete set of the correspondence of Mrs. Walmer's third-grade class, and the recipe for Lucy's Double Chocolatey Brownies?

I thought not.

Back at the work area, Tommy was already gathering up his things.

"End of another grueling day." He stood and stretched. "Let's go." He jammed in the elevator button.

"Tommy, it's not even four-thirty yet."

"So what? Most of those puds downstairs clock out at four and that is after a two-hour lunch." The elevator doors slid open and Tommy stood aside, holding them open. "After you, m'dear."

I glanced anxiously at the clock. "I don't know, Tommy . . ."

"What is this? Are you suddenly planning a career in archives technology? Dreaming of working your way up to the Gerald Ford Library or something? Really, Marjo, what does it matter?"

"Not much, I guess, except that I have this weird fondness for eating, paying the rent . . ."

"Insignifica, M.J.," Tommy interrupted. "In the grand scheme, it matters fuck all. That is precisely the beauty of government work, it *never* matters."

I shrugged and boarded. On the third floor, half the lifers were, indeed, already gone. Of course, though, Smythe and Dorothy were still there. Tommy put on his Ray-Bans, slumped way down and back, as if he were walking into a heavy head wind, and slouched across the floor with his hands jammed into his pockets. He could have been a truly cool vato cruising East L.A. He gave Smythe and Dorothy a power salute as he slid past them. They went into hyper-peeve and exchanged fidgeting looks like a pair of consternated hamsters. I crept past with a weak smile, following Tommy onto the public elevator.

"Hasta mañana," he called back to Smythe and Dot.

I restrained myself until the doors shut, then a few stray giggles leaked out. Tommy gave me his worst bad-ass stare, looking down his nose at me for a few seconds until he too cracked up. For a few seconds there was a giddy exhilaration in the elevator that made me forget all about the SUKs, Teddy Bear blonds, Roger, and the fact that I had no place except Alamo House to go home to. I suddenly wished those big metal doors would never open. I guess Tommy must have felt a little bit that way too, because when the elevator thudded to a stop, he dragged me around the corner to the museum gift shop.

"I have to show you this," he insisted with even more than his usual mania, pulling me over to a rack of postcards. He searched through the photos of bluebonnets and LBJ's bullet-proof limo until he found what he was looking for. He plucked out his favorite and handed it to me. It depicted a giant, cartoon LBJ sitting atop his library and asking, "D'Yuh All Mind If Ah Rest On Muh Laurels?" "Good one, huh?" Tommy asked expectantly.

"Oh, yeah. A classic." I don't know why, but a Tommy who cared what I thought made me nervous.

Suddenly he looked away, staring off into space, his right forefinger raised. "Oh, they're playing it," he burst out. He grabbed me by the elbow and hauled me out of the gift shop. I inadvertently shoplifted the postcard. Out in the museum, Tommy signaled for me to listen. From "The Humor of LBJ" exhibit came the taped punchline to the Big Bopper's story about the elderly deaf gentleman who'd sought his doctor's help with his hearing problem. The doctor had advised him to stop drinking. On a follow-up visit the elderly gentleman, still deaf, had admitted why he hadn't stopped tippling. "Well, Doc, I like what I drink so much better than what I heard." Boundless laughter swelled into applause in the background.

"Did you get it?" Tommy asked, hilarity crinkling his face.

A Tommy who laughed at an LBJ joke *really* made me nervous. "Yeah, Tommy, I got it. About the first hundred times I heard it." I'd been treated to "The Humor of LBJ" every day since I'd come to work. Its charm had not increased with repetition. "Well, see you tomorrow. . . . Tomorrow," I repeated when Tommy did not turn loose of my elbow.

"Hey, I just had a thought!" he blurted out. "You wanna come hear Chuy's debut tonight?" He stared at me, goggle-eyed with amazement that the thought of asking me out should have occurred to him. Was this, I wondered, what he was doing? Was Tommy Chastain asking me out? I stalled.

"You just invented this band. How can you already be playing somewhere?"

"It'll be the same old shit, we'll just throw in the Farfiza organ, the maracas, the headbands. How 'bout it, mujer?"

"Maybe," I answered, thrown off because I wanted to go too much. This had Bad Idea written all over it.

Tommy caught the hesitation, but missed the rest. "Listen, mama, when Los Wavos are playing the Special Events Center and you can't trade your *car* for a scalped ticket, you'll rue this day."

He split before I could decide for sure if he had really asked me out. Before I could even remind him I didn't have a car. At that point, I didn't even have a bike. I set off toward Alamo. A sudden burst of energy propelled me—maybe Roger had called. Annoyed at myself for caring, I still couldn't help hustling the rest of the way up the hill to El Alamo, then racing upstairs to the message board.

The message board hanging above the phone at the top of the stairs was Alamo's communication center. Everyone had her own square on a big cork grid. When someone called or came by and the object of the call wasn't in, a message was tacked onto the appropriate square. I had put my name above an empty square that morning. It was still empty. My spirits drooped. I checked the other messages on the board. Nothing cheered me like a little snooping.

I was happy to see that there were no communiqués affixed to Judith's square. A note in Hillary's box reminded her of the Campus Co-op League's Organic Gardening Task Force meeting that night. Barb had one asking her to call Bobbi if she had any extra tickets to the Holly Near concert. Calhoun Hardware had called Toni to let her know the pipe wrench she'd ordered was in. Byung Duk Soo was advised to "Call Music Department. Your Piano Lab has been changed." The Law School Drink or Drown Committee had left word for Josie Guzman that she had been named chairperson at their last meeting. The other squares were empty except the one labeled Cordelia Mohoric. Her square was papered like Wall Street after a ticker-tape parade. And all the communications were from men. Aha! Towelhead. I riffled through the little vamp's missives, terrified I'd find one from Roger. "Trevor will be by at eight." "Helmut called." "David will drop your syllabus off tonight." "Helmut called *again*." "Trevor wants you to call him."

I turned the corner. Half a sheet of notebook paper was tacked on the door to my room. My unruly spirits soared again: Looseleaf was Roger's stationery of personal choice. I tore it down.

"You didn't come to see me about your duties so I had to schedule you on my own. See me immediately. I'm in the room next to the back bathroom. Toni, House Work Manager."

I found the back bathroom at the extreme rear of the house. The door beside it bore a shellacked pine nameplate with two names wood-burned into it: Pfeifer, Toni. Coker, Barb. From inside, I overheard the low mutterings of a half-hearted fight in progress. I knocked and the mutterings stopped abruptly.

"It's open," a twangy, east Texas voice said. Barb, the blond, and Toni, the brunette, were both nestled on the bed surrounded by a moat of books. Barb's eyes were red from crying and Toni's face was set in lines of grim determination. The books beside Toni were *Projects in Design for Mechanical Engineers* and *Experimental Techniques in Fluid Mechanics*. Barb was flanked by *Start Literacy with You: Grammar for the Elementary School Teacher Educator* and *Topics in Lamination*. A variety of the wrenches Toni, as House Maintenance Person, used in her attempts to keep the Alamo's plumbing functioning lay scattered around the floor. On the wall above them was a poster of Maria Schneider pouting a la *Last Tango*. The opposite wall featured Tina Turner in a black leather playsuit. A huge chart, the "Duty Roster," completed the decor.

"Hi, I got your note about the work schedule. What am I signed up for?" I asked, visualizing myself doing a little light dusting once a week or perhaps gracing the house with a few of the dried flower arrangements I did so well.

Toni quashed that hope. "You should have come in sooner. You're scheduled for dinner tonight." Her accent had answered my knock; it made me think of mean sheriffs in small southern towns.

"You mean to cook?" I asked in stunned disbelief.

Toni nodded.

"Tonight? And dinner's supposed to be served at six?"

She nodded again. Barb averted her red-rimmed eyes from the desperate panic swimming in my own.

Dinner for a dozen. I tried to think of how to convey to Toni just how enormously beyond my capabilities such an undertaking was. Anything that involved browning had long ago been removed from my repertoire. I favored preparations that centered around "Just add water."

"But that's less than an hour away," I whined.

"Judith told us you understood your obligations," Barb said between sniffles. "She usually cooks tonight, but the Campus Co-op League is meeting and she's our House Rep so she said you'd take over."

"Nice of her to let me know."

I staggered toward the door and adjourned to the cramped and dingy kitchen.

It was suppertime minus thirty-eight and counting. I stared into an aluminum pot the size of a small garbage can and wondered how on earth I would fill it. Loaves and fishes came to mind. No recipe books in sight, only a chart telling how to mix tofu with buckwheat groats to get a complete protein. Then I remembered the recipes I'd pilfered. How fortuitous. I took them out and decided that Bunkhouse Chili would best lend itself to quantity preparation.

I cruised the refrigerator in search of ground anything. It was stuffed with leafy green grazing material but not much to center a meal for two dozen around. I dug through the freezer. Behind the mastodon haunches, I unearthed a chunk of something wrapped in white butcher paper with "6 lbs." and a date a year and a half past grease-penciled on it. Six pounds, the quantity was right. Disregarding the expiration date, I unwrapped the bundle and found a freezer-burned hunk of hamburger hard enough to cut diamonds. I tossed it into a pot and ran a stream of warm water over it while I started on a salad.

In twenty minutes of working at top speed and without wasting precious time on washing, I had chopped enough greenery for a Hare Krishna convention. I threw it into a bowl and turned to the chili.

Only then did I notice that the trickle of water had turned into a molten torrent. The hamburger was a soggy mass.

I heard voices from the living room. The little porkers were already waddling up to the trough. I fished out the burger blob and threw it into the cauldron-sized pot. Browning, the first step in Lady Bird's recipe, was a lost cause. The meat had already grayed to the color of wet concrete. I poured in some soy sauce for a bit of color. Then, with passing reference to the recipe, I dumped in paprika, garlic powder, cumin, pinch of sugar, onion salt, Worcestershire sauce, and a cup of ketchup. I was cooking until I hit the last line, "Bring to a rolling boil then simmer on back burner until the cows come home or for 12 hours, whichever happens first."

Lady Bird's homespun humor was lost on me. I didn't have that many *minutes*. I hovered on the crumbling ledge above full-scale panic.

"It's six-ten," someone called. Her voice had the menacing edge of a graduate student ravenous after a grueling day of cross-referencing. It was not a pretty sound. The cows had come home.

I went out to explain my problems and found nearly the whole house gathered in the living room—Alexis, Byung Duk Soo, Toni and Barb, Hillary, Constance. There were half a dozen faces I didn't recognize. I was busy trying to pick out which one might possibly belong to The Weeper when a slight tremor shook the floor.

Like a hugely silent sailing ship, my roommate, Fayrene Pirtle, lumbered into view. It was the first night she'd come down to dinner. All eyes swiveled to take in her great bulk encased in a pair of pink stretch pants and a baggy overblouse that tied in the back with a bow. Fayrene's doughy face flamed scarlet as a handful of Red Hots. Pinioned by the stares, Fayrene stretched a thin smile above her corrugated chins and ducked her head.

Alexis Black Hole leaned over and whispered something to Josie. The law student put her hand up in front of her mouth to stifle her laugh. Fayrene heard the suppressed giggle and turned to head back upstairs.

"Hey, roomo," I called out, stopping her. "You're not abandoning me, are you?"

Along with everyone else, Fayrene looked in my direction.

"Come on, I need help. What can you make that's fast and easy?"

Fayrene paused before answering in a tight, squeaky voice, "Well, most of Maw-Maw's recipes are pretty fast."

"Great, great," I put my arm around her and shepherded her

out of the living room and into the kitchen. I tied an apron around her kettle-drum tummy and pointed her in the direction of the refrigerators. "Please," I begged. "Make something edible."

Fayrene poked around tentatively for a moment, then hefted a huge crockery bowl off the shelf and started pulling jars from the refrigerator. I relaxed a tiny bit and returned to my entrée. The Bunkhouse Chili looked like bunkhouse mattress stuffing swirling in a tomato sauce. I stuck a finger in. It was tepid. I turned up the flame until blue blazes licked out from under the huge pot.

I took the bowl of salad out to the dining room and set it on the sideboard. I caught sight of Judith out in the living room therapizing Toni and Barb. Barb was crying again.

"Listen," Judith was saying, "you two have a very stable, quasi-conjugal dyad going for yourselves that's worth putting in some work on. You're just now getting to the place where conflict can happen and you need to learn resolution, that's all."

When Barb's sniffles created a break in the session, Judith turned to me, "I did mention yesterday that dinner is served at six. Didn't I?" She glanced pointedly at the clock—six-eighteen.

"Judith, you dumped this dinner on me at the very last moment without my knowledge or consent."

"So making it late is your passive-aggressive resistance strategy." She said it in that flat, head-bobber tone that implied total objectivity and automatically made the person on the receiving end of it into a case study.

I retreated to the kitchen. The Bunkhouse Swill was still tepid. Undissolved onion powder and chunks of paprika floated on the top. If Judith wanted passive-aggressive, she'd get it. I slammed down the pot on the dining room table. Silence followed as the graduate women of Alamo House peered into the vat. Hillary spoke first.

"Oh gross, is that meat?"

"I don't know," Judith answered. "Mary is cook tonight."

"Mary," Hillary bawled out. "This isn't meat in here, is it? It's house policy that we don't eat meat."

I reentered. "No meat?" I glared at Judith. "Why didn't you tell me the house is vegetarian?"

"It's not," Judith protested. "I mean, we simply reached a consensus on the meat question. How everyone eats individually is entirely their own responsibility; it's just that as a group we don't eat meat."

"But there's no meat out there except huge, group-sized hunks."

"They date from an earlier phase in the development of the house."

"Yeah," Hillary chimed in, aggrieved. "Back when they were eating the flesh of cows filled with the fright hormones released when they heard their friends being slaughtered. You can just imagine the consciousness level that prevailed back then with everyone's brains clogged with tallow and diethylstilbestrol."

I felt like I'd presented a bunch of New Delhi Brahmans with a pickled cow's head. The mournful Elsie (Love Me, Don't Eat Me) eyes sought me out and I shriveled under their gaze. Then Byung Duk Soo bounced in. I winced as she sniffed at my creation and waited for her rejection as well. Instead, her round face lit up and she heaped a small hillock of the stuff on her plate completely ignoring the salad.

"Very good," she announced, her dark eyes scrunching up with pleasure.

"Mary was the cook," Judith informed her, breaking the silence of the gathering picking over their romaine.

"You make?" she asked, turning to me.

I admitted to the atrocity.

"Very good." In a whisper, she added, "I am liking meat very much. In Korea I am eating meat ebry day. You know what is my favorite American food?"

Without waiting for my guess, Duk Soo burst out, "Hamabooger!"

Hillary glanced over at us with disgust. Duk Soo met her glance with a loud whooshing inward and three fingers pressed over her mouth to express embarrassed apologies to Hillary's offended sensibilities.

When conversation had picked up around us enough to cover my question, I sat down next to Duk Soo and asked how she had ended up at Alamo House.

"Not know what is 'vegatarrian,' " she answered, putting her hand in front of her mouth and trilling out a delicate laugh. "First night, I come down to dinner. I look." She emphasized her search by drawing a line in the air from her sparkling almond eyes out to that first group repast. "But no meat." Dismay dimmed the sparkle for a brief moment before she rebounded from that discovery. "Okay, I think. One night, no meat. Tomorrow, meat for sure. Maybe hamabooger.

"Next night. Steel no meat. Onalee the vegatabow." Duk Soo widened her eyes and jutted her chin forward, reenacting for me the extent of her surprise. "I say, 'Where the meat?' " Lowering her voice, Duk Soo whispered the answer she'd received. "Hillary look at me and she say, 'No meat here. Onalee the vegatabow. We tell you, this vegatarrian co-op.' "

"Duk Soo," Judith interjected wearily, "we *did* tell you about the consensus of group feeling on the subject. We even waited while you looked the word up in your dictionary to make sure that there hadn't been any miscommunication."

Duk Soo chuckled gaily in Judith's direction, then turned back to me and whispered, "I show you what my dictionary say." Taking out a Bic, she began scribbling on the paper towel that served as her napkin. "First I look up this." In a scratchy, butterfly-light hand, she wrote, "vegetarian." "My dictionary say this." She traced out "herbivore" on her napkin. "Not know what is this, look it up. My dictionary say this." The next word in Duk Soo's verbal gymkhana was "ruminant." She stabbed at the word looking at me with the puzzlement that had come over her upon first encountering it while Judith and Hillary had, no doubt, stood by clutching a contract and a room key, waiting to lock her in.

" 'What is this?' I think," Duk Soo continued, still stabbing at "ruminant." "So I look up this too. Come at last to word I know meaning of." Here she scratched out "meditative." "This word I know, means thinking a lot. Sure, of course, I think. Smart women here thinking all time. Good place for me. Quiet. I can listen to records, study for piano. I sign contract. Then, no hamabooger. Ever. Not even the fish. Onalee the vegatabow."

The look of sad knowledge clouding Duk Soo's merry face disappeared as she turned her attention back to the cow pie in front of her. I wished it could have been a "hamabooger."

Fayrene appeared hefting the crockery bowl and attention turned to the mound within. I left Byung Duk Soo to sneak a peak. It was a mottled concoction of maraschino red and white.

"Uh-h-h, what's this?" Hillary asked, waving a finger in the direction of the bowl.

Fayrene looked at me before answering. "Goop Salad."

"Goop Salad?" Hillary repeated. "What is Goop Salad?"

Fayrene began flaming a dangerous shade of red.

"You don't know what Goop Salad is?" I intervened when her chins started to tremble. "Wow, I practically grew up on Goop Salad."

"So, what's it got in it?" Judith asked, peering at me suspiciously. The crowd at her back closed ranks, tightening around her.

"Well, obviously . . ." I looked down at the swirl and saw a rainbow of colors I'd missed at first glance. Along with the red and white there was a distinctly yellow undertone and specks of olive green. I glanced at Fayrene for a clue. She had the paralyzed look of a rabbit frozen in terror.

I sensed a crisis building and almost grabbed Fayrene and Duk Soo and abandoned the inquisition to go out for a "hamabooger." But a voice clearly trained to reach the balcony stopped me.

"Goop Salad is a very personal thing," the voice projected into our midst. It was followed up by a presence that projected even further. It took me a moment to realize who had burst with such flair into the dining room. At first glance I would have said Edie Sedgewick back from a premature grave. It was all there. The

Carnaby Street white vinyl mini-skirt. The hair styled like a twenties cloche. The Queen of the Nile eye makeup with darts of black liner wrapping halfway around the temples. The coltish legs running on forever in white fishnet hose. The truly mod chain-link belt. The chalky white lipstick. The, God help me, white go-go boots.

"Fantastic outfit, Collie," Josie the law student said.

"Yeah," Toni muttered in a husky, unsteady voice, as both she and Barb stared with rapt attention, particularly at the expanse of leg on display. But they weren't the only ones ogling Cordelia "Collie" Mohoric. With the exception of Judith and Hillary, everyone at the table was beaming adoration. It dawned on me then why such a panache-ridden creature would choose to live at Moldering Heights—a built-in audience. Where else except amidst a bunch of college-ruled, carrel-pasty graduate women could she shine so brightly? She had an entire house full of foils. Still, she did appear to be coming to our rescue.

"I mean," she went on, coming to Fayrene's side, "I know what I put in mine." She peered into the bowl. "Yep, looks like our recipes are pretty much the same."

Fayrene looked up at her with an expression that probably wouldn't have been out of place on the face of the little French shepherdess at Lourdes. "You mean," she asked, amazed to be breathing the same air as such an exotic apparition, much less sharing recipes, "you use two large cartons of red Jell-O, three containers of Kool 'n' Kremy whipped topping, a jar of Hellman's Real Mayonnaise, half a bag of miniature marshmallows, and a can of pineapple?"

Collie squinted into the bowl. "And some Spanish olives."

"No!" Fayrene gasped. "I thought only Maw-Maw did that." Fayrene was too overcome by the "coincidence" to notice the collective look of disgust on the faces of the Alamo's discerning diners.

Only Byung Duk Soo joined the three of us in heaping our

plates with Bunkhouse Chili and Fayrene's creation. As I went back for seconds I had to admit it, Goop Salad wasn't half bad.

Around the time I'd gotten my plate down to pink Jell-O smears and orange chili grease streaks, an emaciated Rutger Hauer—ice blue eyes, one pierced ear, and silver-blond hair cut short except for several puzzling tendrils at the nape of his thin neck—came into the dining room.

"Y'all remember Helmut, don't you?" Collie asked the disgruntled residents sitting in the living room bent over their white Styrofoam takeout boxes of tabouli salad and falafel from Habib's. They looked up and stopped being pissed off about the chili and Goop Salad as soon as Collie spoke to them. She had the politician's ability to address a group and make every member of it feel as if she were whispering sweet nothings in her ear alone.

"Guten tag, meine damen," Helmut addressed the group.

"Guten tag, mein herr." The response chimed out.

"Very good. Much better than last time." Helmut rewarded them with a chilly, Herr Doktor Professor smile.

"Can you believe this, Helmut?" Collie pealed out in her crystalline voice. "We actually get to consume a carnivorous substance here within the organically upright walls of Alamo House." She looked over at the takeout diners. "Why can't we make this a regular occurrence?"

Judith sighed patiently and explained in her professionally neutral voice, "Cordelia you knew we were considering the vegetarian issue. You chose not to attend the House Meeting. The house reached a consensus and we have been abiding by it."

"You snuck that past me, Judith, you sly dog, and you know it."

" 'Snuck,' Cordelia? You never come to House Meetings. It would hardly have been necessary to have 'snuck' *anything* past you."

"Well, if they weren't the most stupefyingly boring gatherings ever to be held outside of church walls, I might come. But they are."

Judith and Hillary looked at each other and rolled their eyes just the tiniest bit.

"Cordelia you know if you're always . . ." Hillary burst out, but Judith laid a calming hand on her forearm.

"Cordelia" Judith cut in evenly, the very voice of calm reason, "if you're unwilling to accept the responsibility implicit in the group process, don't you think you might consider officially removing yourself as a participant in that process?"

"Whatever you say," Collie answered, turning her attention to Fayrene and me. "Listen, Helmut and I are fixing to take in an early Fassbinder at the Student Union. Want to come along?"

Though I was dying for a furlough from Stalag Alamo, I heard myself say, "No, I'm still not completely unpacked yet."

"How about you?" she asked Fayrene.

Fayrene lit up. "Oh, I love Fassbinder's work," she chirped as cheerily as if she were accepting an invitation to a Billy Graham crusade rather than to a movie by a notorious German bun-humper. "Which one is it? *Love Is Colder than Death*, 1969? *Gods of the Plague*, 1969? *Why Does Herr R Run Amok?*, 1969? *The Coffee House*, 1970? *The American Soldier*, 1970? *Beware of a Holy Whore*, 1970? *Pioneers in Ingolstadt*, 1970? *Merchant of the Four Seasons*, 1971? . . ."

Fayrene droned on with the filmography of Rainer Werner Fassbinder in a dry, mechanical tone that I was to come to know well. At first, I couldn't make out exactly what it signified. Like everyone else at the spellbound table, I was simply in awe of her prodigious memory.

Right after "*Querelle*, 1982?" she abandoned the robotlike voice she'd used to recite and burst out with a giggle. "Oh, it doesn't matter. I'd see any of them. Because," abruptly she shifted back into her automaton voice, "in Rainer Werner Fassbinder's work we see the conventional chasm that separates most artists from the political realities that govern the workplace bridged. In Fassbinder's work there is an heroic effort to obtrude the public world of the workplace into the private domain of art. Fassbinder's success in making a consistent connection between these two worlds is a very rare one indeed.

"In a Fassbinder film people are not pawns of a benighted history, rather they appear as masters of their own pasts. As far as I can see, Fassbinder's are the only German films of recent vintage which direct themselves to the consciousness of the unenlightened in a purely intuitive, non-didactic way that speaks as the statement of an ever-questing author to a like-minded audience."

Fayrene slumped into her seat like a Pentecostal exhausted from speaking in tongues. She stared down at the napkin wadded in her lap. The stupefied group gaped at her in open-mouthed wonder. Suddenly, the bulb clicked on in my brain.

"Photographic memory!"

Fayrene smiled and nodded shyly. "Well, a person's got to have *some* tricks to get out of Waco." Then, as if possessed again by the spirit of that mechanical voice, she recited once more.

"Rainer Werner Fassbinder was born on May 31, 1946, in the Bavarian town of Bad Worishofen. His father, Hellmuth Fassbinder, was a doctor, and his mother, Liselotte, a translator. He was educated. . . ."

I excused myself halfway through Rainer's career. A great need was building in me. A need to escape. I rushed upstairs. My stash was hidden in a box under my bed. I had to have it. Now. Oh sure, I'd tried to get off the stuff before. Had a brief fling with alcohol. Did a few mandatory drug experiments. But they never really got me off like my own private reserve. Never delivered the oblivion that I craved, and craved desperately at moments like these.

I leaped the last few steps and tore around the corner past the message board. No messages for me. Then I was in my room. Locking the door behind me, I dropped to my knees and hauled the box out from under the bed. I pulled off the camouflaging layer of books that I'd used to keep the extent of my addiction a secret from Roger. I tossed aside great and worthy books by Susan Sontag, Vladimir Nabokov, Günter Grass. My hands were shaking by the time I finally unearthed my forbidden treasure—trash novels.

Thrillers were my vice. When reality became unbearable, I depended on them to bring me narcotic oblivion. Nothing tony and cerebral though, mind you. No tastefully trendy Agatha Christie or Dorothy Sayers. I wanted pulse-pounding, gut-wrenching, mind-frying action that grabbed me from page one, then turned me loose on page the last, never to be thought of again. I wanted terror at every turn. Suspense that made my adrenaline churn and my heart beat in my throat.

Death Works the Graveyard Shift. A promising candidate: Good title. Black and red cover. Drop of blood slipping off the tip of a gleaming knife. The first sentence delivered: "The body lolling in the half-filled tub of tepid water was a cliché. Clichéd perhaps because it was the kind of body that casting directors and sculptors have always used to define muscular male perfection." Great, a hot body on page one, line one. Even better, the body was male. I'd wearied a bit of the ubiquitous shapely, female corpse. A shapely male corpse was a welcome relief.

Soon I was lost. I was on a case.

6

JUST AS I was finding out how the waterlogged hunk got in the insane asylum bathtub, I remembered another mystery I still had to run down. Who was The Weeper? I inventoried the dinner guests. None of the feebs and ninnies I'd met so far could have cried those cathartic tears. Surely I would have recognized her on sight as a soulmate. The Weeper must be a phantom resident, too heart-stricken to eat.

The door rattled. I slipped *Death Works the Graveyard Shift* inside a copy of Doris Lessing's *Briefing for a Descent into Hell*.

"How was the movie?"

Fayrene paused at the door. "Good," she answered, slightly bewildered as she searched her mental files for something under "Opinions: Fayrene Pirtle." Finding nothing, she moved on to other sources. "It was *Despair*. No other film by Fassbinder is based on as polished and literate a script as *Despair*. Tom Stoppard's script plays upon the doppelgänger theme, with all the ambiguity of feeling and values of the final years of the Weimar Republic. Fassbinder follows . . ."

"What happened to Collie and Helmut?" I interrupted her recitation from *Cahiers du Cinema* or whatever source she was plagiarizing.

Her library-paste cheeks flushed pink with pleasure. "They

went back to Helmut's. They invited me to come along, but, you know, three's a crowd. We had cappuchino after the show. It was just, just, just so gemutlichkeit," she gushed before pulling her nightgown out from under her pillow and wafting off to the bathroom.

She returned half an hour later encased in floral-printed flannel from just under her fourth chin down to her swollen ankles and smelling of Wella Balsam hair conditioner. Settling onto her bed like a mammoth brooding hen, she pulled out a bottle of OJ's Beauty Lotion and a cotton pad and began astringing her face until it shone like a waxed Macintosh. Next were the hands, those surprisingly delicate appendages at the end of each ham roll of an arm. She had the hands of a harpist and the nails of an eight-year-old princess. She pushed down the cuticles of all ten shell-pink nails with an orange stick, then filed away at a few corners of the already perfect ovals at the tops. She rubbed mineral oil on each one and buffed them with a little chamois pad, then finished off the whole job with squirts of Jergens, slathering the stuff on up to her dimpled elbows. I figured that that must be the line of demarcation. Anything beyond the elbow joint was territory she'd abdicated control of long ago. She kept the nails and cuticles under close supervision, but beyond them lay treacherous and alien country.

Hair maintenance followed. She brushed her wet hair until it dried, then crackled with static, then fell around her face in soft waves. In the soft glow from the dim bulb, she resembled a hydroponic madonna. All in all, it was a mesmerizing and most impressive toilette.

"Has anyone ever told you," I started off without thinking, "how pretty you'd be if you weren't so . . ." I should have had the euphemism ready.

"Fat?" Fayrene finished gently, laying aside the brush.

"I guess they have. Sorry, I wasn't thinking. I shouldn't have said that."

"No, it's all right. I cain't hep mah wyatt." In her misery, Fayrene's Waco youth reclaimed her and, for just a moment, the accents from those days of moonpies and Big Reds rolled over her again. "It's a hereditary glandular problem, hypothyroidism. My whole family has it."

Outside in the hall, the phone rang. I tensed, waiting for someone to pound on the door, to call out my name. To beg me to hurry, a desperate man was calling to speak to me, to beg my forgiveness and plead with me to come back home to single-family dwelling. Instead, Toni bawled out, "Duk Soo, I think it's for you. I can't make out what this guy's saying."

A stream of high-pitched, rapid-fire Korean followed. Silences between the energetic bursts were short. I tried to get back into my thriller, but Alamo had reimpinged upon my consciousness. I let the book slump to the floor.

"You about ready to turn in?" Fayrene asked in her signature, don't-hit-me whimper.

I nodded and she reached up and clicked off the lamp sitting on the desk between the heads of the two beds. "Well, sleep tight and don't let the bedbugs bite," Fayrene cautioned.

In the darkness, I was immediately swamped by a whining, cringing desire for Roger. I wanted to go home. To sleep with someone who didn't talk about bedbugs biting. Someone who'd never pushed down a cuticle in his life. From the other bed came the almost undetectable rustle of cellophane being stealthily torn from a Peanut Patty. Fayrene's hypothyroidism was acting up.

God, how pathetic, I thought, a whole house full of emotionally crippled losers and I'd end up just as warped as anyone here, if I wasn't already. I was just starting to work into a deeply satisfying melancholia, the kind where wistful tears roll silently down your cheeks and into your ears, when a wave of sound crashed in my head.

Well east coast girls are hip
I really dig those styles they wear

And southern girls, with the way they talk
They knock me out when I'm down there
I wish they all could be California girls

"No, please. Not *every* night of the week," I whispered. But prayers from Alamo House were rarely heard and never answered. Minutes later the cry rang out—"BREW BLAST!"—followed by the scrunching of a half-dozen pairs of Reebok running shoes over the few hardy bits of vegetation remaining in the front yard.

"Hurry, y'all, he ain't gonna hold it much longer!"

The Reebok-fall speeded up. The boys were still in motion when the resonator retch echoed up the side of the house.

"Hey, new technique. The Mobile Blaster! Excellent coverage, Kytes. Best yet, hombre."

A great hoorah went up for Kytes.

I jumped out of bed and fumbled with the window. By the time I had it open enough to stick my head out and yell a few obscenities, they'd dragged their projectile vomiter across the street. My choice epithets were drowned out by David Lee Roth.

Ee-yow-w-w-w, California girls!!!!

"Don't pay them any attention," Fayrene said stiffly. "It only encourages trash like that."

"They don't seem to need much encouragement."

"They're just animals."

"What does that make us? They puke on our house every night and nobody does anything."

"They're beneath our contempt."

"Well, they're having a pretty damned good time down there. Someone needs to step on them a little." Someone, but not me. It wasn't my house. It wasn't me they were yorking on. Let one of the losers-in-residence deal with this nightly indignity.

It was hours later when the next act woke me up. Light shone with a dull, Nile green glow through the panes of the painted-over

French doors next to my bed. A singular giggle also made its way into our room. It sounded as if it had come from the rose petal mouth of a mischievous faun. The whisper of a low, bass buzz told me that The Weeper next door had a gentleman caller.

Normally, I'm as cranky as humans get, stopping just short of loading a high-caliber weapon, when someone wakes me up. But this was different. I felt like Jane Goodall waiting all night out in the wilds of Africa to catch a glimpse of some species of chimpanzee hitherto believed to be mythical. The hour mattered not when the glimpse was offered.

The bass whispers and piping giggles continued. I wondered with a desperate curiosity what on earth could be so amusing. The greenish glow dimmed to a hazy pink. The Weeper had covered her light with a red scarf. I could practically smell the pheromones ricocheting around over there. Two bodies hit the springs of her bed and the giggling subsided. My ears perked up with a disturbingly voyeuristic will of their own. I was fascinated by this person on the other side of the French doors who could one night weep the towering tears of the ages and the next frolic like a debauched wood nymph. A truly admirable range. Here was someone with secrets to share. Someone who'd blazed trails through the uncharted territory of the relationship, who'd slogged through the vale of tears that falls between men and women, and come out giggling. Someone who might be able to give me a few clues on where the whole convoluted journey ended up.

My surging hopes were derailed by the trumpeting of a rogue elephant calling lustily to his mate. A rogue elephant? Trumpeting to The Weeper? And The Weeper answering? I realized at that moment why the basso profundo call of the pachyderm is referred to as trumpeting; that's just what it sounded like: Harry James at age eight sputtering into his first horn. I figured though that the impassioned pair next door were probably hooting at each other through a fist pressed to puckered lips. I tried a tentative toot myself there in the dark. It was small and baleful compared to the joyful caterwauling just a few feet away.

First the low bass trumpet. Then a more sprightly, come-hither hoot. Again, the pursuing bass. The teasing reply.

"This place is weird," Fayrene commented groggily before heaving her bulk over in the inadequate twin bed and stuffing a pillow over her head.

It *was* weird. Still I was jealous. Had Roger and I ever had such lunatic fun in bed? Had *anyone* and I ever cavorted with such heedless spontaneity? In retrospect, my carnal memories seemed as madly frivolous as an est weekend. Just me and another repressed missionary's child settling into our inevitable position while the cannibals and the wild creatures romped with playful abandon through the steamy jungle night.

The calls quieted, replaced by the immemorial symphony of bed springs groaning in joy as one lover shifted position to hover over the other. Then back again. And again. And again. And yet again. Then came a big "whoomph" when the springs took the full load and warmed up for the rhythmic creak, creak, creak that ensued. But they played a different tune from the one Roger and I had always ended up rocking out every night of the week. Then a few nights a week. Then a few nights a month. Then almost not at all.

Instead of the creak, creak, creaks quickening toward a hasty denouement, two pairs of knees and one pair of hands hit the wooden floor and the creaks lost their metallic squeal and took on the rich timber of century-old lumber.

Two words, or possibly one hyphenated (now was not the time to consult reference material), zinged into my mind—doggie style. The melancholia I'd been cultivating earlier burst into full flower. There were only two women in the world not enjoying it doggie style at that moment, Fayrene Pirtle and me. I was sure of it. Emergency cheering up of a highly prying nature was in order. I scraped away at the green paint shielding The Weeper/Trumpeter from my depraved gaze. It flaked off easily under my fingernail. Still my snooping was stymied. There was another coat of paint on the other side of the pane.

That left only one alternate method of cheering up, strongly suggested by the activity across the impenetrable pane. Unfortunately, Fayrene's presence, even sleeping, stilled the downward snuggling of my comforting hand. Like a heretic stretched over the rack, I was wrenched by the powerful pull of two dolorous forces. First was the awful downward drag of having been thrown over for the Teddy Bear blond. It tugged lugubriously on my self-image. Then there were the lusty sounds and, I imagined, smells from my neighbor. They gave my punctured libido a mighty yank that caused a serious realignment of my priorities. From that moment on one need burst to the top of the hierarchy—like Fayrene I suddenly, desperately, wanted to bury myself beneath a mountain of flesh. Unlike Fayrene, I wanted it to belong to someone else.

With that determination came another, equally strong—I would need a guide. I couldn't have these next treacherous forays into the jungle of love ending as miserably as the last one had. I stuffed my pillow over my ears and screwed my eyelids shut. Tomorrow I would find my guide. Tomorrow I would uncover The Weeping Trumpeter.

But there was the small matter of graduate school. I checked in at three classes inexplicably required for a photojournalism degree. First, in order of appearance, a severely dipsomaniacal editing professor, one Dillard Pitsor. Professor Pitsor had a nose like an engorged purple potato writhing with exploded capillaries. He promised to teach us "something that ninety-nine percent of your city room types apparently don't know—how to tell your ass, oh, pardon me, all you delicate sorts, your *behinds* from a weak lead."

Next was Ethics in Media, where a punctilious Professor Lipscomb let us know in ways small and large that he considered our presences offensive, our talent minuscule, and our potential irredeemable. After he passed out the syllabi (a word which he used with theatrical flourish no less than five times during that first class meeting), a frat type stuck his pork-butt hand up in the air. I tried to place him. Imagining those piggy digits wrapped around a bullhorn jogged my memory. It was The Bub. I slunk down in my seat.

"Uh, 'scuse me, Professor Lips-Roam . . ." The Bub paused so that his compadres could get the requisite yucks out of his intentional slip, "Er, uh, *Lips-Comb*," he pretended to correct his use of the confirmed bachelor professor's nickname. "Uh, my *syllabi* is not, like, up to specs." The Bub held up the dimly mimeographed sheet. Lipscomb tore it from his mitt with a great show of contained and trembling wrath, then he turned his back on the chucklehead and dropped a clearer copy behind him. It floated onto the SUK ringleader's desk like the symbolic hanky of a coy maiden. The class roared. I slid as far down in my seat as the human backbone would allow.

In Basics in Black and White, a female professor who asked us to call her "just Denise" pulled at the frizzy hair which had escaped from her Gibson girl bun (styled to go with the lace-collared, mutton-sleeved blouse she wore) and talked about Imogene and Margaret and Dorothea and, well, even little Annie. She muttered at the classic Leica she cradled in her long, expressive fingers like Lady Macbeth delivering a soliloquy to the spot on her hand, then told us all to check the board for our lab assignments.

I was due in Eduardo Suarez's section meeting in Economics 24 in ten minutes. I wended my way across campus soothed by the glossy, primeval magnolia trees and by the strains of "The Eyes of Texas" boinging out from the bell tower. It was from the very same tower that Charles Whitman forever stained the honor of his fellow Eagle Scouts by picking off assorted passersby.

I was only moderately damp and dehydrated by the time I reached my destination a block away. The basement of the Economics Building was cool and dark. So was Eduardo Suarez. The crush was instantaneous. The second I set eyes on his supple Latin hips, his frenzied mat of pansy brown curls, his jaguar agate eyes, the tribal drums began beating a frantic tattoo in my blood and two words flashed through my mind—doggie style. Or possibly one hyphenated word. I hadn't had time yet to look it up.

There was one reference I now knew that I would absolutely have to consult, however, before I set tootsie one into the jungle of love. I meant The Weeping Trumpeter, of course, for I was not alone in my fevered reaction to the delectable Eduardo. Already half the lab, the female half, were battering their wings to shreds in little covert runs on his flame.

"This ees the wet eside," he crooned in his maddeningly accented English, as we toured through the darkroom. A safelight threw an erotic orange glow over the darkened pit. Decades of Dektol developer and acetic acid stop baths had left the sink-lined room smelling like one enormous vinegar douche.

"An this ees the dry eside." Eduardo led us into a hall that opened into a series of tiny closets where all us tyro photojournalists would be loading film in total darkness. From orange haze to total darkness, the photo lab, under Eduardo's tutelage, was fraught with erotic possibility. Though my infatuation was deep and real, it was not all carefree carnality. It did have its serious side: revenge. A fantasy flitted across my mental screen: Enter Roger dressed as Juan Valdez, humble but discerning coffeebean picker. He stands beside some lonely pampa trail while Eduardo, in full gaucho regalia, and myself, clasped lovingly to his heaving chest, caper past astride a high-stepping stallion. Perhaps Roger's moist, spaniel eyes would briefly meet mine. But only briefly, for downtrodden Juan knows the penalty for a peon who dares to covet Don Suarez's mujer.

"Doan especk, choost because it's dark, that this lab will be a siesta time," Eduardo warned. A dozen pairs of southern belle eyes promised slavish obedience to his dictates, and sensual depravities unheard of on the pampa. I clearly needed help, expert help. I had to confer with The Trumpeter. Weeping was inevitable, but that would come later. I wanted a shot at the jungle joy first. I was on my way to oblivion. Eduardo would be the first foothill in the mountain of flesh I craved. He dismissed lab, promising to "esee" us next Thursday. I rushed back to Alamo. I had two days to uncover the identity of my guide.

.   .   .

"Chart?" Judith asked. I'd hated to interrupt what appeared to be an impromptu therapy session she was holding with Barb, who was weeping beside her. "Yeah, there might conceivably be a rooming chart. Why do you want to know?"

"I want to find out who lives in a certain room."

"Just ask me. I'm fairly aware of everyone's spatial orientation."

I hesitated. I didn't want Judith's intervention sullying my search.

"Did I hear someone inquire about a rooming chart?"

The question came from a darkened corner of the room and represented the first words I'd heard from Constance, the prissy egg-timer. "I have it in my room. It was so hopelessly bollixed up that I took it upon myself to redo it."

I was rescued. Judith turned back to Barb and asked her, "Do you feel that your quasi-conjugal dyad with Toni is stable enough to survive what may only be a passing interest in this Terry person?" Barb's miserable snuffles followed me out of the living room.

From the look of her room, all eyelet lace and flounces, Constance Dermott aimed to be the last old maid at the turn of the twentieth century. As befit the graduate woman in the humanities that she was, she didn't wear a speck of makeup or own a garment less than five years out of date. Her lashless eyes, formless cheeks, and amorphous lips all disappeared in her pale face. Her hair was cut blunt like Joan of Arc's.

"All right, then," she murmured, warming to her task. "Where *did* I put that chart?" She shuffled through a stack of baronial crests featuring such oddities as armadillos rather than lions and prickly pear bushes rather than lilies. Under each one was the notation, Society for Creative Anachronism, and the name of a different barony. "Here it is." She unearthed an elaborately drawn diagram with all of Alamo's cubbyhole rooms blocked out. She held it up proudly.

Sure enough, the whole house was mapped out with the names of the occupants done in a swirly calligraphy. My pulse accelerated slightly as I traced my way up the stairs and drew ever closer to unmasking The Weeping Trumpeter. Gleefully, I found Hell Week Heaven. Without pausing to read the names written in my rectangle, I traced a probing finger through the French door into The Weeping Trumpeter's room and read, "Ernest Pierce."

"Ernest Pierce?"

Constance glanced down at the chart. "Oh, Ernest. Yes, he was a rather unsuccessful experiment. The house had fallen on bad times, when was it? Seven? No, eight years ago and, for one summer, we took in male residents. I put Ernest in Room Seven because, technically, that was his assigned room. But, in fact, he roamed shamelessly. It was the source of considerable discord. We never tried it again."

"Eight years ago?" A disturbing thought crossed my mind. "How long have you lived here?"

Constance looked up at the crack running across her ceiling and squinted her faded-moss-colored eyes. "Let's see now. The Barony of Bryn Gwlad, that's Austin and environs to mundanes like yourself," Constance filled me in, "was established seven years ago. And the Society itself had already been meeting for three years then. And, prior to that, I'd been working on starting a chapter ever since I'd been in graduate school. Which was five years. So that makes it, what?"

Fifteen years! In Alamo House? I could not utter the monstrous total. No wonder Constance had lost track of who was living where, she'd lost track of where she herself was living. I thanked her and backed out. Rapidly. *Constance was a living memo to me to make Alamo a very temporary arrangement.* I veered off downstairs. Perhaps some light sustenance, then back to my quest.

Byung Duk Soo and the ever-incandescent Collie Mohoric were in the living room. Duk Soo was playing the piece she was working on on the house piano and Collie was limbering up. Alamo's darling was festooned in a Greek-tunic affair belted at the waist. Pink tights covered the legs she was contorting into unlikely positions. A long, long scarf knotted around her neck trailed down past her knees. If it hadn't been for the scarf I might not have guessed—Isadora Duncan. As Duk Soo crashed out a few chords, Collie grabbed her right ankle and bent the sole of her foot up and around so that she could rest the back of her head against it. What a show-off. I could have done that too. When I was about a month old. And didn't she think the other scarf, tied flapper style around her luxuriant, glossy hair, was a bit excessive?

" 'Scuse me," I said, brushing past her as she stood there making a giant capital "P" with her lithe body.

"Sure." She scampered out to the dining room where she collapsed herself, dropping from the waist to hug her chest to her knees. Several dire notices were taped to the front of the refrigerator: "The Personal Foods are infested. Check through your stuff cuz anything I find tomorrow that's infested, I'm pitching it." Another read, "The tofu in the fridge is *MINE*. Don't anyone touch it!!! Hillary." I bypassed Hillary's oh-so-tempting glop of bean curd and created something cheesy with a mound of sprouts on it and poured myself a big glass of iced Red Zinger tea. My kingdom for a Pepsi and a double-meat hamabooger. I carried my lunch into the dining room where Collie had stationed herself. She hung on to a chair back while she splayed her feet out like a duck and pushed up and down on them.

I attempted to ignore her and chomped into my sandwich. I had a mouthful of sprouts hanging out of the sides of my mouth when I heard it: The Trumpet. The effect was instantaneous and thoroughly disorienting. It was as if I'd heard the Siren's song at K-Mart. I whirled around foaming sprouts like a rabid dog. She was here, The Weeping Trumpeter, my guide, she was here.

I turned slowly for the monumental confrontation and saw only this: Collie, posed like a hood ornament, her body one sleek line, from her toe stretched far behind her, through the curve of her supple back, right up to the uptilted horn of her fist pressed against her lips in just the way I'd imagined that a human might in order to mimic the mighty call of a rutting rogue.

Collie Mohoric was The Weeping Trumpeter? The woman who was to be my guide through uncharted amorous territory?

How, I wondered, my spirits and ravenous dreams of sweet revenge and unbridled libido all sinking, could I have been so mistaken? This chameleon, this Miss Popularity? The Weeper? The Trumpeter? There was no Weeper. No Trumpeter. No guide.

Collie blinked, the hood-ornament trance lifting. She noticed me glaring at her. "I woke you up last night, didn't I? I mean the elephant mating calls did, didn't they? You and Fayrene are right across the French door. Jeez, what a bonehead move. I'm sorry."

I nodded a polite dismissal of her apology, the sprouts swaying to and fro across my mouth. I stuffed the green whiskers in and swallowed the fibrous load. So there was no Oracle at Alamo. My guru was a flighty theater major.

"Men are such trollops," Collie observed affectionately, apparently commenting on her night with Helmut or some other night that had her smiling a secret little amused smile to herself.

Men as trollops. I thought about it for a minute. Roger had proved that he was. And Eduardo? Could there be any doubt about his trollophood? Suddenly, my apprehensions about the Spanish Conquest diminished a tiny bit. This was no exalted grandee I was going after, just your run-of-the-mill male trollop. I wouldn't need a guide for him. Still, just because both Eduardo and Helmut were foreigners, I asked Collie how they'd met.

"He was the t.a. in this directing class I took. Tried to turn us all into raving Brechtians. Sad really when you consider that the only thing half of that class will ever end up directing is a Junior League gala and that the other half will use all that Brecht rhetoric to stage Cole Porter revivals for their friends."

"Well," I asked, just because Helmut was a foreigner and so was Eduardo and there might be some helpful overlap, "how did you get together?"

"Oh, 'get together.'" Collie twitched her eyebrows lasciviously. "I don't know. I guess we both just let mad, impetuous fancy sweep us away. He's a pretty cute guy, isn't he?" She looked to me for confirmation.

"Pretty cute," I supplied.

"No, wait, I know what it was. Vanilla extract."

"Vanilla extract?"

"Sure. I dabbed a little behind my ears every day before class and pretty soon he was dying to nibble on me." She caught my look of incredulity. "Well, it worked with Helmut."

Abruptly, Collie bounced to her feet and shouldered a tote bag bulging with towels and headbands. "Time for class. Talk to you later." With an airy Isadora Duncan-flapper wave over her shoulder, she left.

Vanilla extract, I mused. Love secret of the ages? Sure, if you also happen to look like the young Vivien Leigh.

Still, when next Thursday rolled around, responding to urges I only dimly understood, I proceeded to anoint myself like a piece of streusel. I was also garbed out as flamboyantly as my mudhen graduate woman wardrobe would allow. Every scarf I owned wafted on the douche-scented breeze as I entered the dark depths of Eduardo's lair. Never having been one for team sports, I arrived at the lab early in order to avoid the rush Eduardo was sure to be getting from my classmates. His curls glowed amber in the safelight as he sloshed a print around in the Dektol.

"Buenas dias," I started off jauntily.

He looked up pleased to hear his native greeting. "Buenas dias, señorita . . ."

"Mary Jo," I supplied, wondering if he was getting the full impact of my audaciously prolonged gaze in the dim light.

But Eduardo's eyes were used to the dark, functioned, in fact, as did the rest of his body, at peak levels *only* in the dark.

"Mary Hoe," my conquistador whispered, moving into whiffing range of the extract. "Es un nombre muy linda. Iss a berry priddy name."

Our gazes tangled. The orange safelight playing over our faces could have come from a crackling fire we were stretched out on bearskin rugs in front of. Heated blood pounding through my carotid artery broadcast the scent of vanilla like the Nabisco bakery. I was paralyzed with lust. Eduardo must have shared my sentiments. He whispered huskily that he'd like to see me after class just as the clack of spike heels on the basement steps and the call, "Ed-WAR-do, yew down thar?" announced the arrival of another class member.

I barely had time to nod my agreement. As I turned to unpack my cache of Ilfospeed photo paper, I glanced quickly at the print Eduardo had been souping. A kittenish little coquette peeked coyly through the brownish developer. Eduardo, I thought, you shameless trollop.

7

THAT AFTERNOON at work, I was so lost in anticipation—
Eduardo had asked me over that night to "eshare his work" with
me—that it took a while for me to notice that Tommy was not his
usual bon vivant self. He'd also dropped the Cantinflas moustache
and accompanying lowrider look. I asked how the debut of Los
Nuevo Wavos had gone. He stared blankly at me for a moment.

"Oh. Them. No debut. Allan told me that these new sincerity,
bogus heritage bands made the scout nauseous." He lapsed into
silence.

"So, what's the next incarnation?"

Tommy shrugged. "You tell me. I mean, how do you jolt people out of their collective comas anymore, that's the question. How
do you even raise a blister on the public consciousness?"

Having just barely managed to prick the awareness of one
Latino lab instructor, I didn't feel competent to offer advice on
capturing hearts and minds. I trolleyed down the dimly lit aisles
for the next brown box to strip down and repackage.

Tommy was still in his meditative funk when I returned and
unloaded a sheaf of eight-by-ten glossies. They recorded each step
in Lynda Bird's 1966 makeover masterminded by George Hamilton for their Academy Awards date. In the first shot, Lynda, pa-
tron saint of all dumpy, bookish older sisters of cute, dumb younger

sisters, looked like the chin-shy, nose-ample plain girl the Lord had intended her to be. In succeeding photos her too-low hairline was shaved up to give her more forehead and more of her was spackled over with layers of clown-white makeup. In the last shot, with three pairs of false lashes fluttering above each eye, she resembled either Phyllis Diller or an ostrich made up as a geisha.

"I told you her real father was Big Bird," Tommy commented after spying the After shot. "I wonder how I'd look in dead white makeup?" he mused aloud, picking up the photo. It showed a beaming Lynda looking as pale as a magnolia blossom with daddy-longlegs eyelash accents next to the bark brown George Hamilton flashing his blinding white grin. They were off on their dream date to the Academy Awards, an event which would cause unattractive girls across the nation to put far too much faith in the power of cosmetics and far too little in the power of an important father.

"Like a Kabuki actor gone punk," I answered, plucking the photo out of Tommy's hand and stuffing it, along with several dozen others, into their permanent resting place in a red box. It was not my function to question whether or not the orthodontically perfect George Hamilton merited enshrinement in a presidential library. He'd had his moment with the daughter of a president and a moment had proved sufficient. Such were the wonders of democracy and the strangeness of bedfellows made by politics.

Oblivious to my snappy reply, Tommy began smoothing back his spiky tufts of hair. "I've got it!" he announced. "Joel Grey in *Cabaret*. It was on HBO last week. Très decadent. Do you like it?" he asked, sucking in his cheeks and flaring his nostrils.

"I don't even comprehend it."

Tommy looked off into the far distance, through our eight-foot wall of boxes, into the future of rock and roll. His breathing slowed and all bodily movement ceased as he achieved alpha state. I felt the air around his head warm, heated by mental energy. Then, like the switch being thrown on the Bride of Frankenstein, he came back to life.

"Tommy Berlin and the Vy-Mars!" he announced with a "Eureka!" look on his face.

"The Vy-Mars?" I repeated uncertainly. "Not as in the Weimar Republic?"

"Exactly. Don't look so surprised, my dear. I did pick up the odd fact here and there during my misspent youth."

My dear? The odd fact? I couldn't believe it. Two makeovers in one day. First Lynda Bird going from mudhen drab to ostrich outré and now, right before my eyes, Tommy was transforming himself from a street punk into something out of "Brideshead Revisited."

He glanced around, one eyebrow cocked in aristocratic bemusement, surprised, I'm sure, to find himself in such dingy surroundings, and wondering where he'd mislaid his cigarette holder.

"Mary Joseph, please do close your mouth. Astonishment doesn't suit you at all."

"Certainly, your lordship," I replied respectfully, swept away by the force of this characterization. "Or would you prefer I address you by your full name? Viscount Thomas Berlin Chilltingham."

"Viscount Chilltingham." Tommy auditioned my effort and smiled. "Yes, Mary Jo, that will do nicely."

And thus Tommy Berlin, Viscount Thomas Berlin Chilltingham, was born on the fifth floor of the Johnson Temple. I stuffed the last rakishly grinning George Hamilton into a red box.

"It's working already," Tommy informed me with restrained enthusiasm. "I feel great wells of ennui and cynical detachment opening up in me. I'm entering a whole new phase. My music will be filled with *weltschmerz* and *anomie* and *tristesse*."

"Aren't you forgetting *angst* and *lederhosen*?"

"Sarcasm does not become you, my dear." Viscount Tommy arched a reproving brow. "The music of the Vy-Mars will be a powerful statement about the endless tedium of modern life and one's inevitable yearning for death."

"New Grave music. How peppy."

I flattened out the empty brown box, tossed it on the nap stack, and steered the trolley full of red boxes toward the back row. It fronted onto the glass wall that joined our little hideaway to the Lyndon Baines Johnson Museum. I shoved the pictures of Lynda and George onto the shelf. Far below me, a troop of Catholic schoolgirls in blazers and plaid skirts followed their nuns across the marble museum floor to a display of photos of the extended Johnson sons-in-law and grandchildren. A montage of Lucinda Robb and Patrick Lyndon Nugent fighting over a bowl of popcorn in the timeless way of former First Grandchildren could hardly fail to inspire them. Ditto Claudia Taylor Nugent and Rebekah Nugent, ages six and eight, pretending to play tennis rackets like guitars. The nuns led the schoolgirls away to other displays of historical significance. I hauled down the next brown box and loaded it onto my trolley.

Back at the work area, Tommy was counting out meter with his long, skinny fingers and bobbing his head as he mouthed words to himself. Once he got it right he scribbled down the words: the Viscount was creating. He mumbled aloud,

> *Worms of sodding mediocrity*
> *Invade the corpse of love*
> *Hollowing out the center*
> *Leaving a white, silk glove*

"Still writing those ballads that warm the heart and bring a tear to the eye," I noted. Tommy kept mumbling lyrics.

> *Oh my little porcelain lady*
> *In your black leather gown*
> *You whip the pain from me*
> *If I smile or if I frown*

"Whatever happened to, 'You are the sunshine of my life'?" I asked.

Tommy wasn't there. His mind had gone to the cabaret, old chum. It was just as well since my own mental faculties were vacationing on Passion Pampa. How wistfully ironic that, given my panting anticipation, the most memorable part of that date would turn out to be Collie's reaction to it.

"You got nibbled on!" Collie exploded as I slumped over a predawn glass of hot milk. My hand automatically went to my neck. It was still raw from Eduardo's extensive osculation.

"A hickey necklace," she beamed. "I haven't seen one of those since junior high. It's a good one, isn't it, Trevor?" The wiry, ethnic-looking man at her side nodded approving agreement. He was dark with his hair cut Marine-short everywhere except for several long tendrils trailing puzzlingly down his neck. He wore a tiny golden lightning bolt in his pierced right ear.

I dug through my purse. No mirror. Collie handed over her shoulder bag. It was impregnated with tiny mirrors. Holding the purse at arm's length, I managed to get my neck in focus. It was festooned with strategically placed red suck marks, a string of crimson pearls.

As I handed back the purse, I noticed that the rest of Collie's outfit matched its glittering excess. Beneath a gaudy carapace of costume jewelry—cheap rings on every finger, ruby red glass beads, a clanking multitude of hoop bracelets—she wore a swirling dress of slinky, synthetic velvet tie-dyed with slashes of burgundy red and creosote green. Her hair was frizzed into a savage nimbus. There was no doubt about the persona of the evening—sex-crazed Gypsy Earth Mother from Port Arthur, Texas, Janis Joplin.

"Night, night, Trevor." Collie dismissed her swain with a few kissie gestures around his ears. "Why don't you wait for me up in my room? We've got some girl talking to do."

"Was it the vanilla extract?" she asked eagerly, the second after Trevor left.

Her enthusiasm clashed with my melancholy mood. The evening had fallen considerably short of lurid expectation. "It could have been," I admitted wearily.

"Works every time with the little trollops. What's wrong? Are you worn out or disappointed?"

"A little of both, I guess."

"Who was he?"

"My photo lab instructor."

"A photographer? And he was *malo*?" Collie asked, surprised. "Photographers are usually pretty good. Like to get in the dark and see what develops." She gave a fake yuk-yuk to acknowledge the awfulness of her pun. "What was the problem?" She reached into her mirrored bag and pulled out a bottle of—what else—Southern Comfort. She dumped half a tumblerful into my milk and took a long swig herself. "Makes a great toddy," she assured me.

I took a sip. Then another. Not bad. Certainly better than the toilet bowl cleaner wine Eduardo had plied me with.

"So, tell me about it," Collie demanded again.

"What's to tell?"

"What's to tell! He wanted it, you didn't. You wanted it, he didn't. Good love, bad conscience. Bad love, bad conscience. The variations are endless here in the timeless *baile de amor*. Now, Trevor, for instance. Trevor is just not someone to take seriously. You noticed that didn't you?"

I nodded noncommittally.

"I mean, for a romp, okay, but don't start buying baby's breath, right? What was his name?"

"Eduardo."

"Eduardo!" she shrieked as if I'd named the villain who'd slaughtered her family and raped her when she was three. "Well no wonder. A Latino. Your first? I mean of the unassimilated variety?"

I nodded glumly.

She nodded knowingly. "The Latino Letdown. It's a given. I can see from your neck that he followed standard operating procedure. Your basic south-of-the-border trollop exhausts himself on the hors d'ouevres then, just when your mind boggles at the thought of what could possibly follow such divine delicacies, he hauls out the bean burrito. Take that any way you want," Collie offered as an aside, hiking up the drapey folds of her skirt and sprawling out in earthy Janis fashion over the chairs next to her.

"The fundamental problem with the Latin male," she expounded, "is that once a woman gets prone, that's the end of amor. She has to be upright and resisting for his glands to function properly. He's too tuned in to the preliminaries. The outrageous compliments, the kissing, licking, sucking. Great for as long as you've both got your clothes on, right?"

Too right, I thought bitterly, reflecting on Eduardo's barely perfunctory performance after a truly glorious overture.

"You think, Oh Bliss City, here I come," she continued, reading my rapturous thoughts of only a few hours ago. "Then you end up where? In Piedras Negras. In that sleazy place where the worst of two cultures rub up against each other."

"God, it was so depressing," I muttered. "One minute he was whispering to me about taking me back to 'Arhentina' to meet 'madre' and see 'el rancho' and nuzzling me and calling me," my voice warbled mournfully, " 'Mary Hoe,' and the next minute he was hustling me out of his apartment like I was last week's garbage."

"Very demoralizing. Did he at least buy you dinner first?"

I shook my head no, admitting to the tactical error. "He was in the middle of deciding whether Green Pastures was worthy of me when he started daisy-chaining me with hickies. He ended up grabbing a Big Gulp and a . . ." I winced before admitting how accurate Collie's prediction had been both figuratively *and* literally, "a bean burrito at the 7-11 afterward. I couldn't eat."

"*Very* demoralizing," Collie reiterated, pouring a couple of fingers of straight Southern Comfort into my empty mug.

"I didn't even realize he wasn't that good-looking until it was too late."

"I know. Sometimes they can just stun you with libido."

"Really kind of short. This little pot belly. No shoulders to speak of. These sort of gnarly teeth. Pores the size of . . ."

"All right!" Collie interrupted my rambling. "I get the picture. It was Herve Villechaise instead of Ricardo Montalban. It's all aura anyway. Sexiest man I ever knew was cross-eyed. Of course he did have pores like a baby." I lost Collie for a moment to cross-eyed reveries, but she snapped back quickly. "I really wish you had come to me for a consult before you did anything seriously frivolous. It may already be too late."

Too late. I gulped down the Southern Comfort.

"Perhaps, though, if we take some emergency remedial measures, we can salvage a few shreds of your dignity."

Shreds of my dignity. I sniffed back the tears that had puddled up as I'd told about the bean burrito.

"First of all, lighten up. The only serious damage that can be done is what you inflict upon yourself. Mope and he scores. Don't give the prick the satisfaction. Now, of course, he's not going to call. In fact, the next time you show up in his vicinity he'll avoid you if he can, and if he can't, he'll treat you like a cucaracha."

"God," I wailed, imagining a semester of such humiliation, "what have I done?"

"You took a trollop seriously. Major tactical error. But fear not, I promised emergency remedial measures. You'll have to act fast though. The first one of you to shit on the other will be the one who gets to rub a nose in it."

"That's disgusting," I protested.

"Only if it's your nose."

"No," I stood firm. "Why should I descend to his level? Why can't encounters between men and women, no matter how brief, be humane? Be . . ." I groped, ". . . authentic? With genuine respect for the personhood of the two people involved?" My noble words slurred together. I yearned to put my head down on the table for just the briefest of naps.

Collie glared at me. "Child, you have spent too much time listening to Judith Feldman. Do you think guys like Eduardo spend their time between cruise missions reading Leo Buscaglia and worrying about the 'personhood' of the next woman they're going to be hitting on?"

Blank misery glazed my face in response.

"Not fucking likely," Collie answered hotly.

"What should I do?" I moaned, panicking at the prospect of my "personhood" in Eduardo's keeping.

Collie scooted her chair up closer to mine. "Strike first," she counseled in a low and compelling voice. "Once the Latin male has glimpsed a woman in a horizontal attitude, he becomes convinced that she's dead. You must disabuse him of this notion. Since Latinos basically only care what other hombres think, you will only come back to life for him if you can get a few said compañeros stirred up. In his presence."

"What do you mean?"

"There *are* other guys in your lab, right?"

I thought of the wimpoid crew that the dashing Eduardo had made look like a school of white meat tuna. "Well, sort of . . ."

"Sort of doesn't matter. If they have an Adam's apple bigger than yours, they qualify. Flirt. Be gay. Laugh at their insipid jovialities. Be Scarlett O'Hara at the barbecue."

The thought both compelled and repelled. I owned up only to the repulsion. "I can't do that. Why should I have to play games? If he ignores me, I'll just march right up to him and tell him straight to his face what I think of him." I felt warm and glowing all over and proud of my forthrightness. I lifted my chin again, but my head felt so heavy. I slumped back into a semi-snooze posture, head lolling on my chest.

"Listen," Collie said urgently. "You are missing a vital link here in your understanding of the man/woman relationship."

"I am?" I interjected groggily, not that I hadn't suspected it all along.

"Yes, you're clearly not grounded in The Axiom. It underpins all dealings between men and women. I personally intuited The Axiom in kindergarten when Stevie McMichaels chewed up the little Huckleberry Hound eraser dog I'd given him and spit the slobbery pieces out on me. I didn't bother to put The Axiom into words, though, until puberty, when it became an issue. Since then it has guided every move I've ever made around individuals of the male persuasion."

All my earlier, quashed hopes of guidance through the tangled thicket of sex now foolishly sprang back to life. I hunched forward eagerly and stopped breathing so as not to miss a word. Collie asked casually, "You want to hear it?"

"Yes."

"It really is quite basic, but its ramifications are all-pervasive."

"Yes, yes."

"Okay. The Axiom: Are you ready?"

"Yes!"

"The Axiom: The party of the most interest is the party of the least power."

"Most interest, least power," I mumbled, inscribing the equation on my heart. "That's so callous."

"Callous?" she sputtered. "You're missing the point. It all depends on what you do with the power. Now, who is more likely to use the power in these humane, authentic ways you were talking about? You or Eduardo? Who, in a word, would be nicer?"

I had to admit that it would be me. Hands down. No question.

"Of course you would. So would ninety to ninety-five percent of the female population of the world. Given the power, we'd be nicer. It's just that simple. The trick then, obviously, is getting the power. Which is no trick at all with The Axiom."

"Just don't care." I breathed the secret aloud thinking of Roger and how he had been my slave when he was but one of half a dozen trollops competing for my attention. And how the tables had turned when he became my one and only. What a slut. Collie was right, I should have kept him on the ropes. He certainly hadn't done much for my personhood.

"You're right," I whispered, the truth dawning on me. "You are absolutely right."

"Of course, I'm right. It's so fundamental. The Axiom should be written on every box of tampons sold. A lot more girls fall prey to overinterest than ever get mowed down by toxic shock. But back to the immediate case at hand. Yours. You'd better be wafting the vanilla extract far and wide the next time this lab of yours meets. Make it into your own personal debutante ball and COME OUT," she emphasized.

I enjoyed that vision substantially more than the one in which Eduardo scorned me like a cucaracha.

"What have you got in the way of garbs? Clothes," Collie explained.

"Just the usual."

"That's right, I've seen your clothes. Exceptionally usual. Let me think. What would appeal to the photographer and would-be photographer strumpet?" She fell into silent concentration. Cautiously she began, "Now, if it was just the Latino strumpet we were zeroing in on, I'd definitely advise the Ice Queen, a sort of Evita Lying in State look. But you'll be playing to a mixed audience." Her lovely brow furrowed with thought. She concentrated for so long and in such an intense silence that I began to fear that even The Trumpeter was stumped. I was a hopeless case.

Suddenly, though, she looked up and the light of inspiration was brightening her eyes. "Got it. How about the Ice *Princess*? Romper shorts, my Peter Tosh T-shirt, and trowel on the makeup. The T-shirt will tell all the guys in your class that you're an approachable, with-it, fun-seeker who just might regard sex as a sacrament. These subtleties will, naturalmente, be lost on Señor

Ed. For him, we pencil in the ultra-haughty, die-you-Spanish-dog browline, contour some kiss-my-ass cheekbones, and triple-gloss lips that are sealed to him forever."

Collie positively glowed from the heat of her genius. "Then it's up to you to sparkle. To blink on and off like a traffic light. Just remember that Señor Ed is red, for stop. Alto."

I grinned with delight at the prospect of freeze-drying my humiliator. In the next second, my expression sagged. "Forget it," I shrugged. "That stuff may work for you, but I'm about as glamorous as Frito Pie. There's no way I'm going to pull off a femme fatale."

"You didn't think I was going to throw you out there cold, did you? No, girl, you have got to have the right endorphins coursing through your bloodstream. We'll take care of all that tomorrow. For now, I need copious amounts of Rapid Eye Movement."

Outside, daylight was starting to streak the sky with promises of another equatorial day. Weariness overwhelmed me. We were both lugging ourselves up the stairs when I remembered one last nauseating detail.

"The pictures," I blurted out.

"What pictures?" Collie demanded sternly.

"The pictures Eduardo took of me last night," I winced.

"Photographic evidence of the conquest, I assume." Collie continued up to her room.

"Well, they were sort of au naturel," I admitted as she opened her door.

The room on the other side of the French doors was a fantasy out of *Arabian Nights*. Everything was slinky and tasseled and smelled of clean but naughty bodies and talcum powder. A red paisley scarf was draped over the ornate lamp giving the light the pulsating, flamingo pink hue that had shone through into my dismal room a few nights before. Trevor was curled up asleep on Collie's disheveled double bed clutching a pair of her underpants to his nose.

She started to disappear. "What about the pictures?" I asked, more frantic than I'd intended. "What do I do about them?"

Collie put her head down and thought for a moment. When she looked back up, four in the morning was all over her face. The last thing she said before closing her door was, "I don't know, Mary Jo. There are some mistakes in life we just can't correct."

∗ 8 ∗

I WAS very late to work the next day. In fact, I missed all my morning classes and most of the afternoon work hours. Still I was in time to catch a few hours in the isolation tank where I was merrily snoozing away when jolted awake by the sensation of being watched.

"Mary Jo, were you out debauching yourself last night?"

"Huhmpfff," I answered trying to separate myself from the dream I'd been having in which Roger, in his Juan Valdez peon serape took photos of Eduardo and me doing extensively gymnastic things on the back of a rearing stallion.

"You're asleep," Tommy informed me helpfully, so I worked a bit harder at shaking off the tentacles of the priapic dream. At last I succeeded. "I am not," I replied crossly. "Hand me the stepladder. I relinquish your sleeping chamber."

"I'll never use it again." Tommy intoned the words solemnly.

His reverent inflection alarmed me. "Why?"

"Something happened this morning that changed me."

"I thought the Moonies needed a whole weekend," I said, referring to the only force I was familiar with that could wreak such profound and speedy transformations.

"Don't be tawdry," Tommy instructed me. "Maybe you don't want to hear about it." He was miffed.

"Oh yes, please I do want to hear."

"All right then." He was still mildly aggrieved. Then the memory of whatever had transpired that morning enveloped him in a blissful haze. "Luckily," he began, "or was it fate? Do any of life's major events occur by chance? Certainly an occurrence of this magnitude was destined to be spun on the wheel of fortune. Anyway, by luck or by design, you weren't here and I was. Or actually, the young Viscount was here yesterday. Another piece of good luck because yesterday, I was dressed. A look of casual elegance. Tennis sweater, white wool trousers. Eton hair."

Tommy's spikes were now, in fact, all neatly brushed down and swept forward in the classic English schoolboy cut. It was beyond presentable.

"I was up, awake, you know, beavering away at some new tunes," he recounted, slipping again into the young Viscount, "when Smythe bursts in demanding to know where you are. I informed him that I hadn't a clue. He looks me over and was quite obviously favorably impressed. So he tells me he has a very special assignment for me. Seems the Subatomic Particle . . ."

He referred to Milton, a rather diminutive fellow who worked on another floor.

". . . was out sick. Probably a submicroscopic virus. Smythe was all in a lather because there was going to be a meeting on the eighth floor . . ."

I gasped. The eighth floor! Sacred lair of none other than Lady Bird herself, a region we had heard of in fable but never so much as glimpsed.

"Yes, a meeting on eight and Milton usually helped out in his own minute way with serving refreshments. So Smythe was up here looking for a stand-in. And there I was, representing all that was white, neatly pressed, and right-thinking. Smythe dispatched me immediately to eight."

I grinned with anticipatory glee imagining Tommy, the disguised anarcho-musico bizarro, on the eighth floor. What havoc had he wreaked? I couldn't wait to hear. A tray full of petits fours on the lap of the library director (a singularly pompous and self-important individual)? Maybe a suggestion that they might all enjoy a piece of the electrically charged wedding cake that was occupying so much space on the fifth floor?

"The suite, Mary Jo. You would not believe such elegance exists so close to our own bomb shelter of a floor." He raised his eyes like a fallen angel yearning for home. "Cut crystal, fresh flowers, a view of the city laid out at your feet. And then, she was there . . ."

His eyes unfocused again and I had to prompt him, "Who was there?"

"Bird," he answered, employing the endearment LBJ had used for his wife.

I pressed closer. Tommy's parody of swooning at Johnsonian sophistication was clearly a setup for a wicked lampoon. But it never came. Instead, his gaze grew mistier and he repeated that one syllable:

"Bird."

"Right, Lady Bird," I urged him.

"She came right over to me as I was helping the caterers wheel in the coffee urn, and shook my hand. I mean, it was more than a handshake. She held my elbow and looked, really looked at me. Something passed between us. I know that, while she was in the White House, she met every world leader who traipsed through D.C., but when she looked at me, something unique happened to both of us. I know it. I felt it."

"Have you ever shaken hands with a politician before?" I asked gently.

"No, why?"

"Nothing. Continue."

"It's her eyes really. They stopped putting eyes like those in women. Do you know what her real name is?"

"No."

"Claudia. Claudia Alta Taylor. Claudia, I never realized what a pretty name that was. I found it in the file. Do you realize how much stuff there is about her in these files? There's even recipes of hers, the actual food that she likes to cook." He went to the table where I, daily, transformed bulky brown boxes into sleek red boxes. It was littered with the brittle, pink photostats of Lady Bird's recipes that I had filed yesterday. Mixed in with them were the photos of Lynda Bird's makeover, and mounds of eight-by-ten glossies of Lady Bird and her two birdlets, that I had already filed, the three of them always in some Princess-line mini-dress that displayed their skinny shanks and chubby knees. They were spread all over the worktable; Tommy was undoing all my work.

"Tommy, you're not serious."

"Serious? Mary Jo, I've been in the presence of greatness and greatness has been in the presence of me. Neither one of us came away untouched. There's a reason for everything and, until yesterday, until I met Bird, I was blind to the reason why I'd ended up here. I always assumed it was for my music, but now I see that there's a much higher purpose. Listen, it's in this song. I stayed up all last night working on it. Tell me if you understand what I'm trying to say here."

He composed himself, then began crooning in his scratchy voice.

> Lady Bird, Lady Bird, you high-flying Lady Bird
> You beautified the trails of my heart
> Lady Bird, Lady Bird
> You may be seventy to the world
> But to me you're seventeen
> He was just the court jester
> While you were America's queen
>
> Oh Lady Bird . . .

His warbling trailed out on a note of unrelieved anguish.

"That's as much as I've done. Do you get it?"

"Get it? It's a love song to Lady Bird Johnson. A love song to a woman in her seventies from a guy twenty-two. What's to get?"

"You don't get it." Tommy was crestfallen. "She was the guiding force. It just took one meeting for me to see that. She *was* LBJ. That's what we've got to get across to the world."

"We do?"

"Sure, who else is going to do it? We've got all the material here." He strode over to the worktable massed with photos of Bird and her two daughters with their six pudgy knees sticking out from their three Princess dresses.

"What exactly do you have in mind?"

"Organizing. Getting these files into a really coherent, usable form. People need to know what's up here. So much of it is classic Birdianna."

"Tommy, how do you have any idea of what's up here? You slept through the first three years of the administration."

"That's what I've been doing all morning, perusing the collection. Your system is hopeless, Steadman. It will take scholars forever to dig out the good stuff on Bird. You just didn't really apply yourself."

"You actually care about all this?"

Tommy nodded solemnly.

I watched him warily, waiting for him to explode into hyena laughter.

There was no laugh. Tommy continued with his new Bird Master List. Under Foods, Favorites, he was carefully penciling in "Bunkhouse Chili." He actually appeared to be working. I was shaken.

"That must have been some handshake."

He kept working. Before I dozed back off (I really hadn't gotten *any* sleep the night before), I had one thought—wait until Collie hears about this.

"He's got a crush on Lady Bird Johnson?" Collie demanded, after I'd recounted the unforseeable turn of events at the Presidential Bunker.

"That's sort of what it looks like," I answered.

"I had a cousin, a real young guy, who fell in love with Betty Ford," Fayrene commented, barely loudly enough to be heard over the sound of her thighs rubbing together as we three hiked cross-campus to the swimming pool. "But I guess that's different. She's a very attractive woman."

Collie and I exchanged puzzled glances and we all continued on. With surprisingly little prodding from Collie, Fayrene had joined us in the fulfillment of Collie's promise to pump up my blood with the right kind of endorphins. It was Collie's saying that swimming was the only *other* form of exercise a person could enjoy horizontally that won Fayrene over. She was getting quite a taste for the tiny nibbles of naughtiness that Collie fed her. They teased the sexual energy she and her family had spent their lives suppressing.

The Texas Swim Center looked like a space research center. As we walked in, the tower bells pealed out the evening hour, seven, along with a clanking rendition of "Waltzing Matilda." We followed Collie down to the locker room and Fayrene clicked in another memory tape.

"The Texas Swimming Center was built at a cost of six million dollars eight years ago and could not be duplicated for four times that amount today." She spoke in that slightly robotic voice again. "Modeled after the swimming facility built for the 1972 Olympics in Munich, it boasts the finest, fastest pool in the country.

"The main one-hundred-meter pool contains one and a half million gallons of continually filtered water shimmering fifty feet below the halogen lights that illuminate the Swim Center. The water is kept at a constant temperature of eighty-one degrees year-round. The chlorine and pH levels are monitored by computer to minimize eye irritation. Underwater viewing areas allow coaches to check a swimmer's form."

Fayrene's mini-series on the TSC ended on a note of panic as we entered the locker room. "There aren't any stalls. Changing stalls," she elaborated.

And indeed there weren't. The six-million-dollar facility provided for all the modern swimmer's needs except modesty, a priority item for blimpoid Baptists from Waco. Acute distress wrinkled Fayrene's face.

"How about the toilet stall?" Collie suggested helpfully. One glance told us, however, that there was not room for both a commode and the Pirtle bulk within the stall's narrow confines.

"Y'all go ahead," Fayrene capitulated. "I'll just wait for you outside."

"You're doing no such thing," Collie protested. "You're here to swim and you're going to swim. Now, there's no one else here. Mary Jo and I will turn our backs and it'll be just like you had your own giant changing stall."

I doubt that this line of reasoning delivered by anyone other than Cordelia Mohoric would have worked. But her brimming enthusiasm and determination swept Fayrene along.

"Well, okay," she agreed tentatively. "But don't peek."

"Wouldn't think of it," Collie and I promised. We each took a locker and stuffed our things inside. Then, keeping our eyes trained on a crudely lettered banner with the puzzling command to "EAT GATOR MEAT!!!" taped to the opposite wall, we disrobed. It was only a heartbeat later that a dozen swimmers swarmed in and caught us with nothing on except pubes and belly buttons.

The newcomers had been chatting up a storm and a few fragments bounced off the tiles: "Ew-w-w, y'all, did coach say we'd be doing weights today?" "Ew-w-w, y'all, I hope my weight's down. All I ate today was a chocolate chip cookie." "Ew-w-w, one of those giant ones you get on the Drag? Ew-w-w, they're excellent." Then, finally, horribly, "Ew-w-w, y'all, who are *they*?"

"*They*" were, of course, us, with all our collective glories on grand and absolute display for what could only be the Lady Longhorn Varsity Swimming Team. Fayrene held her panties in front of her. Collie glared at the intruders. I madly ransacked my bag for my swimsuit. This scene might have been somewhat less embarrassing if it had been enacted before a group of mortal women. But swimmer women with their abundance of leg and shoulder and deficiency of hip and belly are not mortal women. Next to them, I looked like an outrider for the Pony Express carrying a month's mail in my saddlebags. Collie, Vivien Leigh in a bathrobe, could have been Olive Oyl gone bulimic in the all-together. And Fayrene. Fayrene was a five-foot-five grub larva, pink with embarrassment across the total acreage of her Rubenesque body.

"Ew-w-w, this is the varsity locker room." The silence was broken by a goddess with blond hair shiny as Christmas tinsel from years of chlorine damage. "Rec swimmers aren't allowed in here. Y'all're supposed to be next door."

Fayrene looked as if she were about to succumb to spontaneous combustion. She was hunched over, paralyzed like a stone gargoyle into a contortion of misery, and flaming a scarlet fever red.

"Be out of your way in a second," I mumbled, jumping into my suit. Collie and I went to Fayrene and, unable to pry her fingers loose from the death grip she had on her bloomers, made her step into her swimsuit by lifting, first one dimpled foot, then the other, into the legholes. As soon as we'd hoisted the navy blue nylon up to her bounteous, yet surprisingly firm, thighs, she dropped the panties and grabbed frantically for the suit. With a few admirably supple wriggles, she wedged herself in. Fully unfurled, the suit had the kind of little skirt on it that overweight women think will camouflage a bit of nature's bounty but succeeds only in making them look like the tutued hippos in *Fantasia*. A couple of the naiads snickered audibly.

"We'll just leave y'all now," Collie said. She threw a towel over Fayrene's shoulders and guided her out. Over her shoulder, she added, "We know you have a lot of anabolic steroids to take. So toodle-oo."

Fayrene's catatonic paralysis still had not lifted by the time we emerged into the swim temple proper. The place itself stunned me. When the gods and goddesses make their comeback, the Texas Swim Center is where we'll all be going to worship Neptune.

Collie grabbed a couple of kickboards and we led Fayrene to the water's edge. The pool was alive with lap sharks hellbent on cardiovascular fitness, the kind of freaks who know their pulse rate, oxygen exchange volume, and percentage of body fat. Collie gave us an encouraging smile, pulled her goggles on, dove in, and motored off. I waited for a slight break in the chain of kamikaze lap swimmers with their menacing Tojo goggles, then slid in, still gripping the side.

"Come on," I shouted with counterfeit enthusiasm to a cowering Fayrene, "water's fine." She edged forward and lowered herself in. A small tsunami engulfed me as she made her aquatic entrance. Once the waters had stabilized, I pushed off attempting to demonstrate what invigorating fun lap swimming was. My crawl was a bit rusty. My flutter-kicking legs felt like a pair of hummingbird wings, but still I was barely moving. Halfway across the pool, a cardiac crisis seemed imminent. A lap shark torpedoed past, leaving me drenched and choking in his wake. I clung to the buoyed rope marking out my lane and coughed up a couple of the chlorinated gallons I'd swallowed.

Fayrene was still clinging to the edge of the pool. Her eyes widened with terror as the sharks zeroed in on her, flip-turned in her face, and pushed off splashing water dangerously close to the upper half of her body, which she was attempting to keep dry. I cut across into the homeward-bound lane and paddled back to her.

"Let's try the kickboards," I suggested, handing her one of the Styrofoam slabs Collie had nabbed for us. Stiff with fear, her back arched above the kickboard like a walrus lumbering about his harem, she put out to sea aboard her flimsy craft. Her feeble flutter kick raised a tepid trail of bubbles. Something about knowing that there was one person in that vast nautatorium who swam worse than *moi-même* renewed my vigor. I kicked up to Fayrene and coaxed her on with a hearty, "Kick, kick. Eat gator meat!"

She stiffened up a bit, poured on some extra fuel, and was rewarded with a surge forward. The novelty of swift, reasonably graceful, self-propelled motion delighted her. She put on another burst of speed and surged forward again frothing the water behind her with a boil of bubbles. Soon, a chunky tug among the sleek sloops lapping past her, Fayrene was chugging away, her head and upper torso still dry as toast.

I too found my own stately rhythm. Once I'd relaxed and settled into my own retirement cruise speed, swimming revealed its secret joy—boy watching. As noted earlier, swimming has an entirely salutary effect on the female body. It does not leave the male physique untouched either. All around me, through blurs of water and motion, long, luscious curves of masculinity—booming Johnny Weismuller chests tapering into whippet waists and corrugated tummies—stroked past. An extravagance of legs trailed out from behind tiny bands of primary-colored Lycra stretched over perky buns and scrotal bulges. Thus diverted, I happily circled, delighted now when a lap shark slithered past.

The only cloud on the bright cardiovascular horizon of my future was the occasional glimpses I caught of myself. My thighs, questionable on land, were twin manta rays rippling behind me in the water. Worse still, I remembered the pull string of my tampon which, even at that moment, might be peeking out of my suit like a small, white ripcord. I quickly reverted to the flutter kick stirring up a flurry of camouflaging bubbles to block the rear view. As soon as I did, a series of lap sharks zoomed past me one after another like drivers who'd been following a hay truck until the yellow stripe ended.

For the next hour I was tuned in to the panorama of gluteus maximi pumping past. Later, it took me a second to realize someone was tugging on my arm. I surfaced.

"You about ready to leave?" Collie asked.

We waited at the edge of the pool until Fayrene steamed grandly up to us, then made soggy tracks for the locker room.

"Some pretty fair fizzy cues out there," Collie commented.

"Pretty fair," I agreed with the understatement.

"Well, anyway, they look good underwater and from a distance," she qualified. "Up close most of them are covered with purple zit scars and their hairlines blend in with their eyebrows."

"Enchanting," I said, fearing for my cardiovascular future.

"That makes it better. Pure aesthetics from afar. What's the scenery matter? We're here to swim, right?"

"Right," Fayrene beamed, flushed with exertion and pleasure. Somewhere on her kickboard cruise, she'd gotten wet and stood before us now dewy and radiant, her hair sleek as a seal's fur, her cheeks pink with vascular suffusion.

"Okay," Collie congratulated us. "You both look like you're positively brimming with the right kind of endorphins. We'll be back tomorrow."

And we were. Fayrene churning the waters with her chubby thighs, I lost in cardiovascular voyeurism, Collie frolicking with the lap sharks. All of us beaming from the blood tingling in our ears by the end of the swim. Then coming back every evening for the rest of the week to do it again. And twice on Saturday. By my next photo lab, I was teeming with endorphins and ready for Señor Ed.

9

"TODAY, chew are debelope chur first roll of film," Eduardo announced to the lab.

The class crowded in a bit closer. The scent and mark of Estée Lauder lay heavily all around, but nowhere more heavily than on me. Collie had made my face a palette for revenge. I'd looked in the mirror when she'd finished and not recognized the person staring back at me. I wanted simultaneously to ask this person for her autograph and to gossip behind her back. Collie assured me that my reaction guaranteed success.

My gaze momentarily crossed Eduardo's and his soulful Latin eyes glazed over with a frostiness that made me want to twitch my antennae in embarrassment. Collie had been so right. Had he looked at me with renewed longing, with fevered remembrance, with anything other than roaring disgust, I would have ignored all Collie's counsel, turned my back on The Axiom. But he didn't. To Eduardo Suarez I was last week's garbage. I hastily reviewed Collie's strategy: "Sparkle. Shine. But selectively. On for any male in the lab except Eduardo. Off for Eduardo. Every time you glance in his direction imagine him sniffing used baby diapers. That will inspire the correct expression of disgust."

I lacerated Eduardo with disgust then searched the lab for someone of the male persuasion to blink on to. Pickings were slim, but rebounders can't care what wall they ricochet off of if they want to end up back in the court. I zeroed in on a scruffy group in the shadows at the back of the lab.

"The best thins in photography are happen in the dark," Eduardo cooed lasciviously to the gaggle melting at his feet.

"Oh, Wardo," one pert coed giggled; a pink headband pulled her blond hair into a style reminiscent of the fabled Indian warrior Cochise. She wasn't alone. They all giggled, each one certain the double entendre had been intended for her. Leaving the despicable Eduardo to his coterie, I made my way to the rogue band at the back.

Eduardo's charm obviously did not extend to the periphery where the disgruntled males of the class were muttering darkly amongst themselves.

"That Bean Head don't know shit from shutter speed. He just got the job 'cuz he's sleeping with Denise," one muttered, referring to our frail and distracted professor.

"Cruel and unusual punishment even for Pantalones Calientes," came the comment on Professor Denise's allure quotient.

"Hey, you go to the Tosh concert?" a scruffian in a muscle T-shirt and a bandana around his neck asked me.

"Huh?" I remembered Collie's Peter Tosh T-shirt and the reason I was wearing it. I blinked on. "Oh, yeah. Wasn't it just reggae-rific?"

"Really. Especially when he invited everyone over to his hotel to share spliffs."

I laughed a gay, knowing, debutante laugh and the circle tightened a bit around me.

Behind me, Eduardo raised his voice to capture the attention of the splinter group. "Chew must to know instinctibbely what to do with chur hands in the dark if chew wan to be esucessful." Out of a haughtily disdainful corner of my eye, I glimpsed Eduardo demonstrating, with a slitheringly sinous suggestiveness, the technique for reeling film onto a developing roll. Several of his adorers had moved perilously close to him and were crossing and uncrossing their legs.

"What a sleaze," one of the scruffians noticed, looking at the bedazzled coeds.

I tossed back my headful of wispy hair which Collie had somehow transformed into a great tawny mane and laughed, a slave to mirth.

The scruffian looked away from the aroused acolytes and back to me with renewed interest. Emboldened, he tried again. "I'll bet he's had a lot of" (nudge, nudge, wink, wink) " 'developments' in the darkroom." I chortled madly.

Soon they all were feeding me lines, doing old routines from *Saturday Night Live*, telling me I looked "mah-velous," calling each other Hosehead or a "wild and crazy guy," saying, "Well, excu-u-u-se me," reenacting whole bits from Monty Python movies. It didn't matter how old and misused the joke, I rewarded each and every one with hebephrenic laughter. Soon the peripherals stopped worrying that the alpha male had cornered all the young breeders; they were getting adoration in its purest form—yucks. No tighter bond exists than between amuser and amused and I'd forged the magical link. Collie, how right you were.

Eduardo shot me a puzzled look of the kind a sheep dog would cast upon a runaway lamb. He honestly couldn't figure out how I might have come to stray from the flock. "Okay, enough lecture. Ebryone, debelope chur negatibs."

"Ew-w-w, Wardo," Pink Cochise murmured, insinuatingly. "Did you bring those reels from your house? I don't think I could get my film loaded onto anything else."

She wilted beneath her headband under Eduardo's ruthless annoyance at her reference to their private developing session. I felt sorry for her. I could have *been* her.

"Hey, you want to get into a dark room with me and see what develops?" the scruffian asked me, playing broadly to his cronies. I was half a beat away from telling him that puns are verbal methane when the Estée Lauder kicked in and I remembered to laugh.

"Sure," I choked out, wiping the tears of mirth from my eyes.

"No," Eduardo burst out, a patient sheep dog pressed to his limits by marauding wolves. "Chee's going to come with me." He threw open the door of the first developing room and stood aside. I entered. "Ebryone, go debelope chur film," he sputtered. An exasperated Eduardo sounded like Donald Duck on amphetamines. He backed me into a developing closet.

"Chew are dribing me crazy!" he exploded the instant the door was shut.

For a second I wavered. It's hard playing a role when your audience is close enough to land spit driblets on you. How, I asked myself desperately, would Collie play this scene? My courage returned and I referred myself to The Late Show.

"What *are* you talking about?" I inquired. I couldn't place the actress I was playing, but I knew she must be from the thirties or early forties at the latest. Even in movies people stopped talking that way after the Second World War.

"Chew know exactly what I yam talking about." Eduardo took to his role naturally. If anything, he seemed a bit overrehearsed. "Chew are making an espectacle of churself. How many of them have you eslept with?"

"Don't be silly." (I wanted to say, "Don't be silly, my dear boy," but even drama has its limits.) "Shall we develop this film or shall we continue this ridiculous scene?"

"I neber thought chew were a cruel woman, Mary Hoe."

For a second, I teetered. The way he said my name, Mary Hoe, tugged at my heart. I almost went back to "being" Mary Hoe. Then I remembered the treatment she had received at his practiced brown hands. No, I was faring far better as this haughty spitfire of a woman with a hibiscus behind her ear and a broken heart in every pocket.

Leaving Wardo with the promise that I might "think" about going out with him again if I was pleased with the job he did developing my negatives, I sprinted across campus and was already pulsating with the right endorphins by the time I met Collie and Fayrene at the Swim Center for our lunchtime swim.

"So, how'd it go?" Collie asked, paddling alongside me. Fayrene churned forward to listen in.

I grinned triumphantly. "Let's just say that The Axiom hasn't been disproved yet."

"You rubbed his nose in it!" Collie exulted.

"Hey, you wanna clear a lane up there?"

All three of us craned around. A kamikaze lap swimmer glared back at us. He looked like a mean Skinhead with his flesh-colored bathing cap and goggles. Fayrene and I dropped back to clear the lane and he flailed past us.

"More details this evening," Collie ordered.

I nodded agreement.

My hair was still dripping when I arrived at the library. I tip-toed out of the elevator onto the fifth floor, trying not to wake Tommy. The sound of frenzied activity reminded me of his trans-formation. I followed the whoomp-whoomp sound of boxes of pa-per hitting the concrete floor. There he was, right in front of the wall of glass with the day's load of patriot tourists five floors below craning their necks upward to watch Tommy frantically pulling red boxes off of the shelves I had so tenderly nestled them upon.

"There's so much here," he muttered distractedly to me as I entered his field of vision. He piled a jumbled stack of papers onto the trolley that had once been my exclusive property and wheeled them over to the work area. The table was buried beneath junk that had gone from White House dumpsters into Government Ser-vices Administration brown boxes into mandarin red display boxes and now back out again. On the top of the pile was a photo of Lady Bird in a bright yellow Princess mini-dress and white gloves hefting a shovel-load of dirt. A grinning man in a suit held an aza-lea bush ready for planting. The Beautification Years.

I pulled out the stepladder and climbed into the isolation tank. It was obvious that Tommy wasn't going to be using it. I drifted off to Tommy's running commentary as he sifted through half a dozen years of Bird P.R. shots: "Oh wow, here she is with Sammy Davis, Jr." "Have you noticed how often she wears yellow? Ah," he chuckled, "the Yellow Rose of Texas." "Hey, Carol Channing's popping her eyes and kissing Bird at the same time in this one!"

My dream blended in with the peevish question, "Well, where is she? Where is Mary Jo?" Where *is* Mary Jo indeed, I wondered, frantically trying to fight my way out of the orange haze of an unending darkroom to answer. I was on the verge of calling out, when I placed the trademark tone and burrowed further into my cardboard hideout. Smythe was outside talking to Tommy.

"Toilet," Tommy answered succinctly.

"That's what you said half an hour ago." The reedy voice of Dorothy Fenecke piped in.

"Yeah, well, I didn't want to have to mention it, but she's having her period and this is a heavy day. I'm sure *you* know what that's like Miss Fenecke. You can just . . ."

"Thank you," Smythe interrupted, hoping to forestall any further elucidation on the topic, but Tommy having learned from me, was not to be diverted.

". . . never be really secure. Really confident. You have to keep checking. Making sure that . . ."

"Yes, yes, we see," Smythe tried again. His voice receded toward the door.

". . . you're still fully protected in a way that only a woman . . ."

That word "woman" did it. A rapid shuffling of shoe leather was followed by the rattling boom of the metal fire door abruptly closing.

". . . can truly appreciate," Tommy called after them.

After a few minutes of silence, I poked my head up. "They gone?" I whispered.

Tommy bent over his stacks of Lady Bird debris. He barely nodded affirmation.

"Thanks," I said, straining to reach the stepladder. " 'Heavy day,' that was good. I could feel Smythe's skin crawling from inside the boudoir."

"Well, the guy had started to annoy me. That was his third trip up. You slept through the first two. He's giving me all kinds of shit about the new direction we're taking here. Funny, when I was napping away my time here, he was happy as a librarian in paste. But now that I'm really trying to get something accomplished, he busts his truss." Tommy shook his head sadly as he picked up a photo of Bird nuzzling black children outside a sharecropper's shack in Mississippi.

"Tommy," I said. He continued looking at the photo. "Tommy," I tried again, this time eliciting a distracted grunt. "It's time to go home."

"You go on ahead," he muttered. "I have to finish up here." I watched him for a minute, debating with myself whether to say anything or not. Somewhere inside of me, I was still waiting for him to break the hyena laugh and cackle for hours about me actually believing this latest act. But as I watched, I knew that wait would be a long one. He wasn't acting. I tried to dredge up a little tact. "You know, Tommy. Tommy. Tommy!" He finally looked up. "I'm starting, just starting, mind you, to get a little worried about you."

"Me?"

"Well, yeah. A little. I've seen you go through a couple of, well, phases just in the time we've been working together and they haven't bothered me. Actually they've kept me amused. But this. . . . For the first time, I really think you're serious."

"Never been more serious." His answer had the pointed brevity of a man anxious to get back to business.

Cynic to zealot in one handshake, it was more than I could deal with. I left him to his labors and headed for home, anxious to make a full report on the photo lab to Collie. We had El Trampa de la Pampa right where we wanted him. All except for one thing. What had ever possessed me to allow that slime to take nudie pix of me?

"Hey, dyke." A SUK distracted me from my worries about what Eduardo might do with the evidence of our night together. He was one of half a dozen brothers slouching on the front porch wearing baseball caps and expensive French Vuarnet sunglasses with neck straps and leather inserts on the side. So handy for blocking out glacier glare or ogling and harassing women. "Where's your Harley, dyke?" came the neighborly inquiry.

"And good evening to you too, my kind sirs," I answered jauntily.

That caused quite a stir of har-hars and execrably bad English accents as they mimicked my greeting between tugs from the bottle of Wild Turkey they were sharing.

As I headed inside, a blubbery fellow on the porch yelled to their head guy, The Bub, "Hey, Bub, how can you tell when a dyke's got a hard-on?"

"I dunno, Schlubber," The Bub individual brayed back. "How *can* you tell when a dyke's got a hard-on?"

"Her tongue's stickin' out!!!"

"Hey, Bub," I called across the street, feeling a little frisky from all the endorphins I'd been exercising into my system lately. "How can you tell when a SUK's got a hard-on?" I scampered into the house and delivered my punchline from behind the screen door. "You can't." Inane, but effective. I slammed the door to screams of "ball-cutting bitch" and "lesbo fag dyke." Even though I considered myself to be a transient at the Alamo, the SUKs braying bonhomie was getting to me.

"Can't we do something about those beefaloes?" I asked the group in the living room.

Judith and Hillary exchanged glances but said nothing.

"I mean, they're over here every night puking on our bushes. They party till dawn five nights a week. Shouldn't we do something?"

"You new people." Amused, Hillary shook her head then went back to misting her diseased fern.

"The situation is impossible," Josie added. "All anyone can do is hang on until they graduate, then move out."

"What? Have you tried?" I demanded.

"Mary," Judith said calmly, "after exhausting all channels, we went to the highest authority in Austin."

"You don't mean . . ."

"Yes, we wrote to Ellie Rucker."

Ellie Rucker, consumer columnist, was Austin's court of last resort. Judith pulled a newspaper clipping out of the desk drawer and handed it to me.

Q. I am steamed. I live in the midst of many frat houses in West campus and for the third night in a row these boys are having a party. They've hired a terrible band that plays unbearable music.

At least once a week they participate in some bizarre ritual in which they chant until 2 in the morning. I thought that after 10 P.M. they had to put a lid on it.

I've waited until well after midnight before I called the police, who informed me that the frat boys weren't feeling very cooperative and in order to shut them up I'd have to file charges!

I have to live next to these jerks for two more months! No way will I press charges against them. They would not respond kindly. What are my rights—if I have any? If a public disturbance law exists, why must I press charges?

Hurry. They just cranked up Billy Idol on their stereo and there's a brawl going on out front . . .

A. Oooh, it sounds pretty bad. We won't print your name.

Unfortunately there's not much you can do. Both the police and a city prosecutor told us you'd have to file charges. And you can't do it anonymously. If the boys across the street ask who filed against them, they'll get your name.

Earplugs? Would that get you through the semester?

As far as noise, the city code says it's unlawful to create noise reasonably calculated to disturb the neighbors between 10:30 P.M. and 7 A.M. But you still have to file a complaint to enforce it.

"The cop is not disturbed so he doesn't have to file a complaint. The person who is disturbed must file a complaint," says city prosecutor Bruce Young.

"The cop can go by and tell them to turn it down but after he leaves, they'll just turn it up again."

Call the police anyway, next time it happens. If you do decide to file charges, at least you'll have the police report to back you up.

"For a week after this came out, the SUKs kept up the noise barrage around the clock." I handed the clipping back to Judith. "The woman who wrote that letter dropped out of school and moved back home."

"Those hominids, can't we . . ."

"We're not saying we approve of their behaviors," Judith cut me off. "We just all need to be aware of the real-world consequences of reacting to them."

I trudged upstairs. Let someone else battle the SUKs, I was just passing through. Maybe Ellie was right: I'd invest in earplugs, then get out as soon as I could afford to.

Fayrene and Collie were waiting for me in Hell Week Heaven.

"Okay, spare no details," Collie demanded. "We want the complete and unabridged story on Señor Ed."

I recounted my debut as a high-spirited spitfire.

Collie was delighted with our success. "Though it really wasn't much of a test, I'm glad to see The Axiom has held true once again," she concluded, pressing the back of her hand to her mouth to stifle a yawn. "Well, compannñeras," she said, standing to leave, "best I be heading off to the bunkhouse for some shuteye. I didn't manage much last night."

Disappointment clouded Fayrene's face. She had settled in for the story hour and didn't want it ended so abruptly. "What about you?" she whined. "What about *your* date last night? Anything to report? Is he a new guy? Is he a weirdo like Eduardo and all the rest?"

Surprised by Fayrene's interest, Collie sat back down. "Well, new to me," she answered, "fairly old to the world. Name's Stefano," she drew out the exotic syllables. "He's Romanian or something quasi-commie. He was on the Olympic luge team and defected. Somehow he ended up in the UT Drama Department. You should see him. He really plays up the Balkan bit with these cossack shirts that button down the shoulder and boots that he tucks his pants into. Does all that qualify him as a bona fide weirdo?" she asked, amused by Fayrene's question. "You tell me, Mary Jo. Is a Balkan defective or an Argentinian who sounds like Donald Duck on speed weirder?"

"They've both got their special appeal," I admitted. "As to which one should be awarded the Weirdo of the Week title, I can't say."

"So, let's have the details," Fayrene demanded, plopping down on her bed for Story Hour.

"Come to think of it," Collie laughed, "old Stefano was pretty sparing on the details. We both still had all our clothes on, including underwear, when he commenced his initial lunge." She paused to reflect. "Quite a feat really, now that I stop and think about it."

Fayrene's eyes widened and she turned a Peanut Patty red.

"Fayrene, you're blushing," Collie noted. "You didn't blush when Mary Jo told about Señor Ed. That proves it," she crowed to me, "my defective is weirder than your gaucho. Scientific Blushometer readings make me this week's winner of the Weirdo Award. Don't worry, Mary Hoe," she consoled me, "there will be other weeks and, I guarantee it, other weirdos."

"Wait a minute," I protested. "You can't just railroad a decision like that. Fayrene hasn't even heard about the first encounter. I'll put Eduardo's strangeness up against anyone's, any day."

"We'll need evidence," Collie cautioned. "Lots of evidence, if you're seriously going to contest the rulings of our judge here." She swept her hand over toward the still-flaming Blushometer. "Isn't that right, Fay?" Fayrene paused for a moment and glanced up at Mel Gibson herding his flock, obviously considering the damage one more weirdo tale would wreak on her eternal soul. She looked away quickly, gulped, and nodded her head vigorously.

I mustered myself together and reflected on the humiliating

evening. In that one moment, however, all the events of my "date" with Eduardo were magically recast. No longer the steps leading down to my debasement, they became the mildly risible means of earning points in this wonderful new competition. "Well, it started off pretty weird. He called these guys," I pointed to my chest, "chichis."

"Chichis?" Fayrene whispered.

"Yeah, he sort of fingered them like they were a particularly interesting brooch I was wearing and he says . . ." Here I did my imitation of the Pampa Prowler, " 'Chew have berry cute chichis.' "

"Berry cute?" Fayrene repeated, beginning to blush.

I winced when Fayrene blushed. My spurt of audacity was drying up.

Then Collie laughed. "Chichis? He said that?" she asked. I nodded, brightening again. She whooped. "What a sleazewad. What a tramp. El Trampa de la Pampa. Look," she turned to Fayrene. "Appears we're registering a Boiler Room Red on the Blushometer, Mary Hoe. Okay, I'll concede defeat. You win this week. But I'm warning you, greenhorn," she snarled at me, "you'd better have something good for next week if you expect to keep the trophy."

"Listen, Collie," I conceded. "I think I'll just retire while I'm ahead. This is more extracurricular activity than I can handle. I'm basically an obsessive monogamist looking for a stable quasi-conjugal dyad."

"Mary Hoe," Collie reminded me, "that's just what you had. And what did it get you? The exclusive right to do the guy's laundry. If that's what you're searching for, get a job at the Kwik-Wash. The pay is better and the hours are shorter."

"Haven't you ever been in a long-term, committed relationship?"

"Sure," she glossed over my question. I made a mental note to grill her on it further. "And, with the typical bad luck of most women, you too will end up in one of Judith's notorious dyads, probably conjugal. And, even before you're through returning all the silver-plated relish trays you got as wedding presents, you're going to be wondering what you missed. So now's the time to find out. The wife who knows that the world is teeming with weirdos whose only goal in life is to make women hate themselves is a happy wife."

"It's not exactly like I'm dying to get married or that I'd be a virgin bride," I protested.

"Dying or not, statistically the chances are pretty good that you will end up married. And you may not be a physical virgin, but you're still a mental one."

"Mental virginity. A most interesting concept. What are you talking about?"

"About you retiring after the first Weirdo of the Week competition."

"Collie, this is a joke, this isn't serious."

"See? That's exactly what I'm talking about. *They're* not serious. Not Eduardo. Not Helmut. Not Stefano. Not Trevor. Not what was his name?"

"Roger," I supplied, a pang shooting through my heart.

"*They're* the joke. None of them are serious. But the competition is. It has to be because if it isn't then they are."

Then Roger is. The equation was self-evident once it was laid out. So was my mission. I could evade it only at the gravest peril to my future, for-real dyad. I had no choice, I would *have* to experience more frolicsome sex.

"Let the games begin."

Collie shot a right-on fist toward the ceiling and Fayrene snuggled contentedly into her bed: The bedtime stories wouldn't end yet.

"So what's the next event?"

I admitted that I didn't have one, that dealing with Eduardo had exhausted my tactical energy.

"Big mistake," Collie cautioned. "Men are like soup, you should always have some simmering on the back burner. Let a guy think he's your only source of sustenance and he'll starve you to death."

"Collie, you're so hard."

"Hard, but right. What's your next occasion of sin?"

I shrugged.

"Okay, when's your next lab?"

"Not for another week. We're supposed to shoot an 'action event.' "

Collie slapped the heel of her hand to her forehead. "Photography assignments, of course. Mary Jo, my girl, you have been given the passport to Encounter Land. With a camera around your neck you can go anywhere and meet anyone. Cameras are like death rays: Point one at a person and they are under your control. I suggest pointing yours at a few of those persons with the enlarged Adam's apples. An action event, huh?" She gazed up at Mel Gibson and the sheep for guidance. The livestock triggered the answer. "A rodeo," she burst out. "It's too perfect. Couldn't ask for more action or more willing men. I'll talk to Trevor, he's a real aficionado of the ro-day-oh. Knows when and where all of these things are held. Hasta lumbago."

Before I could protest, a moped spurted to a stop outside the house and tooted. Collie raced to the window.

"Gypsy Eyes," she called down, "you came! Be right there."

Fayrene and I slipped up behind her. Down in the street was a guy on a red moped who was a slight variation on Collie's recurring motif with his lustrous, dark curls trailing off into one long tendril at the back of his neck and the inevitable earring. Brutal and beautiful. Yeah, Gypsy Eyes fit. Collie, sleep forgotten, was gone before we could quiz her about G. Eyes.

Scarves fluttered out behind her as they puttered away down the street. They looked like two glamorous extras from the set of *La Dolce Vita*, two young hedonists living charmed lives. Sadness could never touch them, never even catch them. Still, when Collie turned to flap me a dramatic wave, a creepy feeling skittered through me. It was the way she was perched on the back of the moped as if she could tell gravity what to do. The way she let those long scarves flutter down around the wheel axle. For a second I thought I was worried about her falling off or pulling an Isadora Duncan. Then I realized it wasn't that at all. What was upsetting was that she truly didn't seem to care.

10

AT DINNER that night, Judith informed us that there was a House Meeting. Fayrene and I were attempting to slink away unnoticed before this meeting got under way when Judith shepherded us into the crowd headed for the living room. Everyone shuffled in like mental ward inmates lining up for their evening Thorazine.

Judith had an easel erected at the front of the room with a large pad of newsprint attached to it. "AGENDA" headed a list of eight items. She glanced around the room counting the house—noted that Collie was missing—then turned back to her chart. Her magic marker squeaked as she forcefully added number nine to the list: "Decide on appropriate negative reinforcers for nonattendance at House Meetings."

I took advantage of the delay to inventory the attendees. Josie Guzman was curled up in the greasy armchair absorbed in a sci-fi paperback. A plume of cigarette smoke fanned out over her head. Hillary, standing on the other side of the easel, glared at her. Feeling the hostile gaze drilling her, Josie glanced up, took stock of Hillary's displeasure, and puffed out a voluminous cloud in her direction.

Esme and Constance occupied the grimy love seat next to the armchair. Esme was busy telling Judith which way to angle the easel so she could read it better. Constance was looking off into the distance, thinking thoughts in Old Norse no doubt. She was studying the language to do research on her dissertation topic, the relationship of the Icelandic Njalssaga to the Ur-Hamlet, an ancient Danish legend that might be the prototype for *Hamlet*.

Toni and Barb were squeezed onto the third cushion of the couch Fayrene and I occupied, whispering in dark tones of dissension that left Barb with a pitifully stricken look on her face. Fayrene was reading a book on cardiovascular swim training.

Alexis Hartwell perched on the edge of the ratty rattan rocker next to me. She kept looking from the sunburst clock to Judith. She obviously had better places to be, better—more useful—people she could be with.

Byung Duk Soo bounced onto the scene headed for the kitchen. Stunned by our little gathering, she froze in mid-bound and asked, "What is?"

"It's House Meeting, Duk Soo," Judith replied. "Didn't you see the notice? As it states in the contract you signed, it's the responsibility of every house member to check the designated message center for notices of housewide interest."

Duk Soo nodded cheerily and continued on her way to the kitchen.

"Duk Soo," Judith called after her.

She stopped and looked back like a startled doe. Her sparse eyebrows shot up to signal interest.

"House Meeting. You stay here," Judith elucidated stabbing the air above our little assemblage.

"Howsameeting," Duk Soo repeated with several vigorous nods, pulling up a chair from the dining room and establishing herself behind me. "I stay," she declared triumphantly.

"Good," Judith dispensed a few of her head-boinger, nonverbal reinforcement nods and Byung Duk Soo beamed.

Judith looked pointedly at her watch. "I guess the only one missing now is Cordelia."

"As usual," Hillary hissed sotto voce.

"Mary," she turned to me, "do you know if Cordelia is planning on joining us or not?"

"Haven't seen her all day," I answered. "I doubt that she even saw the House Meeting notice."

"There were plenty enough in the past that she *did* see and chose to ignore," Hillary huffed.

"Okay," Judith sighed, despairing of the prodigal, "let's get this show on the road, we've got a lot of ground to cover and I for one propose we cover it quickly. I want to try and get a couple more hours in on my thesis tonight. Remember, I'm just facilitating this meeting; it's you all's meeting so you're going to have to lead it. Is that understood?" She looked at us sternly until several heads nodded in understanding and agreement. "Okay, item number one, mail forwarding. Constance, you suggested that item. You take the floor."

Standing, Constance said, "Thank you, Judith," as if accepting the nomination of the Democratic Party. She had a spiral notebook and a letter in her hand. "Now this," she said, opening the notebook, "is where I keep a log of everyone's forwarding address when they leave the house. It's very important," she emphasized, looking around at each one of us, "to leave a forwarding address with me. Sue Jeffers did not do that."

"Wasn't she the one who smelled so bad?" Alexis asked, tearing her eyes away from the clock.

"Bad?" Constance paused, completely derailed. "That depends, I suppose on what you'd term bad. She did have an odor that was not precisely floral. Actually it was more an industrial sort of a smell. Possibly an operator of heavy machinery would have found it quite fragrant."

"She stunk," Alexis corrected her. "Didn't wash her hair either. It like clung to her scalp," she elaborated, shuddering in disgust at the departed Miss Jeffers's lack of hygiene. "And her cuticles were halfway up her nails. I couldn't even eat around her."

"H-m-m-m," Constance pressed a thoughtful finger to her pursed mouth, "I really didn't notice her cuticles. She did go to one meeting of the Society for Creative Anachronism with me. She especially enjoyed the jousting and mead-making. Couldn't interest her at all in heraldic crests, which is my specialty. Still, I think . . ."

"Ladies," Judith cautioned, "we're straying from the agenda. About the mail?"

"Right, forgive me," Constance apologized. "Well, the crux of the matter is that Sue left without supplying me with a forwarding address and now a letter has arrived for her. What are we to do? I think we need to institute a procedure to deal with this contingency since I doubt that this is the only time a case like this will arise."

"I just want to say that Sue left owing the house," Hillary paused and checked her books, "fifty-five dollars and ninety-three cents."

"That hardly entitles you to withhold her mail," Josie said, looking up from her sci-fi mag. "Tampering with the U.S. mail is a federal offense."

"Oh dear," Constance fretted, tightening her grip on letter and notebook, "I was afraid of something like this."

"It's a pretty simple problem, really," Toni stated. "Just trace her through her old college."

"It's not really quite that simple, Toni," Constance answered. "She is persona non grata around the biogenetics department where she was matriculating. Seems she forgot to switch the air conditioner to automatic one evening when she was working late and several dozen generations of fruit flies were frozen to death overnight. She slunk away in disgrace from what I gather."

The details of Sue Jeffers and her mail were beginning to wear on me in ways usually only achievable with a dentist's drill. And still it went on.

"People," Judith shrilled, "let's not get bogged down in specific details here. What we need to be focusing on is the process. We need to establish a process for dealing with situations like this."

"Two suggestions," Hillary said, holding that number of fingers aloft. "One, no one gets their key deposit back until they turn in a forwarding address. And two, right after new members sign their contracts, they give us their parents' address so we'll always have a permanent address for everyone."

"No way!" Esme exploded. "There's no way you're going to get my parents' address. I rooted them out of my life twenty-five years ago and they're not going to start tearing open my personal mail again now."

At that point, the discussion degenerated into squabbles about whether parents or the federal bureaucracy were the bigger meddlers in private lives.

I squinted at the letter that was the cause of this tempest. I squinted harder. I couldn't be seeing what I thought I was seeing. "Constance," I whispered, gesturing toward the communiqué she clutched. "Let me see the letter."

She looked from me to the one-way ticket to Leavenworth in her hand and reluctantly surrendered it. It was true, my eyes hadn't deceived me.

"Excuse me," I said, trying to break into the debates raging around me, "but has anyone looked at this letter?" There was no response. I raised my voice and continued, putting the question to the group: "Do you really think Sue Jeffers is going to care about this?" Only Fayrene was listening as I began to read aloud what was written on the outside of the envelope, "You may already be a winner," I quoted. The hysteria quieted as those words penetrated.

"It's junk mail," Josie deduced. "The Post Office wouldn't forward it even if we *had* an address."

I handed the sweepstakes entry back to Constance, who examined it, muttered, "Oh well, in that case. . . ," and sat down.

"Item number two." Judith "facilitated" us, she didn't lead us, to the next item. "Milk purchase. You brought that up, Toni; I cede the floor to you."

Toni hitched up her cords as she stood, folded one hand over the other in front of her crotch as if she were about to lead us in prayer, spread her legs into a firmly braced, John Wayne stance, cleared her throat, and spoke. "There's never any frigging milk around here." Then she sat down.

No one spoke until Judith broke the silence. "Esme, you're Food Buyer, perhaps you'd like to address Toni's concern."

Esme pressed her thin lips together as if she were trying to seal off some internal pressure leak. Her dark eyes bulged in their sunken sockets. She flipped feverishly through a looseleaf note-book on her lap filled with mimeographed sheets. Ripping a sheet out, she waved it above her head like a banner.

"Here it is, guys," she announced, her voice crackling with suppressed rage. "*Your* food order for the past week. I did not buy milk because milk was not on my order sheet. And *why* was milk not on my order sheet? For the answer to that you will have to ask Hillary, who makes up the order sheet supposedly in compliance with house wishes." She closed her eyes in an expression of saintly forebearance and let her hand fall.

"Well?" Toni asked, turning the inquisition to Hillary.

"I cut the milk order back because the week before I had to throw out a whole gallon that went sour."

"The refrigerator wasn't working week before last, *that* is why the milk went bad," Toni explained in exasperated tones.

"Well, we were still ordering too much. We already have tons of cheese and other mucus-producing dairy products." Hillary's voice began to rise.

"It's the only source of protein we have," Toni moaned.

Hillary clucked and rolled her eyeballs. "You've obviously been reading too much FDA propaganda, Toni. Americans eat way too much protein. You should look at the dairy lobby's budget sometime."

"Irregardless," Toni countered, "we should order milk every week."

Hillary glared at her. "Every week *I* order tofu and *it* never shows up, but I don't make a huge issue out of it, putting it on the agenda and everything."

"I've told you, Hillary," Esme groaned, "we can only buy tofu in gallon containers. You're the only person who eats tofu. One gallon is too much."

"Yeah," Hillary shot back, "well, why do you keep getting soy sauce when I specify tamari?"

"Because they're the same damned thing and tamari costs twice as much."

"Is that why you won't get the cold-pressed oil either?"

"No," Esme answered forthrightly, "it's because your damned cold-pressed oil costs *ten* times as much as plain old Mazola. If I bought all the things you ordered, Hillary, all we'd have to eat is tofu with tamari and cold-pressed oil."

"While I agree with you on those particular items, Esme," Constance said, back from the dead letter file, "there *is* such a thing as false economy. That Spree dishwashing liquid you buy for fifty-nine cents a quart, you have to use half a cup of the product to make any bubbles. Why can't we stick with Joy?"

"Same for that Pulvo cleanser you've been buying," Barb hitched a ride on the train of thought chugging past. "It's like trying to clean your sink with goldfish gravel. Why don't we just get Ajax?"

"Since we're on the subject of food buying," Toni added, "why don't we ever have any Grape-Nuts?"

"Have you read the label on that shit?" Hillary's retort was drowned in a flood of other longed-for foodstuffs. "Why don't we ever have any picante sauce . . . raisin bread . . . wine vinegar . . . sesame crackers . . . elbow macaroni . . . Velveeta cheese."

"Velveeta cheese!" Hillary expelled the name of the foul cheese food product and scrutinized those gathered for the offender who had uttered such blasphemy. Fayrene withered beside me, her face lighting up with that familiar red dye number two crimson blush.

"I just thought," she whimpered, "since you were taking suggestions and all."

Hillary gave her the acidulous look that food purists reserve for known consumers of cheese food products and the litany continued. "Why don't we ever have . . . turkey . . . mangoes . . . Popsicles . . ."

No one else noticed Esme's internal pressure building dangerously as the harangue raged around her. She seemed to rise like a dark dirigible clad in violet sweat pants and yellow muscle shirt with "The Dicks Shall Rise Again" written across her droopy breasts until, swollen with rage, she towered over us. The bickering stopped and everyone looked to Esme.

"The reason we don't have any picante sauce, or Grape-Nuts, or Ajax, or mangoes," she burst out, her voice crescendoing dangerously, "is because I'm a lousy, goddamned food buyer!" With that, she hurled down her Food Buyer's notebook. It bounced off the coffee table springing the ring binders loose and spraying two years of grocery lists across the floor. Esme had already stormed out, slamming the screen door dramatically behind her.

Fayrene and I looked at each other like thunderstruck children huddled under the bedcovers while their parents have their first screaming fight.

"Item number three," Judith droned on as if Esme had just excused herself to get a drink of water. No one else took any more notice of the incident than that either.

"Weird," Fayrene whispered to me. I nodded.

Dramatic though it had been for Fayrene and me, the others were apparently inured to Esme's blowups. As the meeting dragged on, the items grew so excruciatingly tedious that I began to detect the wisdom of Esme's histrionics. I forced myself to listen, searching for something I could take theatrical exception to and storm out myself. It was like trying to concentrate on the scenery in west Texas. Everything swept past me in a flat, undistinguished, hypnotizingly dull muddle. I kept pushing my foot to the floor to speed out of this wasteland, but the meeting did not accelerate its mournful pace.

Behind me, I heard a muted snuffling. Duk Soo was slumbering blissfully through the proceedings. In front of me even Hillary seemed a bit dazed and road weary. She dug at her scalp, examined what she'd unearthed, then pried it off her fingernail with her teeth. I wondered if ovo-anorectic vegetarians were allowed this one dispensation from their prohibition on eating meat products.

"Listen, people, this is an important one." Judith stabbed item number nine with her magic marker until the easel wobbled. Hillary jumped up to save it from collapsing and Judith stopped drilling it. "I mean, if we can't expect at least a minimal level of commitment from residents, this house is just not going to work. And what can be more minimal than, at least, attending House Meetings?" Her voice had taken on a keening edge.

"That's why we need to get fairly sanction-oriented about this. We need to message to non-attenders that we, as a house, are not taking kindly to the statement they're making about us, about what we're trying to do here. So, does anyone have any input? Suggestions for negative reinforcement of this behavior?"

"How about an extra cleanup?" Josie suggested. For just the barest fraction of a second, I caught Judith give a judgmental wrinkle of her nose. Then it was gone. "Okay," she boinged, "okay. That's an idea."

And that's a chair and that's a rug, I thought to myself.

"But we need to consider the time element here. First of all, there are how many?" Judith did a quick head count. "There are ten of us here. Each one of us has put in. . . . What is it now? My God, it's almost ten-thirty. Three hours apiece."

"That's a collective thirty hours. In essence then, she owes the house thirty hours." Josie announced the total and Judith boinged her head in response like a charade player signaling to a teammate that she was on to something. She did everything but touch her nose and wave a finger at Josie. She didn't need to though; the message was clear enough already—crucify Collie.

It appeared that if Judith were to have her way, Collie would end up digging new sewer lines for the house.

"What's Judith got against Collie?" Fayrene whispered to me.

Who could say? All I knew was that the dynamics of our warm sisterly nest sharpened dramatically when Collie breezed in from her date.

"Jeez, another House Meeting," she exploded. "I thought you all just had one last month. Kee-rist, one a *year* is enough for me." She had her dark hair slicked back and pomped in the front with just a dark curlicue flicked onto her forehead. She took off the Salvation Army thrift shop wino raincoat. Underneath, she was dressed all in black—a baggy black overblouse with tight, tight black capris. It took me a minute, but the way she was drunkenly slurring her words tipped me off.

"Judy Garland!"

"Took you long enough," she answered soberly.

"Somewhere over the rainbow," Constance crooned jokingly in her madrigal singing voice, a big grin lighting her face as she turned from the last three hours of tedium.

"Bluebirds fly," Collie throbbed in a choky Garland voice, looking faroff and splaying her fingers out in a spastic reach for the happiness that was always just beyond her grasp.

"Brewbirse fry ober the rainbow," Duk Soo woke up to chime in an operatic voice that made the paint curl and eardrums pound.

Collie threw an arm around her and another around Fayrene. Josie, well into her second six-pack, Constance, and I all joined in for the big finish. "Why then, oh why, can't I?"

Across the street, horns honked and a volley of beer bottles was launched, shattering on our front porch.

"A simple 'bravissima' would have been sufficient," Collie yelled out the screen door.

"If we can finish this last agenda item," Judith facilitated through clenched teeth. "All in favor of a reciprocal payback for missed meeting time." Judith and Hillary raised their hands. Through stares and brow furrowing, they managed to prod Toni, Barb, and Constance into raising their hands as well.

"What are we voting on?" Collie interrupted the hand count.

"Whether to stick you with thirty hours of cleanup for missing a House Meeting," I explained.

"Me? I didn't even know there *was* a meeting until I walked in just now."

"The only difference your not knowing made," Hillary added snidely, "is that you missed *almost* all of the meeting instead of all of it the way you usually do."

"Hillary," Collie said with mock alarm, "such hostility. Someone must be waving Big Macs over you at night while you sleep." She turned to the group at large. "Listen, is this for real? You really want me to wash dishes for thirty hours because I missed your little confab here? I mean, what critical decisions did I miss out on? Last House Meeting I was at three months ago the key issue was whether or not to buy Grape-Nuts and up the milk purchase."

"That's what we talked about tonight!" I blurted out in amazement.

"And did P.M.S.me throw her notebook down and stomp out?"

"Yeah." I began to see why no one else had been terribly moved by the scene.

"The individual issues are not what's important." Judith took the floor again with her put-upon teacher voice. "It's working through them as a house. That's what's important. That's what we should be protecting here." She acted as if she were talking about baby seals.

"But thirty hours?" Collie retorted. "You have got to be kidding."

"No, Cordelia," Judith went on, "we're not kidding." They locked gazes like two battling rams fighting over the harem.

I leaned over and answered Fayrene's big question: "Judith wants to be queen bee."

"Shall we put it to a vote," Judith asked. "All in favor of sanctions for noncommitment." Judith and Hillary shot their hands into the air. Alexis, Toni, Barb, Josie, and Constance studied the cobwebs in various distant corners of the room.

"All opposed," Collie called out, speeding up the process. Fay-rene and I joined her in a reach for the sky.

"What is this? Are all the rest of you abstaining?" Collie asked the cobweb studiers.

"This is a question that really needs more thought, more analy-sis," Constance equivocated.

"So abstain," Collie said. "We still win. Three to two. Thanks guys," she said to Fayrene and me. "Let's go get a beer."

The three of us trooped out as Judith was folding up her easel and decamping in an icy fury. We cut through the overgrown back alley strewn with garbage that connected us and our next-door neighbor, Satori House. We rarely had any truck with the Satori heads except to frequent their soft drink machine stocked with equal parts Pepsi, Sunkist Orange, and Shiner beer. Forty cents, your choice.

Next to the dented and abused machine was a galvanized steel washtub. A sign smeared by many beer dousings read "Dump Your Unwanted Beer Here." From the smell of the swill accumu-lated within, it appeared that some imbibers had contributed used beer as well as the dregs from their bottles.

"What is that?" Fayrene asked, wrinkling her pink nose like an acutely offended bunny.

"It's Hillary's," Collie explained with no hint of rancor toward one of the two voters in favor of her enforced servitude. "She gets people to dump that last little bit that's always left in the bottom of the bottle. Then she collects it and uses it in her, of course, organic garden to trap slugs and rolly-pollys. She sets the beer out in jar lids and the slimy things crawl in and drink themselves to death. That way she doesn't have to rain chemical death on her lettuce."

Collie thumbed in four dimes and dislodged a Shiner. I fol-lowed suit.

Fayrene eyed the Sunkist Orange with longing but, wanting to be one of the girls, she too pulled a Shiner out of the machine. Then Collie dumped in another handful of change and took three more for the road.

"Hell of a deal. Two-forty a six-pack."

Back at Hell Week Heaven, we were just settling in with our brews when Collie jumped up, cried out, "The cowboy lecture," and exited into her room through the French doors.

Fayrene took a sip of beer, made her bunny face, and, dreaming of a Big Red, took another. "This is the first whole bottle of beer I've ever had that was completely mine."

"You're kidding."

She shook her head. "I've had sips before of other people's, but never a whole bottle all to myself. My parents don't allow any kind of liquor in the house. I used to spend a week in the summer with my Aunt Eustace in Waxahachie. She ran the Salon de Belleza beauty salon there. It was just like that beauty shop where you took pictures. Anyway, Aunt Eustace always had a beer in one hand and a rattail comb in the other. Ladies there still like beehives and bouffant hairdos that are all teased up and sprayed. I used to sneak sips of her beer every so often. I thought that once you got to be a certain age, you just automatically started liking the taste of beer. I just wanted to see if I'd gotten to my age yet." She looked at the bottle in her hand and laughed her slow, sweet laugh. "Looks like I haven't made it yet."

"You will," I assured her.

"Yeah, hanging around with you and Collie I'm sure to."

"To Aunt Eustace." I held my bottle aloft and Fayrene clinked hers against it.

As she sipped down a thimble or two of beer, I noticed something. "You're losing weight, aren't you?" Looking at her now, I wondered how I could have failed to notice earlier. Her polyester pull-ons were positively drooping and she was down to two and a half chins.

"It's the swimming," she beamed. "I've yo-yo dieted ever since I got too big for anything but elasticized waists. But exercise is the key. Since we've been swimming every day, I've lowered my set point. Have you read about set-point theory?"

I confessed that I hadn't. Fayrene was halfway through a

verbatim quotation of the latest article she'd read about set-point theory when the French doors swung open and Collie burst in again.

"I fall to pieces," Collie warbled as she threw open the doors. She was resplendent in a white cowgirl outfit with fringe on the bottom of the skirt and around the yoke of the blouse as she belted out the C&W classic. Curving red arrows were embroidered above the pockets and ruby snap buttons ran between them.

"Patsy Cline!" Fayrene, who'd grown up with the doomed songstress's music, cried out the hallowed name.

Collie smiled, acknowledging her fan with a dip of her head. She'd gotten rid of her Judy Garland do and had one of those teased jobs that Aunt Eustace specialized in. "I hear there's a certain someone with us tonight who's fixin' to go to her very first rodeo."

"Trevor found one," I concluded.

"That's right, darlin', and we'll be headin' on out this very weekend. But before we do, there are a few things you'd better have straight in your head about cowboys." Collie plopped down on the bed beside me and grabbed a Shiner. She dropped the twangy accent. Expositions on The Axiom were serious business not to be approached in alternate identities.

"First off, forget about actually meeting any real cowboys. I grew up with the genuine item and haven't seen one in ten years. What we'll be talking about are mostly these yahoos in black pickup trucks with the wheels big as satellite dishes. They like to think they're cowboys and are the most sentimental creatures on earth. They believe, or want to believe so hard that it makes no difference, in all that Code of the West bullshit. You go into one of these guys' room or mobile home or wherever and there won't be a scrap of paper in the place. No indication that he's ever been exposed to the alphabet. Except, he'll have every book that Louis L'Amour ever wrote. And they'll be annotated cause he's educating himself about this code.

"Ignorance and sentimentality. Two very powerful forces. Send a c-boy a throw-up syrupy Hallmark card and he'll tape it on the dashboard of his truck right underneath his Skoal a-leetle-pinch-is-all-it-take spitoon and keep it there until he dies of lip cancer.

"Number two, c-boys love to suffer. They learn six new ways to hurt every day listening to the radio and they're dying to try out every one. All of which means that if you treat a c-boy mean, if you two-time him, fuck his best friend, clean out the joint account and use it to buy bolo ties for your new boyfriend, he'll blubber about you in honky-tonks from here to Bangor, Maine."

"Collie," I attempted to remind her, "I don't want a snuff-dipping love slave. All I'm going to be doing is taking a few pictures at a rodeo."

"Steady on, Steadman," Collie cautioned me, "because any woman who even *breathes* the same sage-scented air as a man of the Western persuasion needs to be thoroughly grounded in these basics I've outlined. I've seen too many good women go the way of the buffalo with these marauders. Is that understood?"

"Sure."

"Good. Now, I want you to absorb this right down to your toenails, then we'll figure out what you're going to wear."

I adopted a thoughtful, receptive posture and Collie stood for her final number of the evening.

"I fall to pee-ces . . . Each time I hear your name . . ."

11

THE RODEO Trevor had decided on was an all-black affair held out in nearby, rural Bastrop. Somewhere along the forty-minute ride, we—Collie, Fayrene, Trevor, and I—crossed the line that divides the west from the south. The countryside went from scrub oak and mesquite to pine and magnolia. Summer was making its last stand out there with an equatorial humidity.

"Collie, these jeans are cutting me in half," I whined from the back seat of Trevor's Peugeot. Fayrene looked at me with empathy. Though she was currently sporting a wraparound skirt, which she was wrapping around more and more now that her polyester pull-ons would no longer stay aloft, she still knew a thing or two of clothes that bound. "I told you," I continued. "I'm a full-figured twelve. What size are these anyway?"

"They're stretch. One size fits all and they're just right on you. If your toes aren't blue, they're not tight enough for cowboys. Trust me. Without my guidance you'd have looked like you were recruiting for the Sierra Club."

"Collie, you keep forgetting, I'm here to take pictures. Period."

"That doesn't mean you have to look like you wear Gore-Tex lingerie."

"Oh, Collie," Trevor soothed, "don't harangue the little dove, she and I are both here for purely aesthetic reasons. In my case, of course, there is the further motive of wanting to learn all I can about the tragically neglected role of the black cowboy in the history of the West," Trevor sniffed.

"Well, there it is, scholars and aesthetes," Collie announced.

Ahead of us, on the right side of the highway, was a ramshackle arena tacked together from scraps of mismatched lumber that had long ago weathered to a dispirited gray. A string of bare bulbs lighted it in the sultry night.

The photos I eventually printed from that evening synopsize what followed fairly well: Collie, Fayrene, and Trevor mugging. Collie and Fayrene mugging while the omnisexual Trevor's attention is caught by a well-filled pair of men's Wranglers passing by. The black faces gleaming in the night, smiles revealing white teeth outlined in gold, dark hands waving bottles of Baby Chams pink-tinted malt liquor at the camera. Young, black, country boys pinning contestant numbers on one another's backs. Trevor offering to help. A bucking horse frozen at the apex of a jump. A contestant crumpled in the dirt. A covey of old black men in suspenders and white shirts leaning against the arena fence. A disgusted roper tossing his lariat to the ground as a calf dances away from him. A terrified bullrider clinging to a mammoth beast making a dive for the earth's core. And then Harlan. One long-lens close-up of his Gary Cooper grin beneath the wide brim of his silver Stetson, sweat-dampened curls flipping up above his ears.

Here the photographic record thins out a bit. Harlan's was the only other white face in the crowd. He was the stock contractor, the person who brought the opposing team—the quadrupeds—to the rodeo. When I stepped into the arena to begin taking photos, he rode up and told me that if I was "inturested" he could put me in the best, safest spot in the arena for "making pitchers." Lacking any great affection for homicidal bovines, I accepted. Without any further ado, he swept me off the ground and up onto the horse behind him. It did prove to be a superior vantage point. The first thing I noticed from that height were the little crinkle lines, white against his tan, around his eyes. I couldn't overlook a truly admirable pair of shoulders either.

"Yew a Yankee?" he asked after our initial exchange.

"Hardly." I laughed the gay, debutante laugh that had worked so well in photo lab. "I'm from New Mexico."

"Jest like I figured, a Yankee. Don't matter though, I like your action."

"My action?" I inquired coquettishly, noticing Collie and Fay-rene nudging one another and pointing in my direction. I smiled their way and flipped my brain to "Record" so that I could share every precious word with them later on.

"Sure, your action. Like a horse's action. Yew know, the way your butt moves when you walk."

I trilled my amusement. Collie would love it. All in all, I en-joyed the rodeo considerably more than I'd expected joggling around on the back of Harlan's horse and waggling little covert waves to Collie. The whole improbable scene seemed like a skit I was acting out for her benefit. I suppose that that feeling, along with the Baby Chams Harlan had been feeding me, accounted for my lack of alarm when Collie, Fayrene, and Trevor approached at the end of the performance and announced they were leaving.

"Y'all go on ahead," Harlan urged them. "I'll carry your run-ning buddy home."

Running buddy, I liked that. Collie and Fayrene and I were just that, we were running buddies.

Harlan ordered his underlings to round up the stock and we took off. The cozy Baby Chams trance lasted through the ride to his "spread" where, he said, he needed only to stop off to feed the stock he kept there before zipping me on into "the city." During the ride, I was lulled by the mindless inanity of about two dozen C&W songs with their inevitable spouse-cheating, lover-meeting, enemy-beating lyrics. I began to come to a little with my first glimpse of "the spread"—a mobile home sitting on blocks in the middle of an acre of weeds. I began to fear that I'd bought "el rancho" again.

"Haven't got around to building the ranch house yet," Harlan explained as he pitched hay. Next he insisted a cup of coffee was necessary before he could make the drive to Austin. His aluminum abode was furnished with a tangled mess of bull ropes, chaps, stiff riding gloves, rigging bags, dirty dishes, soiled clothes, drained beer cans, a TV set with tin foil wrapped around the rabbit ears, and, in a hallowed corner, the complete works of Louis L'Amour. A belt with the name "Darlene" tooled on it was draped over a lampshade. I began to wish I'd cut short this cross-cultural junket. That wish flowered into a fervent yearning when Harlan removed his hat and, in so doing, added twenty years to his age. He was bald, Friar Tuck bald, with luxuriant sandy brown curls on the side and not so much as a stray filament wandering across the gaping dome atop.

He leered at me and I knew I was doomed. My Weirdo of the Week entry was coming up. Like Collie's defective, Harlan lunged for me and, hopscotching over the wreckage, carried me to bed. The trailer rattled as I landed on the grimy sheets. It rattled again as Harlan landed on me. His hand was inside my bra before I'd stopped rebounding. The instant my nipples responded under his calloused, rope-burned fingers, he moved the hand downward to attack my pants zipper and began a furious rubbing thereabouts.

"Maybe we should slow down a little?" I muttered against the teeth he was grinding against mine.

"Cain't now, darlin', this big ole thang here won't 'low it."

Needless to say, the "big ole thang" turned out to be the wildly overbilled boner he freed from his jeans. I suppose he thought that the sight of his range snake alone would be enough to inflame any cowgirl, because he promptly dispensed with his symbolic interpretation of foreplay and attempted to move on to the main event.

At the same time that I started reviewing my class in personal defense, the attack and its prime impetus withered. Harlan must have thought something had happened, however, for he cut loose with an ear-splitting "Lordee, God, I can see!!!" A few seconds later he was snoring.

Dawn revealed the true grunginess of the sheets as well as

the person sharing them with me. Could that be the Gary Cooper grin that had entranced me last night now hanging slackly open? I dressed swiftly and shook Harlan's shoulder.

"Not now, darlin'. I'm worn smooth out. I'll letcha have some more sugar after I'm rested up." Then he slumped back into his coma.

I shoveled out a phone and called Alamo House. A groggy Fayrene answered. She perked up immediately as I explained my dilemma and took down directions to the aluminum abode. I spent the next hour leafing through *Kid Rodelo*, *The Cherokee Trail*, *The Strong Shall Live*, and *Mustang Man* until I heard a car pulling up outside.

As I opened the door, Harlan croaked from the bed, "Leave your number by the phone, darlin'. I'll call you real soon and we'll do it again."

Right.

Collie and Fayrene were in the front seat of Trevor's Peugeot. I piled in the back. "Ride 'em, cowgirls," I directed them, sliding into a recumbent posture. "Make like steaming green horse turds and hit the trail. Pronto."

"One question, then you can go to sleep," Collie asked as we hit the open highway. "Was it a Weirdo of the Week award winner?"

"Oh, at the very least I should claim the award," I assured them. As I fell asleep, I was already framing up my account of my night at the Rodeo of Love.

12

I WISH I could say I learned my lesson with Harlan. But I didn't. I was out every night with my running buddies. Mostly I trailed after Collie making the rounds of the clubs and the drama school parties. Just collecting the ones that ricocheted off of Collie left me with too many takers for meaningless encounters. Like any other sport you dedicate yourself to unstintingly, Weirdo of the Week exacted a toll. Heretofore I'd always been a grade grubber of the most meretricious sort. I was the kind of kid who had a galaxy of stars after her name on the summer reading chart. The kind who sewed a little pouch on the front of her pajamas to demonstrate marsupial mothering. All for extra credit, of course. The grade was all. For me, there were only two marks—A's and head in the oven.

By absolutely ignoring my classes and never even buying the accompanying books, I had managed a feat that eluded even the masses of chuckleheaded fraternity and sorority mutants who stream through the school: I fell behind at the College of Communications. A monolingual Aleut and I are the only two students to have accomplished this to date.

It shouldn't have shocked me, but it did. Coming up on midterms, I realized just how much in arrears I was academically. The little grind in the the kangaroo suit deep within me panicked. To placate her, I made a pilgrimage over to the great rusty monolith that was my college and tracked down my professors to see about setting my accounts straight.

Professor Lipscomb peered at me over his half-moon glasses. He took them off and let them hang on his concave chest by a little gold chain around his neck.

"So the prodigal is here to make amends," he gloated.

"If that's possible, sir." The little nurd in the kangaroo suit was really antsy about those non-A grades I was coming close to sullying her record with.

Lipscomb warmed to my obsequious sniveling and sent me off with a penitential assignment and a warning that his midterm was going to be a "bear."

As I wandered the labyrnthine halls, the kangaroo-suited weenie lurking within me came into her own. I was cowed and repentant. How could I spend half a semester just listening to Collie? How could I have gone so wrong? I rapped timidly on my editing professor's door.

"Min," a weak and distant voice responded.

Was that "C'min" or "Jusamin?" I couldn't decide. So, cautiously and without sound, I opened the door and peeked around the corner. Professor Pitsor was bent over, shoving something hurriedly into his bottom desk drawer and slamming the drawer shut with a sloshing clank. Towers of paper high as my shoulder encircled him. "C'min!" he blared out, rising up. His piggy little eyes were glazed and his tuberous nose engorged with blood. I moved in front of his desk.

Like a sedated rhino, he swung his head in the direction of the door I'd just come in and shouted out once more, "I said, c'min! Dammit." The last he muttered under his breath. It was a breath that filled the room with a dangerous volatility.

I cleared my throat. "I'm here, Professor Pitsor."

"Uh, so you are." He swung his gaze in my direction and stared at me, his head weaving as if he were having difficulty supporting the weight of his nose on his spindly neck. "Slipped in on me, eh?"

"I've come to talk to you about . . ." I vaguely remembered him saying that his assignments would consist entirely of writing articles. "About the articles for your class."

"Articles," he echoed me. "Whuz your name?"

"Mary Jo Steadman. Sir." The little nurd made me add that last flourish.

"Right, right. Thought it was." With an unsteady hand, he pulled out a notebook with "Attendance" written on it and flipped through several lists. I braced myself for the moment when he discovered I had missed nearly all of his classes this semester.

"Steadman, there it is," he announced. I looked down and watched him draw a trembling finger under my name. All the spaces for attendance checks beside it were blank. I swallowed hard. It could really be the head in the oven this time, the little nurd warned me. Then I noticed something odd. None of the other names had any marks beside them either.

Pitsor sucked in a deep breath that left him momentarily sitting upright. "I haven't gotten around to handing it back yet, but your investigative series was top rate. Really, top rate. Refresh my memory again. I remember your name and that you did an excellent job, but what was your subject?"

At that critical moment, I noticed that those towers of paper sheltering Professor Pitsor were articles. Hundreds of them, the accumulated outpourings of all his classes. Not one of them had a mark on them. I glanced at the title on the top of the nearest stack.

"Strip mining, sir," I answered with appropriate modesty. "The whole question of lignite safety."

Pitsor nodded and stroked his chin. "Really top rate. I'll just go ahead and enter your grade right now while it's still fresh in my mind."

I did have to lean forward and guide his hand back to the proper line so that he wouldn't write the A in next to Marcia Steeles's name. As it turned out, the A extended for two lines in either direction anyway so that four other students got in on my free ride.

"That all?" he asked, his glassy eyes focusing briefly on mine.

"That's about it."

"Bye," he waved, leaning over toward that bottom desk drawer again.

Professor Denise was far less amiable. "Come in, Mary *Hoe*," she said with a pointed waspishness when I poked my head around her door. I didn't have to strain to figure out where she'd heard that particular pronunciation of my name. Frazzled tendrils of hair trailed untidily from the Gibson girl bun perched, slightly askew, atop her head. She had on the same high-collared, mutton-sleeved blouse trimmed in lace at the neck and wrists, but it had lost its starchy white freshness. Professor Denise looked as rumpled as her blouse. Both needed a good pressing. Her voice was oddly strained as she bid me enter, then added, "I've been expecting you."

She had? "You have?"

"Yes, it appears that you've been doing some, uh, most, uh, *interesting* work in lab." I gulped. Outside of the rodeo pictures, Eduardo had been doing all my assignments for me. In return I allowed him to drool on my knuckles once a week. It was all very unwholesome. "But you haven't deigned to come to lecture for, let me see . . ." Professor Denise flipped through *her* attendance record. "Weeks. Months, it looks like."

"Yes, well, that's what I'd like to talk with you about," I began lamely, but she cut me off.

"Been too *busy?*"

I didn't like the way she was putting key words into italics. I'm not especially astute at picking up cues from people, but there was no way to miss with Professor Denise. She was handing out annotated volumes with my name on the cover and a bloody knife plunged into it. The waves of animus pouring off her screwed up my menstrual cycle for the next three months. I theorized that Eduardo, El Trampa de la Pampa, was the probable cause. My canny guess was confirmed when I spotted one corner of an eight-by-ten sticking out from beneath a stack of contact sheets. Only a few toes were visible, but they were my toes. I would have recognized my distinctive gnarling anywhere. I knew that they were attached to my nude and supine body in one of the shots Señor Ed had taken of me before I'd been subjected to the Latino Letdown.

Professor Denise stared at me waiting for a response. Her fingernails were now raking spasmodically across my toes and a light film of perspiration glistened on her upper lip. My heart went out to her. I knew what it was like to have the green-eyed monster gnawing at your entrails.

"Listen, I'm sorry I haven't been to your classes. I really did enjoy the first few lectures."

"You *did, did* you," she shrilled. "You can't *imagine* how that pleases me."

If there ever was a woman who needed The Axiom, it was Professor Denise. I felt obligated to share it. "This semester has been fairly chaotic for me." I took in a deep breath, steeling myself against the animosity that rained down on me, and plunged forward. "I found the man I'd been living with in bed with someone else."

Shock briefly replaced hostility on Professor Denise's forgettable face.

"So I was on the rebound for a while. Then I learned an important lesson: The party of the least interest is the party of the most power." I felt like I was throwing out a lifeline. The inner nurd hopped around screaming at me like an enraged troll for talking to a bestower of grades in such a fashion.

I wish I could say that my compassion was rewarded. That Professor Denise instantly clicked to Collie's wisdom and that we ended up going out for a beer together, but such was not to be. Professor Denise sent me out of her office with enough work to ensure that I wouldn't have time to mess around with Eduardo or anyone else before the onset of menopause. She assigned me a paper delineating Imogene Cunningham's influence on the work of Judy Dater. Another one that would show that Georgia O'Keeffe was the true force behind the work of Alfred Stieglitz. Another one tracing the development of the Zone System. And there was a midterm three days hence to study for.

Thus burdened, I staggered home. If I did nothing but study, research, and write for the next seventy-two hours, I might have the barest of chances of salvaging the little nurd's academic record. If I didn't, Southern Union Gas would be the only mourner.

I was well into cram hyperspace when Collie tapped on my door that evening with an invitation to a Drama Department party. I shooed her away and continued stuffing facts and liftable phrases about Imogene Cunningham into my head. Even the nightly Brew Blast barely raised a welt on my concentration, although I did notice that the crew carrying Kytes across the street for the evening's purge had gained in number and in volume. I was aware, but like all the other crammers in the house, only peripherally, that their depravities were louder and lasted longer than usual.

Around seven the next morning, after a couple of hours of sleep, I stumbled downstairs for coffee. Fayrene padded down behind me. A grief-stricken group composed of all the house members except Collie was already clustered in the kitchen. I asked what the matter was.

"We've been violated." Judith spoke for the group.

"A gang rape? Here?" I was stunned.

"I was speaking figuratively," Judith said, stiffly.

When it became apparent that Judith wasn't going to elaborate any further, Duk Soo took me by the hand and led me, through the kitchen, into the backyard. Fayrene followed. The thicket of bamboo that normally sheltered the backside of the house was gone. We'd been scalped.

The bamboo, dense and fast-growing, had shielded us from the tireless scrutiny of The Moorland, the high-rise apartment building directly behind us. The Moorland teemed with foreign petroleum engineering students learning how to do tricky things with their country's oil. Long absence from wives and girlfriends, combined with our wantonly unveiled faces, had driven the petrocrats to the brink. They kept high-magnification binoculars perpetually trained on our back windows in the futile hope of picking out a female form from behind the Bamboo Curtain. With the bamboo gone our backside was nakedly exposed.

Duk Soo pointed to The Moorland. It glinted in the sun like a rhinestoned Porter Waggoner stage costume. Duk Soo made her chubby fists into two circles and held them to her eyes to suggest binoculars. Then she trained them on an Alamo House bedroom window that faced The Moorland and dropped her jaw in a show of lascivious amazement.

"My room," she explained, pantomiming the ceaseless ogling that the bamboo scalping had exposed her to. "You know where bamboo is gone?" she asked, deep wells of red rage splotching her lotus blossom skin. Without waiting for my hypotheses, she took me by the hand again and led me to the front yard. There, across the street, was our bamboo. The Sig Up parking lot had been transformed into the Mekong Delta. A banner wafted in the morning breeze high above the tropical paradise. WAIKIKI WACKOUT it read.

"The SUKs stole our bamboo." My statement of the obvious was noticeable for one significant fact: I'd used the word "our." To be stripped of our bamboo was one thing, but to have it stolen by the Cro-Magnons to provide ambiance for a "Waikiki Wackout" was quite another. I looked back at Alamo. Clustered on her porch were most of the residents: Constance in her housecoat; Toni and Barb in the matching T-shirts they slept in; Josie just waking up with her first cigarette; Hillary in her flannel grannie gown; Judith clutching a terry bathrobe about her. Upstairs, Collie, who didn't bother with sleeping garments, poked her head out of my window and asked what was happening.

"That's too much," she responded.

It was an obvious statement of fact, but Collie's words seemed to galvanize something in all of us. We had certainly endured a host of indignities and might have even ignored this latest one without Collie's announcement. After all, what were we but a houseful of graduate women? Each one of us had at least sixteen years of schooling in the twin arts of the female academic—long suffering and reducing reality to a three-by-five index card. But Collie pointed out a limit to us and we all knew that the SUKs' brazen ruffianism had pushed them way over the foul line. From that moment, little flames of insurrection began to be lighted.

"Those jerks," Fayrene whispered. The first one to break the silent paralysis we had all fallen into, she walked up to the edge of the street, bent over, and hurled a rock across. It clattered across the bamboo-enclosed parking lot.

Duk Soo tugged at my sleeve and gestured for me to look up again. I glanced around toward The Moorland. Amidst the flash of binocular lenses trained on us, I noticed one lonely pair follow Fayrene as she walked a ways into the street. Then, as she turned and came back to us, the binoculars flashed again. The binoculars stayed on her every step of the way.

There was a caucus about what to do, what our response should be, but I bowed out. The slaughter of our bamboo *was* a violation, and I *did* feel personally defiled, and I *had* begun to identify with Alamo House, but I also had to study. The little nurd gave me no choice. And so, stoked up on caffeine, I retreated to my room.

Hours slid by as I immersed myself in the gaseous pronouncements of critics attempting to infuse photography with the methane stink of Real Art. I copied their words verbatim. With one paper down (the Imogene Cunningham/Judy Dater opus), I moved on to some flat-out studying, loaded for Professor Lipscomb's bear.

Late that afternoon, I was motoring through the complete history of the evolution of the Helvetica Bold typeface when the first electric squawk pierced my eardrum.

"TESTING. ONE, TWO, THREE. TESTING. TESTING."

It came from the Mekong parking lot across the street. I pinched off a blob of waxy pink Ear Stopple and pressed a wee cornucopia into either side of my head. Then I bore down. I was breezing through the mechanics of web offset printing when the trembling started. It came up from the floor through my feet and the chair. The cold coffee in my mug began to shimmer with a series of concentric rings that quivered across its surface. Groggy from binging on junk facts, I thought for a moment that Austin might be experiencing her first earthquake. But no. The pounding wave of sound that pulsed through the house was the cause. The SUKs were checking their granite-crumbling party sound system.

Out in the hall, other stymied studiers gathered. We stood for a moment, battered by noise. Further work was out of the question. With no other avenues open, I came up with a timeless solution: "Let's make brownies."

We trooped down to the kitchen. In the living room, Josie, Fayrene—just back from the library—Alexis, Esme, and Hillary were clumped on the floor around Judith who was seated above them on a chair. It looked like story hour at the library, but I recognized the configurations of group therapy a la Feldman. Even though it was eighty-five degrees outside, we shut the front door. It cut the noise enough that we didn't have to bellow to be heard. Forgetting our brownie mission, Toni, Barb, Duk Soo, and Constance drifted over to Judith's session.

"To me," Esme was saying, "it's a pretty obvious attack on the power of women. We threaten them, it's that simple."

Judith glanced away from Esme, who had been receiving the full jolt of her undivided attention, and looked at us newcomers. "Find yourself a place anywhere. We all decided to convene an emergency session to work through some of our feelings about the bamboo and the noise. Esme's just shared what I think is a very valid insight. Any of you have anything you want to throw out?"

"Yeah," I chuckled, a bit dingy on caffeine and sleep deprivation, "a hand grenade."

All eyes darted from me to Judith. The beginnings of smiles faded away when the group registered Judith's expression of puzzled disapproval.

"That's a fairly disturbing thought, Mary," Judith said evenly. "Would you like to explore some of the feelings behind it?"

I rolled my eyes heavenward in exasperation and pronounced those most deadening of words, "I was only kidding."

Duk Soo burst into laughter. "Onalee kidding. I understand now, throw hand grenade to fraterrary. Good joke," she beamed. Then, her smile fading, she added with a hissing solemnity, "Better idea."

"Okay," Judith bobbed. "Okay, if you two feel up to owning those feelings of destruction, you're entitled to do so. Anyone else?"

For the next half hour the group batted around terms like womb envy and homophobia, misogyny and aural rape.

Finally I felt compelled to ask, "Have you ever considered that they might just be a bunch of asshole throwbacks?" My hypothesis met with a chilly reception.

"Of what productive use would negative labeling be, Mary?" Without waiting for my riposte, she turned back to her little tutorial. "I'm getting a real strong feeling that we need to be making a response to some of these behaviors. Anyone have any thoughts to share?"

"Nuke 'em back to the Stone Age," I contributed with rousing gusto.

"I think, Mary," Judith informed me in a chilly tone, "that we're looking for feasible alternatives here. For *appropriate* responses."

Still punchy from nearly twenty-four hours of cramming, I nodded to signal my withdrawal of the nuclear option. "You're right. We're low on plutonium anyway."

"I could write a really scathing editorial for the *Texan*," Alexis said. "I'd have to pull a few strings, but I think I'm in good enough with the editor that he'd run it for me."

Shivers of delicious, girlish glee ran through the group at such a bold plan. I thought back over the past week. To the best of my recollection, there had been three "really scathing" editorials about fraternity excesses.

"You might want to consider," Constance put in, "the danger of tarring the entire Greek system with the same brush in writing the editorial. What I mean is, fraternities are actually founded upon the highest of ideals and I imagine that some of them must surely live up to those ideals. You wouldn't want to issue a blanket attack on a whole system."

"Really," Hillary asked, "is it even truly fair to criticize any system unless you have a better alternative?"

Heads nodded as they considered her point.

"Oh, don't worry," Alexis assured us. "I wouldn't write a blanket anything. Too many publishers are old frat rats. It's safe to blast the SUKs though; they're such a bunch of illiterates, I couldn't possibly jeopardize any job contacts."

"You know what would really focus attention on this incident?" Hillary burst out with a febrile show of ovo-anorectic enthusiasm. "A hunger strike."

"That's an option," Judith commented nondirectionally.

"Yeah, we could all go on a strict fast and consume nothing but wheat grass juice which I can get in bulk at the produce place. Okay, that will keep our electrolytes in balance. Electrolyte imbalance, that's what got Bobby Sand." Hillary was aglow with the prospect of getting ten other women to look like her. "The media will eat it up. I mean who ever thought twice about Dick Gregory before he started fasting. And Gandhi. My God, look at all the Oscars he got for a few hunger strikes."

Judith nodded with sage wisdom. "I hear you, Hillary, and that's a very valid approach. Why don't you and a couple of the others interested in a hunger strike form a committee and report back to us. Any takers?"

Fayrene with her lifelong interest in dieting was a natural. As she raised her hand, I noticed that the Michelin Man rolls of flesh around her upper arm had disappeared. Although her voluminous overblouses and wraparound skirt camouflaged losses as well as gains, it was quite clear that Fayrene was dropping some substantial tonnage.

"Come on, people," Judith prompted. "We're just brainstorming here. Go ahead and throw out any ideas that occur to you. Don't self-censor."

"Well, all right." Constance surrendered to her coaxing. "This may be a bit excessive. But, we might write a letter to the Interfraternity Council."

"Okay, okay," Judith nodded. "We sure could. We surely could do that."

"Why don't we just call the police?" I asked.

The entire group fell silent.

"We've already discussed that alternative," Judith finally answered in the tone of a mother explaining to her child why "we" don't pick "our" noses at the dinner table. "We don't consider the police to be an appropriate option at this time."

"As opposed to a hunger strike?" I asked.

Judith withered me with a glance that didn't bother to be nondirectional. In no uncertain terms it said, "Take a hike."

I retreated to the kitchen. As the discussion veered off into the wisdom of "not descending to their level," I pulled out Lucy's recipe for Double Chocolateys. Pretty soon everyone out in the living room was telling stories about what jerks their old boyfriends were. I, meanwhile, was getting after it with the Hershey's cocoa and the Pet evaporated milk all to a sonic boom accompaniment.

> *I've been all around this great big world*
> *And I've seen all kind a girls*
> *But I couldn't wait to get back in the states*
> *Back to the cutest girls in the world*
> *Eee-yow-w-w-w-w-w!*
> *I wish they all could be California girls*

I was just approaching the "Add nuts" stage when a question bellowed forth drowning out the band.

"Why the fuck hasn't anyone called the cops?"

Collie was home. I quickly poked my head around the door.

"That would escalate the situation to an untenable level," Judith answered calmly. "The group has decided against that posture."

"Great, then 'the group' can just get themselves a discount rate on hearing aids. I'm calling the cops."

Not too many minutes later, a beefy policeman was standing, legs braced wide apart, in our front door. He was a football and brew kind of guy whose playing days were in the recent past but whose drinking days went on. He introduced himself as Patrolman Dunders then shouted over the din, "What seems to be the problem here?"

Collie turned to me in disbelief. The asphalt on the street was undulating from the sonic battering and he was asking what the problem was. "Why are you yelling, Officer?" Collie asked.

"Because of the noise."

"That's the problem, Officer."

Having been led, through clever use of the Socratic method, to the source of our contretemps, he pulled a citation book out of his back pocket. "Okay, I'll go over and have a little talk with them."

"I'll go with you," Collie volunteered.

"I will too." Fayrene and I spoke simultaneously.

Judith and Hillary sat, rigid, in the living room. The rest of Alamo's merry crew was gathered on the porch as we trooped off after Patrolman Dunders. Ahead of us the Waikiki Wackout flickered beneath tiki torches strategically located at each of the six kegs. I recognized the ferretty face of Kytes, the Brew Blaster, stationed at one of the kegs stoking up for that night's defilement of our greenery. His tumorlike stomach pooched out above a grass skirt. Yes, many of the jolly Sig Ups were sporting grass skirts and slaying each other by parting the blades, flashing brothers and sisters alike. Fayrene's jaw dropped as she was treated to a parting of the foliage.

"You ladies wait here," Patrolman Dunders directed, leaving us on the sidewalk as he strode up to the front door. Dunders leaned heavily on the bell. A brother bolting out to retch on the front lawn accidentally answered the bell. As he weaved back into the house, our man Dunders collared him, yelled something into his ear, and sent him back into the house. Collie and I exchanged grins, pleased to see action being taken.

Shortly, a basketball-headed brother appeared at the door

pulling a suit jacket on over his grass skirt. It was The Bub individual. A pink umbrella was propped open behind his ear. He
swatted it away. Patrolman Dunders gestured toward us huddled
on the sidewalk, then toward Alamo House huddled across the
street, then over to his rioting brothers.

The chastened Bub nodded with grave officiousness. Collie gave
me a giddily triumphant "okay" sign.

Dunders kept on pointing and speaking and Bub continued to
nod with appropriate chagrin. And then, just when we were really
beginning to believe that it was possible that right would triumph,
that our shrill cries would be heard, Bub stuck his hand out with
the back side up. To our amazement, Dunders slapped the top of
his own down on it, then they both rolled their hands over until
the tips of their fingers were touching. Next they performed the
little maneuver kids do to accompany the joke that goes, "What's
this? Give up? A spider on a mirror." After doing the spider on a
mirror with their fingertips a few times, they intertwined their fingers, bent their arms at the elbow, and pushed against each other
with their shoulders.

"They're doing the goddamned Sigma Upsilon Kappa handshake," Collie whispered in horror.

Patrolman Dunder's back quivered for a moment before he
shoved his brother Sig aside.

"How creepy," Fayrene said, watching our rescuer embrace the
enemy. "It's like *Invasion of the Body Snatchers*."

"Yeah, he's a pod person all right," Collie said as we watched
Dunders and Bub bat each other on the arm a few times. Patrolman Dunders was grinning as he started back toward us. He quickly
readjusted his expression into one befitting the stern interceder on
behalf of justice he was supposed to have been.

"I lodged your complaint with the head honcho there, Bub
Wilkers, and he promised he'd hold it down to a low roar."

In the parking lot behind Dunders and in our full view, a triumphant Bub Wilkers was racing back to the party. He stripped
off his jacket as he ran and was whirling it over his head as he

danced into the fray. So much for low roars. I looked across the street at my fellow residents clumped under the yellow bug light on the porch. Hopeful expectation gleamed on their faces.

"Well, thank you, Officer," Collie said.

Before the words were fully out of her mouth, Patrolman Dunders was scurrying off to claim the foaming cup that Wilkers was holding out to him.

"What? Is that all?" I sputtered. "But they haven't lowered the sound level one decibel."

"They will, Mary Jo," Collie soothed, dragging me away. "They will."

By the time we were halfway across the street, a couple of sisters were wrapping a grass skirt around Patrolman Dunders' ample waist and he was shimmying toward a keg. The group on the porch witnessed his defection, hope draining from their strained, bookworm faces.

"We should have known better," Barb moaned.

"Of course a policeman would be on the side of the white, male, patriarchal infrastructure," Toni growled.

"Yeah," Josie added, "probably if we bothered suing, we'd end up with a Sig Up judge."

"Probably" was the unanimous conclusion.

"Oh stop being such weenies," Collie ordered. "Things are right where we want them now." She led us inside.

"And where's that?" I inquired. "Midterms start tomorrow. No one in the house can study. We'll all be a bunch of deaf dropouts. *That's* where we want things?"

"No, out of official hands," Collie explained, her lovely fawn eyes widening mischievously. "That's where we want things. This strip of Pecan has just been declared a DMZ."

Identical blank looks covered our faces.

"Okay," she demanded, "who's going to call and complain now? About anything?"

We could offer no candidates.

"No one, right? The Zone-Outs next door at Satori wouldn't

notice a fire bombing. That leaves us with what? Frats and sorority houses. They all sign nonaggression pacts so they can take turns annihilating the surrounding neighborhoods. And the SUKs are certainly not going to report anything. Not with Patrolman Dunders over there hulaing his fat butt off. Don't you see? We can do anything we want."

"But all we want to do is study, Collie," Constance whined.

"That was before. Now we have a once in a lifetime opportunity for revenge. To get back at those hominids for puking on our lawn every night, for calling us dykes, for keeping us awake with their sleazoid music."

"For stealing bamboo," Duk Soo added.

"For wrecking my bike." All eyes shifted to the mangled machine still wrapped around our one pecan.

"You're right," Barb agreed, her chronically red-rimmed eyes taking on a strange and disturbing glow. "We've been suffering in silence long enough. We're on our own here. No one's going to ride up to rescue us."

"Collie," Constance asked, "what do you suggest?"

"First, a reconnaisance mission. Who's game?"

"You mean actually go over there?" I asked.

Collie nodded gleefully.

"I guess the question is, then, which of us could blend in."

Collie, the chameleon, was a natural. Duk Soo, who wanted desperately to wrap herself in black and make an assassination run, had to be eliminated: There were no Korean sorority girls. Constance and Esme were too old. "Barb? Toni?" I asked.

"Yeah, I'll go," Toni volunteered. "I'd like to kick one of those assholes' balls up his throat."

We decided that Toni would probably not be a good mingler. Barb wouldn't go without Toni and Josie declined altogether.

That left Collie, Fayrene, and me. Fayrene hestitated. "I don't think I'd really, you know, blend in," she explained, waving vaguely at the area between her ankles and chin.

"Fay, face it," Collie countered. "You're in the normal range now. As soon as we get you out of your maternity wardrobe you'll be as close to normal as anyone wants to get."

A momentary look of panic darkened Fayrene's face, then she caught Collie's radiant smile and reflected it back. "Sure, I'll go," she whispered.

"Great, we might be able to use the Pirtle photographic memory. Of course, you're going," Collie said to me.

"Of course."

"You'll make a killer sister. Okay, Tiffany," she christened me, "and Sissy," she named Fayrene, "and, of course, I'll be Muffy. Let's get to work."

13

COLLIE'S CLOSET would have done Edith Head proud. It was stuffed with the trappings of the many personas I'd seen and some I had yet to enjoy. But tonight we were going for less flamboyant fare. Surprisingly, she had an ample stock of Oxford cloth and khaki items. In minutes, she and I were outfitted in the romper shorts and Oxford cloth shirt uniform of the UT sorority girl.

Fayrene was a more difficult camouflage problem. Although she had shed considerable weight, she still wasn't down to a size that even Collie's most commodious pair of rompers could accommodate.

"Y'all go on ahead," she said dispiritedly.

"No way, José," Collie/Muffy replied pertly, already getting into character. She plunged back into her closet and, with a chorus of rustling, reemerged triumphantly holding a grass skirt.

"Uh, I don't think so, Collie," Fayrene said, backing away.

"Oh come on, Sissy, y'all'll make a killer wahini."

Fayrene shook her head.

Collie let the skirt fall. "You're right. It's a fire hazard anyway." Back into the closet. "This is it!" she exulted, holding out a muumuu printed with purple orchids outlined in gold. Silhouettes of muscular men on outriggers and palm trees bending before a tropical breeze adorned the background. Fayrene's eyes moistened as she beheld the garment.

"It's beautiful," she breathed.

Contrary to the muumuu's typical effect, in this one Fayrene looked somewhat slimmer than she actually was. We unbraided her hair. Still crimped from the tight braids, it fluffed out around her head with a Polynesian authenticity. Collie crowned her with a wreath of laurel leaves that Isadora Duncan occasionally wore, then decided that something was missing.

"A tan!" she announced, diving into her cache of cosmetics and coming up with a tube of Natur-Bronze. She smeared it over all of Fayrene's dough-colored exposed parts. Then she "balanced" the effect with some eye makeup. When she was finished, Fayrene was gorgeous. Just plain, flat-out beautiful.

"If only Gauguin were alive to paint you," Collie pronounced the verdict.

"Let me see, let me see," Fayrene demanded, scampering over to the full-length mirror. She was speechless, then, in a quiet voice, "Is that me?"

"It sure is, Little Leilani," I assured her.

"Come on y'all," Collie whined in pitch-perfect girl Greek tones, "we've got some serious partyin' to do."

"Collie," I observed, "you do that so well, it's almost frightening." And it was. Her voice, her posture, her whole being had changed. As good as she was at getting into characters, she was doing Muffy so well that it went beyond acting. "You know, I just realized something. Muffy is the only character you've done who's not doomed."

"Guess again," Collie answered, with a somberness that seemed to come out of nowhere. "She's the most doomed of them all."

The capering spirit bubbling through us a moment before went a bit flat until Collie picked it up again.

"Y'all," Muffy/Collie harangued in nasal tones of sorority distress, "all the brewski's gonna be gone. Not to mention that mondo cute-orif Biff Patterson."

"Ew-w-w, incredible babe," I said getting back in the spirit. "Let's party hearty. You ready, Muffy?" I asked Fayrene.

"I thought I was Sissy."

"And *I'm* Muffy," Collie corrected.

"Right," I corrected myself, committing our assumed names to memory. "Sissy, Tiffany, and Muffy Go to the Waikiki Wackout."

Hoots of derision met our appearance downstairs. If frat rats were the enemy, sorority girls were fifth columnists, despised collaborators that none of us at Alamo House could ever truly understand or forgive. We crept out the back door and circled around through the alley. Crossing Pecan Street a block up from the Sig house, we cut back through the alley that ran behind the parking lot. Finally we were peering through what had once been our bamboo curtain. The band was off taking a break.

"Okay," Collie hissed at us. "We'll fan out and generally reconnoiter the situation. Then we'll focus in on weak spots, points of vulnerability where we can attack. Shall we split up?"

"No," Fayrene answered firmly.

"Fine, we'll stick together. Sissy? Tiffany? Y'all ready?"

"Ready as I'll ever be," I answered and we slithered through the bamboo. The bachannal whirled around us. My courage grew with every drunken frat rat who stumbled by oblivious to us.

"Props," Collie reminded us. We made for a tiki torchlit keg. A group that included "head honcho" Bub Wilkers; the tubby Schlubber; Opie, a freckled redhead, of course; and Brew Blaster Kytes had coagulated around the keg. Bub was speaking as we ventured near.

"Oh yeah, Heather Steiner, what a Grub Queen she is. Had to slide about half a bottle of Chivas into her first though. Then I just smoothed her on into the sack." Bub stopped to down a manly swig and adjust his, no doubt swollen, equipment.

"You got off light," Schlubber chimed in. "Took me near a *whole* bottle of Chivas before I could tear me off a chunk."

They shook their heads in silent commiseration over the impenetrable vicissitudes of love.

"What about that Shannon Andrews?" Opie indicated a young woman passing by held securely beneath the arm of a Neanderthal with a heavily underslung jaw and a jowly chin.

"Ew, what a troll!" Kytes spat out.

"Who are you kidding?" Bub whooped. "You'd snake her away from Bulldog in a second if you thought she'd mug."

Kytes shrugged in modest recognition of his omnivorous sexual appetite. "Well, sure, a butt date's a butt date."

"All right!!!" The brothers held brews aloft to toast the immortal words. "To the Sor Whores!!!"

"Oh, uh, 'scuse me, girls," the ever-suave Bub said, noticing us lurking behind him for the first time. With mock chivalry, he pulled his cronies away from our access to the keg. "Didn't see y'all there."

Collie gave him a cutsie-pie smile that said, "I have an IQ of thirteen and I love Chivas." It made my blood run cold and Bub's hot.

"You a Tri-Delt?" Schlubber asked. "Tri-Delts got all the good-looking women. Hardly ever come to our parties. You a Tri-Delt?"

"Ew-w-w, gag, no," Collie said with ultimate disdain for Tri-Delts. "We're all QPs."

"Kewpies?" Schlubber asked blankly, looking at his buddies for help.

"Guy," Collie whined. "Quid Pro Quo." She said it as if stating the obvious caused her actual physical pain. I was afraid that she'd gone too far; surely even these chuckleheads would snap. But no, only her tone penetrated.

"Oh yeah, right," Schlubber nodded. "I got paddled so hard my first semester I was shittin' outta my nose and I *still* never learned all them Greek letters."

"There's really only three important ones anyway," Kytes piped up in his reedy voice.

"You said it, bro," Bub agreed with an excess of manly vigor.

Then the group of them crouched down together and began chanting, "Sigma Upsilon Kappa, Sigma Upsilon Kappa. The others are the crapper, but we are the capper." The chant grew louder as other voices picked it up. Soon it was a booming chorus. "SIGMA UPSILON KAPPA. SIGMA UPSILON KAPPA. THE OTHERS ARE THE CRAPPER, BUT WE ARE THE CAPPER." All around us beefy boys had gone into huddles, their arms thrown around one another as they howled out those three letters. Finally, at some signal I was unable to discern, the chanting groups screamed the sacred letters one last time, then rammed their heads together. Really cracked craniums. I began to understand why SUKs didn't manifest many of the finer sensibilities. They all staggered away laughing and attempting to focus.

Bub weaved his way back to Collie. "Come on, you Kewpie doll, you, I want to show you the Trophy Room."

A stab of panic pierced me as Collie walked away with Bub's tree trunk of an arm fallen around her shoulders. Sliding around under that yoke, she called back to us, "Y'all check out the party. Be back in a minute." Then she winked.

The wink allayed some of my fears and I reminded myself that espionage was a dangerous and a dirty business. Fear came with the territory. Neither Fayrene nor I was attracting much attention, so we roamed at will. We discovered that the majority of the female partygoers were Chi Gammas—CGs. The Sig Ups, however, invariably referred to their guests as "Sleazies." As in the much-repeated bon mot, "What's the mating call of a Sleazie?" "I dunno." "Oh, I'm so-o-o drunk."

Out beyond the perimeter of flickering light cast by the tiki torches, we stumbled upon our first significant find.

"Uh, pardon me," I apologized, disentangling myself from the cat's cradle of arms and legs I'd fallen into. At my feet were Brew Blaster Kytes and Shannon Andrews, whom he'd been maligning earlier. He *had* snaked her from Bulldog. The briefly disturbed couple were back at it before I was on my feet again, slurping over one another with many sucking noises. Standing still in the darkness, Fayrene and I realized that we were surrounded by couples suctioning various body parts. It sounded as if we were lost in the Everglades and all around us creatures were pulling their large feet out of the muck.

"Oh, I'm *so-o-o* drunk," came the call, high and shrill. Then an answering, "Shlu-u-u-urp-p-p."

Fayrene moved closer to me in the darkness. I attempted to be analytical. "Appears to me that the three key ingredients for a frat party are noise, darkness, and beer. Okay, we've already tried to eliminate the noise. Not much we can do about the darkness. That leaves the beer."

"I've already done what I could about that," she said, turning me back to the tiki-lit area. All four unattended kegs were leaking a foaming lake of beer onto the parking lot.

"Nice work," I congratulated her. Even as we watched, though, the spillage was noticed and alarmed SUKs splashed through the foam to staunch the flow.

"Oh Tiffany, Sissy, yoo-hoo, where are you?" Collie stood on the porch yodeling out into the darkness.

"She means us," Fayrene explained.

At the porch, Collie took both of us by the arm and led us into the dark and fetid lair of Sigma Upsilon Kappa. It smelled of old beer, dirty socks, and degrading sex and made Alamo look like a designer showcase. Collie led us forcefully back to a door with "Trophy Room, Keep Out" scrawled across the torn veneer. I wanted desperately to comply. "Come on, Collie, let's get out of here," I hissed.

Ignoring me, she opened the door. Bub was sprawled out on a battered turquoise vinyl couch. He held a black book embossed in gold. As the sign had promised, the room was filled with trophies. Trophies, all small, all tinny-looking, and all in alcohol-related shapes—mugs, martini glasses, and an infinity of beer bottles. No football, baseball, or basketball. Not a lacrosse racket or even a little bowler in the lot. I picked up a miniature barrel of sour mash complete with XXX bronzed on the top. The plaque read: "Kentucky Derby Days 1953. To the winners of the Mint Julep Chugathon, Sigma Upsilon Kappa."

"Y'all are just not going to believe this," Collie burst out with her newly acquired Flower of the South perkiness. "But Bub here was showing me his membership book and it's like packed with really maximally important people."

"I told you that," Bub grunted from the couch. His shirt was unbuttoned and he was clearly not pleased to be having company. "But you wouldn't believe me. Now you gotta go and show everyone. That's private. Confidential. Prohibido. Verboten." He mumbled on, a multilingual drunk.

"Oh, Bubkins," Collie soothed, "it won't hurt just to let my sisters take just the teeninesiest peek. It's not like they're going to be able to memorize the names and addresses of all the important and influential parents in there or anything." Collie made serious eye contact with Fayrene as she spoke. Fayrene looked over at the book Bub was grasping, then back at Collie, and gave a nearly undetectable nod of agreement.

"Oh, awright. Take it." Bub surrendered the black book and Collie rushed it over to Fayrene. They huddled together, flipping pages as fast as Fayrene could gobble them up. Collie erupted with an occasional comment like, "Ew-w-w, Bubkins, you didn't tell me that your daddy used to be governor."

"Okay," Bub announced, "that's enough. Makes me nervous when anyone around me looks at books too long. Get rid of your friends, Muffy, and start mugging me."

Collie shifted her eyebrows from me to The Bubkins. I shook my head frantically.

"Muffy," Bub said threateningly. Collie yanked her eyebrows in his direction again. Searching my mind frantically for topics of interest, I approached Bub. Football would have been a good one, but I'd only just recently learned why burnt orange was such a popular color around the UT campus. How was I going to divert the priapic Bub until Fayrene could memorize their membership book? The Trophy Room abounded with inspiration.

"Bub," I slurred his name and my gait, "you would not believe how wasted I was last weekend. Sissy and Muffy and I put away a case and a half."

"Thas nuthin'," Bub responded. "Kytes and me and The Schlubber finished off an entire keg by ourselves last Saturday. We were so pissy-faced it wasn't even funny. 'Bout half of it ended up across the street on the dykes' front yard."

I had to pretend ignorance of the custom I knew only too well.

"Yeah, big bunch of lesbos live in that old house across the street. Glasses and fat asses, heh-heh-heh."

I pivoted, removing my capacious can from his view.

"Kytes is like, what's he call it? Oh right, a projectile vomiter. Guy can puke farther'n you can throw a baseball. So we haul 'im across the street ever night to blast the lesbos."

"Har-har-har," I joined in Bub's belly-jiggling laughter. Suddenly the laughter stopped and a confused and angry look came over Bub's features. "Hey, Muffy," he bawled. "Put that book down and come over here and play Snake in the Grass with me."

Snake in the Grass? Grass skirt? The prospect was too stomach-turning to contemplate. Collie glanced back at him. She and Fayrene were less than halfway through the book.

"Oh yeah, but you know what's really fun?" I had to repeat my question a few times to break into Bub's concentration on Collie.

"What?" he finally growled at me.

"Throwing back flaming shots of tequila. Bet you never did that."

"Bet you I did."

"Yeah well, we were doing that over at the house the other night and my record was," I picked the first number that came into my head. "thirty-seven."

That got Bub's attention. "Thirty-seven flaming shots?" he asked skeptically. "Looka that there." He indicated a trophy on the shelf behind me. I picked it up. It featured a shot glass with tongues of cut tin fire leaping from it. The plaque read: "To Champion Flame Thrower, Bub Wilkers, 36 Consecutive Shots."

"I don't believe you tanked thirty-seven shots," Bub said belligerently. "After thirty-six they had to take me to the hospital. Told me later that my brain was clinically dead for half an hour. I ain't believin' thirty-seven shots." He'd become surprisingly agitated over this affront.

"Gee, it's a darned shame we don't have a couple of gallons of tequila right here to settle this."

"Open that shelf," Bub ordered.

A sick feeling rolled over me as I approached the shelf. I stalled for time, deliberately opening the wrong one.

"Not that one!" Bub yelled.

"What is this?" I inquired politely, not wanting to rile Bub any further. "Must be a model of Carlsbad Caverns with all those little stalactites? Or is that stalagmites? No, it's 'c' for ceiling, stala*c*tite. 'G' for ground, stala*g*mite. Hey, wait. Those things aren't either one. Those are . . ." I slammed the door shut, the sick feeling turning into a rolling nausea.

Bub was whooping in delight at the greenish hue I'd taken on. He sucked in a calming breath. "Yeah," he gasped, "they're rubbers."

"*Used* rubbers," I corrected him primly. He didn't miss the note of censure.

"Well, why the hell d'ya think we call it the Trophy Room anyway?"

"That is so disgusting," I began, then had to stop. Had to take one little peek just to make sure that I'd really seen what I thought I had. I peeked. Sure enough. "There's women's names written on them!"

"Hey, the Grub Queens themselves do the writing. Later on we compare handwriting samples. How else are we supposed to verify a Butt Date? You wouldn't want unprincipled guys running around claiming strikes on every Sor Whore in town, would you?"

"It's just too noble for words."

"If you're finished snooping, open that cabinet."

I did. It was filled with gallon bottles of generic tequila.

"Haul una grande over here, Sugarplum. We're going to find out exactly what kind of a tequila drinker you really are."

"Gosh, I'd love to, but I can't really get into it without my special, good-luck shot glass."

"Listen, Baby Doll, we've got two games we're going to play

here. It's going to be either Flaming Shots or Snake in the Grass. Take your pick."

Collie glared at me. Fayrene had her face squinched up and had broken a light sweat. She still had half of the book left to memorize. Collie jerked her head in Bub's direction. I hoisted up a gallon and headed on over.

Let the games begin.

Grimly, Bub filled two smudged shot glasses, then pulled out a Bic lighter and ignited them both. "Down the hatch." He held his shot aloft and the blue flame danced over the surface of the liquor. It danced all the way down his gullet. He slammed the glass on the table and scratched a mark underneath his name. The other column, "Kewpie Doll," was apparently mine.

I picked up the glass and the blue flame skittered toward my hand. "Now that I think about it," I temporized, "it was Singapore Slings that I drank thirty-seven of. If you happen to have three kinds of rum and some orgeat syrup, we could . . ."

"Drink!" Bub bellowed.

Startled, I downed the shot. In one sweeping, blistering bolt, all my autonomic processes stopped dead. The little blue flame was the coolest, smoothest thing about that particular tequila. Eyes watering and nose running were the first two bodily functions to kick back in.

"Breathe!" Collie reminded me from across the room.

I did and Bub bent forward to scratch one mark on my column. "We're going to have to pick the pace up here a little." He pulled out half a dozen more smudged shot glasses and lined them up in front of us. He ran the bottle across them. "Okay, this'll be a sprint. Whoever finishes their four shots first gets a bonus point. Got it?"

I nodded to indicate that I'd grasped the concept.

He drew his lighter across the tops of the glasses and a wall of flame shimmied along them. "On your mark." Bub hunched forward as he counted down. "Get set. Go!" He grabbed one blazing glass after another. In his frenzy, I was able to overshoot a couple of shots onto the wall in back of me. But he was watching for the last two and I had to slam them down the hard way. We both banged our glasses onto the table at the same moment.

"Hey, a tie! You're a real go-for-it chick, Kewp," Bub congratulated me.

I tried to pretend to smile, then realized that I was already grinning like someone with a tiara on her head and an armful of roses.

"That means," he said, splashing tequila into the glasses, ashtrays, and both of my shoes, "a tie-breaker!"

"Salud!" I toasted him, holding up my first glass. He flamed it for me. It was down the hatch before I remembered that I was only supposed to be pretending to compete. I tossed the next two behind the couch. Bub was already finished and watching me, so I had to down the fourth.

"I won by a, ha-yuk, *long* shot." He grabbed the scorecard and drew nine wobbly lines on his side and eight on mine. "I'm beating." His mouth hung open slackly as he stared at me. I noticed mine had assumed the same relaxed posture. Bub upended the tequila bottle and managed to fill three of his glasses and one of mine. "Go!" he called out. Not bothering to flame these shots, he threw back two in rapid succession. I was no longer able to make my hand grip. Terror trudged numbly through my paralyzed body. The jig was up. We'd all be forced to play Snake in the Grass. I tried to warn Collie of impending doom, but my mouth would not form words.

Bub reached for the third shot, after which he would reach for me. Soon I'd be nothing more than a tiny stalactite in the Sigma Upsilon Kappa Trophy Room. Or was it stalagmite? No, it was stalactite. Tequila-deadened fear slogged through my veins. Then Bub leaned his head back, sloshed in the tequila, rolled his eyeballs back, and dropped the glass on his forehead. Clonk!

At the same moment, Kytes burst in carrying a limp and dripping rubber. He rushed to the cabinet and tacked it up. "Hey," he said, noticing his fallen comrade, "is Bub experiencing clinical brain death again or what?"

"No," Collie assured the little Brew Blaster, "he's just napping. See, listen to him snore. Brain-dead people don't snore. Okay, Tiffany, oopsadaisy." She grappled with me, finally hauling me to my feet. Fayrene, her fingertips pressed to her forehead, scanned the last page, and slammed the book shut. At the door, I paused.

"Tell Bub he won," I declared magnanimously.

Outside, the Waikiki Wackout was going off like Krakatoa. I stumbled, hanging limply between Collie and Fayrene. They were forced to lower me to the parking lot pavement for a short rest.

"I'd say the mission was a success," Collie noted. "Shall we call it a night?"

"Yeah," Fayrene agreed. "We'd better take her home."

Her was me. "No!" I protested, jerking my head up from my chest. "I'm having fun. I never thought drinking could be so much fun. I wanna bop till I drop! Party till I puke! Do it till I can't do it no more!"

I searched my memory for more T-shirts to quote, stopping only when I saw the band retake the stage after an extended break. The lead singer appeared to be a member of some fallen aristocracy with one hand pressed into the pocket of a threadbare jacket so that just his thumb showed. The other hand trailed a cigarette as he growled into the microphone, "I wish they all could be California girls . . ."

"Tommy!" I screamed, staggering to my feet and pushing through the crowd.

The look of heavy-lidded ennui lifted as my co-worker spotted me. I felt like a weary traveler seeing a familiar face in a strange land.

He put the microphone back on the stand and crouched down at the edge of the stage to take a closer look. "God, it *is* you." He hopped down in front of me. "I would never have figured you for someone who'd get wasted at a frat bash."

"Hey, well, lissen to the pettle call the kot . . ." I shook my head. "Lissen to people in black houses . . . What are *you* doing here?"

"Gainful employment."

"Yeah, but . . . the SUKS?"

"I know, I know. But this is how Christopher Cross got his start." Tommy paused to consider. "There may be a lesson there. Well, anyway, *I'm* not getting sloshed."

"You're not singing much either," I tossed back.

"I should strain my vocal cords for this?" He gestured at the crowd. They were all so messed up on alcohol, drugs, and hormones that they wouldn't have noticed if five guys with chain saws had been playing.

"I see what you mean."

"You still haven't told me what you're doing here. Wasted."

"Wasted?" I objected. "I may be the teeninesiest bit tipsy."

"You are paralytic."

"Maybe it's just the intoxicating nearness of you." I laughed. Scarlett at the barbecue. The liquor was talking. For the first time in my life I was seriously flirting and it had only taken a healthy chunk of a gallon of tequila to do it. I wondered vaguely how I could have let twenty-seven years slip by without engaging in this dangerously delightful activity. It suddenly seemed like the most wonderful thing in the world to be doing and Tommy the most wonderful person to be doing it with. I attempted to bat my eyelashes, but a slight delay between bats when I commenced to doze off ruined the effect.

Behind us the band started playing something moderately slow and instrumental. After being buffeted about for a while by Greek couples engaged in vertical foreplay on the dance floor, Tommy suggested we dance.

I listed drunkenly against him. "Are you taller than you are at the library?" I asked, surprised at how far I had to reach for his shoulder.

"No, you're shorter when you're drunk," he explained.

"Oh. How *are* things at the library? I've been sort of busy lately."

"About the same."

"So you're still . . ." I tried to think of a tactful way to say "obsessed with Lady Bird."

"Working on the Bird Collection," he filled in for me.

I nodded. I searched for a way to ask him if he was really serious about all that but lost the thread of the conversation and we just swayed around the parking lot for a bit. Somewhere amidst all the swaying a terrible weariness came over me and I snuggled up against Tommy's jacket front for the briefest of rests. He put his arms around me. It was immeasurably cozy.

Suddenly the band picked up the tempo and the pillow of Tommy's chest began pitching wildly beneath my head. I was jolted into a fast dance. Once I caught up with the rhythm, it was great fun. Tommy yo-yoed me back and forth in his long arms, twirled me around like a music box ballerina, and rolled me out in looping spins. I was at the far end of just such a spin when I lost contact with Tommy's hand and went gyrating into the frenzied crowd.

I finally managed to bring my body to a halt, but my head kept twirling. I felt obliged to apprise Tommy, Collie, and Fayrene, wherever they might be in the human maelstrom swirling about me, of one salient fact: "I'm soo-o-o-o drunk," I wailed.

Ominous rustlings disturbed grass skirts all around me as SUKs turned to respond to my call. A dozen brothers were closing in when Collie broke through the tightening circle they were forming around me.

"It's that darn herpes medication, Tiffany," Collie called out. "You know how susceptible it makes you to alcohol."

The brothers faded back into the night, but my equilibrium seemed to have been fatally unbalanced. I was wobbling noticeably by the time Collie, Fayrene, and Tommy reached me.

"Grab her," Collie ordered Tommy at the precise moment when I felt my legs clock out for the night.

Tommy obeyed, scooping me into his arms. I had to laugh. It was such a cliché. Who would have ever thought that I, Mary Jo Steadman, would be swept off her feet? It really was too silly. Tommy seemed to be amused as well. He was laughing.

"You are really cute." The words popped out of my mouth. "Really cute." I was going to qualify that assessment. Warn Tommy that it was only valid for one night, but I was drawn once more to that cozy spot on his jacket front.

"Looks like our little party girl just reached Saturation Fun Levels," I heard Collie observe from what seemed a great distance.

Tommy put his face next to mine. I could feel his breath when he spoke. "Oh yeah, she's out."

I was framing the objection I wanted to raise when I realized that they were right.

· 14 ·

"THE BATTLE has been joined." Those were the first words that penetrated my consciousness the next morning. Actually it turned out to be late the next afternoon. I'd slept the day away.

"Are you coherent?" Collie asked.

"No," honesty compelled me to answer. Though it jarred my cerebral cortex to move my eyes, I couldn't help noticing a few additions to the decor of Hell Week Heaven. "What are all these klieg lights doing up here?" A battery of the things had been erected along our windows.

Fayrene joined Collie. Both of them perched on the edge of my bed like two sorority sisters about to announce their engagement. Possibly to each other. "You missed the good part last night," Fayrene said. Her exuberant glow was hurting my eyes.

"Collie," I requested wearily, "pretend that suspense has already built to an unbearable peak and just *tell me* what happened last night."

"Okay. You were out before we got you back into the house. It was great coming in with the corpse of a fallen comrade. Your martyrdom galvanized our cause. Everyone was *electrified* into action."

It was hard for me to imagine any Alamo residents other than Collie "electrified," but I didn't interrupt.

"Fayrene gave her report of what you two had reconnoitered

and of your analysis of frat party essentials. You know, noise, darkness, and beer. We'd already tried to do something about the noise and Fayrene told of her attempt on the beer. Then, after we learned about what was going on beyond the tiki torches, we knew we had the key."

I looked at the lights with new understanding. All of them were marked on the back with an orange longhorn and *UT Drama Dept.* "You floodlit the Waikiki Wackout."

"Like Radio City Music Hall," Collie burst out. "There were two of us on every light. Then I gave the signal and the place lit up. Great freeze-frame action. Bare SUK buns glistening in the light at various spots among the foliage. Groups gathered around mirrors snorkeling up ungodly quantities of controlled substances. At the precise moment the lights came on, in fact, our own Officer Dunders had a coffee stirrer hanging from his nose. We *did* immortalize that, didn't we Fayrene?"

Fayrene nodded and patted my Nikon, which had apparently played a much more active role in this *coup de frat* than I had.

"You would not have believed how rapidly such a saturnalia could grind to a total standstill. We were all impressed. The SUKs, though, grew quite surly. They shouted and yelled obscenities. They threw rocks. Officer Dunders acted swiftly to stop that by reminding them of the number of compromising positions they had all been caught in.

"Anyway, all those mega-kilowatts of light proved just the ticket for pooping their party. The sisters, as soon as they could get dressed, were the first to leave. Then Tommy packed the band up. After that, it was a pretty dreary affair. We did get to witness a brew blast. But somehow, fully illuminated, Kytes just didn't show his usual exuberance."

"Good, Collie, good," I mumbled, joy piercing the fog of pain coiled around me. I was already slipping back into sleep when I remembered the midterms I had missed that day and the papers I hadn't finished. At least we'd won.

It was early the next morning when I came around again. The

klieg lights were gone and three large tumblers of water were sitting by my bed. I drank them all, then struggled downstairs. I wasn't up to school yet, but I figured I could handle a day of rest at the library.

Halfway down, Alexis Hartwell intercepted me.

"You're not planning to go to work today, are you?" she asked frantically.

I admitted that such was indeed my purpose.

"You can't. Tommy called yesterday while you were out and we arranged everything. He's going to sneak me into the library to do a story on what he calls the Secret Presidency."

"The Secret Presidency?"

"Yeah, sure, Lady Bird's. He's been telling me about all this fabulous material he's uncovered up there. It'll make a fantastic story."

I tried to figure out what it was about Tommy's inexplicable obsession that could possibly have interested a Black Hole like Alexis Hartwell.

"Tommy promised that Bird herself would personally see a copy of my story." She shook her two trembling fists around her ears in uncontrolled delight. "Lady Bird Johnson reading my story! Lady Bird Johnson, owner of . . ."

The cause of her journalistic fervor dawned on me and we finished her last sentence together. ". . . of KTBC-TV."

She popped up, ready to set off, a brave little networker inching forward toward her career goals.

"How are you going to pass yourself off as me?" I inquired. "There's only about half a foot difference in our height."

"Oh, no problem. Tommy says no one ever pays any attention to you on the third floor anyway. They won't notice."

"That's true." As doubtful as I was about Tommy's Bird Deification Project, I was happy to have a reason to spend the rest of the day in my flannel nightgown.

As soon as morning classes were over, everyone spontaneously gathered in the living room. A strange, keyed-up gaiety that I never would have thought Alamo residents capable of generating pervaded the house. It was like being backstage at a Junior League gala right after a successful first act. We all were goosy and hyped up, waiting for the curtain to rise on the next act, anticipating SUK response and planning retaliatory measures.

Only Judith and Hillary remained aloof from the fever that gripped the house. "Still playing war, I see," Hillary sniped as she walked in on our strategy session, pulling off her gardening gloves as she went.

"Well, no, actually that's not it at all," Constance sputtered.

"More like giving those fuckheads what they deserve," Esme clarified.

"Listen," Josie cut in, sucking a little eloquence from her Lone Star bottle before continuing, "I thought we'd agreed that no action whatsoever would be taken except in the eventuality that the SUKs cross our property lines."

"That's right," Toni confirmed, "but we want to be ready, have our contingency plans all in order."

"Yes-s-s," Duk Soo added sibilantly, "have pungee sticks ready."

"Duk Soo" Hillary chided her. "We told you, no pungee sticks. That's a sick and disturbed idea."

"Not making to kill pungee sticks. My friend, Vietnam, show me how to making onalee to hurt verry bad pungee sticks. Not to kill." She looked around the room hopefully, smiling broadly, but couldn't drum up any support for her suggestion to mine the front yard with sharpened, manure-dipped sticks.

Hillary paused at her door to listen to the discussion. "You guys remind me of my little brothers. Why don't you just build a fort in the front yard and throw cherry bombs."

"Cherry bombs," Collie burst out. "Thanks, Hillie, we hadn't thought of that."

"How incredibly de-evolved." Hillary slammed her door behind her.

Collie hastily wrote "cherry bombs" at the bottom of a list

that contained such classics as "the unordered pizza" and "flaming bag of shit on the front porch."

I'd been astounded at the virulence and extent of the revenge schemes harbored in the scholarly minds of my housemates. It seemed that everyone gathered around me had bloodlusted in her heart, hatching grim and gory plots of reprisal against perfidious lovers, arbitrary dissertation committee members, condescending professors, tyrannical fathers, overly familiar bosses, mean brothers, wolf-whistling construction workers, haughty waiters, and snide salesmen. An unsettlingly large number of these plots involved castration and boiling in oil. I had to conclude that repression is not without its price. The Night of the Lights, as Constance christened it, had been the first time any of these gentle nuns of academe had acted on the corrosively hostile impulses simmering within them for decades. The experience had been a heady one.

"Fellow illuminati," Constance began, pressing a knuckle against her pursed lips to stifle a giggle caused by the audacity of her wit, "I propose that we break for dinner and await the counterattack."

"Dinner!" Josie echoed. "I totally forgot. It's my night to cook."

It was a first at Alamo. Revolting as it might at times be, there had always, hitherto, been dinner on the table as near to six in the evening as was humanly possible. More astonishing, though, than Josie's announcement was the reaction: No one peeved out. Even Esme was good-humored. "No problem, we'll just slap together some sandwiches." Only Judith, coming in late from a meeting of her doctoral committee, and Hillary were annoyed.

"Listen, folks," Judith requested of the crowd foraging in the kitchen. "I think that this catharsis thing you're doing here vis-à-vis the SUKs actually has some healthy growth aspects. This almost ritualistic ventilation probably serves several latent functions that verbalization or left-brain-type processing couldn't serve. But, still, we're based here on a system of reciprocal responsibilities and when that starts breaking down, the whole house structure goes with it."

"Are you going to have a sandwich or can I put it up?" Esme asked, holding up a five-pound hunk of cheddar for Judith's inspection.

Judith splayed out her fingers in front of her three or four times, sighed with weary resignation, dropped her hands to her sides, and left the kitchen. Constance, Toni, and Barb exchanged concerned glances. They were putting down their cheese and sprouts to follow the retreating martyr, when we heard ominous crunching in the backyard.

"Sh-h-h-h," Collie hissed, silencing everyone. We froze and pricked up our ears like startled deer. The crunching turned abruptly to crackling.

"Fire!" Collie screamed as we all stampeded out the back door.

A roaring bonfire and the catcall, "Here's your bamboo back, dykes," greeted us. I recognized the pubescent cracking of Kytes's voice, ringleading in the way marginals like to do. Though the blaze was quite spectacular for a few moments while Collie and the others scurried about discovering that the garden hose was rotted through, the dry bamboo burnt like crepe paper. By the time the first few drops of water hauled in pans from the kitchen reached it, the fire had burnt itself out. But it had been a fire. A crude, but potentially dangerous counterattack, it was exactly what we had all been waiting for.

"What's it going to be?" I asked Collie.

"Tomorrow's some big game isn't it?" she asked.

"The Horns are playing Baylor," Toni answered. "One of the biggest."

"Perfect." Collie declared. "Perfect for Constance's scheme. Wouldn't you all agree?"

The scheme she referred to was one Constance had concocted for a Society of Creative Anachronism knight who had gone errant after winning her heart. It met with unanimous approval.

"I don't think it will disappoint," Constance said modestly.

"Hey, guys, don't you think that one's a bit extreme?" I asked. "I mean we're getting into the realm of property damage here."

"You think those fuckwads were worried about property damage when they torched our backyard?" Esme asked with more than her usual belligerence. "Property damage, shit. We could all have been burned to death."

"Yeah, right!" The mob rallied and I was swept along with it. So much so in fact that I ended up being the one to supply the chief agent of mischief to carry out this scheme. It required a white, Anglo male capable of acting straight. Collie, in her vast masculine acquaintanceship could come up only with gays, weirdos, and foreigners. The rest of the house's connections with men were so tenuous that they couldn't bear the weight of the favor we had to ask. Collie suggested Tommy Chastain.

"Seems to me," she cooed, "that young Mr. Chastain would be only too eager to offer you a helping hand."

Tommy was surprisingly receptive. His interview with Alexis had gone well and he was in an expansive mood. Besides, after experiencing them at close range while playing at their party, he too despised the SUKs. Sure, he'd be glad to help.

Once that was out of the way, I thanked him for carrying me home from the Waikiki Wackout.

"So, you survived."

"Just barely." A strange awkwardness entered the conversation, the kind of awkwardness that could forever destroy fifth-floor frolics. I scurried back to the safety of our old relationship. "I hardly remember anything about that night."

"You don't?" I couldn't tell if he was disappointed or muffling ecstatic relief. I told him I had to go report his answer to the group and hung up, still wondering.

We all settled in the living room and stayed even after I'd told them Tommy had agreed. It was odd to congregate for something other than group therapy or a House Meeting. Duk Soo started tinkling around on the piano. Then Constance brought out some madrigal songbooks and asked if anyone else sang. Of course, Fayrene had had ample experience at Waco First Baptist; she was assigned the soprano parts. Toni reluctantly admitted to a misspent youth as a Church of Christ alto. The rest of us sort of filled in wherever we could. With Constance leading, we ripped into "What Ayles, My Darling?" The effect was surprisingly euphonic. We segued into spirited renditions of "Hey Ho to the Greenwood" and "O Care Wilt Thou Torment Me."

Only gradually did a certain familiar clanking register on our collective consciousness.

"They're rolling in another keg." Collie identified the sound. We all knew what it meant: Where there was a new keg at the SUK house, a Brew Blast couldn't be far behind.

No one reacted. Like homeowners on an airport flight path, we'd stopped noticing an annoyance we were powerless to change. It took a second to apply our new militance to this old grievance. At first we thought we should save ourselves for the big assault on game day. But the Brew Blasts had passed unpunished for too long. We were batting around sanctions when Hillary emerged from Judith's room.

"I hate to disrupt your puerile fantasies with such mundane realities," she said, "but I need a couple of volunteers. Satori House is complaining that my beer trough is overflowing. I need two strong backs to help me carry it over to the gardens tomorrow for my slug traps."

Eyes lit up all around the room. "We'll trap some slugs," Fayrene said under her breath.

"Well? Volunteers?" Hillary prompted.

"Oh sure," Collie answered. "We'll move the beer trough for you. We promise. Don't we?"

Universal agreement.

Hillary knit her eyebrows together in suspicious dyspepsia and left.

"Too fitting," Constance crowed.

"Shall we arm ourselves for the evening's reprisal?" Collie inquired.

It wasn't hard to understand why even filth-tolerant Satori had objected to Hillary's tub of beer, used and otherwise. An entymology lab of many-legged creatures floated in the stinking vat. It took five of us to heave the sloshing trough out of Satori, through the back alley, into Alamo, and up the stairs to Hell Week Heaven.

While we waited for Kytes and the brothers to get primed, Toni, our sole engineering student and house maintenance chief, calculated lift factors, trajectories, and pi times gallons in the trough. Then she positioned us in what she claimed would be the optimum spot and demonstrated the exact force we would need to create the perfect arc. Given the condition of our windows, plumbing, and every other malfunctioning appurtenance touched by Toni's handiwork, I was skeptical. But, rather than dampen the festive air with doubt, I kept my silence.

We hoisted the tub onto the windowsill, turned out all the lights, and waited.

We'd almost started to worry that on this of all nights Kytes and company might not be making their regular pilgrimage, when the front door of the SUK house burst open and they poured out carrying Kytes battering ram style.

"Get ready," Toni hissed. We bent down and shouldered our noisome burden.

"Hang on Kytes!" our chum, Bub Wilkers, exhorted the Human Volcano as they rushed him across the street.

"Lower," Toni ordered us. "Squat down lower." We recoiled, drawing the yeasty charge back.

"Ew-w-w-w, his stomach's tightening up," one of the brothers carrying Kytes bellowed. "He's fixing to let fly."

"Steady," Toni commanded, as we trembled under the weight of beer and bug bodies.

And then: Kytes's seismic retching. The splattering of befouled foliage. And Toni, "Wait, wait. Okay, NOW!"

We sprang up dumping beer and bugs in a stinking waterfall out the window. For once, Toni's engineering was impeccable. The whole troughful cascaded onto the unsuspecting frats, drenching them in a decoction nearly as bad as the one they'd been spraying on our landscaping for the past few months. A dead slug slithered down Kytes's forehead. The stunned silence was broken by the sound of gagging.

"You've really done it this time, you cuntlappers," Wilkers screamed up at us. "You're going to pay for this. Really pay." A volley of rocks crashed against the dowdy dowager's olive-drab flanks, but the SUKs were in too much of a hurry to get to a shower to do any serious damage to the house. Besides, their threats couldn't touch the elation that seized us when we saw our tormenters drenched and festooned with bug parts.

Toni was particularly pleased as she basked in Barb's admiration for her engineering prowess. "Some of my everyday projects don't always work out," she admitted. "But when it really counts, I usually come through."

"Most handsomely indeed," Constance agreed, slapping her on the back.

"I'd say this calls for a celebration," Collie announced, digging quarters and dimes out of her jeans.

We were pulling long-necks out of Satori's cooler, when I realized that this was the first totally happy night I'd spent at Alamo. That night, we were triumphant. We'd bitten the ankle of the overlord. And always, at the center, making it happen, was Collie. How she did it, I couldn't say, but somehow she wrapped us all in the spell of her golden gutsiness and made us feel it was ours as well.

We emptied out the machine that night.

FOOTBALL GAMES WERE, at best, a mixed blessing for Alamo House. Left to ourselves, we would have taken no notice at all of the sport and UT's participation in it. Collection of individualistic oddballs that we were, there was only one characteristic we all shared: None of us had ever witnessed a UT football game. Nor had we any desire to do so.

Living so close to the campus, however, forced our involvement. Early on the morning of any game, fans flooded the neighborhood. They lined the streets with their Continentals and Mercedes and polluted the landscape with their burnt orange, double-knit Sansabelts and blazers. Female fans, on the other hand, favored New England-type woolens—starting in September, when temperatures were still regularly over a hundred degrees. They'd soak their Shetland wools in sweat and die of heat stroke, but the fannettes *would* wear the woolens of autumn.

The hours before and after games were like living on Bourbon Street during Mardi Gras. And then, for an all-too-brief time while the game was actually being played, there was peace. The fraternity houses emptied. The fans stormed the stadium. Pecan Street was abandoned. We opened windows normally shut against the incessant aural barrage, and unaccustomed breezes blew through the house. Duk Soo played albums with musical nuances that could be heard at no other time. Constance seized those hours for particularly troublesome translations from Old Norse. And Judith confronted the latest criticisms of her dissertation committee, communications she couldn't face with David Lee Roth screaming in the background.

Far off, at Memorial Stadium, bursts of cheering boomed out like distant cannon fire in a battle that would, all too soon, reach us. Inevitably it did, with the front line coming right up to our porch. We hated it when "the Horns" won. The ensuing melee was always a lot worse than if they'd been chastened a bit on the playing field. Either way it was a major monstrosity. All the fans, cranked up on beer and mob pheromones, streamed out of the stadium, got into their cars, and drove them into our neighborhood. Far into the night, for blocks in either direction, the streets would be clogged with drunk, yelling, honking, mooning, vomiting, horny Hornophiles.

But that day, following the Bamboo Bonfire, we were willing to endure it all for those few hours of freedom while the occupying forces were away. As usual, after a pre-game morning of beer absorption, all the brothers jumped into their cars and sped off to pick up dates bundled up against the inclement weather. Temperatures had chilled dangerously into the mid-eighties.

By noon, Pecan was a ghost street. We all gathered at the windows lining Hell Week Heaven.

"Mary Jo," Fayrene asked nervously, "just how reliable is your friend, Tommy?"

"He's totally *un*reliable. You think we could get a *reliable* person to go along with this?"

"Probably not," Fayrene admitted. "But where is he?"

"He'll be here," I assured the fidgety group.

"I have my doubts about this whole scheme," Esme snarled.

Constance sniffed her nonverbal aggrievement. "I can't see why. I've spent the past eight years working out all the details."

"What I mean," Esme continued, "is, what contractor in his right mind would go ahead with this without a large deposit?"

"The one Tommy heard about," I supplied crankily. I was

nervous enough already without Esme contributing her own permanent load of free-floating anxieties. "He handpicked him for sleazy operating practices and greed. All Tommy had to do was to mention over the phone a few of the bigger names in the book Fayrene memorized and the guy was ready to go."

"I just knew that book would prove useful," Collie said. A lone car pulled onto the street below us. "That him now?"

I groaned. It was indeed Tommy pulling up in his 1957 Bel-Air two-tone station wagon with Tommy Berlin and the Vy-Mars still painted on the side. He got out. Everyone else groaned. He was wearing, in addition to his Ray Charles Ray-Ban wraparounds, a black and white striped, Buddy Holly short-sleeved acrylic sweater with contrasting red turtlenecked dickie, shrunk-to-bind black chinos that exposed half a foot of white sock, and black platform shoes.

"I told him to dress Greek," I moaned.

"He must have thought you said 'geek,' " Collie said.

Seeing us clustered at the window, Tommy wiggled his fingers jauntily in our direction. I flagged back a limp wave and we all sank a bit lower beneath the windowsills.

"Not much point in witnessing the rest of this fiasco, is there?" Hillary, who had stopped in briefly to ask where the hell her old beer was, announced triumphantly. "Esme, I'm going to make up the food order. Anyone else want to come downstairs and input on it?"

Toni, Barb, Alexis, Josie, and Esme struggled to their feet. The sound of a diesel truck stripping gears as it maneuvered into the SUK parking lot stopped them. A magnetic sign on the side of the truck read, A.J. Hawkins, General Contracting. A potbellied man in khaki swung out off the bed of the diesel.

"You Berlin?" he asked Tommy.

Tommy darted forward, his hand extended. "Yessir, and you must be Mr. Hawkins."

"The costuming is all wrong," Collie commented, "but he sure does have that two-faced, suck-up fraternity act down cold."

Hawkins eyed Tommy suspiciously. "You got anything to prove who you are?"

"How's that?" Tommy asked, gesturing toward the station wagon with the Tommy Berlin name on the side. Without allowing any further inspection or reflection, Tommy ushered the man back to the empty parking lot. "Listen, I told you, we've got to hurry to get the pool dug out before Jasper Jr. gets back from the game. The governor," Tommy stopped to laugh at himself, "I mean the ex-governor—we still like to call him Governor around Jasper Jr.—wants it to be a surprise. Well, the hole part anyway. Enough so that young Jasper will know he'll never have to swim in a pool with anyone of questionable sexual persuasion." Tommy added, confidentially, "If you know what I mean."

Hawkins nodded. "I know *just* what you mean. Haven't used a public convenience in a year. If Rock Hudson can get that stuff, it just goes to prove that no one's safe." He walked to the back of the truck where he flipped up a canvas curtain.

"Vamanos," he yelled, and a crew of brown men in straw hats with little dingleberries hanging off the back hopped out. "Andale, andale. Pronto, pronto," he speeded them along. "Y'all better andale or I'll call Immigration and y'all'll be having a white Navidad back in old Mayheeko! Vamanos! Immigracion! La migra!" The men scurried about as Hawkins directed, unloading various gas-powered machines with rotary blades. Hawkins conferred briefly with Tommy.

"Oh Olympic size, at least," Tommy answered, always loudly enough so that we in the balcony could hear. "Oh yeah, make the sucker just as big as you can. Don't scrimp on the governor's son. Bring it right on up to the edge of the parking lot."

"Where are you boys going to be parking once you got a pool on your lot?" Hawkins asked.

"Look around," Tommy directed his attention to the deserted street. "Plenty of room on the street. This parking lot's just a waste of space."

"Mas grande," Hawkins bellowed at a Mexican national operating a machine that cut into the asphalt like a knife through a pan of Double Chocolateys. The man sliced right up to the house. As soon as a rectangle the size of a tennis court had been incised in the black top, Hawkins got on his walkie-talkie and a few minutes later a huge machine with the jaws of *Tyrannosaurus rex* rolled up Pecan Street.

"That's the biggest back hoe I've ever seen," Fayrene breathed. We all looked at her, perplexed. "Daddy used to operate one," she explained.

The machine was just as efficient as it was mammoth. The speed with which it excavated an Olympic-sized hole where the SUK parking lot had been was astonishing. Somewhere in the cloud of dust raised by the gouging behemoth, Tommy and the Bel-Air disappeared. Only J.W. Hawkins and a hole that sloped down to a final depth of twelve feet—suitable for safe diving—were left.

"Oh God, what have we done?" Josie stared, terrified, into the abyss. "We can be cited for criminal and civil trespass, breach of contract, tortuous interference with contractual relationships, intentional infliction of emotional distress, slander of title . . . I'll never be allowed to practice law," she concluded, her eyes glittering brightly.

Her distress puzzed me as I'd always assumed, judging from her sci-fi and beer "study sessions," that never practicing law was her career goal.

"Don't be such a weenie," Collie counseled forcefully, bringing the distraught Josie back to her senses. "If it ever comes to that, which it won't, you can blame everything on me. I sure as hell don't ever plan on practicing law."

The scrape of the back hoe was answered by the far-off booming of the fans' cheers. The hoe had gouged out a gaping pit where so many eardrum-piercing parties had once been held. A hillock of rubble now covered the front lawn.

"We'd better prepare for their crude and unimaginative reprisals," Collie cautioned. "Even though they'll never be able to prove anything, they'll know it was us."

We spent the rest of the game scrounging scrap lumber to use for house reinforcements. We were raiding a pile in the alley behind Satori when Collie jerked her head up like a sniffing hound.

"Hear that?"

I stopped and listened. The cheering booms were coming closer. A car streaked past on the adjacent street, its horn blaring, beer cans flying out the back windows. We passed the order to retreat. Grabbing our lumber, we ran to the house, locked ourselves in, and waited on the second floor. We didn't wait long. Minutes later the first of the SUKs came tearing to a rubber-burning stop just short of the chasm that had opened in their absence. Abandoning their BMWs, Trans-Ams, and giant-wheeled trucks on the street, they all gathered around the excavation and peered over the rim in stunned wonder. J.W. Hawkins approached them.

"Now which one of you fellows is the governor's son?"

Bub "Brain Death" Wilkers stepped forward. "Well, my dad used to be governor."

"Surprise!" Hawkins called out. "Your daddy's giving you a swimming pool."

"But he knows I hate to swim," Bub answered numbly. "Always have."

"Well, he musta forgot," Hawkins countered with a rapidly growing belligerence. "Cause he got your chairman of special projects to set it all up. And I've got a signed contract to prove it." Hawkins waved the document in front of Bub's blanched visage.

"We don't have any 'Viscount Berlin' here. You got taken."

"No, son," Hawkins informed him. "*You* got taken. You've got a perfect Olympic-sized hole dug here. Now, it's no concern of mine what you do with it, but I cain't take it back. You understand?" What there was to understand was Hawkins' tone, which had taken on a dangerously currish quality. "Cause if you don't quite grasp the situation, I'll just have to explain it to your daddy. His mind is so sharp in these kinds of matters."

"Do whatever you want," Bub said, looking slowly from the bas-relief parking lot over to Alamo, then back again.

"The synapses are firing," Collie said in a muffled squeal.

"I will," Hawkins promised, slapping the bogus contract against his horny palm. "I will indeed. And don't you think I won't. Vamanos!" he grunted at his colleagues and, with dingleberries flying in the wind, J.W. Hawkins departed.

"Horns rule!!!" The shout echoed around us, followed by a cacophony of honking as a stream of cars bottlenecked where the Sig Ups had abandoned their vehicles in the middle of the road in front of their eviscerated parking lot.

The shock was wearing off and the rusty gears of the SUK mind began turning. "You Alamo bitches did this!" Bub gave voice to the dawning cognition, reaching around and hurling a handful of excavated rock at the house. Further retaliation was prevented by the angry snarl of cars pushing against the roadblock of SUK vehicles. The brothers mounted up and fanned out in search of the parking places that exist only in the lore of a bygone era.

The rest of the day was quiet, or as quiet as it could be in a neighborhood lousy with rabid football fans having group hysteria. After hitching rides back from parking spaces throughout the city, the brothers came home and set to immediately filling back in J.W.'s twelve-foot hole. Around UT, parking takes precedence, even over revenge.

"We should charge them," Collie announced, as we viewed the sweating SUKs. "They'd pay Nautilus an exorbitant sum for the superior kind of deltoid development they're getting down there."

But the instant the brothers had their autos stowed on their new parking hump, they turned their barnyard energies to revenge. Finesse and imagination were totally lacking from their rock-chunking reprisals. In that first round, we discovered that a photographer was an absolute deterrent. As soon as I appeared with the Nikon and a long lens and commenced to clicking, these sons of bankers and politicians dropped their rocks and we were safe. For the moment.

The next few weeks were times of high drama for the olive-drab dowager with Constance running around shouting "Aux armes, citoyens!" every time we were hit. The SUKs' crude retaliations—throwing trash in our yard, breaking windows, stealing our bikes, starting a fire under the porch—coalesced the house. We struck back with an assortment of deplorably juvenile tactics.

We were in the backyard, readying a giant bag of manure we'd cadged from Hillary's organic compost supply, when Judith passed by. She looked more grief-ridden than ever now that no one joined in her therapy sessions anymore.

"Have you all ever thought about dealing directly with the anger you're displacing through all these junior high school rituals?"

"What anger, Judith?" Constance asked.

"Well clearly yours for Lancelot," Judith answered, referring to Constance's knight errant. "And, Mary, yours for Roger."

It had been so long since I'd thought about the little slime that it took me a minute to recall him to mind. When I did a melancholy yearning for the swans of Travis Heights pierced me.

"Don't you think you ought to be working through some of these feelings instead of projecting them onto men you've never even spoken with?"

We considered her words.

"I mean, this is the level of awareness of junior high school girls who," she paused to scratch quotations marks into the air, " 't.p.' a 'cute' guy's house."

"You mean that custom of strewing toilet paper all over the trees and house," Constance clarified.

"I never did that," Barb sniffed. "Of course, I was never in the right clique."

A chorus of "me neithers" greeted the confession.

"They accidentally did it to our house once," Fayrene said. Her voice was still soft, but it had become audible, having mysteriously grown as her bulk had continued to shrink. "We lived across the street from the quarterback. It rained that night and all that pink toilet paper just kind of glopped up. We had a horrible time getting it down. I think there's a few shreds still up there. Turns gray and looks like moss."

"Thanks for the great idea, Judith," Collie said. "We'll add it to the list."

Judith shook her head with weary tolerance and left us to our puerile retrogressions. That night, the SUKs danced on the bags of manure we left flaming on their doorstep. The next night our garage was broken into and our washer and dryer were filled with concrete. Fortunately, though, insomniac Esme went out to lull herself to sleep with a rinse cycle so we caught the concrete before it had a chance to set up. The next night, since rain was forecast, we t.p.ed the SUKs' few spindly trees. They barely seemed to notice.

Soon even Duk Soo was ready to cut back on the raids. We spent the week clearing away the debris and planning for the next siege. Though our spirit remained high, school began claiming warriors. Gradually we slipped from being Freedom Fighters back to being students. But vigilant students, ever ready for the next attack.

· 16 ·

"HAS ALEXIS said anything about when the article is coming out?" Tommy assailed me with the question just as he'd done every day since he'd sneaked Alexis up to our sanctuary to witness the full flowering of his Birdmentia.

"Uh-h-h, no, she really hasn't. She's been super busy with a bunch of projects." Actually, since Alexis and I had never spoken about any subject other than Alexis Hartwell, I had no idea how the article on Tommy's collection of Birdianna was progressing.

A loud clanging announced that the freight elevator was in operation. This was a most unusual occurrence as Tommy and I were its sole users. It banged to a stop and the doors creaked open. A furious slap of shoe leather and the scent of Lilac Vegetal brought Smythe into our work area. Dorothy teetered after him. Another first, the four of us gathered together with no one in hiding.

"What's the meaning of this?" Smythe demanded, slapping one of his miniature hands against the copy of the *Daily Texan* he gripped in the other hand.

"The article," Tommy exulted, reading the pummeled headline. "It's out."

I peered around his shoulder to catch a glimpse of the article in question. " 'Secret Presidency' of Lady Bird Johnson Revealed by Library Worker."

Transfixed, Tommy ripped the paper from Smythe's grip and began reading aloud.

Could the real LBJ have been *Lady Bird Johnson?* That's what Thomas Chastain, an archivist at the Lyndon Baines Johnson Presidential Library maintains. Chastain, 22, known to music fans as Tommy Berlin of Tommy Berlin and the Vy-Mars, has spent the last several months at his part-time archivist's job organizing a collection of material about the former First Lady.

"I don't think there can be any doubt about who the power behind the throne was," Chastain said. "I mean with all this new stuff coming out showing what an oaf Lyndon was, you have to start wondering how he got to the White House and managed to stay there."

The collection of what Chastain calls "Birdianna" is conclusive proof to him that there was a "secret presidency" guided by the skilled and gentle hand of Lady Bird Johnson. That collection, housed on the fifth floor of the Library, contains such mementos as three boxes of the actual cake served at Lucy Johnson's White House wedding; hundreds of copies of many of Lady Bird's favorite family recipes; swatches of designer samples used in selecting the fabrics for the redecoration of the White House Treaty Room.

"That's it?" Tommy asked, outraged. "That's all? She left so much out. I showed her everything. She didn't mention the letters, the pictures . . ."

"The writer of this article was here?" Smythe demanded. "On the fifth floor?"

"Of course," Tommy answered his pesky interrogator. "How else could she really appreciate what we've got up here?"

"You heard him, Miss Fenecke," Smythe said almost decisively. "Bringing unauthorized persons to nonaccess floors," he read the charge. "That alone is enough to have you fired."

"Fired?" Tommy echoed.

"Fired," Dorothy assured him primly. She looked away and horror drained her face of all color except the two perfect polka dots of rouge on her cheeks. "Oh, Mr. Smythe, down there. Look." Dorothy pointed a tremulous finger at the window behind Smythe. Down below us, an assortment of individuals wearing expressions of carefully cultivated cynicism masking their basic Beaver Cleaver naiveté were storming onto the museum's marble floor.

Tommy identified the intruders. "Reporters."

"Look what you've done," Smythe said to Tommy waving a quivering hand in the direction of the invading mediots. "Where's your . . . your . . . hideout?" Smythe spat out. "I know it's up here somewhere."

"Sir?" Tommy asked.

"Where do you hide when I come up here on inspections? I need to know. Right now." He glanced feverishly up and down the long rows of red boxes.

Below us, the attacking reporters stopped dead center, right on the eagle in the presidential seal inlaid into the floor. They held out sharpened pencils and began counting up. One, two, three, four, five. Half a dozen graphite lances tilted up at us.

Smythe withered away from their thrusts. "Tell me, dammit." He pleaded with the vicious courage of a cornered rat.

"Mr. Smythe, you'll have to face them sooner or later." Dorothy spoke, an old-time starch in her voice that brought Smythe back to his panic-stricken senses.

"Of course, Miss Fenecke." He drew in a deep breath that swelled his sunken chest until it was almost level with his knobby shoulder blades. Then he hissed it away, deflating back to the scared bureaucrat he was. "You're through, Chastain," he promised Tommy. "You might as well pack up right now."

"I'm not through," Tommy informed his superior coolly. "The collection is still incomplete. I can't leave yet."

"It's never been done before in a presidential library, and almost never in the whole of civil service, but I'll see to it that you are fired." Smythe trained his beady eyes on Tommy and spoke in a low and menacing voice. "You'll never work in library science again, Chastain. Not as long as I'm alive."

Dorothy tightened her chubby little hands into fists and pressed them against her ample bosom.

"Oh, Smythe," Tommy sighed, "why are you pressing me to do this? You really leave me no choice. Step this way, please."

We retreated back to the work area. Below us, the reporters loaded onto the elevator and headed for the third floor to await Smythe. At the work area, Tommy pulled a Xeroxed sheet of paper out of a file folder marked "Safety Net." He held it out to Smythe.

The proffered sheet was a copy of an invoice for the refreshments served that fateful morning when Tommy first met his high-flying Lady Bird. As I recalled, he'd said there were a total of five having coffee and doughnuts that day with the Bird. The bill for their rendezvous was $3,000. I blinked and tried to get the zeros to disappear. They refused to metamorphose into either an exorbitant but still believable $30, or even an unbelievable, but not for the government, $300. The total remained $3,000. I leaned in closer and squinted at the figure. One tiny zero had been penciled in. The addition was initialed with a near-microscopic "R.S." Smythe.

Tommy whisked the sheet back into his folder. "Now, much as I would hate to do so, Mr. Smythe, I *would* take this bill to the press if I were forced to leave before my collection was in order. Imagine, if you will, the howls of indignant and overburdened taxpayers if they were to find out what kind of money's being put out around here on coffee breaks."

Smythe's mouth wriggled around for a few seconds before he clamped it into a tight seam, turned on his heel, and stomped out with Dorothy wheezing and clacking behind him.

Tommy hurried to the dumb-waiter shaft and stuck his head down to tune in to the proceedings on the third floor. "The reporters demand to see the fifth floor!" Tommy cried jubilantly. His expression abruptly changed. "Oh no, Smythe is telling them that this is a nonaccess floor restricted exclusively to scholars working on library-approved projects." He looked away forlornly, but a trail of assertive voices pulled him back to his listening post.

"They demand to speak with the director." He relayed the good news to me. Tense minutes passed as we listened like Resistance fighters clustered around a crackling shortwave radio. Finally, "They're coming!" as he announced the arrival of the liberation forces.

In a trice our dim and deserted floor came alive with reporters, photographers, and a television crew. The voices of all these seekers after the truth reverberated across the concrete expanses uniting in one mighty chorus, "Where's the wedding cake?"

Surrendering to the people's right to know, Tommy guided the crew back to the red box filled with little white, heart-shaped boxes that held tiny packets of red foil-wrapped pieces of wedding cake and had me demonstrate their edibility.

And that is how I ended up in a front-page picture the next day biting into one of the slivers of cake above a caption that read, "Not the Freshest, Maybe the Most Expensive." The accompanying article, which I ingested with my breakfast, went on to detail precisely how much it cost taxpayers each year to keep the electrically charged cake, cloth swatches, recipes, stacks of blank White House stationery, letters from outraged third-graders, and photos of the Lynda Bird makeover all in pristine condition.

"Mary Hoe, you're a star," Collie said. She squeezed in beside me to read the article. "Hey, I've got a Weirdo candidate."

"You do?"

"A pip," Collie promised me. "But we have to wait for the Blushometer to wake up to judge if he takes the title away from Charley." Charley, a business accounting major with a fondness for black leather underwear, had been Collie's last award winner.

Though Fayrene was not thrilled at being awakened, she came around quickly when Collie announced she'd reeled in a candidate. Collie's enthusiasm for a potential classic was catching.

"Okay, well, I met him—are you ready for this?—on a shuttle bus. Yesterday. It was five o'clock. I'd just finished my dance class so all I had on was tights and a leotard."

"Collie," I admonished her, "you're such an exhibitionist."

"If you'd prefer to cast aspersions on my colorful bohemian character, we can forget my little tale altogether."

"No, Collie," Fayrene moaned on cue. "Don't interrupt her," she warned me.

Satisfied with the degree of interest evinced, Collie went on. "So there I was tired and sweaty and the shuttle bus was, of course, packed. There was no place to sit down, so I ended up hanging from a railing on the ceiling and swinging myself in this guy's face who's sitting down right beside where I'm standing. In passing, I'd already given him the half-second evaluation upon which mates are chosen and futures decided, and had concluded that he was not bad. He had these sweet tendrils of hair on the back of his neck and a dangling-chain earring."

"Of course," I interjected.

"Anyway, there we are lurching along, everyone packed up against each other trying to pretend they're alone on the Serengeti or somewhere. Suddenly I start getting this very warm feeling in the old hinter regions. So I look down and this guy is laser-beaming my crotch. Now we all have gotten a prod in the back with an unidentified blunt instrument, right?"

Fayrene nodded as if she were the object of endless proddings.

"But this," Collie continued, "this was so blatant. So I just laser-beamed him right back. Forced him to acknowledge what he was doing and that I was on to it."

"Great," Fayrene and I applauded her forthrightness. "Then what?"

"Then he looks up like he's coming out of anesthesia, very embarrassed, very *discomfited*, and he turns these adorable cocker spaniel eyes on me. My heart just *melts*."

"Yes, yes," we prompted.

"And he says, sort of startled, 'Wow, I'm really sorry. I just couldn't help staring at the conformation of your pelvic girdle.' Of course, my mouth is dropping. I can't believe this. My pelvic girdle? 'You'll have surprisingly easy births,' he tells me, 'for an ectomorph.' Are these classic opening lines?" Collie demanded of us.

"Classic," we answered.

"Hall of Famers." She returned to her narrative. "Naturally, I'm interested."

"Naturally," we urged her on.

"When the bus clears out a little, I take the seat next to him. Pretty soon we're talking and riding and back at the Drama Department. We keep on talking and transfer to another bus. Then we're walking and talking. Before I know it, we're at his house. Duplex actually. Basically, a nice little place. Pretty neighborhood. Huge live oaks and pecans everywhere. But what a sty. The extent of its tawdriness, though, did not sink in until later. Upon first viewing, I was still mesmerized by Cocker Eyes."

Fayrene and I were both nodding our heads, feasting on the details that make a story real. Collie continued.

"He confesses that he is dying for a closer inspection of the incredible conformations of my pelvic girdle, so we retire to the bathtub for a sudsy frolic. Quite a nice bathroom. Candles everywhere, no lights. A huge bubbly bath and these truly serene swans etched on the glass shower doors sort of patrolling us."

Swans? Cocker Eyes? How many more animal clues did I need?

"This 'guy,' " I asked. "He wasn't in anthropology, was he?"

"Oh, I don't know, something like that, I guess."

I could not account for the sick feeling coiling around my intestines. Nor could I keep myself from asking, "Well, how was he?"

Collie held her hand out and gave it a rocking-boat, so-so warble. "And that's being charitable. He had the finesse of a battering ram. I wanted to call it to his attention that the moat drawbridge was already down."

"Collie," I whined, "you slept with Roger."

"Roger? Your Roger? I guess the new haircut and earring

threw me off. Though I did sense something familiar about his particular brand of insufferability . . ."

"Collie, how could you?"

"What do you care? You left him."

"Collie," I protested, "I loved him. Doesn't that mean anything to you?"

"It means you put up with a slob who was nada in bed. Who acts like making a woman come is something you learn in doggie obedience school. Besides, he had a beard when I first met him and men with beards just don't register with me."

Tension crackled in the air. A major confrontation was building. My reaction was swift and sure. I sidestepped it, ducking into another issue altogether.

"I hate that word."

"What word?" Collie asked.

"Come."

"Me too," Fayrene agreed eagerly. She was as fidgetingly anxious to avoid confrontation as I was.

"What would you prefer?" Collie asked. " 'Denouement'?"

"That's an improvement," Fayrene said. "But 'flowering' is better."

" 'Flowering'?" Collie asked.

"You know," Fayrene stalled. "Like in, 'the seed of desire blossomed in a cataclysmic flowering deep within her.' 'Awakening' is also nice. So is 'shuddering fulfillment.' "

"Don't take this the wrong way," I said cautiously, grateful for an excuse to abandon my anger. "But that sounds an awful lot like romance novel talk."

"So?" Fayrene countered defensively. "Are they so much worse than what you read? *Death Works the Graveyard Shift?*"

"They're not worse or better or anything," I said, apologetically. "I was just curious. I've never actually read a romance novel before."

"Me neither," Collie jumped in.

"I've been reading them since I was a little girl," Fayrene confessed. Basking in the attention and still anxious to avert conflict, she added, "I even have some here."

Secretly pleased to have taken the spotlight in a Weirdo of the Week competition, Fayrene feigned reluctance as she tugged her treat box out from under her bed. Tossing aside a few camouflaging Peanut Planks and Chicken Bones, she uncovered a solid tier of paperbacks. Their covers were a cloud of puffy pastels and searing reds billowing out behind some flinty-eyed rogue hovering in the vicinity of a heaving bosom. Collie and I dove into Fayrene's box of literary candy.

"Oh, these are great," Collie said, sorting through the pile. *"Deny the Tempest, Forbidden Embraces, Defiant Desire."*

"Passion's Torment," I added to the list.

"Hey, I've got a *Tormented Passion,"* Collie called out.

"There was also a *Passionate Torment,* " Fayrene informed us helpfully.

"Listen to this," Collie ordered, as she commenced a dramatic reading from *Deny the Tempest,* " 'You're magnificent, he murmured, awed by his first sight of Heather's alabaster torso and high, proud breasts. He bent toward her, slipping one reverential hand beneath the excruciatingly delicious weight of her breast and lifting its dark-apricot center to his lips. The touch of his tongue against the maddeningly sensitized tips was unholy ecstasy. A wave of pleasure pulsed through Heather again, leaving a spiraling vortex of desire whirling at the core of her throbbing desire.' "

"Yum-yum, 'throbbing desire,' " I responded, thumbing through *Reap the Wild Wantonness.* "How about, 'her secret inner moistness'? Or 'the delta of her womanhood'?"

"Not bad," Collie commented, continuing her perusal of *The Agony of Ecstasy.* "But I like," she read aloud, " 'Her everdeepening chasm aching to be filled.' "

"What about him?" I appealed for equal time, turning to my

selection from *Surrender to Oblivion*, "What about 'the rigid evidence of *his* throbbing desire'?"

"Or," Collie skimmed *Passion's Promise*, " 'the pulsing shaft of his manhood.' 'The hard male length of him'?" Collie stopped hooting and asked, "Fayrene, tell me one thing, does anyone ever say boner in romance novels?"

"You guys . . ." Fayrene whined.

"That is what we're talking about, isn't it? The erect male member? I mean, given the circumlocutions, I can only assume."

"What's this mean?" I interrupted with my own need for a Romancespeak translation. "Let me summarize. First, there's this big juicy scene where he's caressing, adoring, cradling, cupping, fondling, celebrating, debauching, blessing, tantalizing, kindling, and rekindling her body. Then they switch and she works on him a while and performs something called 'the ultimate act of loving' and at the end it says, 'She tasted the sea.' What's that supposed to mean?"

Fayrene reddened and started gathering up her books.

Collie laughed. "It means he lied."

"Oh-ho," I said, the dawn slowly breaking. "So 'the ultimate act' is . . ."

"Yep," Collie finished, "she gummed the salty sausage."

"You guys are so gross," Fayrene sighed.

"Tell me," Collie asked. "Why can't they just say boner?"

Fayrene slid the box back under her bed clearly regretting that she'd ever hauled it out. "Love isn't always just Weirdos of the Week," she answered with prim indignation.

"God," I wished fervently, "I hope not."

"That's true," Collie conceded, "it isn't always weirdos. But it's *never* the way it is in those books. They have no bearing whatsoever on the reality of what happens between men and women."

"And Weirdos of the Week do?" Fayrene countered. "I think everyone creates their own reality and if you just go around looking for exotic neurotics then that will *be* your reality. It's fun listening to the stories and all. Maybe it's even fun for you while they're happening. But some people couldn't live through them. If that's the way it really was going to be for me, I . . . I guess I'd just rather be alone all my life." Fayrene's words trailed off into silence.

Collie stared at Fayrene for a long time. I expected her to make some zingy reply, but she didn't. Instead, she looked away as if trying to remember what we'd been talking about, grabbed up a book, and pretended to be interested in it. "Hey," she asked, "what was that part about him 'adoring' her body?"

Fayrene checked out at least seven of the eight corners in the room before she reluctantly answered, "What part? The heroine always gets adored eventually in romance novels. It's part of the formula."

"Always?" Collie echoed, opening up *Deny the Tempest*. "I could stand a little adoration in my life, even if it is vicarious."

Our interest started out half as a joke, as a feeble way of making up to Fayrene, and half as a way to divert me from thinking about Collie and Roger dallying beneath my swans. But, that evening, instead of our usual trip to the Swim Center for endorphins and aqua ogling, we were seriously snuggled up with a few Shiners and a little *Fiery Ecstasy* to keep us warm.

"He laved her body in ardent kisses," I read, "adoring every silken inch of her with a worshipping tongue." That worshipping tongue flickered across my lobes and drew me into a world far removed from those pesky swans.

17

WE NEVER DID award a Weirdo of the Week that night. I was glad. Even if he had pierced his ear and grown neck tendrils. Even if he had been glad to ditch me, I still couldn't bring myself to think of Roger as a Weirdo. It pained me to hear the man I'd once pined for rated "nada in bed." Not terminal pain, mind you, just a few passing winces. What hurt most was Collie's attitude, her casual dismissal of my feelings.

From that evening, Weirdo of the Week competitions slacked off. One reason was the Roger entry. The other was, we lost our Blushometer. Or were in the process of losing her. It all started so subtly that Collie and I never noticed until it was too late. I *had* noticed the twin glints emanating from the thirteenth floor of The Moorland that morning we found our bamboo gone. I remembered how they had tracked Fayrene's progress. But how could I have known then that those glints were from the binoculared gaze of one Rashid Al-Hamur, the Creep of Araby.

Who knows what the lonely Persian Gulfer was watching for and how he knew he'd found it that morning in Fayrene? Perhaps it was a gait slightly less bold and aggressive than that of the other American women he'd tracked. Perhaps the modesty of Fayrene's fat wardrobe, flapping as it did on her waning frame, attracted him. It could even have been the remaining Pirtle bulk itself.

Though Fayrene was only a shadow of her former self, she could still eclipse most other UT coeds. Whatever it was, it drew Rashid to cull Fayrene from the herd. He must have studied her comings and goings for a couple of weeks after the initial sighting before he took to appearing on the corner Fayrene turned each day on her way to school. Eventually he worked his way up to the edge of the lawn. He would wait there until Fayrene came out, then dog her footsteps.

One nearly brisk morning in mid-November, Fayrene and I were leaving the house together, I to the mausoleum, she to her library classes, and there he was. Fayrene was by now quite aware of his intentions and blushed as he turned his limpid Middle Eastern eyes on her. One thing I had to give Rashid, he *was* good-looking in a swarthy, sheik of the burning sands way.

"Why will you never talk to me, Miss?" he pleaded unctuously as we sailed past him. "I am a stranger in your country, Miss. I seek only companionship. Only a friend to talk with."

Fayrene slowed down and gave me a look of confused desperation. Why, for all she knew, he could be one of her Sunday School stories come to life. Lord Jesus Himself disguised as a poor wayfaring stranger cruising for true Christians. I stared sternly ahead and motioned for her to keep moving. She picked up speed.

"It is because I am not a Texas boy, Miss, that you will not speak to me. Not even tell me your name. Every day I tell you mine. I tell you I am Rashid Al-Hamur. And every day you ignore me. In my country that is a great insult. I am sure you would not be so cruel if I were a rich, fraternity boy."

"That's not true," Fayrene stopped. I attempted to urge her forward, but Rashid had landed a solid shot. "I can't stand fraternity boys. And my name's Fayrene so don't call me 'Miss' anymore."

"Farina," he repeated in syllables of awed wonder. "It is the most beautiful name I have ever heard."

"Fay*rene*," she corrected him. "Farina is a goopy cereal with lumps in it. That's what the mean kids used to call me at school."

"Fay*rene*. Fay*rene*," he repeated after her, falling in step with us. "Forgive me, beauteous one, my English is so bad especially when I am in the presence of such loveliness."

I felt my breakfast rise in my gorge, but Fayrene just looked straight ahead and stifled giggles. Rashid spotted the stifled smile and coiled around so that he could face her and dog our footsteps at the same time.

"A smile is fighting to be free on your beautiful face," he teased her, tickling the corner of her mouth. "Give in to laughter, to joy on this morning as beautiful as you are."

"Why don't you give in to disappearance, Rash?" I suggested.

"If that is the wish of Fayrene, I will leave, never to return again. Never to seek after her friendship. What is your wish, Fayrene? Do you wish me to disappear forever? Just say the word and I will be gone, never to return."

Fayrene rolled her eyes and frowned comically like a stressed-out ten-year-old.

"So," Rashid announced triumphantly. "You do not share your friend's wish for my disappearance."

"I don't even know you," Fayrene whined.

"That is easy to remedy. Come with me to my room. I will make special Turkish coffee for you and show you maps of my country."

"I can't do that," Fayrene protested in girlish tones. With a dawning horror, I realized that she was flirting with The Rash. "I have to go to class."

"Then I will call you and we will arrange another time."

"It's a free country." Fayrene capitulated and The Rash vanished like a psychosomatic case of eczema.

"Fayrene," I asked, astonished, "Why didn't you tell him to get lost?"

"Well, because he's a stranger in our country and he just wants to be friends . . ."

And he's the first man who's ever paid any attention at all to you. I occasionally amazed myself with my insensitivity. I tested to see how far this had already gone. "He's not bad looking."

"Do you think so?" Fayrene snapped up the test comment and, for the first time since I'd known her, I saw Fayrene's face come fully alive. Dreams that had been suppressed under all the fat she'd shed shone on her face. Rashid, I thought to myself, you may be the lying dog I think you are, but you spoke the truth today; Fayrene really is a beauteous one.

"Yeah," I answered. "He's pretty cute."

"He is, isn't he? Did you ever see *The Wind and the Lion* with Sean Connery and Candice Bergen?"

"Not *that* cute," I interrupted, but it was already too late to short-circuit the fantasies powering through her mind.

"Oops, here's my class." As Fayrene veered off to "New Frontiers in Cataloguing," I felt like the mother of a mildly retarded girl about to go out on her first date. I was worried.

At the library, I braced myself. I was sure that Tommy would be sunk in a funk about the coverage his collection had received or, rather, failed to receive. Instead, he was zipping around the floor like a hummingbird on deadline.

"Yo, steady Steadwoman," he hailed me.

"Yo, Chastain," I responded. I prayed that his next incarnation would not be as Rocky Balboa.

"Did you see the article in yesterday's paper? You know, the one with the picture of you yomping into Luci Presley's wedding cake."

"Yeah, I saw it, Tommy, and I'm really sorry about it. I know how hard you've worked to get your 'collection' taken seriously."

"Sorry? M.J., I made the papers. The whole world and especially the MTV scout now knows about my fanatical devotion to Lady Bird Johnson. Smythe's already been up three times this morning. Papers from all over the state have called. Steadwoman, it worked. And you helped. I could kiss you."

Then, in a rush of hummingbird exuberance, he almost did kiss me except that Smythe burst in. He whom I suspected of shaving, flossing, and re-talcing every day on his lunch hour had a two-day stubble of wispy red hairs and the wild, disheveled look of a man coming rapidly unhinged. Dorothy followed. Her wig askew, she wrang a tiny, damp handkerchief of Irish linen in her hands. They were enough to momentarily take my mind off Tommy's deception.

"You, you," Smythe stood in the walkway stabbing a finger toward Tommy.

Tommy glanced over his shoulder. "Are you addressing me, Mr. Smythe?" he inquired courteously. Smythe lurched forward to the work area. His hands clasped and unclasped spasmodically, rising almost of their own will toward Tommy's throat. Dorothy plucked at Smythe's crumpled shirt to hold him back. The homicidal hands fell to Smythe's sides.

"You, you've ruined me," Smythe croaked. "Thirty-three years in library science. Twenty of them with the presidential libraries, starting right out at the top with JFK's. And, in all that time, not a blot on my record. Not a smudge. Not a smear. Now this." Smythe's eyes bulged. "You told them what we actually have up here." Dorothy restrained Smythe's desperate lunge toward Tommy.

Smythe slumped. "The director just called me. The Friends of the Lyndon Baines Johnson Library Society just called him. They're, heh-heh," he chuckled mirthlessly, " 'very unhappy.' Heh-heh. Consequently, the director is 'very unhappy.' So 'unhappy,' "—with every repetition of the word, Smythe's tone gained a little manic energy—"in fact, that he's asked for my removal. I'm being transferred, Chastain." He addressed his adversary directly. "Transferred to the . . ." A shuddering sob cracked his voice.

Dorothy trembled in an agony of indecision for a moment, then threw motherly arms around the broken Smythe. Smythe looked up, stunned by the sensation of human touch. His eyes, burdened with career devastation, found hers. They locked. Time stopped. Time started again and Dorothy gave Smythe a comradely clasp and a clap on the back.

"Transferred to the . . ." His voice was trance-like. He couldn't take his eyes off of Dorothy. She adjusted her wig to a less rakish angle, ". . . the Richard Milhous Nixon Library."

"Oh, tough luck," Tommy commiserated.

"If they take you," Dorothy piped up, "I'll . . ." She looked at the bewildered Smythe, stiffened her spine, and continued. "I'll apply too. They don't get many applications there at San Clemente. Not like here. I'm sure I'll be accepted."

"You . . . ," Smythe stammered, ". . . you would do that? Deliberately exile yourself to the Richard Milhous Nixon Library?"

Dorothy drew herself up to her full five feet and answered with prim candor, "For you, Mr. Smythe, yes, I would."

The last we heard as they stepped together onto the freight elevator was, "Please, call me Reginald . . . Dorothy."

The instant the elevator doors clanged shut, I cornered Tommy. "Just what did you mean when you said, 'It worked'?"

He tossed off his jacket and tugged the Windsor knot on his tie.

"You faked this, didn't you? Right from the beginning? I knew it. You never fooled me."

"Of course I did," Tommy replied blandly, pulling the links out of his French cuffs and rolling up the shirt-sleeves. "I had to. Your face is an open book. You couldn't be devious if your life depended on it."

"I can so. I can be downright conniving."

Tommy laughed. "No, you can't. That's one of the things I like best about you."

That comment stopped my probe for details cold.

Tommy yawned and ruffled his Eton hair into spiky tufts. "I knew there'd be news guys swarming all over this place once they found out what was actually up here. So, Steadly, mission accomplished. That MTV scout is going to have an eye out for Tommy Berlin and the Vy-Mars. Besides, I truly like The Bird."

I wanted to dig farther into motivation, but Tommy clambered groggily into the cardboard dorm, then uttered the words I'd feared I'd never hear again, "Think I'll take a nap."

Happy to have things back to abnormal, I set to work rectifying the havoc he had wreaked in his catastrophic bureaucratwho-cares stage. I tossed out the new catalogue he'd created with its dangerously accurate descriptions of what was actually contained in the red boxes we'd been enshrining and reinstated the high-blown euphemisms. "Little Slivers of Luci's Wedding Cake" became, once more, "White House Nuptials, Artifacts." Tommy's snores cheered me as I set about burying forever what we'd unearthed.

All the next week, we teetered just at the brink of breaking into national news. Reporters still snooped around on the third floor. I have no doubt that, had Tommy chosen to ride out the publicity wave, we would have gone national. But, apparently, all Tommy had ever wanted was to be noticed by the scout. He snoozed serenely through a number of critical meetings between the local press and the library director. His goal was to appear on MTV, not a Senate Subcommittee hearing on waste in the presidential libraries.

"Cultural history" was generally offered as the reason for the enshrinement of the more marginal items Tommy had brought to light. For the benefit of persistent journalists, there were a few conference calls with curators from around the country. The one that finally placated the aroused reporters was with a curator at the Colonial Village in Williamsburg. He revealed that they were keeping in deep storage a lump of Boston Brown Bread believed to have been left over by the Founding Fathers from the First Constitutional Congress. After that, I saw no more hell-bent-for-leather types storming the first floor brandishing steno pads.

Then one day while I was storing some eight-by-tens of Luci showing her pals how to do the Pony at a White House slumber party, Tommy awoke, his old frisky self again. He peered with sleep-reddened eyes over the edge of the slumber barricade, took a look around, and observed, "It's so damned *pristine* in here."

"Surely you jest," I answered, wading through the swamp of crumbling papers and broken-down boxes to hand him the stepladder. He crawled out and took in a big lungful of LBJ Library air.

"No, it is. Everything here is filtered. All the impurities have been removed from the air, from the source material. Have you noticed that we haven't filed one obscene letter? One crudely scrawled missive full of venom and derangement? Do you really believe that the only letters that arrived at the White House were written under careful supervision by right-thinking schoolchildren?"

"Probably not," I hazarded a wild guess.

"Of course not!" Tommy thundered. It was good to see his demented dander up again. "A serious historical deficiency gapes before us." He flung his arms wide taking in the shelves of sanitized debris. "We must redress this deficiency for the sake of generations of Americans yet unborn." Throwing himself into the new crusade, he sat down and pulled out a stub of pencil that he had in the pocket of his motorcycle jacket. He loved the garment's "uniquely Taiwanese look" with its two dozen zippers implanted in crackling black vinyl. How he could stand to wear nothing but bare chest underneath it was beyond me, but it did contribute to the jacket's bleak post-industrial appeal.

"Paper," he requested. I handed him a few sheets of loose-leaf and he began scribbling. He would pause from time to time, look up, mouth words, then scribble some more. After a last quick reading, he handed the sheet to me.

> Consuela Arguello
> Hotel Tropico
> San Juan, Puerto Rico

> President Linton Panes Johnson
> White House

Washington, D.C.

Querido Juansonito,

Why have you not written? Why do you not return my calls? Have you forgotten our noche de amor en San Juan?

I believed you, President of the mightiest country on earth. Who would think you would lie to a little hotel maid? Why have you not sent for me as you said you would?

Our son is now already eleven months old and each day he looks more like you. Cousin Estrella even said, "You know, Consuela, your little Lintonito with those great big Dumbo ears and that little chicken lips mouth, he looks just like the President of the United States of America." He does too. He's even got a little squint and his hair is starting to get thin on top and his smile has your way of sinking into his face.

Querido, I understand it's a hard job running the most powerful country on earth, but it's not easy being an unemployed hotel maid and mother of a bastardo either. Please can't you take just a few minutes to write, to call, anything.

Siempre Amor

Consuela

"I don't know, Tommy," I cautioned him as he filed the letter away under "Correspondence. Re: Foreign Affairs." But Tommy wasn't listening; he'd already dug out a few sheets of high-quality bond and was slipping one into the ancient Smith-Corona that had been put out to pasture on our floor.

Dorian Peters

789 Telegraph Hill

San Francisco, CA

November 2, 1964

Cher Lyndon,

Let discretion be our watchword.

I know I can never expect you to answer this. National security and all. I understand. I really, really do. The thought that perhaps the St. Christopher's I've enclosed might, for just a moment or two, hang around your neck is enough for me.

I hope that the simple inscription, "To El B.J.," will not give anything away to "Goony Bird," as you so amusingly called her. Though I can never hope for more, I must admit that I'll always go to The Baths praying that lightning might strike twice for me.

Ever,
Dorian

"Oh now, Tommy," I protested. "That is really too much."

"I don't know about that," Tommy answered, filing Dorian's letter under "Correspondence. Re: Domestic Affairs." "I think we've seen recently that history is a pretty fluid commodity. It kind of rises and falls with the tide of public opinion. If the public ever needs a randy president with an illegitimate Puerto Rican son and bathhouse assignations, he'll be right here waiting for them to fish him out. Come to think of it, I'd be just about the right age to be Lyndon's illegitimate Puerto Rican son."

Tommy's eyes lighted with a strange fire. "Lyndon's son," he whispered to himself. "That's it!" he exploded. "Oh, this is epochal."

"Epochal," I echoed. One hesitates to appear ignorant of the epochal.

"Yes! Right before your very eyes, Mary Jo, you have witnessed the last link in the chain being forged."

"I assume you mean this media jamboree you stage-managed," I probed.

"Oh, the P.R.? Yeah," Tommy answered distractedly. "That's worked out great, but I always thought it was for Tommy Berlin and the Vy-Mars. Wrong. They were wrong. I can see that now."

Tommy appeared to be seeing a lot, none of it visible to me. He sunk into a concentration trance that intensified until waves of hot mental energy undulated out from his head and the light over our work area flickered, dimmed, then burst into powerful illumination when Tommy proclaimed, "Little Lyndon and the Great Society!" Euphoria beamed from his face as he turned to me.

"Don't you get it?" he asked. "Look, everyone's tired of this moldy Euro-Bowie decadence. It's morning in America again, right? And who better to ring the alarm than Little Lyndon?"

I could offer no candidates.

"God, don't you see how perfect this is?"

I furrowed my brow to indicate that I was trying to bring it into focus.

"Me, the goof in the papers. In love with Lady Bird. It's such a natural for me to now segue into a band devoted to those happy Johnson years. Little Lyndon and the Great Society," he breathed out the name, officially christening his latest incarnation.

"I like it." I was drawn into his creative fever.

"We'll declare war on nihilism. War on ennui. War on cynicism. We'll be bright, peppy, and upbeat."

It was very disorienting to listen to a spiky-haired bongo board in a black plastic jacket talk about being peppy and upbeat, but Tommy somehow bridged that gap for me.

"I've got nearly a full repertoire already. I already know 'Moon River,' 'The Impossible Dream,' 'Love Is Blue.' I have them all in my K-Tel collection," he said, as if that explained everything. " 'Blue, blue, my love is blue,' " he muttered as he toddled off back to his cardboard boudoir and retired for the morning.

With Tommy's cerebral heat switched off, our floor grew even chillier than it usually was, which was chilly indeed. When I noticed my fingers turning blue, I left Tommy to his musical reveries and slipped downstairs to thaw my outer extremities. I headed for the only place in the Presidential Mausoleum not cryogenically cooled—the ladies' room—taking with me a little something from Fayrene's stash, *Rendezvous with Ecstasy*.

After a couple of sizzling chapters, the danger of frostbite passed and I headed back to the fifth floor. I knew something was wrong the moment I stepped off of the elevator and whiffed Lilac Vegetal hanging heavily on the air. I rushed to the work area, but Smythe and Dorothy had beaten me back. They stood around the cardboard fortress like two geriatric children on Christmas morning stunned by what Santa had left for them. Tommy, dazed from sleep, rose up to greet them.

"Aren't you guys supposed to be in San Clemente?"

"The transfer isn't effective for another week. Aren't *you* supposed to be working?" Smythe asked with a snottiness inspired by his newfound love. Dorothy beamed beside him.

"I got tired. Hand me that stepladder, will you?"

No one moved.

Tommy zipped up a half dozen zippers that rasped noisily in the pregnant silence. "Br-r-r," he rubbed the crackling vinyl of his jacket. "Cold in here."

"You can be fired for this, you know," Smythe informed him gleefully. "Sleeping on the job. It'll take a while, but it can be done."

Tommy leveled a gaze at him so threatening that Smythe backed up a bit, leaving Dorothy exposed to the line of fire. When Smythe ducked into a defensive crouch, Tommy broke the gaze, snorted a laugh, then bent down. With Smythe watching, thunderstruck, he got a grip on the bottom box in the barricade, paused for dramatic effect, then upended the whole structure. The flattened boxes flipped over in the air landing with a gratifying "whoomp" at Smythe's feet.

"Save yourself the effort," Tommy said casually. "I quit. This job's cutting into time I should be spending on my music. Besides, I can sleep better at home."

Like Samson emerging from the ruined temple, Tommy trod over the pile of boxes. He picked his sunglasses up off the table, flicked the stems open, and placed them over his defiant eyes. He pulled out his keys, removed the elevator key from his Hello Kitty keychain, tossed it at Smythe. Then Tommy Chastain took his last long walk out of the Lyndon Baines Johnson Presidential Library. I stood there with Smythe and Dorothy and watched him leave.

An era had ended. I could have cried.

18

I LOITERED AROUND the library for a while after Tommy left. The floor had never seemed so quiet. Even when he'd been sleeping, there was always at least his Kodiak bear snore every now and then to hold back the silence. Now it closed in around me.

Without Tommy, loafing on the government payroll was no fun. I stuck the pictures of Luci doing the Pony into a red box and trolleyed back for a new box. Puzzling over what he might have meant about liking my lack of deviousness and just how far this "like" went, I dug into the box and was up to my elbows in pictures of babies being baptized before I realized it.

There weren't a lot of them, maybe a dozen at the most. The only thing that distinguished the little groupings of radiant new mother, squalling infant, father, assorted relatives, and man of God clustered around a baptismal font was that the president of the United States stood with them. I studied the names and faces to pick up a clue as to how one hooked the leader of the Free World into watching your wee one get water poured on its bald little head.

I flipped through all the pictures and didn't recognize a single name, except one, Fairchild. But then everyone knew who the Fairchilds were, a kind of Texas cross between the Borgias and the Ewings. I didn't have to wonder how old Creighton Fairchild had managed LBJ's grinning appearance in his granddaughter's baptism picture. One of the best-known, but least officially substantiated, rumors of the many surrounding LBJ's rise to power had it that Creighton Fairchild had largely masterminded and financed it. The eight-by-ten glossy in my hand seemed pretty fair substantiation.

I stared at the mother in her black velvet pillbox hat, inclining her willowy, patrician figure slightly over the bundle of baby wrapped in a crocheted white afghan she was cradling. She was an unutterably lovely woman, delicate and haunted. But what was most arresting about her was her hold on her child. She gripped her baby with such a restrained tension that the knuckles on the fingers peeking out from under the afghan were a strained and jutting white. Just as the mother's attention was absorbed by the baby she seemed almost to be protecting, her husband's was directed toward his father, the formidable Creighton Fairchild. Even LBJ's eyes were cutting over to the senior Fairchild at the moment the shutter clicked. Only white-maned, beetle-browed Creighton himself, out of the whole entourage, was staring directly into the camera with a withering scowl.

The photograph had a doomed, mythical quality that made it seem far older than a quarter of a century. Not the Waltons, I thought to myself with a shudder and flipped on past it. By comparison, the other families all looked like ones you could see any Sunday lined up at Luby's for fried okra and baked fish. I shoved the whole christening collection into its little red coffin, then stopped dead and went back to the Fairchild baptism.

One further glimpse of the mother's luminous face and I knew I didn't need to go any further. Still, I flipped the photo over to the caption taped on the back and read through a long list of Fairchild names until I came to this line: "Little Missy Fairchild is wrapped in an ivory afghan trimmed in imported Irish lace and knitted by the baby's maternal grandmother, Cordelia Mohoric."

I turned the picture back over and looked at it until I couldn't tell whether it was Mrs. Fairchild or Collie under the black velvet pillbox. By then it was time to go home.

Outside, a blue norther had blown in.

Collie was on the phone when I got to Alamo. Crying. She turned her head away from me as I crept past her clumped on the stairway and went into my room. Fayrene wasn't home.

A few minutes later, Collie barged in. No trace of tears dampened her face or spirit. "So what's new at the Petrified Bakery?" she asked brightly, flopping down on Fayrene's bed. I felt like we needed to be introduced.

"You okay?" she asked when I continued staring. "Hey, guess what? I have to go home for a few days."

Home? Alamo was home.

"Back to Houston," she clarified, lighting a clove cigarette.

"Those'll give you cancer just as quick as regular ones."

Collie drew in deeply as if the spicy taste was enhanced by the information. I couldn't stop looking at her, studying her. I wondered how I could ever have missed it; she was every inch the heiress. It was there in all her gestures, the line of her nose, the way she spoke, the way she acted. So why the big secret? I wanted to know, and I wanted Collie, who had never told me a true thing about herself, to tell me.

"What?" she asked me, feeling my eyes on her. "What is it?"

"You tell me." My knowledge was so apparent to me that it seemed to fill the room. I was sure she'd tell me everything. That she'd be a little embarrassed at first, then relieved to finally have it in the open.

She was now clumped on Fayrene's bed watching her smoke rise and acted as if she hadn't heard me. "Hey, you didn't even notice. I got my hair cut today." She ran her fingers through her hair completely unaware that her exposed secret was filling the room.

I was dumbfounded.

"You won't believe this guy I met while I was there," she chattered on. "He could be a candidate. He, Glen, geek name, huh? was there, at the haircutters, getting a, brace yourself—BODY WAVE. A body wave! The guy had already body-waved every other part of himself. He was one of those rippling, pumped-up bodybuilder types. So there he was, he's got on a muscle shirt with all his biceps and triceps and deltoids and everything hanging out and his hair is all soaked with perm solution and rolled up on rollers. It was hysterical."

It wasn't even mildly amusing. Not as related in the frantic tone Collie was using. "Where's Fayrene?" she asked, glancing around quickly. For the first time I noticed that her dark hair had blond roots.

"Out with The Rash," I answered. "Their first date, I guess."

"It's not the first, Mary Jo."

"It's the first I know about."

"I think she thinks you disapprove."

"What?" Some of the depth charges of emotion lying unexploded around the room blew up in my response. "Disapprove of a slimeball Mideasterner who probably believes that any woman who's not tarped from the part in her hair down to her pedicure is a whore? What's to disapprove of?"

"I know," Collie agreed. She stubbed out her cigarette in my turtle shell. "But you have to cut your friends a little slack. Let them make a few mistakes. Don't you?" Collie looked at me and for an instant the frantic camouflage went out of her gaze.

I didn't say anything.

She stood up, walked over to the French doors, and paused. "Well, don't you?" she asked again.

I nodded and she went into her room to pack, closing the doors behind her.

Then I had to take a long time out to lie on my stomach on Fayrene's bed and look out the window thinking about Collie and Tommy and Fayrene and the Creep of Araby.

By the time I got around to the final topic, it was nearly one o'clock and the couple in question strolled up the sidewalk. They paused right beneath the window I was stationed at. And there, in the yellow light from the bug bulb, he lunged at her. From my vantage point, I could see Fayrene's eyelids flip back like window shades and roll around on their sprockets. Throughout Rashid's extremely vigorous osculation, Fayrene held her eyes open in shock and wonder.

Barely giving her time to breath, Rashid slipped a heat-seeking brown hand under her tent top and captured a Pirtle mammary. Fayrene was stunned by the swiftness of the attack. Before she could protest the initial incursion, the rapidly spreading Rash had flipped up her top, yanked down her bra, and began suckling away for all he was worth at the same time he deployed a hand south-ward for a brisk rubdown in the crotch region.

"Rashid!" Fayrene cried out in indignation, swatting his bur-rowing head from her bosom and staking down the tent top again.

Rashid emerged, his hair brushed forward. "You inflame me, Fayrene," he implored her. "You know that you have toyed with me all evening, exciting me beyond what any man can bear. It is painful for a man to be so aroused without any release. Is it in your Baptist religion to be so cruel?"

"Rashid," Fayrene whined, "I explained all that to you before. The Lord Jesus Christ frowns on any premarital stuff."

"Surely your Lord cannot be so cruel that he denies his chil-dren the joy he meant for them to take in their bodies."

"Baptists don't believe in joy. At least not in bodies. Not in our congregation back home, anyway."

Rather than parry this statement of dogma, Rashid made an-other lunge, attaching himself tight as a tick to Fayrene's neck. I was reassured as long as her eyes were open wide, but when they fluttered shut, I had to restrain myself from running downstairs and holding a smoldering matchhead to Rashid's butt. The SUKs saved me the trip. Just as it seemed Fayrene was feeling what *Rendezvous with Ecstasy* called "the sweetly languorous, all-forgetting sweep of a surrender she could not deny," the SUKs bolted out of the darkness carrying Kytes in the prescribed battering ram posture.

"He's fixing to heave!"

"Not so damned loud, Schlubber. We don't want the dykes hauling out their cameras. Puke quiet, Kytes."

Kytes responded by letting fly with a sonic boom level retch.

"My shoes!" Rashid shrieked.

"Ah, sorry, pardner," Bub apologized. And they were gone.

Rashid's ardor was replaced with a different kind of heat. He steamed and fumed as Fayrene fumbled with the hose to rinse off his shoes. "My socks!" He let fly with a stream of curses that his ancestors had developed for camels who did unpardonable things, and stomped off into the night.

I quickly climbed into my own bed and pretended to be asleep. Fayrene sniffled into her pillow for a good long time before falling asleep.

Collie came back Sunday night. I'd been stewing all weekend about her really being this Missy Fairchild person and was ready to start demanding some answers, but she was so preoccupied and gloomy that I couldn't. Her short visit home had changed her. She was chain-smoking clove cigarettes and biting her nails. I tried to tease her, to dull the nervous edge she'd taken on. But jocularity was a frequency she seemed to have stopped receiving.

"I need to think," she said, dismissing me. I left her in a clove-choked funk in her voluptuous bedroom.

The Brew Blasts, starting with the one that had landed on Rashid's foot, kept up all that week. In giddy anticipation, everyone waited for Collie's reaction as the attacks grew more and more blatant until they at last approached pre-Bamboo Outrage levels of excess and defilement. When Collie took no notice, the group's gravity seemed to give out. The pull of gravity sucked us all back into our own private revolutions around our own private planets.

I trudged through the next few days. Collie and Fayrene had taken to haunting their bodies without really inhabiting them. Both of them went around like consumptive Victorian heroines heaving great sighs and focusing on distant horizons. With no one to talk to, I began calling Tommy. Funny, now that we didn't work together anymore, we actually talked more than we ever had when he was lying in state on the federal payroll.

On Friday of that grim week, I came home and opened the

door to Hell Week Heaven. Fayrene was gone. Something was wrong. It took me several unsettled minutes to figure out exactly what it was, then several more to process the implications. When I had, I turned to the French doors and pounded. Though I'd resolved to leave Collie alone until she gave me some indication that she desired human contact, I couldn't wait. This was an emergency.

"H-m-m-f-f-f," she muttered.

"Collie, you there?" I asked at the same time I opened the doors. She was there, in the exact position she'd been in when I'd left her five days ago. Same clothes. Same dark intensity. "Come here," I urged her up and off her bed and into my room.

"You notice anything missing?" I asked.

She looked around warily and shook her head no.

"Mel Gibson and the sheep," I prompted her.

She searched for the icons that had graced our walls since the day Fayrene moved in, but they were gone.

"It's an ominous sign, wouldn't you agree?"

"Sweet, blond Jesus," Collie said distractedly. "Dispossessed by the Creep of Araby. Yeah, that is no wayno."

I was cheered by her response. "What are we going to do?"

"Do?" Collie inquired as if she were not familiar with the meaning of the word. "Why do we need to 'do' anything?"

"It's pretty obvious," I answered, growing slightly frantic at her inability to comprehend that we had an emergency on our hands requiring swift intervention. "Those pictures were the last bricks in the fortress Fayrene had built around her body. Rashid is probably, at this very moment, massing for the final assault."

"So?"

"So! Rashid and Fayrene? Fayrene's first time? It would be hideous. We have to save her."

"Have to save her?" Life crackled back into Collie. "You remember that big, fat woman who was with Fayrene the day she moved in?"

"Sure."

"You happen to recall who that woman is?"

"Fayrene's mother; but Collie, I . . ."

"I don't remember hearing that she'd died."

"Collie, I'm not trying to act in loco parentis here, I just want to spare her some guaranteed heartache."

"Who are we to decide? Who are we to look into someone's life and say what's best for them? Who ever knows anyone well enough to make that decision?"

I was wounded by Collie's reaction. "I don't know, Collie, I thought the three of us had gotten to know one another fairly well."

Collie made one of her drama school expressions designed to be read in the balcony. "Yeah, we probably do know each other fairly well and even then, there's more about me that you *don't* know than you *do* know and I think that's true for most everyone."

"But truer when someone is working overtime at being an enigma, isn't it?" I asked.

Something dangerous flickered in her eyes as she glared at me. I noticed the dark circles around her eyes and how bone-weary she looked. She hunched forward the tiniest bit and folded her arms in front of her. Her hands gripped her elbows so tightly that the knuckles strained white and jutting as her mother's had been at her baptism. Everything in her expression and posture forbade me to pursue the topic. I didn't like being forbidden.

"Cordelia, how did you get your name?"

Her expression changed. I expected anger but got this sort of hurt betrayal instead that, momentarily, made me ashamed. But Collie recovered. She drew herself up, and answered. "My mother has never revealed to me what hallucinatory substance she was under the influence of when she named me. The closest I've ever been able to come to a reality-based source is a Saint Cordelia, an early Roman martyr who died after a gaudy assortment of pagan tortures including having all her teeth pulled out rather than renounce her faith or put out for the centurions. And that's about all I know about that," she concluded with a gay little smile as she breezed back through the French doors, shutting them behind her.

I don't suppose that, until that moment, it had fully sunk in that Collie was an actress. It wasn't just something she studied at school, she *was* an actress. A good one. She'd almost gotten me with that set piece about her name. I'd almost believed she'd told me something about herself. But now I knew better.

"Fuck it," I whispered to the French doors closed against me. Fuck the whole house. I'd gotten far too mired in the lowrent melodrama swirling around me. If Collie wanted to be this century's greatest living enigma, let her. But let her tantalize someone else with the mystery of her past, the romance of her present, the tragedy of her future—I was through. And let Fayrene stumble down the primrose path unescorted. I had had enough. I needed a break.

With that in mind, I slammed out of the house and headed over to the Student Union where I signed on for a canoeing trip that would get me out of the house for four whole days over the Thanksgiving holiday. Four days away from the Brew Blasts, the scolding notes on the refrigerator, Constance and her inevitable three-minute eggs, Esme and her snarling asides, Barb and Toni cooing or hissing at each other, Hillary nibbling at her dandruff flakes, Judith and her head-boinging, Fayrene and her deflowering, Collie and her decline. Everything. Besides, there was already talk afoot of stuffing a pumpkin with various whole grains for Thanksgiving; I didn't think I could face a vegetarian Thanksgiving.

I was cheered by the depth of Fayrene's distress when I announced my plans.

"Four days?" she wailed. "Is that including," she gulped, "nights?"

"No, I'll portage back every night." I laughed to soften my sarcasm. "Of course, it includes nights." After being out in the cold for the past week, I was warmed by Fayrene's attention.

She gave me a look of concerned terror.

"I'll be fine," I assured her.

I wasn't. The first day of the trip, J-stroking down the Guadalupe River, was the longest of my life. I'd been randomly paired with two computer science majors who'd come along to find out if there was life out where the cathode ray tubes didn't beam. For Chuck and Bert, there wasn't. Not life as we know it. Not life as I could endure it.

They started off slow, sprinkling otherwise normal conversations with stinky little anchovies of computer jargon.

"Okay, let's boot 'er up," Chuck called out to buddy Bert as we set off. Behind us, floating on an inner-tube arrangement they'd rigged up, was a cooler full of "system-essential supplies"—a six-pack of Mello-Yello, another of Mountain Dew, a couple of bags of pork rinds, a couple dozen bags of Sugar Daddies, and several boxes of Tic-Tacs.

"Oh wow, component interface problems," Bert observed as the three of us tangled paddles. We separated to perform our own gawky, ineffective strokes that succeeded only in angling our craft directly across the flow of the river. Other novice canoers streamed down upon us buffeting our canoe and creating a monstrous bottleneck. It took a while, but I finally understood enough of their language to get us under way.

"Power up, Bert," I barked at the helmsman to make him go. Then, "Power down," to get him to stop his wildly flailing movements. With stop and go under control, we headed down the river. Bert and Chuck's combined personal charisma was more than enough to ensure that we had the whole river to ourselves. The entire flotilla accelerated rapidly past us as soon as they came near enough to overhear a few key phrases like "RAMs of K," "addressable memory," and "I/O status byte." And then I was alone with them. If Sartre were to rewrite No Exit for the eighties, this would have been his mise-en-scène—stuck on a canoe with two pasty-faced, sugar-crazed, monomaniacal computer drones.

I made it, barely, through the first day and night. But, going into the second day, I started to lose it. Their laughing at numbers was what did it. Bert would make some witticism about an 8080 then Chuck would come back with a howler about the oh-so-laughable 3001. Suddenly, I too laughed. I knew that if I didn't get off that canoe soon, Chuck and Bert and I and the whole gang down at the Computer Center would just chuckle our way into the Silicon Valley together. The situation called for drastic action and I responded. In the parlance of the Lone Star State, I *tumped* the canoe over, just gently leaned to my right side and kept on leaning.

Chuck and Bert came up sputtering, but, with their first words, I knew they were all right. "We'd better access that shore over there," Chuck suggested.

"I'll log on to that program," Bert seconded the plan, and we swam for the nearest bank. Chuck drove us back to Austin in his battered Toyota. I felt mildly guilty about ruining their holiday until we got within sniffing distance of the nearest disk drive. Their only concern instantly became sneaking into the Computer Center to log some free time using the faculty code they'd recently cracked.

They dropped me off and I dashed up the stairs. The outing had demonstrated to me how precious the human drama was. Once again I cherished my place in it and was eager to get the show on the road. I was just as eager to change out of the soggy blue jeans that were chafing my legs. My buoyant mood fizzled when I discovered the door to Hell Week Heaven bolted from the inside. I was about to pound, when Collie popped her head out of her room and stopped me.

She gestured me toward her. "Fayrene is with Rashid," she whispered in my ear.

" 'With' him?" I asked.

Collie nodded and pulled me into her room.

"Now? In there?" I asked in an urgent whisper pointing to the French doors.

"Yes," Collie hissed. "Keep your voice down."

"I knew this was bound to happen. That was why she was so upset about me leaving. It doomed her to sweet, savage surrender."

"Mary Jo, don't get all febrile. It might be wonderful."

"With The Rash?"

"What's the difference? Like, what's the difference whether

you die of colorectal cancer while you're watching 'Hawaii Five-O' reruns or whether you check out hang gliding over the Grand Tetons?"

"Collie, I'm going to go on blind faith and assume you have a point here." I didn't like the way she was rambling or the way she clutched my hand.

"There's no difference, ultimately. Is there? You end up at the same place. All of our tickets are punched for the same destination. I mean, we're all going to die. It's only the route, the number of stops you make along the way, that makes any difference." Collie was much too intense about her life-as-a-bus-ride theorem.

"Uh, listen, Collie, have you slept any since I left?" I asked gently.

Before she could answer we were interrupted by the single most gripping sound that one pair of humans can make and another can overhear—creaking bedsprings. Collie and I both stopped breathing and devoted ourselves wholly to eavesdropping on Fayrene's deflowering. Our eyebrows jumped together at the sound of a particularly vigorous creak. It was followed by a few more puny creaks, then silence. I saw my wide-eyed, breath-holding expression mirrored in Collie's face. I leaned over close to Collie's ear and whispered.

"Pretty short ride."

But already we were listening again, our ears pricked and our hearts steeled for what we both feared we would hear next— Fayrene's weeping. The silence dragged on, then the bedsprings heaved mightily as they received the burden of Rashid's weight being transferred off of Fayrene.

"If that turdlick gets up and leaves," Collie whispered fiercely. It cheered me to hear the old pepper in her voice again.

The springs creaked once more as they uncoiled when The Rash got to his feet. Coins jangled in a pocket as he pulled his pants on. His buckle clanked as he fastened it. The springs creaked one last time.

"He's putting on his goddamned shoes," Collie hissed frantically. She was her old self again. It made me forget all about LBJ watching her being baptized.

There were heavy footsteps, a bolt being drawn, a door opening, a door closing. No words had been spoken on the other side of the French doors.

"The slimewad left." Collie was stupefied and mad. "Just like that. He up and left."

Outrage allied us. It wasn't as if we had never been players in a dismal scene just like the one that had transpired next door. It was intolerable, though, that Fayrene should have to endure one on her very first time.

We listened for other sounds then: the pop of the Valium bottle being opened, the click of a revolver chamber being spun, the whack of a noose being tossed over a high beam. But there was nothing. We waited, barely breathing, not moving, for ten minutes.

"You think she's all right?" I asked.

Collie shrugged. We worried. As the minutes passed, we worried seriously. We had to know how Fayrene had fared. I remembered the night when I'd tried to do a little surveillance work from the other side of the French doors, when I'd scratched away at the paint to catch a glimpse of the person I knew then only as The Weeping Trumpeter. I concentrated and recalled the exact pane I'd scraped at and the exact place. I explained to Collie and we both got down on our hands and knees as I scratched softly with my fingernail. The paint chipped away and we had a tiny window into the next room. By angling around, I finally got Fayrene into my limited line of vision. She was sitting bolt upright in bed, moonlight streaming around her sweet soft face, which was set into the first hard expression I'd ever seen it wear. I moved away and Collie took up my position.

"Is she pissed, apoplectic, or pensive?"

I had no explanation for the grim expression.

"We'd better go and find out." Collie had completely abandoned her noninterventionist stance of letting life's little bus ride wander whither it may. We tapped gently. No response. A heartier tap. Still nothing. Finally Collie tried a full-blown pound. From deep within the pit of a darkened Hell Week Heaven came an answer.

"Go away." Then a moment later, "Please."

"Well, looks like you bunk with me tonight," Collie said. She dug out an extra nightgown and we made a nest for me out of her abundance of pillows.

"Collie," I asked as she switched off the light. "You know what you were saying, about me not really knowing you . . ."

"Forget it, Mary Hoe. I didn't mean it. My endorphins were screwed up or something. You know me. You do, don't you?"

It might have been easier to blurt everything out in the dark. To tell her I'd seen the picture and knew who she really was. But that suddenly didn't seem to have much to do with her question.

"Oh wow, I'm exhausted," she said, plumping up her pillows. "I can't keep my eyes open another minute." She switched off her light, dove under the covers and pantomimed a woman falling into deep and immediate sleep. It was one of her less convincing performances.

I stayed awake for a long time. Collie was awake even longer.

19

EARLY THE NEXT MORNING, I intercepted Fayrene on her way downstairs. She was gnawing on a Slo-Poke and carrying her box of romance novels. Her once-soft features were still hardened into a mask that would have looked nice on Easter Island.

"Need some help?" I asked. I scooped a fevered load off the top and followed Fayrene back to the dumpster in the alley.

"You're not going to throw all these away, are you?"

Fayrene didn't answer. She tossed the rakish, ruggedly lean heroes with mocking green eyes flecked with chips of smoldering agate as well as the high-spirited heroines, their eyes flashing defiance, into the overflowing dumpster.

"This really goes against the grain for me," I joked, setting down my load for disposal. Fayrene's colossal silence made me nervous. "You know, I come from a family where the third law of thermodynamics is, 'Matter is neither purchased retail nor thrown away.' You could at least sell them."

"No," Fayrene exploded. "No other woman should ever read these. They're just lies and fantasies."

"I thought that was taken for granted."

Blotches of bright red broke out around Fayrene's nose and eyes and tears brimmed above her lower lids. She ran inside.

"Fayrene," I called after her, "I'm sorry." I followed her back inside and up the stairs. The door was locked by the time I reached it. It took my sunlight-stunned eyes a second to adjust to the dark-ness. When they did, I noticed Collie huddled at my feet talking on the phone in low and desperate tones. She slammed the phone down, looked at me for a moment, then bolted for her room.

Both my retreats now shut off, I sank onto the top stair and wondered what was shaking with Chuck and Bert down at the Computer Center. I might have "tumped" on them too soon.

Over the next few days, Fayrene restocked her Treat Box and went after it like a shrew trying to eat several times her own body weight at once. Day after day it went on. Fayrene brooded on her bed in a nest of Peanut Pattie wrappers, devouring Little Debbie cakes and staring out the window, watching for the Creep of Araby. I tried numerous approaches: sympathy, cajoling, frank concern for her health—both mental and physical—just plain good sense, and more sympathy. Nothing worked; the tears only poured down faster. Desperate, I fell back on inane prods.

"Why don't we just hook up an i.v. of Eagle Brand condensed milk?" I asked as she gargled down a fistful of Reese's Pieces.

She answered me with a hurt and bewildered look and the next day a six-pack of Eagle Brand appeared in the Treat Box. She slugged it down, the most densely caloric substance known to man, like it was Diet D.P.

Of course, all Swim Temple outings had ceased. At precisely the worst possible moment, just when Fayrene's set point was sky-rocketing, her ballooning body was denuded of all the right endor-phins. She hung up her wraparound skirts and brought out the polyester pull-on pants again. Though they were still baggy, I knew she had every intention of filling them out to their seam-splitting fullest.

"Fayrene," I whimpered, "he's not worth it. The guy was a Weirdo. Tell me the story," I pleaded. "We'll laugh about it and you'll get the award this week. It's not a tragedy unless you turn it into one." I wished for Collie's gift of alchemy, her ability to some-how transform the heavy, leaden stuff of life into solid gold skit material.

But it seemed Collie herself had lost that gift or was unable to apply it to her life. She languished on the other side of the French doors like a Tinkerbell no one believed in. The only evidence of her continued existence was the fog of clove-scented cigarette smoke that exhaled from her room. That was the variation on self-destruction she had chosen to play. For a rich, contrapuntal effect, Collie had also stopped eating. As Fayrene waxed, Collie waned.

The only time Fayrene tore her eyes from the window during those dismal days was when the phone rang. Though it hadn't been for her since the night Rashid had had his way with her, she always looked from the phone to me with imploring Lillian Gish eyes and I always shuffled out to answer it. And always it was for someone else.

Like jackals sensing their prey weakening, the SUKs closed in. Particularly fond of adversaries who are down, they brought the full weight of their bovine intellects and energies to bear on revenge missions.

It was early December and winter was finally getting serious about settling in the day the SUK reprisals crescendoed. The security guards had chased me out of the library after work that day and I was forced back to the house.

I'd come to dread crossing the war zone that used to be our front yard. Last week I'd returned to find the burnt-out stump of the spindly pecan still smoldering. Toilet papering was too advanced for the SUKs. No, they had to torch our lone tree. All that remained of my crumpled bike, still chained to the stub of charcoal, was the scorched frame and the stink of burnt rubber.

After that, I'd resorted to sneaking in through the back alley. But those zany SUKs had surprises waiting there too. A few M-80s in the back dumpster and we had most of a ton of garbage bedecking the alley.

Needless to say, I was wary that day as I turned the corner and came up Pecan. Still, I was not fully prepared to find that, there on our front dirt, a miniature Hoovertown had sprung up. Instead of honest, but luckless, Great Depression hobos, however, quite another species had taken up residence. Every city has its strain of street person. In Austin they've earned the name "drag worm" for their habit of hanging out on the main drag across from the university and panhandling students.

I slowed down and started to turn away. Maybe I could find a comfy library carrel to curl up in. But it was already too late; the worms had heard the clink of one coin tapping against another in my coat pocket. Before I could flee, they were upon me.

"Hey, man, spare change?" asked a fellow who looked as if he'd never recovered, psychically or hygenically, from Woodstock. On a dirty piece of clothesline, he led a gray-spotted mutt with a blue bandanna tied around its neck. As he held out his palm, he transferred a can of Colt 45 to his leash hand.

I handed over my change and bolted for the safety of the front door. In order to reach it, though, I had to run a gauntlet of the drag's most virulent panhandlers.

"Hey, momma," a black worm with no front teeth stuck a shiny palm in my face. In his other hand he gripped a can of Colt 45. "You fine. Gimme uh quar-tuh."

I whirled away from him and faced a worm dressed entirely in incompletely cured animal hides stitched together with rawhide strips. "Hey, Miss," Natty Bumppo hissed at me. "Miss, c'mere. I jus wanna ask you a question. Miss. Why are you running away? Do I scare you? Why should I scare you?"

Why? Just because you've got serial killer eyes and a skinning knife strapped to your thigh? I raced into the house. Fayrene was at the door. She cracked it open enough for me to slither inside, then slammed it shut on an invading hand. The hand dropped a can of Colt 45 and withdrew.

Before I could ask for an explanation, Fayrene dragged me over to a window. We peered through a gap between the boards. Across the street The Bub was passing out tall-boys of malt liquor to my assailants.

"The SUKs are paying those street whacks to harass us?"

Fayrene nodded. "They get extra cans if they make us shriek."

I didn't need to ask why no one had called the police. I'd seen how fast the typical drag worm could vaporize when an officer of the law appeared. There's no way of telling how long the panhandling and harassment jamboree might have lasted if the SUKs hadn't killed their own golden goose. Seems they put Kytes on double grog rations and the spectacle of the little toad abusing our few surviving sprigs of greenery was more than even dumpster-diving drag worms could tolerate. They decamped.

It was lucky that the SUKs hoisted themselves on their own petard like that because none of us was much inclined to take affirmative action anymore. Collie had been the center stake keeping the gaudy circus tent of our resistance aloft. When she crumbled, the big top sagged back into a puddle of mismatched patterns and clashing colors. Attendance at Judith's therapy sessions picked up. I stumbled into one as Judith was "guiding" Barb, Toni, Esme, Hillary, Josie, Constance, and Duk Soo through an expression of their feelings about the ongoing abuse.

"I think the fuckers ought to be drawn and quartered," Esme volunteered with a throaty, pirate gurgle.

"Uh-huh, uh-huh," Judith boinged back at her. "I think we can all get behind you on the emotional content of your solution. How about it?" she cheer-led the group, happy as a clam now in the high tide of misery swamping the house.

"Oh yeah," Toni snarled. "Those pricks are an affront to humanity. They should be staked down with wet rawhide in a hot sun until their body parts are ripped asunder."

That suggestion won wide and rousing approbation. Then Judith brought everyone back to their senses.

"Now that we've vented a lot of the very real, very valid feelings that we're all experiencing, I think we might want to begin focusing on a few real world, workable responses to the situation."

"Pungee stick!" Duk Soo offered. Looking around hopefully, she added, "Hire assassin?"

"Heh-heh." Judith let her off with a little light chuckle. "No, I think we've all learned the futility of response-type responses to aggressive, juvenile behaviors with the same sorts of behaviors." She lifted her eyebrows and looked from face to face until each one nodded, until every one of them had recanted the Cordelia Mohoric heresy. Only then was she willing to welcome them back into the damp and clammy fold. "Your thoughts?" she asked.

"Have we completely abandoned legal alternatives?" Josie asked. Hillary glared at her and Josie waved the cigarette smoke twining toward the organic anorectic off toward Constance who merely pressed a tightly balled fist against her mouth and coughed softly.

"Don't look to me for answers," Judith said, holding her palms out to the group. "I'm just facilitating here."

"Forget the cops," Toni counseled. "They're part of the same patriarchal infrastructure that produces and supports fraternities."

"You know," Constance began dreamily, "often the most effective protestations are those which are lodged symbolically. I'm thinking now of the Kaiser Wilhelm Cathedral in Berlin. It was bombed into a hollow, charred shell during the war and the Berliners chose to let it remain in its devastated condition as a reminder to the world."

No one said a word; instead they all turned to Judith.

"I like that!" she exclaimed after a dramatically sufficient pause. "We could simply leave the house and yard in *their* devastated condition as a statement to the world." Immediately the scramble was on for everyone else to jump on the sanctioned bandwagon.

"It's perfect," Judith went on. "I mean, in this era of ground-losing, women need a symbol, a reminder of the oppression that lurks, forever waiting for us. I motion that we leave all the evidence of misogyny just as it is." The motion was heartily seconded and unanimously passed.

I stumbled away. I was going to be living in a memorial to oppression? With obelisks of charred tree trunks and an altar of dried vomit?

It was hard to imagine the house becoming less appealing, until ominous rumblings issued forth from the plumbing, the warnings of an angry god displeased with our offerings of Tampax. Toni was called out for crisis intervention. Her pants dragged down to mid-crack level by an assortment of wrenches, she marched down to the basement to do battle with the groaning god of the ancient pipes. Toni lost. Decisively. All the toilets backed up. Toni made a tactical withdrawal to her room and refused to answer the door. Hillary announced that there were no funds in the treasury to hire a plumber and that she would have to wait for the next Co-op League Meeting to request an emergency loan. Satori House next door became our outhouse. We had to shower in university locker rooms.

A few days later I came back from a morning jaunt over to Satori, careful to avoid the charcoal sculptures and Kytes's used food creations, snatched the *Daily Texan* off the dining room table, and turned to "Apts. for Rent": I was vacating the Kaiser Wilhelm Memorial to Oppression Boarding House. I spotted a promising "Effic. Near shuttle bus rts." that would be vacant at the end of the semester. Even though it was the cheapest thing listed, I'd still have to find another job in order to afford it. But I had to leave. There was no longer any other sane alternative.

Constance, Esme, Barb, and Toni were waiting on the doorstep when I arrived. By the time the landlord showed up, Duk Soo and Josie had joined us for a look around. None of us even made it across the threshold though. The landlord informed us that a more enterprising seeker of shelter had shown up early that morning with deposit in hand. And, quite frankly, he was looking forward to having the next Barbara Walters, Alexis Hartwell, as his tenant, starting next semester. Even if she could "talk the ears off a mule." Barely looking at each other, we fellow traitors slunk away. I angled off toward the campus. I'd put off the odious chore long enough; I had to find out if there was any hope of my continuing in graduate school.

The tower bells were pealing out "Greensleeves" as I cut

across the West Mall. The day was gray and a slicing wind blew trash up against my ankles. For the past couple of days, I hadn't wanted to venture out into the cold for a cross-campus shower. Consequently, my hair was plastered in oily strands against my head and areas where limbs joined my body were vaguely itchy. Yes, I was enchanting and felt every bit as sparkling as I looked. Then, I caught sight of the back of a nuzzling couple, and my heart leapt.

I was sure that the nuzzlette ahead of me was Collie. It was her slender, dancer's figure. Besides, the man she was with had odd little tendrils of hair trailing down his back and I caught the glint of an earring in his ear. Collie had recovered! She'd scored a weirdo this week! Hope was born anew. I raced ahead to intercept her.

Too late I recognized my clean-shaven ex. "Roger!" I gasped as I came abreast of the couple.

"Mary Jo!" he gasped back.

The slim, dark-haired woman with him bore an amazing, though inferior, resemblance to Collie.

"Are you Mary Jo?" the sooty-lashed beauty asked. "Roger's told me all about you."

All? Oh, that stung. She and Roger exchanged glances of deep and fond understanding. My colon tightened.

"Mary Jo, I'd like you to meet Chloe Beaumatin, my fiancée."

Fiancée? Had I heard right? I looked at the dew-kissed Chloe and one thought surfaced—I couldn't imagine Roger expecting her to pick up his underwear. She was too pretty. Is that why she, not I, had won Roger? A cleaver of wind cut into my eyes and I blinked back tears. The bells pounded their tune into my heart and there, in that broken and trampled space, I sang inwardly along:

> Bong, bong, two, three—Alas my love, you do me wrong,
> to cast me off discourteously. Bong, bong.
> When I have lo-oved you so long,
> delighting in your comp'ny.

Okay, so the delight time had been dwindling there toward the end; I still wasn't prepared to meet the future Mrs. Roger Halpern.

"I'm so happy for both of you." I said the words in a monotone as if I were reading cue cards, one at a time. But I said them. We exchanged a few more bits of wooden, pro forma dialogue, then they walked off into the shining vista of their shared future.

He never picks up his socks! He's nada in bed! I wanted to yell after them. I even raised my fist. Then I remembered my greasy hair, my questionable body odor, and I stopped. With the bells hammering in my head, my arm frozen in the air, I felt like Quasimodo trying to flag down Esmeralda.

All the way to Communications Building A, I berated myself for becoming entangled in Weirdo of the Week competitions. I should have stayed in my single-family dwelling and plugged the holes in the dike that was leaking on my relationship with Roger. Of all the men I'd met and been exposed to in the past three months, only he had proved himself capable of a permanent commitment. It should have been to me. It *could* have been me—secure, safe in a real conjugal dyad. Watered by my tears, orange blossoms and baby's breath bloomed in my heart, but they weren't for me.

I was so demoralized by the time I reached the Communications Building that, instead of walking around to the front, I slipped in the side door and took the stairs up.

"Enter the phantom student!" Professor Lipscomb announced when he caught sight of me lurking at his door. "And, pray tell, to what do we owe the honor of the most unexpected pleasure of this visit? H-m-m-m?"

Professor Lipscomb, I sent the message telepathically, my heart is breaking, please ease up. He was not receiving.

"H-m-m-m?" he wheezed again through his nostrils.

Visits to other professors were worse. The J-School faculty had massed for my expulsion and I had no defense. I was sitting in Professor Denise's office, pleading for another chance, when her phone rang.

"Denise Kleppers," she began smartly. Then her face and manner fell. She swiveled her chair so that her back was to me.

"Do you think this is entirely appropriate?" she hissed into the phone. "Do you realize that you are about one f-stop away from being fired? I don't think I can save you this time. Not with what's downstairs." She listened, then heaved a mighty sigh. "Oh, all right." She turned to me. "It's for you." The frost in her voice could have cracked a boulder.

"Me?" I stammered. She held the phone out to me like a sub-poena. I knew I was dead if I took it, but I did.

"I haired chew were in the building." Donald Duck on am-phetamines.

"Uh, yes." I couldn't have choked out another word even if I'd wanted to with Professor Denise sitting there strafing me with killer gazes.

"Today chew will lairn the cost of toying with a man's hairt."

"Okay, okay, I believe I've met that course requirement."

"Come to the low-bee and see for churself."

"Low B?"

"Low-bee! Low-bee!" Eduardo yelled.

"Of course, the lobby. Certainly. Good-bye." I reached out and cut Eduardo off in mid-rant. "Just checking with me about a grade on a project," I lied to Professor Denise. "He thinks I deserve a low B." I slid out of my chair. "I have to go now and pick up the project I got the low B on. It's in the low B. Lobby," I quickly corrected myself. "Down in the lobby." I backed out of the office and rushed downstairs before Eduardo could call back. He was not helping my chances for academic survival.

The front section of the downstairs lobby, the part that faced onto the glass walls at the front of the building, was entirely en-closed by portable room dividers. Their backs all faced me as I made a rapid approach. They were the kind of dividers that stop about knee level. Poking out from under one section, I recognized Eduardo's shoe. I'd had ample opportunity to acquaint myself with his particular model during our noche de amor when I'd knelt before him and slipped it from his foot. My colon ratcheted shut a few more notches and I had to force myself forward. Eduardo must have heard my reluctant footsteps for he popped out from behind the dividers.

"Choost in time," he greeted me. There was a glitter in his eyes of the kind that makes me change seats on buses when I detect it in strangers. It made me extremely uneasy when Eduardo clamped me around the shoulders and whispered in my ear, "Come right this way. I choost finished." He forcibly guided me toward the front of the dividers. I did not want to go. Besides the glitter, Eduardo, el suavecito, hadn't shaved for days, his breath smelled like he'd been eating Alpo, and the fingernails he clawed into my shoulders were as long as Howard Hughes'.

"Eduardo, I know that cultural misapprehensions have clouded our relationship in the past," I said soothingly. I talked to him the way you would address someone on top of a tall building holding a high-caliber rifle with a Zebra scope attached. "But I think if you just sit down and . . ." Shock silenced my Voice of Reason monologue as I came face to face with a sixteen-by-twenty blow up of my left breast complete with puckered aureole.

I looked around and found myself encircled by a corral of my own flesh. Eduardo's photo exhibition featured me in an assortment of dreamy, pre-coital poses, all nude. (There were no post-coital shots of me, depressed and disappointed, huddled in Eduardo's car as he chowed down on a 7-11 burrito and sucked up a Big Gulp.)

Short of any hard-core pudenda displays, it was all recorded: the mole on my right hip, the little hairs around my nipples, my saddlebags. My cellulite was enshrined, photographed, printed, mounted, and displayed for all to see. Between moments when everything around me went dark, I read the title of the show: AWAKENING. Beneath the white, block letters was a shot Eduardo had taken of me at the very moment I had knelt before him to take off his shoes. I could not believe the saucy, naughty kitty look he'd caught on my very face.

Darkness swam up around me and I reeled backward into it. Eduardo caught me and hissed into my ear, "Now do chew know the cost of toying with a man's hairt?"

The acrid smell of his breath brought me around and I lurched from his grasp to struggle outside into the lashing wind. My thoughts seethed. They boomeranged from embarrassment that would make a bison blush back to unreasoning rage.

Inchoate fury swirled through me attaching itself to Collie the way molten sugar spins around a stick into a tacky glob of cotton candy. Collie had conned me. How could I have ever listened to her? Followed her advice? Now my academic career was in ruins and my social life was an extinct species. The man I might have shared my future with if I hadn't fallen under Collie's pernicious influence was marrying a winsome poppet. And, as a direct result of Collie's coaching, my fleshly delights were being exposed to the world. I cringed with a bit more of the totality of my being as I imagined Professor Lipscomb, Tommy, Alexis Hartwell, the guys in my photo lab—anyone—waltzing through the lobby of Communications Building A. Collie was responsible for this. I scurried back to the place where I slept and would now hide. I could no longer bring myself to think of Alamo House as home.

The first hint I had that the day's catastrophes were not at an end was the robin's egg blue, classically restored Mercedes Benz parked in front of the house. In the rear window was a parking sticker for the River Oaks Country Club. River Oaks is a Houston neighborhood hermetically sealed against incomes under six figures and skin tones darker than a tennis flush. A middle-aged Chicano driver sat in the front seat. I had to break through the cluster gathered at the front door peering outside to get into the house.

I hurtled upstairs already knowing what I'd find: Collie packing. Fayrene was in the tasseled room helping her.

"So," I asked, my voice alive with something that felt composed of equal parts rage, betrayal, and wicked mischief. "Dancing back to Fairchild Manor?"

I looked to Fayrene expecting surprise. It wasn't there. Nor was there any on Collie's face. They glanced at each other. For the first time Collie looked to Fayrene for help.

"She's going back to Houston," Fayrene answered me, though she never took her eyes off of Collie.

"In a chauffeur-driven Mercedes," I pointed out.

Collie jerked her bony shoulders and the corners of her mouth up. "I'm leaving," she said as if that were supposed to absolve her of everything. When I didn't say anything, she added, in her life-is-a-cabaret voice, "Gotta keep on rolling, keep on pushing. That old, lonesome highway is a calling me again." She arched her eyebrows at me to include me in on the joke, but I just stared back at her. My life wasn't currently any goddamned cabaret.

I watched in smoldering silence as she pulled out her "garbs"— the white satin Patsy Cline western shirt and fringed skirt with the red embroidery; the Isadora Duncan tunic and scarves; Vivien Leigh's fluffy white bathrobe; Janis Joplin's psychedelic tie-dyed outfit; the Marilyn Monroe spike heels, sundress, and white blond wig—and packed them away, every one of them.

A spurt of jealousy gushed into the bath of caustic elements I was seething in. Collie had no serious worries. She was going back to a cushy, assured future. She had the freedom to pursue any whim that crossed her mind. Meantime, I had "Greensleeves" boinging in my head and a grudge nudie show starring my own dimpled body hanging in a public lobby. Collie was packing up to sail off back to River Oaks opulence and I had to walk half a mile for a shower and machete my way through a garbage-strewn alley to use a toilet. After toying with any betendriled, earringed male who captured her fancy, she'd end up safely married to some adoring stockbroker who would spend his life pampering his pet bohemian. I couldn't even hang on to Roger Halpern and was losing my grip on my minimum-wage job.

Collie and Fayrene shimmered like an oasis in the blood-colored light from Collie's red scarf-draped lamp. Bit by bit, the scarves came down, the pillows were boxed up, the fringe and tassels were thrown away and Alamo's wavy green Sheetrock walls were exposed. Blinking and biting my lip, I siphoned off the tears puddling above my lids as Collie and her voluptuous room disappeared. In the end, Collie was just a rich girl with a few stray rebellious tendencies. Fayrene left with a loaded box and headed downstairs to the Benz. The Benz.

Collie stopped and stood square in the middle of the French doors. "The only way to travel, huh?" She raised her eyebrows and nodded out toward where the chauffeur was rearranging her belongings so that they all fit in the trunk.

I'll admit it—before Collie spoke, my heart was ready to be softened. Anger, jealousy, betrayal, and rejection are not the easiest emotions in the world to sustain. I was ready to flush them. I would have, could have, if Collie had made any half-assed attempt at apology, even explanation. Saying "The only way to travel" to someone whose only means of conveyance was currently wrapped around a scorched pecan tree stump did not qualify in the reconciliation department. Collie's staggeringly flip comment took me so by surprise that I was sabotaged into a snarlingly direct statement.

"You pimped me, Collie. Me and Fayrene. All of us." My voice quivered with the rage I was trying to deny. Once it was out, though, there was no use pretending it didn't exist. It all spewed forth. "What were we to you, Weirdos of the Week? Are we all going to become amusing little vignettes to regale your Junior League friends with back in River Oaks? Was Alamo just an out-of-the-way stop on your personal bus ride, Collie? Huh? Was that it? Huh?"

She shrugged. She shrugged! She stood there in her gaunt and luminescent beauty and shrugged. That tore it. I went for the jugular.

"You are such a phony, Collie. Playing the bohemian, passing out all that great advice about men, lecturing on The Axiom. Party with the least interest. It must have been a whole lot easier for *you* not to be terribly interested with Fairchild Manor to retreat to. Hey, *real* great advice. Obviously you apply it to your 'friends' too. You'll be pleased to know that Roger is marrying someone who looks exactly like you. Kind of a nice tribute, huh? Couldn't have the real thing so he took the next best . . ."

"Roger!" Collie exploded the name incredulously. "Roger is so immaterial. Is he why you're mad? Is that the . . ."

"No!" I cut her off. "No. I'm mad because you used us, used Alamo for your little tour into oddity. I'm mad because you get to cruise back to River Oaks. Because I have to live here with the weirdos and the frat rats and the plumbing that doesn't work and . . ." I bit down on the inside of my mouth to keep from crying. "Because I don't get to leave."

Suddenly, Collie could have been some sorority girl from a prim and perfect background with a BMW and five hundred a month to spend at Benetton's gawking at the oddball chaos of my life.

The tears seeped up again. I chomped down on the inside of my mouth and sealed off the pain. I couldn't handle it. I froze out the pain and what was causing it. I froze out Collie. "Bye." I walked into my room.

She didn't say anything for a minute. Pausing for dramatic effect, I figured, and that made me despise her. Then, softly, "You shouldn't crucify your friends."

"Friend?" I asked in a neutral, dead voice. "You were right, I never even knew you."

"You knew me." She closed the French doors between our rooms.

I listened to Fayrene and Collie clomp up and down the stairs while the chauffeur stayed at the car packing away the props Collie had used during her extended Alamo tour. I could hear everything they said.

"Can I help you with anything else?" Fayrene whined when they'd finished.

"No, thanks, that's about it. I'll take the rest of the stuff with me on the plane tomorrow after I get through checking out of school."

"Want me to get you a beer from the machine?" Fayrene's voice reclaimed its cowering Waco twang.

"No, thanks. I guess I just need to be alone for a minute." Collie sounded a bit shaky herself.

"I could sweep for you," Fayrene offered with a cringing servility that made me want to scream at her.

"No!" Collie snapped. "I don't want you sweeping for me or getting me beers or anything. I just want to be left alone."

You bitch.

"Uh, oh-kie," Fayrene whimpered. Alamo's ancient floorboards groaned beneath Fayrene's heavy footfall. I winced as the doorknob turned. I was not up to facing a five-foot-five spineless slug. Fayrene stepped in. Her face was varnished with tears. That annoyed me. I was managing to keep *my* loose ends tucked in.

"She's really leaving," Fayrene choked out.

I could feel Collie next door waiting for my answer. I had to get away. I stalked out, pausing beside Fayrene to hiss, "She was never really here."

Downstairs, Judith had a brood settled around her and was asking, "How does the group feel about what Toni just said?"

Esme answered. "I think she's blocking a lot of feelings about her father and projecting them onto anyone in a position of authority. That's why she can't deal with losing control."

I slid into the greasy armchair at the edge of the group. For the first time, I was in the mood for the Judith Feldman Bitch and Moan Hour.

Constance turned to me and whispered, "Is Collie really leaving? Was that really her chauffeur?" I nodded yes to both questions.

"Should we address Toni's concerns here?" Judith asked Constance pointedly.

Constance smiled and lightly touched her closed lips with the tip of her finger. For a few more minutes they chewed the cud of Toni's authority complex. The comments grew progressively less detached and more personal until they zeroed right in on Mr. Pfeifer, Toni's father. Finally, Toni cracked. Sobbing, she admitted,

"Yes, I hated that self-righteous, hypocritical, bible-thumping son of a bitch. The only person I hated more though was my mother, who bowed and scraped to the son of a bitch."

"We hear you," Judith cooed, a pleased look lighting her face. Barb scooted over close and put her arms around Toni, who was snorting and hiccuping. I was riveted. As though the quadrupedal sounds of Toni's misery had called Fayrene out of hiding, she oozed into the group, tears still rolling down her doughy cheeks.

"Fayrene," Judith asked in her smarmy take-your-troubles-to-Jesus voice, "would you like to talk about it?"

Fayrene nodded and gulped several times, stopping to take a few swigs of Eagle Brand condensed milk from the can she'd brought with her. Calmed enough to speak, she proceeded. I knew who her tears were for, but since the name Cordelia Mohoric was anathema in Judith's gatherings, Fayrene did a quick substitute and bawled, "Rashid never called."

"That slime," Esme burst out.

"What level of commitment had you reached in your relationship?" Judith guided the discussion into a more productive avenue.

"The deepest," Fayrene whimpered.

"Are you saying that you and Rashid had intercourse?"

Fayrene nodded guiltily as if she was confessing in front of Waco First Baptist prior to rededicating her life to Jesus. She stared down at her hands, wadded up like old Kleenex in her lap.

"What are you feeling now?" Judith probed. "Rejection? Anger?"

"I guess," Fayrene mumbled in mucoid misery.

"What had you been expecting from the relationship?" Judith spoke to her gently.

Fayrene shrugged and squashed her mouth into one side of her face, then the other.

No one spoke. Fayrene's nose turned red. Two spots flamed on her cheeks and the tears rolled in earnest again.

"What had you been expecting from the relationship?" Judith repeated.

Fayrene sniffed back her grief and wiped her hand over her cheeks. She hung her head and tears dripped off her nose onto her knotted hands. No one breathed. Then, in a puny and muffled voice, she answered the question. "Friendship, I guess." Louder, she affirmed her response. "I just wanted a friend."

That pulled everyone's switch and eyes all around me misted over. Mine went first.

"So we're all wallowing in it again?"

I hadn't heard Collie come in. Her hair was swept back in a ponytail with a perky fringe of bangs up front. She had on a short-sleeved blouse with a Peter Pan collar and a full skirt, Bass Weejun loafers and anklets. She looked like the perfect fifties coed. I was not in any mood, however, to appreciate the fun she was having with fashion. Everyone gaped, hanging in suspended animation like atomic particles trying to decide on a valence. Ever the puppy dog, Fayrene perked up visibly.

"I wonder," Collie mused aloud. "Have any of you stopped to consider that for the last twenty years since people have been therapizing things to death we've created some of the most screwed-up humans ever to inhabit a planet. I mean, is there a correlation?"

Something surged through Collie's emaciated body. I probably could have figured out what it was if I hadn't felt such hostility toward her. But, at that moment both she and Judith repelled me in equal measure.

Collie glared at Fayrene. "What are you blubbering about? Because that Mideastern scum sucker boinked you and now he doesn't want to know your name?"

"Collie," Judith interrupted ferociously, "Fayrene has undergone a psychically devastating episode."

" 'Psychically devastating,' my butt," Collie countered. "It's only as 'devastating' as she makes it. Looks like, with your help, she might just be able to run it up into one major scarring catastrophe." She looked back at Fayrene. "But it's not. Sex never is. Never can be. It's too damned funny. If you want to cry, get a newspaper. But don't fucking cry about fucking." Acetylene sparks leaped out of Collie's eyes with a heat hot enough to resolder the connection between her and Fayrene.

"Listen," she went on, speaking to Fayrene. "I'm going to let you in on a little secret: Everyone's got a tragedy. Everyone. Even those yahoos across the street, if they put their minds to it hard enough, even they could find something in their lives to leak a few wet ones over."

"That may be true, Collie," Judith said, "but don't you imagine that it's more comfortable 'leaking' them in a baby blue Benz?" It stung to hear Judith take my position.

Collie didn't even glance at Judith. She went right on staring at Fayrene. "There is no hierarchy of suffering," she said. "The only extra points you get for hurting are the ones you award to yourself, so don't bother. It may be true that people with money or looks or whatever may not hurt as bad. It may also be true that the Homecoming Queen's mother gave her an enema on the kitchen table every day of her life and Bub Wilkers across the street there may be dying of leukemia. But we'll never know. The only safe assumption you can make is that if a person is upright and thinking, they're ripped apart about something."

Fayrene's eyes were big as Peppermint Patties when Collie finished. She may not have processed text and subtext, but she had definitely been warmed by the heat of Collie's message and by the fact that it had been for her. So, when Collie said, "Fay, Mary Jo, could I talk to you guys for a minute," Fayrene bolted out of her chair. Me, I was nailed in place by animosity and by the stares that turned my way waiting for my answer.

"Can't," I finally said, breaking through the tractor beams of attention and vaulting to my feet. "Have to go somewhere right now." It was true. Alamo had become a murky tank for me strewn with hooks. I had to get out before I bit on another one and took in someone's line.

I went to the garage, "borrowed" Constance's bike, and pedaled furiously into the night. I did not want to, would not allow myself to think about any of it. I'd known where Tommy lived since the first day we worked together. I'd wanted to go there since he'd left the library. I turned off Pecan and arced across campus over to Speedway. Shuttle buses blasted by spewing carbon monoxide in my face. I pumped on past the fire station and post office on Forty-second, down the hill there, across the light at Forty-fifth, and I was in Tommy's neighborhood. I took a right onto Cicada.

He lived in a hovel behind a hovel, a garage apartment with the emphasis on the garage. I stood outside with dead leaves and pecan hulls up to my ankles and looked through the window. He sat in a rocker with a couple of the back braces gone, his fingers curled around the neck of a guitar, mouthing words. I wondered what in hell I was doing and walked up to the door. He answered like we'd had a long-standing date.

"So, what's up at Sunnybrook Farm?" Golden light streamed around his back.

I told him "mucho de nada" and he asked me in. His place was littered with costumes from his various stage incarnations: Kenny of Kenny and the Attractions had left a pair of saddle shoes and a zoot suit jacket; a headband and a pair of maracas were all that remained of Chuy of Los Nuevo Wavos; Viscount Tommy Berlin had deposited a collection of eyeliners and nail polishes along with some white flannel trousers and a few tennis sweaters; Little Lyndon appeared to be in the process of gathering together some buckaroo paraphernalia. The thought flitted across my mind that Tommy was a male Collie, but I evicted the little insight asking it never to return.

I told Tommy I'd come to use his shower. He showed me into a mildewed little closet and tracked down his one clean towel. When I was through, he gave me some old jeans and a T-shirt of his to wear. I left the T-shirt untucked to hide the fact that I couldn't get his jeans to button around my belly.

We made popcorn and watched an old war movie with Van Johnson because Van reminded Tommy of his hero, Durwood Kirby. Mostly I just sat and watched the picture and listened to a continuous mental replay of Collie's last few scenes. Tommy kept working on his Little Lyndon repertoire, singing "Love Is Blue," except that he substituted "goo" for "blue": "Goo, goo, my world is goo." My world felt pretty gooey. I was grateful to Tommy for just letting me sit there, catatonic, and goon at his TV. Without my even asking, he pulled out the sleeper sofa and fixed a bed for me, which I also accepted with gratitude. I couldn't face Collie's final farewell when she left the next morning.

For most of the night, I lay on the lumpy sleeper listening to the comfortingly familiar sound of Tommy snoring across the room and trying to uncross the emotional wires shorting out inside of me. Early that morning, with just enough thin winter light leaking in to illuminate Tommy in the posture I was most familiar with—fast asleep, his hair sticking out like a newborn chick's—it hit me. All of Collie's various personas came home to roost and I finally realized what they'd all had in common: madness, untimely death, or suicide.

I grabbed my dirty clothes and jumped into them, oblivious of the goose bumps raised when I stepped onto the oil-stained concrete floor. I left Tommy a note and made a running takeoff. For, in that moment of cognition, I had realized who Collie was doing yesterday when she'd staged her farewell confrontation with Judith. The ponytail, the Peter Pan collar, the demons shrieking beneath the tiara of the Golden Princess, the girl who seemed to have it all, but who had only sorrow—Sylvia Plath. Of course, she'd been doing Sylvia Plath.

I pedaled faster, harder, until my lungs burned and my thighs felt quivery. I dropped the bike in the front yard in a hillock of dried vomit and raced into the house. No one was up yet. I stopped dead still in the living room at the precise spot where Collie had stood last night and listened to my heart pound in my ears. I wiped my sleeve across my nose which was running copiously, took several deep breaths, and debated whether I could go forward. Whether I could walk into the kitchen with its giant black widow of a gas stove sitting there, waiting. Enticing. I thought of Collie's dead, flat voice yesterday and considered going up to get

Fayrene to come with me. No, walk, I ordered myself, and my feet obeyed.

I made it to the kitchen door. It was closed. I swallowed hard. The kitchen door, in all the time I'd lived at Alamo, had never been closed. I held out a numb arm and pushed against it.

The windowless kitchen was dark, especially the corner holding the stove. I sucked in a long breath, reached out for the light, and switched it on. My hand had obeyed, but my eyes were screwed shut when the light went on. Fear hammered my pulse up to a manic level. I forced my lids apart and directed my vision toward the stove. Toward the floor in front of it.

Roaches scattered in every direction across that floor making for baseboards and crevices. But that was all. Light shone back dully from the scratched and pitted linoleum.

I breathed again and tore upstairs. On the second floor, I skidded past the telephone. Her door was slightly ajar. I ran to it and burst in. The room was empty. All that was left was the stink of clove. Collie was gone.

· 20 ·

DID I SAY Alamo was in a slump before? Well, I was wrong. It was only after Collie's departure that I learned what a slump was. We got down so low that we could roll over and lick a lizard's hindquarters. Even the SUKs got tired of oppressing us because we bore their taunts and humiliations with such stoic indifference. Everyone in the house except for Judith and Hillary was making getaway plans.

Only Fayrene actually seemed content, in a low-keyed, philosophical way. Ever since that last night when Collie pulled her out of Judith's therapy session, she had been different, suffused by an enduring strength she hadn't had before. I was dying to ask her what Collie had told her, but I refused. I knew that was just what Collie expected me to do. I wasn't going to be her pawn anymore.

As for school, I could no longer face it. My consumption of thrillers with black and red covers rose alarmingly. Occasionally I could force myself to put in a few hours at the library. But, all alone up there on five, I started missing Tommy, then Roger, then Collie, then even Smythe and Dorothy, who had both sailed off for San Clemente. Their last day of work, a big party was held on three by all the other lifers. I wasn't invited, of course, but I listened to it via the elevator shaft and felt left out of even that.

The only bright spot on this bleak horizon was Tommy, and I was consciously not letting that flame burn too brightly. We alternated between acting like either Romper Room playmates or ancient tribal enemies, either cavorting madly or eyeing one another warily, each of us unsure of the other's motives. Certainly neither one of us was going to be the first to risk actual physical contact. At times we'd break down and just be humans. It was during one of these rare moments that I told Tommy how pissed off I was at Collie, what a phony she was. That kicked something off in him.

"Do you know that in all the time I worked at the library," he told me, "I never once visited the museum? Took the tour? I finally did it last week. It was worse than I thought it would be. There's this slide show about old Lyndon that seems like it was written for Charlton Heston. But they couldn't get Chuck to play the part so here's this chump with big ears and chicken lips standing in. I mean, it had the swelling-chord soundtrack and a picture of Lyndon teaching little Mexican schoolchildren. The only trick they missed was water into wine.

"I just sat there watching this Disney version of the most efficient political machine ever put on earth and thinking about what the Bopper had actually done, what the man had accomplished." Tommy looked at me with this expression of earnest puzzlement on his face that broke my heart.

"Okay, so LBJ *was* a phony," he finally blurted out. "So he *was* anything that would get him a round of applause, a few column inches, or a vote. He still did the right things. He got the bills passed. He made a lot of lives better. He may have been an unevolved political shark, but he did a few of the right things. Do you see what I'm getting at?"

Only too well and in too many ways. Tommy's story was a parable for me. It sliced through the hardened layer of my resentment. I had to admit that Collie too had done a few of the right things. However questionable her motives, she had managed to transform Alamo's misfits from passive lumps into spirited humans.

Still, it's a lot easier to be abstract and forgiving about a president than it is about someone who's slept with your boyfriend. Okay, ex-boyfriend. Still.

The night he told me that story, I went back to Alamo and found the house deathly silent. Only the wispy sound of Fayrene's infernal humming wafted through the halls.

"Where is everyone?" I asked her.

"Library. Studying for finals," she informed me.

I tried again to figure out what was so different about my roommate. It wasn't that she seemed particularly happy. She was too distant for that. It was almost as if she were beyond both happiness and sadness. She had this kind of majesty that made it impossible for me to imagine her ever moping her way through a twelve-pack of Little Debbies again. She seemed transfigured, that was it.

"Want to go swimming?"

"No, I do not want to go swimming," I snapped. "All right, tell me," I sighed, surrendering to the inevitable.

"Tell you what?"

"Tell me what Collie told you before she left."

"I think that's for Collie to share."

"Don't make me pry," I begged. But Fayrene merely kept on with her beatified smile as she sorted through the Treat Box, tossing crinkly bags into the trash.

"Need a few cans of Eagle Brand?" she asked, as she chunked them into the trash.

"I think I liked you better as a catatonic."

She smiled and waltzed out of the room with her *Fantasia* swimsuit and a towel tossed jauntily over one shoulder.

As the afternoon wore on, I lost myself in *Death of the Homicidal Kind*. Try as I might to resist, the sound level outside kept intruding. Finally, I was forced to get vertical and check on the situation.

Across the street, Bub Wilkers and Schlubber were unfurling a giant banner across the parking quagmire. Recent rains had transformed the unpaved lot into tire-rutted muck. It was criss-crossed with boards being used as walkways. The banner read, BLOW OFF FINALS BLOW OUT, and was illustrated with two bottles of MD 20/20, smoke curling out of the tops.

The SUK's Mad Dog 20/20 Finals Party was a thing of legend. It was the SUKs' annual academic suicide ritual and they liked to take everyone within a ten-block radius of the house with them. Constance had spoken of it in tones of dread. Alamo residents had tolerated this assault on the bell curve for years, gobbling Di-Gel and doubling up on appointments with their therapists at Student Counseling. From what I'd heard, though, the Mad Dog Finals Party didn't usually take place until later in Dead Week, on the precise night before most finals were held. I wondered why they were being so conservative this year and holding the bash early.

Hillary provided the answer at dinner that night. "Oh yeah, we were talking at the last Campus Co-op League Meeting about maybe circulating a petition to block the Mad Dog Party this year. Then someone said they'd heard from someone on the Interfraternity Council that the SUKs are on scholastic probation. Seems they all did so bad on midterms that if they really do blow off finals, they'll blow off the house too. They're having the party early this year so they can actually study for finals and maybe pass a few. They have to or the house will be suspended. Pass the zucchini loaf, please."

That semester's Mad Dog Finals Party may have been born premature, but at nine that evening it came into the world screaming.

Ee-yow-w-w-w!!! I wish they all could be California girls!!!

The major suspect in *Death of the Homicidal Kind*, the one I'd put my money on, had just turned up in the detective's hot water heater closet with an ice pick through the jugular. I had to nail another suspect before the whole book ran away from me, but the noise outside was interfering with my concentration. I went downstairs and headed for the dining room where I could put a few more walls between myself and the SUKs.

I paused on the porch and watched the party preparations in progress. Jasper Bub Wilkers was supervising. A couple of cauldrons had been set up on boards spanning the mud and Opie was methodically opening gallon bottles of chromosome-altering MD 20/20 and dumping them into the vats. Kytes was pulping lemons and limes with his bare hands and squeezing the citrus mess into the tubs.

Schlubber appeared dragging a garden hose through the mud. He trickled a thin stream of water into each cauldron with his brothers watching carefully. When approximately a cup of water had been dribbled into the thirty-gallon container, Kytes yelled out, "Whoa! Don't dilute it too much or it'll take all fuckin' night to get the Grub Queens *so-o-o-o drunk*." All four of them chimed in on the last two words trilling them into the cold night in wavery falsettos. Remembering their female co-vivants, Bub yelled orders to a freshfrat and he scampered away. He reappeared carrying two ten-pound sacks of sugar. One was dumped into each cauldron, stirred, and their special party punch was ready. The band was just arriving as I went inside: The decibel level had only begun to climb.

The whole Alamo crew was gathered in the dining room clumped over books, note cards, rough drafts, monographs, and Xeroxed handouts. Everyone was busily highlighting, underlining, notating, editing, rewriting, and memorizing. It was the graduate women's version of a Mad Dog Finals Party.

Esme and Constance barely glanced up at me as I settled in with my mystery. Duk Soo beamed me a fast but blinding grin before refurrowing her brow and plowing back into *The Inversions of the Dominant Seventh*. Judith had a cup of black coffee by her side and was frowning at the notes her dissertation committee had made on her latest draft. By my rough calculations it would have been number six in what appeared to be an endless series.

Josie was propped back in her chair with her feet up on the table exposing the pages of her civil procedures text to light for the first time. Hillary tapped her on the shoulder and, startled, Josie teetered precariously close to tumping over for a moment.

"Could you either please stop smoking or study in a private place?" Hillary asked her. Josie crushed out her cigarette with a theatrical flair and picked up the long-neck that was sweating water rings onto the table in the airless, overheated room. Then she plunked the bottle back down and pulled a Slim Jim out of her shirt pocket. With much crinkling, she unwrapped and began gnawing on the chunk of fat and beef by-products.

"Ew, how can you eat that?" Hillary provided a satisfyingly predictable response. "Especially when you're drinking beer? God, do you have any idea of the nitrosamines that are flooding your system at this very moment?"

Josie held the stick of animal offal in front of her and snapped off another bite like a frog catching a fly.

Judith peered at them over the tops of her glasses. She maintained that she needed them for reading, but they were almost clear plastic and seemed designed more for disciplinary effect than vision correction. Anyway, she peered at the two squabblers until Hillary retreated to her books shaking her head in disgust at the carcinogen factory across the table from her.

As soon as that little brush fire was stamped out, Barb and Toni began spatting off in the corner. They hissed at each other in low voices.

"People," Judith said menacingly in their direction. Toni shot her back the kind of look that explains why policemen are loath to intervene in domestic squabbles.

Alexis flounced through the room trailing clouds of Diorissima behind her. She settled in beside the downstairs phone located at the edge of the dining room and proceeded to conduct a very loud, very lengthy interview—Hartwell-style.

"Hi, Melinda? This is Alexis Hartwell with the *Texan*, do you have a few minutes to talk now? . . . Great. What I had in mind was a feature about what it's like to be a six-foot-four champion women's basketball player. First of all, is it hard getting dates? . . . It's not! Well I wish you'd tell me your secret. The last five guys I went out with were such losers. I just found out today that Donald has been sleeping with my news lab partner. You think that doesn't hurt? I don't know what it is, men are so threatened by me. They respond to the exotic, the siren within me, then they can only perceive me as an archetype. They never get to Alexis Hartwell, the person. But wait, enough about me. We're doing you here. What about motivation? What motivates Melinda Gaines, premiere ladies basketball player? . . . You too! I remember when I was in first grade watching Huntley and Brinkley and saying to myself, 'Someday it's going to be Huntley and Hartwell.' I remember that! And I was only, what? . . ."

"Six years old," Esme called out to her. We'd been treated to the What Motivates Alexis Hartwell monologue before.

"Do you mind?" Alexis asked huffily, turning her back to the crowd at the table.

We had just managed to block out Alexis's stream of revelations when the band across the street began warming up. As the amplified chords trembled through the house, the leashes on simmering tempers snapped and the group got surly.

"Will you shut up, Alexis?" Esme screamed. "We know more than we ever wanted to about your motivation and love life and Five-Year Plan and every other damned thing in your life."

"Melinda," Alexis spoke evenly into the receiver. "Don't move a muscle. I'm going to hang up and call you back on another phone." She looked at Esme and said pointedly, "There's too much interference on this one."

She banged down the receiver, stood grandly, and addressed us: "I can hardly wait to move out of this dump. You all have been jealous of me from the day I moved in here. You're such a bunch of losers that you can't stand having anyone around who isn't a loser. Anyone who's not going to end up in some moldy classroom or library or some dumpy place like Alamo House, because that's where all of you are headed and you know it. Alamo House is where you all belong. I never fit in here because I wasn't a loser. The rest of you fit in perfectly. I mean, Christ, none of you even has a boyfriend." She stopped, used her pinky to remove tiny smears of lipstick from the corners of her mouth, held her head up proudly, pivoted on her heel, and stomped out.

The deathless strains of "Louie, Louie," that mandatory party anthem for naughty boys, pounded into the silence that followed Alexis's indictment. Breaking with tradition, Bub made it painfully easy to decipher every word of the version that he rasped out:

Ah u.t., u.t.-tie,
Aye-yi-yi-yi
We gotta grub now
Well a duck's a duck and a suk's a suk
One likes to swim and the other to fuck!!!

Bub's keen rhyming ability failed to cheer anyone. The thudding bass loosened plaster causing a fine sifting of dust to rain down on our heads. We all just sat there blasted into a stupor by noise, Alexis's too-true diatribe, and the futility of it all. It was sad and alarming. I wondered what Collie would have said to Alexis. I started to make a joke about organizing a chapter of Losers Anonymous, but it was too feeble and too close to true to say out loud. I just didn't have Collie's talent for putting the starch into limp people.

Constance shut the book in front of her. A puff of dust rose as it closed. Esme shoveled the papers in front of her into a file folder. Judith took off her dust-coated glasses.

"Anyone care to trek over to Belmont for a shower?" Josie asked. The Co-op League still hadn't found a plumber willing to take on the repair of hundred-year-old plumbing for what the League could afford to pay.

"Might as well," Constance said. "We won't be getting much more studying done tonight."

Murmurs of assent followed. I declined. Everyone gathered up towels, washcloths, shampoo, conditioner, Buf-Pufs, loofahs, tweezers, razors, shaving cream, hand lotion, body lotion, face lotion, baby powder, deodorant, antiperspirant, Tampax, Kotex, and panty liners and trooped outside for the hygiene excursion. A wave of sound rolled in when they opened the door.

Ah u.t., u.t.-tie, hey, we gotta grub now!!

I trundled upstairs and sat in the dark letting the music bludgeon me.

Well, uh gimme a pi phi, a tri delt, a gamma
Cuz I got the nail and I want to hammuh!!

In the parking lot below me, Bub and Schlubber were having a chugging contest. Bub won and let out a victory howl. One by one, the other brothers joined in until they were all baying at the moon like, well, like mad dogs. I lay back, stared at the ceiling, and thought about the past semester from the moment I'd first walked into the olive-drab dowager. Collie figured in nearly every frame worth remembering from then on. I thought of her limbering up at breakfast decked out in a leotard and an assortment of Isadora Duncan strangler scarves. In that shot, reflecting Collie's golden glow, the graduate women of Alamo looked like a bunch of madcap, brainy bohemians. In the takes without Collie, particularly the one tonight with Alexis telling us off, we looked exactly like what she'd called us, losers. Oddball, bookworm misfits with little more than the obscurity of a dissertation topic to distinguish us.

Had it all, all those times with Collie, been fraudulent? Like LBJ? I pricked myself. I didn't have a chance to mull on those questions because Fayrene whipped in at that moment and threw on the lights.

"Oh, sorry. Didn't think you were in here." Her hair was still wet. The whole room filled up with the smell of Wella Balsam conditioner. Every exposed bit of her was pink and flush with vitality.

"Have you been swimming all this time?" I asked, oppressed by her new exuberance.

She smiled benevolently at my whimsical jest. "No, I did some work on the new retrieval program I'm writing, did the Par Course twice, then I went swimming."

"Making up for lost time?"

She beamed and nodded, "Yes."

"I was afraid of that."

"Mary Jo, I know how it is when you're in the dumps, you don't even want to get out of bed. But Collie was right, that's exactly the time you need all those endorphins the most."

"You want to save these Mohoric insights for the biography you will no doubt be writing?" The edge on my voice was sharper than I'd intended and a bit of Fayrene's bloom faded. She sagged momentarily onto her bed. Then, abruptly, the pink returned to her cheeks and kept on returning until they were flaming a candy apple red.

"You don't know anything about Collie," she blurted out.

"It's not like I didn't give her a chance to fill me in." I kept my voice casual, but it was an effort.

"She wanted to tell you."

"Tell me what?"

"Who she was. Why she was here. Why she had to leave."

"And you know all that. She told you, but couldn't tell me."

Fayrene nodded. "She could talk to me because I'm not . . ." Her rosebud lips squirmed around, finally forming the word, ". . . normal."

Though I didn't understand, my hostility cooled.

"You're normal," she explained. "Collie didn't think you'd understand. She was afraid you'd reject her."

"*I* would reject *her*?" I repeated, flabbergasted. "Let me make sure I've got this right. The Golden Girl from River Oaks? The chameleon goddess from one of the richest, most powerful families in the country? She was afraid that I would reject her?" I started getting mad all over again at the snow job Collie had done on Fayrene.

Fayrene handed me a scrap of paper with a phone number written on it. "Well, anyway. That's where she is if you want to call. It's a clinic." For the first time Fayrene's newfound equanimity faltered.

I stared at the number. "What kind of clinic?"

"They think she's crazy. That's why she came here. It was her last chance. But they said she wasn't improving."

"That's perfect," I said once the shock wore off and I figured out what Collie was pulling. "A secret mental condition. The perfect dramatic ending. Count on Collie for a big finish." I wadded the scrap of paper into my pocket.

Fayrene shook her head, pityingly. She looked away. "Collie was right. She said you wouldn't understand." Fayrene studied me. "You really don't know what it is to truly hate yourself, do you?"

"What has Collie got to hate? She's beautiful, rich, men drop at her feet . . ."

Fayrene closed her eyes in disbelief. "How stupid. People don't live in their bodies. They live in their minds." She stared at me, perplexed, then turned to the window.

I stood beside her but didn't really see what was happening down on the muddy parking lot. I thought about Collie and Marilyn Monroe and Sylvia Plath. I'd always thought people who killed themselves were kidding in some way. Fayrene was right. As depressed as I may have ever gotten, I'd never come close to wanting to extinguish Mary Jo Steadman. I didn't know at all what that

was like. I thought about Collie's personas, the brassy theatricality
that underpinned all of them. It suddenly seemed much more like
desperation.

Ah, u.t., u.t.-tie
Aye-yi-yi-yi
Hey, we gotta grub now!!

"What is he doing down there?" Fayrene asked, directing my
attention to the SUKs.

Kytes, always a bit more eager to prove himself than the others, was executing a quick squat-thrust on the board he and his
date had been dancing on. Once prone, he performed a classic 'gator. He was in mid-hump when the board slid out from
beneath him like a greased tiddly-wink, tumping him and his
partner into the muck. Even I felt a wince of sympathy for
the little toad as he landed, face down, in all that motor oil-
enriched mud.

But Kytes, acting brilliantly on some idiot savant insight,
turned the whole situation around. He didn't stand up and grimly
wipe the sludge off to an accompanying chorus of catcalls. No,
Kytes stayed right where he was and *wallowed* in the oozing stuff.
Wallowed, then rolled over and *bayed*. His teeth gleamed starkly
white against the black mud streaking his face as he let out the
quintessential feral, mad dog howl. His date, plopped down in the
mud on her expensively upholstered keister, stared in dumbfounded wonder as the ferrety Kytes let loose with a mastiff wail
that drowned out the band.

The band stopped playing. The brothers tiptoed across the
catwalk of boards and surrounded Kytes. Kytes stared up at them,
a dachsund encircled by a pack of wolves, and cut loose with his
blood-curdler yell again. A signal, probably originating with Bub
Wilkers and transmitted by pheromone down the dominance hierarchy, passed through the brethren in that instant.

The signal said that this was to be one of those group-sanctioned times of lunatic spontaneity; one of those carefully measured out moments that they would look back on and cherish in later life. It would stand as proof that, somewhere beneath the vested pinstripe, the heart of a real rip-and-tear renegade, a total wild ass, once beat. The notion of renegade spontaneity is, of course, completely ludicrous when speaking of members of a group more closely regimented than an order of Trappist monks. Still that illusion had to be cultivated and, in Kytes's lucky stroke of in-tuition, an opportunity to meet the quota of wild-assed lunacies presented itself.

Bub Wilkers fell to his knees beside Kytes and began baying along with him. Once the official sanction had been given, the rest of the brothers went down like a herd of wounded buffalos. They got down there and commenced to *root*. Pretty soon they were slagging each other with handfuls of liquid earth. Then the mud wrestling started.

"Oh man," an exuberant and encrusted Schlubber yelled out. "This is going to become legend!" Then he leapt back into the fray envisioning, no doubt, his future reputation as one of the fabled Sigma Upsilon Kappa Mad Dog Mud Wrestlers.

"The tragedy of hormonal excess."

Fayrene nodded at my comment unable to tear her eyes away from the mucky spectacle. I picked up *Death of the Homicidal Kind* and went back to reading. I had a lot of escaping to do. Try as I might, though, I couldn't stop thinking about Collie. What if everything she'd told Fayrene was true? What if it wasn't? How much did it really matter? I was trying to figure that one out when Fayrene squealed.

"Oh no!"

I jumped up behind her and echoed her sentiments. For, just rounding the corner, was the Alamo contingent. Their faces beamed from the combination of a good scrubbing and the possi-bility that the silence that greeted them might mean that the Mad

Dog Party had broken up early. Steam from their shower-warmed, clean, powdered, depilated, and deodorized bodies perfumed the night air. Crystal droplets of water fell from their glistening, still wet hair.

The SUKs spotted them long before they took notice of the SUKs. Bub was the first to rise out of the primordial ooze and scoop up a Guernsey-sized patty of mud. One by one, working swiftly and silently, the others followed suit and moved into place at the edge of the parking bog, where they waited.

I cranked furiously on the window ready to shout out a warning. The handle came off in my fist. Toni had repaired it last week. The other windows she'd worked on were stuck shut. Fayrene and I could only watch helplessly.

The shower patrol was ambushed just as they drew abreast of the parking lot. As the Suks rushed them, they froze, unable to make sense of these mud-covered Cro-Magnons running toward them. In that instant of hesitation, they were lost. Bub led the attack. He dumped a slurpy handful on top of Constance's gleaming head, then hugged the mesmerized medievalist in a mucky embrace. The SUKs swarmed over their pristine prey. Kytes unloaded his haul on Judith's head, then hugged *and* kissed her. Schlubber glopped a big gushy muffin on Hillary and engulfed her skinny frame in a wave of mud and blubber. Opie grabbed Esme. Everyone else swamped a partner and hugged them until it was impossible to tell our *Homo sapiens* from their *Homo erecti*.

It brought to mind the rape of the Sabine women. Our housemates' shrieks pierced our hearts, but it was over before we could move. As the marauding band ran off, Bub called over his shoulder, "Bet you girls are sorry you ever dug up *our* parking lot!"

Stunned horror stretched Fayrene's face. In the time I'd known her, I'd witnessed that face attain every shade imaginable from the palest baby butt pink to flaming incarnadine. Now I saw it achieve a hue I'd imagined to be completely beyond Fayrene's spectrum—rage-pale clam. In a voice that trembled through clenched teeth, she said, "We have to do something." Each word came out whole and separate, with an equally ferocious emphasis.

"You're right," I agreed as if she'd just explained gravity.

"We'll have a party. For Alamo House. For us."

"For Collie." The name slid out as smoothly as if I'd been planning to say it all along.

THE TROOPS RETURNED muddied but unbowed. Judith immediately began lobbying for what she called a "dramatic representation of the dehumanizing forces at work here." She wanted everyone to let the mud dry on themselves, then to stand outside as a kind of *tableau vivante*, all of them caked with dried muck.

"What a stupid idea," Fayrene blurted out, her cheeks still pale with outrage. "Do you think those animals care how dirty they get the doormat they wipe their feet on?"

All the muck-globbed heads swiveled to stare at Fayrene. Most of them didn't know her voice could raise above a self-effacing whisper.

"We can't just lie around and take this . . ." She paused for a beat before spitting out the word, ". . . shit." Jaws dropped. Hearing Fayrene Pirtle use that mild vulgarity was, for most of the group, like seeing Jerry Falwell do the Dirty Dog. She had everyone's absolute, undivided attention.

"We've got to do something," she insisted. "We've got to have our own party, louder and longer and wilder than any those . . . SUKs could even dream of . . ." She paused. Her transfigured expression was stronger than ever as she lifted her head and gazed heavenward for more divine guidance. "And we're going to have this party on the very night before the heaviest day of finals. We'll see to it that those damned SUKs don't get in a lick of studying. They'll flunk their finals and the house will be suspended!"

Stunned silence met Fayrene's proposal as everyone attempted to readjust their concept of the Peanut Patty to include such an impassioned plea. Judith was the first to recover.

"I think we're all feeling a need to make a statement here," Judith said. "But a lot of us don't have a whole lot of time right now to be spending on anything, much less a party."

"Oh bull," Fayrene burst out. "Look at all of us, we're reliable, diligent grinds. It's our turn to hand a paper in a day or two late. To postpone an exam because of pressing personal reasons. We've all built up a lot of extra credit. We can afford to use some of it."

Muddy heads slowly nodded. "Yeah."

"The time has come for us to rise UP OUT OF THE MUCK, not to wallow in it!" A smattering of "Amens" answered Fayrene's blistering, washed-in-the-blood intensity. I tried to reconcile the stemwinder in front of me with the Slo-Poke-munching slug who'd inhabited my room for the past few weeks. The transformation was inspiring and disorienting. The inspiring part infected me.

"Maybe Tommy's new band would play," I suggested.

"That's good. That's very good," she approved. She looked to the crowd for more support.

"An anti-frat party, that's a hell of an idea," Toni declared. Barb nodded vigorous confirmation. "We can invite all the women in the Radical Lesbian Coalition. They'll party till dawn if it'll cleanse the campus of one fraternity asshole."

"The Society will love it!" Constance burst out, a white grin opening in the middle of her dirty face.

"The Society?" I prompted.

"The Society for Creative Anachronism," she elaborated and I nodded remembering her jousting, wenching, battle-axing medieval buddies.

"Yes, please get them to come," I encouraged her. "In full battle dress. With weapons."

"I suppose," Hillary began, trying to hide her enthusiasm, "that I could involve the Co-op League. We might even get them to sponsor it. Invite all the co-ops and maybe throw in some food."

"Fantastic idea!" Fayrene blurted out. Hillary flowered beneath the flood of unqualified approval, so much more replenishing than the meager reinforcement bobs that Judith doled out.

"Yeah," Hillary continued, "I could cut a stencil over at the office and run off handbills on the mimeograph then post them at all the houses tomorrow when I put up the League notices." The full force of Hillary's impressive organizational capacity was brought to bear on the party. We set a date—day after tomorrow—and a time—sunset to sunrise. Names were suggested—Sweet Revenge Party, Fratricide Night. We settled finally on the Flunk-a-Frat Party-a-thon. Hillary noted it all and promised delivery of party announcements by tomorrow morning.

"Oh give me a whopping big stack of 'em," Esme requested. She flicked off a clump of the mud that had dried on her ziggurat hairdo. "Everyone at the department hates frat rodents. I'll hand out notices in the anthro and government departments too. Big anti-frat contingents there."

"I could take some around to the clubs," I volunteered. "And get Tommy to pass the word amongst his following. Greeks aren't terribly popular with them."

"I tell friends from many lands," Duk Soo, her shiny black hair dulled with mud, volunteered. "Everyone hating frarinaries."

"And what about Collie's drama friends?" Fayrene inquired.

"Great," I answered. "Nothing like a little guerrilla theater to spark a party."

The guest list grew as suggestions continued to stream in. Militant lesbians, nuevo wavos, unreconstructed hippies, medieval anachronisms, it was an odd and unlikely coalition with one thing in common—we all loathed fraternities.

Alexis, who had been quietly contemplating the irreparable harm the sludge on her face was doing to her pores, suddenly came to life. "My God," she muttered, "we've got a genuine populist movement starting here. I think that if I play up that angle, I might be able to get five hundred words out of it and put an item in the *Texan* tomorrow. With that kind of publicity this thing could really take off, then I'll be right here to do the series on the movement." Her eyes glazed over the way they always did when she was framing answers for Barbara Walters and we lost contact with Alexis.

"Oh no," Fayrene wailed. "We've forgotten one thing."

"What?" we demanded.

Fayrene glanced furtively in either direction then whispered something. What we heard instead was the SUKs' version of "Louie, Louie."

"What?" we tried again.

"Liquor," she answered, yelling into a sudden break in the music.

"You're right," I agreed. "We're going to need alcoholic amplification if we want our guests to achieve the cerebellum-scrambling decibels necessary to render study or sleep impossible. Let me work on it."

"Bear in mind, Fayrene," Judith cautioned, "that we have no discretionary funds whatsoever left in the treasury."

"From now on, Judith," Fayrene said, her voice dead level, "I'd appreciate you, all of you," she turned to the rest of the group, "calling me Fay. I've always hated Fayrene. As for the liquor . . ."

"As for the liquor," I interrupted. "I have an idea how we might get around it. Why don't you all go shower again and I'll talk it over with Fayree . . . with Fay." They slipped out the back way, cutting through the alley to avoid the SUK house, and set out to demuck at Belmont.

I discussed my liquor procurement plan with Fay and she deemed it inspired. Then I attended to an even more critical element—noise. I called Tommy.

"A Flunk-a-Frat Party-a-thon," he echoed. "That is a toda madre, Steadwoman. A truly boss idea. I love the concept. It'll be the perfect event at which to introduce Little Lyndon and the

Great Society. Yeah, I like it," he affirmed. My party-a-thon spirit soared.

The next day I unveiled the strategy for providing the party with the needed liquid megaphones.

"I don't know," Hillary objected. "I don't think I should get the League involved in something so ethically questionable."

"There's also the very real danger," Josie put in, "of a defamation of character suit."

"Oh, stop being such a bunch of weenies," Fay blew up. "We're never going to specifically say who we really are or specifically who we're really supposed to be, so quit worrying."

Criticism muzzled, everyone listened intently as I outlined the plan of attack. Then we grouped into pairs, divvied up the neighborhood, and went to our rooms to dress. Not many of us had the correct romper shorts, knee socks, and oxford cloth shirt disguise, but we came as close as we could by sweeping our hair into ponytails, wearing our most conservative clothes, putting on every piece of gold jewelry we owned, and troweling on makeup. Downstairs, everyone grabbed a big, brown grocery bag and we hit the street.

Fay and I let the more timid take the areas right around the house, so we had a fair hike before we reached our designated sector. It was in a nice, upper-middle-class neighborhood north of campus. Since this whole thing was my idea, I took the first house. I sucked in a deep breath, installed a perky smile on my face, blanked all intelligent thoughts from my mind, and stepped up to the door of a two-story, red brick Colonial number. A sweet-faced old lady answered the chime.

"Hi," I greeted her pertly, tilting my ponytail from one side of my head to the other. "Our sorority is having a scavenger hunt," I trilled, "and we only have three things left on our list."

"Scavenger hunt?" the old lady asked. "Didn't know they still had scavenger hunts. Thought they went out when all that disco dancing came in."

"Tee-hee. Well we still have scavenger hunts and my partner and I have almost everything on the list."

Fay held up her empty bag and I pulled a sheet of paper out of my pocket. "All we're lacking is," I pretended to study the blank sheet, "is a subscription card to *Ramparts* magazine; a grape Fizzie; and a partially full bottle of liquor."

The old lady turned quizzical, watery blue eyes on us. "Now, what was that again? *Ram's Hearts* magazine? No, I don't believe we ever took that particular publication. Then there was a what? A grape Fizzie? I believe the grandchildren used to use those. But we stopped keeping them in the house since Tammy went off to A&M. She's studying engineering, if you can believe that. What was that last item?"

I looked down at the paper pretending to search for the third item. "A partially full bottle of liquor."

"Let me see, I might be able to help you with that one." She left us and went back into the house. Fay lifted her eyebrows at me and I lifted back. A few minutes later, the old lady shuffled back carrying a half-empty bottle of Riunite. "Does wine count as liquor?" she asked.

"Oh sure," Fay answered, holding out her bag. The woman dropped it in.

"Sorry I couldn't help you with those other items. Good luck."

"Oh this is grite," I burbled, borrowing Fay's old accent on great. "Thanks a ton." We backed away from the door and rushed toward the sidewalk.

At the next house, Fay scored half a fifth of sweet vermouth that had sugar crystals forming on the neck. We mixed the two wines together so the bottles wouldn't clink in the bag. Then it was my turn.

It took two rings before we heard halting footfalls approach the door. It swung open. "Professor Pitsor." He weaved unsteadily in the doorway, struggling to bring me into focus. "Mary Jo Steadman," I prompted him.

"Right. Yes, you did that trenchant series on strip mining. I'm sorry I haven't gotten those articles back to you. I'll bring them with me to class next time we meet. See you then. Goodbye." He had the door half shut before I could wedge my foot in.

"Classes are over, Professor. Anyway, that's not why I'm here." The door smashed my foot but I couldn't let him get away. In this particular scavenger hunt, the dipsomaniacal Professor Pitsor was the Holy Grail. Pitsor oozed back around the door.

"It's not?"

"No, actually we're on a scavenger hunt." I slipped into my preset spiel. "We only have three things left on our list: a subscription card to *Ramparts* magazine; a grape Fizzie; and a partially filled bottle of liquor."

He breathed heavily for a moment, inflating then deflating his purple tuber of a nose. "Got it," he proclaimed at last. He threw the door open wide and turned around.

"Oh no," I whimpered. There, behind him, like the towers of ungraded papers in his office, were towers of old magazines stacked over every square inch of his living room. He roamed through the chest-high piles finally stopping at one flanking his brown and white checked sofa. "Here they are." He plucked the top copy off the stack and held it up. It was one of the last issues of *Ramparts* magazine ever published. He leafed through it, fumbling awkwardly with the pages as if he had on mittens in addition to the ever-present buzz. Finally he slapped the magazine down.

"Forget it," he muttered. "That's too much like work." He disappeared, then returned with a three-gallon bottle of generic vodka. He opened the screen door and held out the unopened bottle. "Oh wait," he said, withdrawing the prize. "You said 'partially' full bottle, didn't you?" He broke the seal and searched behind him. Whisking a coffee mug off an old pile of yellowed *National Observers*, he glugged the vodka in, then twisted the cap back on.

Fay gaped at the hugest bottle of liquor she'd ever seen as Professor Pitsor handed it back out to us. "I didn't even know it came in three-gallon jugs," she breathed.

"Does if you buy in quantity direct from the warehouse," Pitsor informed her helpfully. I quickly bagged the bottle in question.

"Thanks so much," I effused. "We're sure to win now."

"No problem." He smiled benignly as we faded down the walk. "Can't understand why the school is kicking you out. What did you ever do to Denise Kleppers? She portrayed you as the biggest menace to hit the campus since Charles Whitman."

I shrugged. Kicking me out? Only total avoidance of school had kept me in such ignorant bliss. I can't say I didn't expect *or* deserve it.

"Oh well," he sighed, shutting the door. "Great strip mining series."

"Don't think about it now," Fay ordered me before I had a chance to slump into a depression about my future.

"Yeah, it's a little late at this point," I admitted.

A dozen blocks later, we had a full, sloshing load. In addition to the Riunite, the sweet vermouth, and Professor Pitsor's generous contribution, we had acquired a puddle of mezcal complete with mummified worm; a stalagmite of Gallianos left over from Harvey Wallbanger days; some cheap port; some cheaper burgundy; several bottles of scotch donated by a man who proudly announced he no longer drank "the blended stuff," and a bottle of peppermint schnapps. "Tastes like alcoholic mouthwash," the schnapps contributor said as he dropped the bottle into my bag.

Back at the house, the firewater was flooding in. Fay and I added our cache. Hillary had shown up with the announcements in our absence and half the house had fanned out across the campus and environs delivering and posting them. Alexis was at the *Texan* writing the article that would appear in tomorrow's paper. Only Judith sat, alone and uninvolved, working on her thesis. The house was humming again.

Deep-seated, hormone-rooted impulses kicked in that night and we all did what we could to make Alamo presentable. Company was coming! Infected by this new morale high, Toni strapped an arsenal of wrenches and augers onto her pants and strode off, down into Alamo's troubled bowels. A few hours later, she emerged and announced that our guests would have facilities, then she and Barb went upstairs to take the first shower Alamo had known for weeks.

The plumbing miracle really boosted esprit de corps. Our only worry now was the weather. The band and dancing were going to be outside in the vacant lot next door and a cold front had hit. There was talk of building a bonfire, but we were still concerned that we might not meet our objective if partygoers got too cold to stay around all night and distract the SUKs from their studies.

Our fears were laid to rest the next morning. Summer, still down in Cozumel laying in some tropical stun rays to stagger Austin with next August, chose the very day of our Party-a-thon to send an advance man back up north. Just to remind the River City who *owned* that town. It was T-shirt and party punch weather. We were ready by seven that night with both. After extinguishing the small flash fire that resulted when we combined all our scavenged liquors and mixers together with several gallons of Co-op League-supplied juice and a handful of grape Fizzies, we ended up with a surprisingly potable decoction. Flavor was really a minor issue though as, after the first swallow, taste buds ceased to function anyway.

Tommy showed up in time to sample the first batch and declared it a first-class paint and inhibition remover. He had *become* Little Lyndon with his very own Mr. Potato Head, too-small cowboy hat, and a gabardine western-cut suit appropriate for presidential leisure wear or pumping gas. The Great Society was decked out in white shirts, skinny ties, and dark suits from Goodwill. Tommy had even recruited some backup singers. All three had Clairol Raven's Wing Black hair ratted into towering helmets that flipped up at the ends, four pairs apiece of ostrich-eyes lashes, chalky pink lipstick pale enough to bring out the yellow in their teeth, A-line mini-dresses, and patterned white hose guaranteed to make any leg look like it belonged on a piano.

Burly roadies muscled equipment into place out on the vacant lot. I was pleased to see them set up a wall of forehead-high speakers along the sidewalk, all pointing toward the SUK house.

"Borrowed the sound system from the Brown-Outs," Tommy explained, referring to a local heavy metal group.

"Good work. You'll be pleased to know that the showers are fixed. I won't have to be traipsing over to your house anymore."

"I thought you might have gotten kind of partial to my plumbing." Tommy gave me the kind of smoldering roguish look that goes so nicely on the covers of romance novels. Against my conscious will, my autonomic nervous system made me complete the picture: I blushed, my bosom heaved, and I felt irresistibly drawn to this dashing rake in the gas station attendant suit.

"You know, it's too bad you don't remember anything about that night at the SUK party."

"Well. . . . Actually, it's not a complete blank," I admitted.

Tommy stepped closer. "So tell me, what do you remember?"

I gulped air. It was getting to be now or never time. "Dancing with you."

"How was it?"

"Nice. I liked it."

Tommy put one hand on my back and moved me into dance position. "Want to try it again?"

We started swaying to the squawks of the band running sound checks. In mid-sway, Tommy bent me backward in his arms. "You inflame me, you haughty wench," he breathed into my face. Then he kissed me.

I'd read in *Love's Reckless Passion* about bones turning to jelly and whirling vortexes of desire sweeping through women at the first kiss and dismissed it as romance propaganda. First kisses just had never been much for me. Heretofore, all I had ever been aware of during that awkward initial osculation was excess slobber and having my lips ground against my bicuspids. With Tommy it was the Jelly Vortex.

"What can I promise you, my darling?" he asked. "Gilded nights in the back of a two-tone, Bel-Air station wagon? Salacious songs dedicated to you? Merely ask and it all shall be yours." Before I could answer Tommy was called away.

I stumbled off dazed by my first jelly vortex kiss and by the fact that it had been planted by a man in a Mr. Potato Head hat. The guests were arriving. By foot and by car, they came. Soon Pecan was clogged with the aging VW vans of unreconstructed- and neo-hippie co-opers and the classically restored Studebaker Metropolitans and Karman Ghias of the trendier nuevo wavos.

Constance's SCA friends appeared en masse and in full chain-mail battle dress. They headed immediately for the vat of liquid megaphone and dipped in with their tankards.

A mob of Vy-Mar/Attractions fans showed up and clumped around the stage we'd improvised. They were a bit diffident at first about Tommy's latest incarnation. But when he and The Great Society ripped into their first number, a heavily synthesized "Moon River," the fans were bewildered and repelled. Knowing bewilderment and repugnance to be the indisputable signs that musical frontiers were being pushed back, and wanting always to be the first into the breach, the fans churned themselves into a frenzy. By the time Little Lyndon dove into his next number, "To Dream the Impossible Dream," the fans were foaming at the mouth and wetting themselves in their excitement over being THE FIRST to discover Cardigan Rock.

Tommy beamed as he jumped off the stage during an instrumental interlude and came over to capture me in a headlock. He pulled me to him and kissed me again. "It worked!" he exulted. "You thought I was out of my mind, didn't you? Admit it."

"Could you narrow down the time frame for me a little?"

"My Bird phase. But it worked. There's the proof." He pointed to a plump woman with the hair shaved off both sides of her head. What hair remained had been teased into a tornado funnel touching down on her forehead. A small chandelier hung from one distended earlobe. She was grooving ardently to The Great Society's beat.

"Look," Tommy directed me delightedly. "She came and she's

buying it. No bogus heritage here. No new sincerity. She's read the newspaper stories. She knows of my devotion to Bird and to all things Johnsonian."

"Who is she?" I interrupted his rapture.

"The scout from MTV, who else? What did you think this was all about anyway?"

Before I could hazard a guess, he asked, "Are we going to have an affair? Give me an answer next break." He kissed me and hopped back onstage to announce a personal favorite of the Big Bopper and to say that Mary Jo Steadman had requested it.

"Raindrops Keep Falling on My Head," he crooned the odious title.

I don't know how he did it, but Tommy *almost* managed to make me like that song.

The whole repertoire, candy-ass as it was, was played at decibel ranges capable of opening clogged sinus passages. That was on Our Side. The speakers were pointed toward Their Side. On the SUK side of the monster sound amplifiers the pavement was buckling.

The noise might have triggered a mass exodus from the SUK house to the library except for the fact that their study technique was, of necessity, a loud one. It centered around the chapter grind drilling his brothers on the answers he'd worked out to stolen exam questions. Far too noisy for the library. Consequently, the SUKs were trapped.

Merrymakers continued to stream in: Duk Soo's friends from many lands included, first and foremost, herself dressed in her national party togs: a billowy creation in hot pink that puffed out beneath her armpits then went all the way to the ground in a pastel cloud. A dozen Taiwanese men who looked like they'd be superior in Ping-Pong and engineering tagged along behind her.

Mixed in with that crew were a handful of the world's champion revelers—Brazilians. As soon as the beat reached them, they all leaned their shoulders and upper torsos as far back as their supple spines would allow. They looked as if they'd been caught by a strong head wind as they followed their gaily waggling pelvises into the fray, spreading Carnaval wherever they went.

Old-time hippies did what came naturally as they felt the good times moving into high gear: They removed articles of clothing and whirled them over their heads. The men got their consorts to crawl up onto their shoulders and prance through the crowd.

Seeing the festivities take off animated Little Lyndon and the Great Society even further. They dug back into Kenny and the Distractions' repertoire for some burn up the gym floor, sock hop rock 'n' roll. After a few of Tommy's sweaty originals, the crowd metamorphosed into a great, drunken, dancing bear roaring at the moon in an excess of pleasure.

At ten, the SUKs sent a couple of white-jacketed butlers over. Fay and I braced ourselves as they ricocheted from one madly stamping dance crew to the next until they were finally directed to us. We were at the punch vat fortifying our brew. The two black gentlemen marched solemnly up to us, dutifully registered the complaints of their bosses, then faded into the dancing melee, each one grabbing two partners apiece. Fay and I went on feeding the monster in the vat.

At eleven, a beefy squad of SUKs led by The Bub stormed across the street, swinging baseball bats, golf clubs, and drinking trophies. The sprawling amoeba of a crowd engulfed them, then spat them out like rejected food particles. Dazed, they wandered back across the street. I glanced over at Fay and she beamed back at me: It was working, the SUKs were definitely not studying. Without thinking we both yelled the same thought at the same time: "I wish Collie were here."

One of Constance's medieval friends, a sweet-faced, roly-poly man wearing a monk's robe and tonsure, interrupted us and, with much toe-grinding in the dust, asked Fay to dance. Fay shrugged and grimaced. "I don't really know how," she shouted her confession.

The elfin-faced monk grinned. "Good. I don't either," he hollered back. "Let's check out the refreshments."

Fay shrugged, grimaced agreement, and, with a backward

glance at me, left with the round monk to sample the heavily organic spread put out by the Co-op League.

Constance danced up. She was decked out in a Lady of Shalott outfit with a high dunce cap trailing a long chiffon scarf and earmuff buns. She seized my hands in hers and squeezed them. "A rousing success!" she shouted, looking over at the SUK house where the brothers were gathered at the front window staring furiously at *our* excesses. "Right shall triumph yet," she vowed jerking a plucky fist up in front of her face. Then she whirled off to join in a quatrain being performed by her friends to the bobby strains of "Never on Sunday."

At midnight, Little Lyndon and the Great Society took a break and the Brown-Outs took over. They were dressed in dancing tights and wader boots with sashes around their waists and minuscule torn T-shirts shielding the area around their nipples. They had rooster haircuts and guitars shaped like chubby lightning bolts.

"We're the Brown-Outs," they screamed into the microphone and, for a brief second, I actually pitied the humans on the other side of the speakers. Had we gone too far? I wondered. The second passed and it was myself I pitied as the Brown-Outs ("We get our name because one of two things always happens when we play—there's a power failure or someone messes their pants") screeched and roared into their first number.

The crowd seemed oddly inured to and energized by the auditory assault. I noted that the fourth vat of party punch was empty and went inside for the necessaries to brew another one. Tommy helped me, then we went for a walk. Ten blocks away, the Brown-Outs were still killing tender vegetation. Tommy was ecstatic about how well Little Lyndon and the Great Society had been received. Allan, his friend who slept with the MTV scout, had told him the scout thought they were even better than The Bruces, a gay band that dressed in bolero jackets and wedgies.

I wondered why I had never noticed that Tommy's nostrils

were shaped like two perfect teardrops. I wondered if he was going to kiss me again. He did. Again the jelly vortex. Yeah, we were definitely going to have an affair. And it would be sweet ecstasy and screaming agony. Suddenly, I wanted very badly to talk to Collie.

At one-thirty, the Brown-Outs leaped off the stage with sweat and scarves flying and Tommy went back on, ripping into "Up, Up and Away." I stood back and surveyed the revelry.

Hillary was entangled in a crew of unreconstructed hippies and their younger acolyte hippies-in-training learning the old tribal dances. She was following the lead of her partner, a lean, balding man in a Mexican wedding shirt. He was executing a series of moves that called to mind a Tai Chi dancer being electrocuted.

Judith stood off on the sidelines with a bearded and bemused crowd of her fellow psych grad students. They pointed surreptitiously at various amusing displays of human foiblery and whispered a running commentary to one another.

Esme had stationed herself directly in front of the stage and was attempting to get a lively round of slam dancing going, except that everyone she touched backed precipitously away. The nuevo wavers were working out on the Swim, the Twist, the Cool Jerk, the Pony, and other dance classics from Great Society days. Toni and Barb were happily oscillating at the center of a crush of women in work shirts and Frye boots. Duk Soo, in her hot pink balloon dress, was getting down with a compactly built Taiwanese with a calculator slapping against his thigh.

Josie, cigarette in hand, along with a few core members of the Law School's Drink or Drown Committee, had taken up a permanent spot by the vat of party punch. Alexis scurried about, notepad in hand, screaming questions into merrymakers' ears about what they thought the significance of this populist uprising to be. Constance led an armored and gowned group in a spirited pavan. Fay daintily nibbled the edges off of a party cookie offered to her by the tonsured monk.

As I glanced from one Alamo resident to the next, a great, warm, party-punched wave of feeling for all these bright, quirky, feisty, idiosyncratic, eccentric women swept over me. In that moment, I loved them all, every maddening one of them. Collie, I wished, you really should be here.

Little Lyndon was going to town on "Climb Every Mountain" when I went inside and climbed the stairs up to the phone. I sat on the top step for several minutes, my hand on the receiver, the scrap of paper Fay had written the clinic number on in front of me. Finally, I dialed.

The phone rang long enough to remind me that it was three-thirty and the whole world was not up having a party. For a second, I considered hanging up. But it was too important. I really *had* to talk to Collie. Now.

"Kenneth Blaney Clinic, how may I help you?"

Deep in my heart, I hadn't truly believed that Collie would be where Fay had said she was. I asked to speak with Collie Mohoric. When that drew a blank, I tried Missy Fairchild and was told that all the residents were asleep and to call back in the morning.

"But I can't. I have to speak with Missy now. I'm leaving for Tierra del Fuego in the morning. They don't have phone connections. I just heard about Missy. I'm her oldest friend. It would be just so therapeutic for her to hear from me." I continued on in this vein for a bit longer, until the woman at the other end interrupted with an indulgent chuckle to say that she'd put Missy on. I suspected that she figured anyone who'd go to the trouble of coming up with Tierra de Fuego really cared.

"Hello." Collie's voice was more than sleepy. Even at her first moment of consciousness she was more charged up than the average Chihuahua dog.

"Collie, it's me, Mary Jo." I didn't want to give her the chance to hang up or to just not say anything. "We're having a party. Hear it." I held the receiver out so that she could pick up Tommy crooning "The Impossible Dream."

"Alamo is having a party?" she asked, still groggy.

It was wrong. Collie didn't belong in a place where they'd flatten her manic zest. "Collie, you shouldn't be there."

There was a long silence on the other end and I thought about all that I didn't know about Collie. Finally, she spoke. "Most of the time I'd agree with you. But it's hard work being a phony and sometimes I need a little rest between acts."

"Collie, I never should have said that. I didn't mean it. I was jealous. I wanted someone to carry me off in a Benz. I didn't know where they were taking you."

"It's just a short stay. Get my endorphins balanced or something. Make sure I don't eat too many sleeping pills again."

"Again? Collie, why?"

"Why? I guess that's what I keep coming back here to figure out."

"But you didn't want to go, did you? They sent you."

"My family? Yeah. But just because they notice when I'm going into a black dog phase before I do. Hey, it's not so grim here. All the drugs a person could ever want, plus I get to catch up on the soaps."

"Collie, you shouldn't be there."

"Hm-m-m-m, well. . . . What's new?"

I told her about getting kicked out of school.

"Best thing that could ever happen to you."

"Right, a real lucky break. I had to pull some strings to do it."

"No, really," she insisted. "What does a photographer need college for anyway? I mean the editor at the *Beeville Herald* is not going to want to sit around and talk about what Man Ray was *really* trying to say. All he's going to want is to see some pictures. So get a job with the *Texan* and take a shitload of the things."

"Good career counseling. Hey, you should have seen this place crumble when you left. We need you, Collie. We need your theatrics, the gaudy glitter of your many personas, the benefit of your experience as a camp follower in the Weirdo campaigns . . ."

"Oh, you flatter me," she trilled. For a second it was like old times, the wind of her spirited excess blowing through our banter.

In an instant it was snuffed out. "The nurse is signaling for me to hang up. She can get in a lot of trouble for even letting me talk to you."

"Collie . . . I really miss you."

"You do?" She sounded surprised.

"Yeah, I really do. I should never have said all those things I did. I was a total ass."

"Oh well. If we both apologized every time we were total asses, there wouldn't be much time left for anything else. Look, really got to go."

"Collie," I stopped her. "Don't let them turn the jokes into tragedies."

"You too, Mary Hoe. Hasta lumbago."

"Hasta then, compañera."

I went into my room and watched the party. Though the ranks had been thinned considerably, the die-hards were still down there dancing to Tommy's music. Among them was the MTV scout.

Across the street, the SUKs seemed to have surrendered. Most of the house had gathered on the second-story balcony where I'd first glimpsed them. They were downing brews and looking haggard and stunned that anyone had actually out-partied them, and to such devastating effect. Then there was a brief caucus and all the brothers perked up before they went downstairs, leaving their leader alone on the balcony. Bub grabbed his bullhorn and pointed it our way.

"Hey, I got something to say!" he bellowed. Tommy stopped singing and the band quieted down so we could hear.

"Uh . . . Hey, y'all probably think you're real smart, doncha, for shuttin' us out with your party. Okay, okay, I admit it. We're gonna flunk. No two ways about it. Our asses are out of school. The house is history. But don't go thinkin' you won. You didn't win."

Obscenities greeted Bub's pronouncement. Down in the SUK parking lot, grinning brothers wearing Panama hats, baggy shorts, and huaraches were carrying suitcases out to the cars. The crowd quieted when Bub started up again.

"I'll tell you why you dings didn't win. Cuz you'll never win. You can get all the degrees you want, but when you finally get out into the world we'll be there. Running it. When you want a loan, we'll be there. When you go to buy a house, you'll have to come to us. We're gonna make the laws and run the people who run the government. Wherever you go, we'll already be there. Waiting for you. Naw, you didn't win diddly squat tonight and you never will. See you in the next cartoon, losers!"

Bub slung himself over the balcony and dropped into his brothers' waiting arms. On signal, the SUKs revved up their engines and unfurled a banner that read "MAZATLAN OR BUST!!!"

"Vamanos, hermanos!" Bub circled his hand in the air several times, then brought it to rest pointing south toward a sunny Pacific beach.

Just as the beefkabob caravan was about to roar off, however, a black stretch limo with smoked glass windows pulled around the corner. It slinked to a stop at the edge of the parking lot blocking the exodus. Bub jumped out of his Bronco and, flanked by other outraged brothers, stormed over to the limo.

"Hey, dickhead, you wanna get the fuck outta our way," he inquired.

Slowly the back door of the limo swung open. A silver-haired guy who reeked power stepped out. Bub's jaw dropped.

"Daddy!"

"Governor!" his cronies added.

The former governor straightened up. Bub wilted visibly before his father's tall-in-the-saddle presence. The governor studied his son. His son's friends. His son's fraternity house. Then he turned and studied our devastated dwelling. With each second that ticked by, the silence on Pecan Street deepened and The Bub shrunk a bit more. Finally the governor spoke.

"Dickhead?" he asked softly.

Bub commenced quaking.

"Dickhead!" the governor thundered. Bub throttled into a full cower.

"I didn't know it was you, Daddy," Bub whined.

The governor massaged the bridge of his nose, the picture of straining paternal patience. No one moved. No one breathed. "Son, when are you gonna break the factory seal on your brain?"

Bub attempted a grin that went all spastic and shrugged.

"Do you think you're gonna get charged for the mileage you put on what little you got up there between your ears?"

If Bub hadn't spent the past few months torturing us, I might have felt sorry for him. As it was, I hoped the governor had a whole flock of zingers to whip on the fruit of his loins.

"What are you doing here, Daddy?" Junior piped up, the booming Bub vocal cords now gone reedy with fear. "You're supposed to be in Washington lobbying for that depletion allowance."

"Does the name A. J. Hawkins mean anything to you?"

"He's that crazy man who dug up our parking lot. I can explain about . . ."

"Don't," the governor ordered. "I've already got this whole deal down here checked out. Talked to some of my old friends around campus. Didn't like what I heard, Jasper. Y'all are gettin' your asses kicked out of school."

"School," Bub laughed weakly. "You always said yourself, sir, only piss-ants need school."

"What the hell you think you are, boy? You got no family bidness to walk into. *This* is my bidness." He waved his arms toward us. "Every sumbitch who can punch a ballot, that's all in the world I got. You are alienating my constituency, peckerwood." He stabbed a finger at the house. "These women vote!"

"Oh, them," Bub chortled. "They're lesbians. Man-haters."

"Well, if you're supposed to be a sample of the material, Slick, I'd say that'd be a real smart way to go. Jesus. Biggest damned mistake I made in my life was raising a rich man's son. You're a pussy, Jasper. I've paid your way and bailed you out all your life. Well, that's over." He looked back at the other SUKs in their Hawaiian shirts and yelled to them. "It's over for all of you!"

"Hey, Bub," Kytes called. "Let's get the show on the road."

"That you Kytes?" the governor asked, nailing the little weasel with a glare. He pulled a document out of his jacket pocket. "This here's a warrant, Kytes. For your arrest. That little set-to back home in Odessa you left for your parents to clean up." He pulled out a dozen more. "I've been in touch with all you all's folks and they're 'bout as fed up as I am. There's not a one of you thugs isn't in some kind of deep shit and gettin' in deeper. Well, boys, the news here today is, the ride is over. Your parents aren't going to be paying the freight for you any more."

The brothers looked at one another.

"Oh, believe me, boys, it's over. Your daddies are with me. We figure we got one chance left to turn you parasites into something worth the sperm we wasted on you. We've even hired someone to help us do that." He turned to the limo. "Mr. Hawkins." The door opened and the sleazebag contractor stepped out.

"Hi-dee," he greeted the gathering.

"Boys, meet your new house mother."

Hawkins cleared his throat, hurled a loogie at Bub's feet, and nodded. Then he turned back to the limo and leaned inside. He whipped the CB radio mike out and switched it on. "Venga la troque," he ordered. Seconds later his truck rumbled to a stop in front of the SUK house. The back flaps flew open and a dozen Mexicans of the undocumented worker variety surged out.

"And meet your new pledge class," the governor introduced the smiling brown men before turning back to his captive audience.

"Here's the deal, gentlemen."

I watched and waited, as transfixed as the SUKs down there on the parking lot goggling at the governor and the illegals.

"For the duration of the next semester your sorry asses belong to me and to Mr. A. J. Hawkins. You and your new pledge brothers will spend each and every day working side by side, doing exactly what Mr. Hawkins says you do. More'n likely it'll be the kind of college work I did. Digging postholes, pouring concrete slabs, chopping brush."

"This is insane." Schlubber snorted and shook his head. "You can't do this."

"Oh, probably not alone," the governor speculated. "But with your parents' full cooperation and with some help from my many old friends around the state in law enforcement, I can. Of course, you all do have a choice. You can either spend your semester with Mr. Hawkins or you can spend a lot longer in whatever jail wants you most. Because the legal shield is down. Not one a your parents is going to pay another lawyer another dime to keep your butts out of jail if you leave here today."

"Can he do that?" Schlubber asked Bub.

Bub, who had that brain-dead look again, nodded. "He's a goddamn honorary Texas Ranger. He can do anything."

"Mighty fine." The governor grinned. "Looks like we all understand each other now." He put his arm around his shattered son and addressed the group. "You know, boys, I think some good has already come out of all this. Y'all are finally on your way to becoming bona fide Texans."

His son looked over at his father and asked numbly, "How's that?"

"Well, you've already taken the first step cuz it's by God certain that every one of you will always, no matter where you go or what you become, you will always . . . remember the Alamo."

Scattered applause went up from our side of the street. The governor turned and bowed to acknowledge the cheers from his newest constituency. "Pleased to make your acquaintance! Name's Wilkers," he shouted across the street. " 'Preciate it, if you'd keep it in mind next time you see it on a ballot." He grinned and made his eyes twinkle. Behind him Mr. Hawkins was herding his crew, delighted brown and stupefied white, into the SUK house.

It was over. After months of struggle, we'd won. Something inside of me sagged. It had been an immensely long night. I walked slowly downstairs tripping on ghosts all the way. Collie was there, curled up on a step with the phone, crying; bounding up the steps, calling for me; pulling me and Fay down, out to some adventure. I went out the back way, through the kitchen, past the big black stove. The awful morning when I'd expected to find Collie there seemed a long time in the past. I knew I had decided: I was leaving Alamo House. All I wanted now was a private place in which to make my farewells to the olive-drab dowager.

Out in the backyard, I breathed in the cool air exhaled into the darkness by pecan and magnolia trees. The little patch of land behind the house shimmered in the ghostly illumination of a "Moon Light" half a block away. Moon Lights, erected in the shape of the Lone Star, had glowed all over the River City around the turn of the century. Most had ceased functioning and been toppled decades ago. The Pecan Street light, miraculously, was one of the few still standing. Eighty years later it continued to bathe our backyard in a spooky radiance.

That light fell on something I hadn't noticed in all the turmoil of the past weeks since the Bamboo Outrage. They looked like a row of luminescent dog penises poking their glistening tips through the dark soil at the rear periphery of our yard. I stepped closer and bent down, surprised by the loamy squishiness and fertile smell of the ground beneath my feet. I reached out toward the pale projections, almost afraid that they would feel fleshy. I touched one and laughed. Out loud. Up at the Moon Light. Up at The Moorland where a few late-night pairs of binoculars still flashed. It was the goddamned bamboo. It was growing back. At this rate it would be as thick and dense and as binocularly impenetrable by the end of Christmas vacation as it had ever been.

"You're growing back," I whispered stroking the tender little shoots.

"Who are you talking to?" Fay knelt down beside me on the ground.

"The bamboo, it's coming back."

She crouched over to touch the new growth, marveling at its stubbornness.

We sat in silence under the Moon Light until I asked, "What are you doing for Christmas vacation?"

"I don't know. Go home to Waco, I guess."

"We could go to Houston," I suggested, seeing clearly in that moment exactly what had to be done. "We could go get Collie."

Fay straightened up quickly. "And bring her back here?" She was excited.

"She belongs here. She'll do a lot better at Alamo than she will in some damned clinic. She's just not a mental health kind of person."

Fay nodded in thoughtful agreement. "Okay. Houston it is. I'm sort of surprised. I'd assumed you were moving out."

I shrugged and pointed at the baby bamboos, "What the hell, if they're going to all the trouble of coming back for Alamo House, it's the least I can do."

Besides, the olive-drab dowager still held a certain charm for me—I was certain she'd be cheap.

ALAMO HOUSE

A Reader's Guide

SARAH BIRD

To print out copies of this or other
Random House Reader's Guides, visit us at
www.atrandom.com/rgg

A Conversation with the Author

On a steamy evening in early May, Sarah returns to Seneca House Co-op for Graduate Women to visit with current residents about life at a UT co-op. Sarah lived at Seneca House in 1974 and 1975 while getting a graduate degree at the University of Texas and then again in 1983 when she went undercover and moved back in to gather material for the book that would become Alamo House.

The first change I notice is that where parking around the university was once difficult, it has become impossible. No wonder I haven't returned in the years since I left 2309 Nueces. I find a spot far from the house and amble back through the West Campus neighborhood of century-old houses and towering pecan trees being rapidly crowded out by snazzy new condo developments. I pass the intersection of 24th and Nueces, site of a favorite old haunt, Les Amis, a sprouts and herbal tea emporium that I knew had been torn down some years back. What I hadn't fully realized was that the counter-culture icon had been replaced by— altogether now—a Starbucks. It is a too-pointed reminder of the mourning for lost innocence quality that all such strolls down Memory Lane are prone to. I imagine that twenty-five years from now some current West Campus dweller will be recalling with misty fondness the golden Starbucks of his youth and lamenting its replacement with a drive-through Botox station.

An afternoon shower has turned the city into a steambath. I recall the permanently wilted state I existed in while living at Seneca where a few ancient window units churned futilely against the heat and humidity. In fact I further recall, to my astonishment, that my room did not have one. Only someone who has lived in these latitudes can understand the significance of the AC issue.

As I approach the house, something seems very different. Before I can figure out what it might be, an attack of nerves hits as I realize what an essentially bizarre mission I am on. I try to imagine how I would have reacted when I was a resident of Seneca House to the invasion of a decidedly mom-looking suburbanite into my stronghold of bohemianism. I picture the group of high school seniors I spoke to the week before and decide that the giant "Whatever" expressions on the silent faces pretty well covers what I can expect.

On the porch I note the same assortment of dead and dying houseplants that festooned it when I was a resident. A new addition is a serious-looking lock with a security code keypad on the front door. Given the abandoned shopping carts, bundles of clothes hidden in the brush, and homeless men roaming the alleys, this seems a wise innovation.

I brace myself for the sauna and mildew factory of my memory, and knock. The first major surprise is that, after a worryingly long wait, an amiable young man wearing glasses and a yarmulke answers.

"You're not the health inspector, are you?" he asks, nodding at my notepad where I've written the words "dead plants." The dozen or so residents clumped around a long dining room table chuckle agreeably.

They're joking, I realize with intense relief. I pretend to jot furiously. "Yes, I am and I'm shutting you down for a number of violations."

I'm back. With one stupid joke, I've stepped over the threshold and back in time more than a quarter of a century. I'm momentarily disoriented by both this time travel experience and because the dining room is now where the living room used to be and the kitchen has been turned on its side and . . . Oh my God! Most peculiar of all, the house is cool. It's delightfully, pleasantly cool with not the slightest hint of the mildew-cumin-incense odor that defined my Seneca experience.

The pleasant young people are staring at me. Deeply grateful for their surprising friendliness, I blurt out my strange errand. They don't find it strange in the least. Everyone shifts over and I take a seat at the table.

"Can I get you something to drink?" Kavan Modi, 24, a graduate student in physics originally from India, asks.

"Are you hungry?" Liz Rivera-Dirks, 21, studying computer science, adds, indicating her plate splashed with the remnants of something that looks very much like vegetarian chili.

I assure them I'm fine and plunge in, noting the most obvious difference that had occurred to me when Adam, 27, an Israeli-American philosophy major had opened the door: "The house is co-ed."

Tanisha—"I'm the only white Tanisha you'll ever meet"—fills me in, the house went co-ed in '92 and they now have seven men and twelve women.

"The first summer I lived here," I tell them in my best grizzled old-timer voice, "we had trouble filling up the house and let guys in. It was a disaster."

"Why?"

"Lots of romantic turmoil," I answer, telling about the Lothario from Venezuela who left a trail of broken hearts and unwashed pans in his wake but not about my sweetheart. How his summer at Seneca almost, but not quite, saved us. I glance at the stairway at whose top I spent far too much time huddled against a phone receiver, weeping, after I lost said sweetheart to the clutches of Scientology and he left for Los Angeles. Once embedded in that world he took up with an actress who dumped him for another actor who then dumped her and so on in a daisy chain of betrayal that extended right up to some of your better-looking Oscar winners. Let's just say, if I'd only had the fore-sight to harbor a truly nasty STD, Penelope Cruz would be at her gynecologist's right this moment.

"Everyone just sort of decided that guys upset things too much and that they didn't carry their weight," I say, glossing over the summer of the green toilets and sodden phone receiver. "So, how is the co-ed thing working out for you all?"

"I had a pretty crappy experience," Chad Wood, 23, computer science, says. "I dated this girl then she started sleep-ing with this guy down the hall and I was stuck living with her."

"It's just difficult living with someone you're in love with," Kavan interjects.

"I would call it hell," Chad maintains.

"When you're in love with someone," Kavan continues, "you tend to spend a lot of time with them and that's not good for the group as a whole." Such thoughts seem to come naturally to Ka-van and it's not surprising to learn that he is the Labor Czar, the person responsible for assigning jobs, making sure everyone does their chores and assessing fines when they don't. I ask if they still have "Labor Holidays," and everyone groans at the diabolical oxymoron.

"What did you used to do back in the day?" someone asks.

I like repping for my "back in the day" peeps and recount endless hours spent scraping mildewed windows with razor blades. Window work doesn't figure into the picture much any-more. I comment on how good the house looks and learn that a fire five years ago led to major reconstruction, including the

blessed addition of central AC. The AC has had the added benefit of making Seneca the most popular of the Inter-Campus Council's eight co-ops.

"What is room and board now?" I ask.

"Six hundred and two dollars."

I'm surprised at how low the figure is since a plank in a laby-
rinthine university dorm can cost far more and private dorms
will run two to three times that amount. I begin to look at my
old co-op in a whole new light, the light shed by a parent's brain
sizzling away trying to figure out how to pay for college. Seneca
House starts to seem like a place where my thirteen-year-old son
might possibly, one day, be very happy.

"What about food?" I wonder. "Given that the house is
so much more diverse than when I was here is that reflected
in the food? What do you eat that might be out of the ordi-
nary?"

They consider this and Liz answers, "Steamed buns."

A sign from God. My son's favorite food is exactly this Chi-
nese delicacy of puffy dough and red bean paste or barbecued
pork all in a handy microwaveable format.

"Mole, curry, Thai. Kavan makes a really good Mee Siam,
Thai noodles with tomato and coconut milk sauce."

This all sounds a vast improvement over the unpronounce-
able whole grains and other bulk food items perpetrated "in the
day." I recall an intense yearning from that time for a meal with
identifiable components, something mass feeding does not lend
itself to.

"The worst was peanut butter casserole," Christy volunteers. "It had zucchini and other vegetables in this pool of oil."
There is a group shudder at the memory. Okay, so it's not all
steamed buns.

"Was the house always Seneca Falls Co-op?" Leela Ellison,
who chose co-op living after a spell in an apartment with a
manic-depressive roommate who never bathed, asks.

"Actually, the name changed while I was living here. When I first moved in it was Varsity House or something fairly dopey like that. A movement was started to change it and since the house was all-female at the time, a feminist slant was favored. Lilith House, Suffer Jet City, Sojourner Truth House. Though I do recall a contingent that lobbied heavily for Middle Earth. Eventually Seneca Falls House was chosen in honor of the first women's right convention held in Seneca Falls, New York in 1848. Somehow the Falls got dropped and the official sign read Seneca House."

"So why did you call the book *Alamo House?*" Liz asks.

I laugh and answer truthfully, "That was the publisher's decision. They pretty much gave me two choices: Magnolia House or Alamo House. There was a lot less awareness about Texas at that time, a sort of general crunching together of Texas and the South. Joking with my editor, trying to get him to see how wrong, how 'Southern' Magnolia House was, I said, 'Why don't you just call it Kudzu House?' Unfortunately, the joke was lost on him. He was very disappointed when I informed him we don't actually have kudzu in Austin. Of course, my hardcover publisher for *The Mommy Club* wanted to put a saguaro cactus on the cover of that book and wasn't pleased when I informed her that saguaros only grow in some tiny area in Arizona. But tell me, do you still have the same problems we did with the fraternities?"

"What fraternities?"

That is when, looking out the front window, I realize what is so very different: the twin fraternities—both evil—that used to squat across the street are gone. The entire block they occupied is vacant. A parking lot. I think of the beefy crews who tortured us with all-night parties, obscene epithets, and raids on the bamboo jungle that once surrounded the house. Apparently one house burned down and the other was put on a sort of permanent probation for hazing violations. Then, or so the story goes, according to Mr. R., 27, a Mexican-American law student wearing a T-shirt with the Hindu elephant god Ganesha on it, when the national chapter sent money to jolt the monster back to life, the officers absconded with funds and went on safari to Africa!

I love this unverified story and answer with one of my own, recounting how when *Alamo House* was first published I received a call from the president of the national chapter of the house that the SUKs were based upon. (I add that I found it very telling that they were able to identify the house simply from the depredations mentioned in the novel.) At first I was slightly worried that they were going to sue me. But only slightly as they would have been dipping into some of the shallowest pockets imaginable. But no, the president had called to tell me that they were putting copies of my novel into every chapter across the country! As a cautionary tale!

"It's different now," the irrepressible Mr. R. assures me "Every time we have a party that sorority back there, Pi Beta Phi, I think it is, calls the cops."

"The Greeks are calling the cops on you!" I explode. This is *too* delicious.

"Oh, yeah." They tell me about the mammoth blow-outs Seneca hosts: two, three bands, five kegs, open to all comers.

"This is so amazing," I gasp. "There we were, all these timid graduate women just tortured mercilessly by these Greek thugs. The police would come over and trade secret handshakes with the guys and there didn't seem to be anything we could do to retaliate. So, essentially, my novel is this big revenge fantasy. And now, here you are living my fantasy. The Greeks are calling the cops on Seneca House."

Even as I am delighting in this better-than-fiction twist, Kavan, the Labor Czar, leaps out of his chair, bolts across the front room, and out the door. I worry that he might have deep hidden Greek attachments that I've offended. Instead, a moment later he comes back. He'd seen the homeless man who had been hanging out in the laundry room putting cleanliness next to scariness and run out to issue a stern warning about spending his spin cycles elsewhere.

I take the opportunity to visit my old room upstairs with its current occupant, Suzanne Julian, 21, a particularly kind sociology major from San Antonio who wears her graciousness as lightly as the stud on her tongue. The room, a converted porch that once housed three and had the fiendish ability to amplify both noise and heat, is now a serene hideaway for one with gleaming new wood floors, leaky walls all nicely sheetrocked, and plenty of blissful AC pouring in.

As I note and photograph the changes, Suzanne talks about how she moved in because of a desire to be involved with an "intentional community." How she was excited about the commitment to cooperation and being respectful of everyone's needs that participation in such a community implies.

This, too, seems the realization of a fantasy, this one implicit, in the book I wrote. The felicitous phrase "intentional community" rolls around my brain as I say my good-byes and head back outside. The Austin evening has cooled. I bounce back to my car far perkier than when I'd left. The "dowdy dowager" I'd described in *Alamo House* seemed considerably spruced up in ways that go far beyond AC and new floors. Ready to forge her way through the new millennium or, at the very least, I hope, long enough to get my son through college.

READING GROUP QUESTIONS AND
TOPICS FOR DISCUSSION

1. Circa 1800, self-styled "Texans" fought for their independence from Mexico in the Battle for the Alamo. At the time, the Texans branded themselves revolutionaries. In what ways can the contemporary Texan women in this novel also be described as revolutionaries?

2. Feminism creates a strong sub-theme throughout *Alamo House*. Discuss Mary Jo's ambiguous feelings about feminism.

3. Alamo House is located on Pecan Street, which Mary Jo thinks is a prodigious metaphor. Discuss the idea that the women in the house were "nuts." Do you think they were? Or were they independent and self-expressive?

4. Among the many women who lived in Alamo House, Mary Jo, Collie, and Fayrene are quite distinct from each other, yet their threesome friendship made sense. Discuss the dynamics between these three women.

5. Collie is the novel's most enigmatic character. Did you find her enigma enticing, repulsive, or both (like Mary Jo)? Who do you think Collie really is—Marilyn Monroe, Janis Joplin, Sylvia Plath, or Cordelia Mohoric?

6. Much of Mary Jo's time is spent on the fifth floor of the LBJ Presidential Library. Yet, as an archivist, her work includes stacking small pieces of petrified wedding cake rather than filing important presidential memorandum. Discuss possible political messages behind this paradox.

7. There are many examples of perfect femininity given throughout the novel: Mary Jo's collection of Ladies' Home Journals, the SUKs anthem of "California Girls," and the infamous females that Collie imitates. Do you think that only one of these can be the correct example of feminine perfection? Is there such a thing as feminine perfection? Can a woman be both Marilyn Monroe and Sylvia Plath?

8. Mary Jo leaves Roger for Alamo House because of Roger's sloth. Yet, Alamo House is a much dirtier establishment, and Mary Jo ends up committing to live there by the novel's end. What happened to her obsession with cleanliness? Was it simply a problem in her relationship with Roger, or was it something else entirely? What do you think signals this change in the book?

9. Collie tells Mary Jo and Fayrene that the only way to relate to men is through The Axiom: "The party of the most interest is the party of the least power." Is The Axiom correct? If so, how? How do Collie's experiences with men embody and/or defy The Axiom?

10. Collie states "Men are such Trollops." Do you agree with this statement? Who in the book would you describe as a trollop? Do any of the women qualify? Or, as Collie's evaluation seems to imply, are women always nicer than men?

11. Collie and Mary Jo engage in a lot of casual sex, as well as the SUKs across the street. What do you think about this

part of the story? Although *Alamo House* was written in the mid-1980's, there is no mention of the AIDS crisis that was beginning to grip the country. Do you think these students were unaware of the crisis, or simply thought themselves immune to it? Would these attitudes be acceptable within current social norms? If written today, what sexual attitudes might the characters in *Alamo House* exhibit?

12. Do you think Alamo House's retaliation against the SUKs was well-deserved? Or do you think they went overboard? Did you ever find yourself in a similar situation in college?

13. During an ad hoc house meeting, Mary Jo narrates, "For the next half hour the group batted around terms like womb envy and homophobia, misogyny and aural rape." Given these basic points of 1980s feminism, how do you think feminism is depicted in *Alamo House*? Is it shown as something that advances or hinders the progress of women in society? How do you see it?

14. Collie and Tommy are the two most important people in Mary Jo's life after Roger. In what ways do they influence her life for the better? For the worse? Which one do you think enables her to become a better person?

15. Fayrene shows up at Alamo House as a Bible-beating virgin. Yet, a few months later, she loses her virginity in a one-night stand with an Arab national. What does this signal about the change in her character? Do you think this is due solely to Collie's influence on her? Why or why not?

16. After Collie's departure, Fayrene tells Mary Jo that Collie did not tell her the truth about her identity because she's "normal." What do you think Fayrene meant? Was it a compliment or not? Do you think Mary Jo is "normal"?

17. At the end of *Alamo House*, the women engage in their own Battle for the Alamo. Unlike the original battle, the women win. Why were the women successful? Was it simply ingenuity, or something else?

George R. Jones

About the Author

SARAH BIRD is the author of five novels: *Alamo House*, *The Boyfriend School*, *The Mommy Club*, *Virgin of the Rodeo*, and *The Yokota Officers' Club*. She lives in Austin, Texas. Book clubs write perfumefactory@earthlink.net to find out about a possible chat with Sarah.